You Can Hear the Ice Cracking

You Can Hear the Ice Cracking

a Novel

Robert Lefever

Book 2: Lizzie

c 2015

Published by RL Books, a trading name of Doctor Robert
Limited, 58a Old Brompton Road, South Kensington,
London SW7 3DY, UK
Registered number 7852730

First Published in 2016

10 9 8 7 6 5 4 3 2 1

Text Dr Robert Lefever 2016

A CIP catalogue record for this book is available
from the British Library.

ISBN 978-1-871013-93-1 (Hardback)
ISBN 978-1-871013-92-4 (Paperback)
ISBN 978-1-871013-91-7 (ebook)

Cover design by Paul Maley
Typeset in 10.25/14pt Versailles by Falcon Oast Graphic Art Ltd.

Acknowledgements

Gisela Stuart, in a conversation, inadvertently gave me the title. Ian Gregory, in another, set me on a fertile path.

Doctors advised me. Professor Oscar D'Agnone, Dr Oliver Foster, Mr John Grindle, Dr Jonathan Boreham, Dr Charles Alessi, Dr Anu Jain, Dr David Lomax, Dr Sam Barclay and Dr Mark Jenkins were generous with their time and expertise.

Patients and friends guided me. Dan Donovan, Jonathan Prime, Titus Searle, Gail Thompson, John Graham, Joan Allman, Loliya Harrison, Robert Batt and Lorraine Manley gently pushed me back into line.

My brother Andrew, a lawyer, corrected me and advised me.

The talks in Book 1 are based on entries in my *Diary of a Private Doctor*. The references to various psychological approaches in the other books in this five-volume novel, *You Can Hear the Ice Cracking*, come from my privilege in meeting many distinguished therapists personally in four attendances at the four-yearly *Evolution of Psychotherapy* conference established by Dr Jeffrey Zeig and on my notes on training courses run by Dr Richard Bandler and by the late Dr William Glasser. I am very grateful for the training I received from all these insightful therapists.

I have also drawn on the notes I made for the *MSc in Addiction Psychology* training course at London (South Bank) University that Professor Geoffrey Stephenson and I established. I drew on many resources, particularly the delightfully illustrated 'For Beginners' series of books on various psychologists. I have also drawn on extensive information on SMART Recovery that provides an alternative to Twelve Step approaches. The excellent articles in *Wikipedia* have been a continuing important source in gaining information and understanding in my work as a counsellor and trainer.

Errors that occur in this book and in other volumes of *You Can Hear the Ice Cracking* are mine and mine alone.

Paul Maley's genius for illustration, Pouya Hosseinpour and his remarkable gang at Nocturnal Cloud and Colyn Allsopp and his patient team of typesetters at Falcon all helped to turn my literary dreaming into physical reality.

To all these wonderful people I owe a huge debt of gratitude.

To my wife, Pat, I owe my life and my inspiration and my particular thanks for her patient editing skills.

Disclaimer

You Can Hear the Ice Cracking is a work of fiction. All characters and events portrayed in this book come solely from the imagination of the author. Any resemblance to real people, living or dead, or to any actual happenings in the past or present, are entirely coincidental.

to
Simon and Diana
Graeme and Avril
Jeffrey and Aline
with love.

Time Flies

In the text of Book 1 and Book 2 there is no time interval between each set of asterisks, the time interval between each section marked oOo is one week and each book covers six months.

In the text of Book 3, Book 4 and Book 5 there is no time interval between each set of asterisks, the time interval between each section marked oOo is two weeks and each book covers one year.

oOo

Part 1

No! . . . No! No! No! . . . NO! . . . She's awake! She's awake! . . .
Just as I was when the locum anaesthetist was chatting to his
assistant about football instead of concentrating on *me*,
Lizzie, his patient . . . I can't operate. I'll never be able to work
again as a surgeon. I can't put the knife in . . . I'll never get
over the fear that the patient might be awake. I can't operate.
I can't. I can't. I CAN'T . . .

* * *

What a girl! What a girl! . . . I'll tell you this, Phoebe Finch
. . . I thought they'd stopped making them like you . . . But
they haven't . . . You're my very own Phoebe . . . And you
always will be . . . I recognised and respected my parents'
self-sacrifice and I recognise and respect yours . . . I'll let you
go . . . now . . . for your sake . . . if that's what you want . . . I
love you . . . But don't think for a minute, even a nanosecond,
that I'll leave it at that . . . We belong together . . .

* * *

'Father, I'd like to ask for your advice . . . Where do I go from
here?'
    'Wherever you want, James. – It's your life.'
    'Yes . . . I mean . . . What would you do in my position?'

13

'Ha! – There's a very old answer to that very old question. – I wouldn't start from where you are.'

'Fair enough. – But, if you *were* in my position – right now – what would you do?'

'It's impossible for me to answer that. – I'm not in your position. I never have been. I'm not you.'

'Oh.'

'It's not that I'm being unhelpful. – It's more that I recognise your right to live your own life, make your own mistakes – and learn from them – just as your mother and I had to.'

'I'm not aware that either of you ever have made any mistakes . . . You wouldn't have got where you are . . . professionally or personally . . . if you had.'

'On the contrary . . . Everyone makes mistakes – all the time – but we try not to make the same mistake too many times.'

'How do you stop yourself?'

'Pain.'

'Huh?'

'It becomes too painful to go on making the same mistake – time and time again – and keep hoping that the result will somehow be different . . . Magically.'

'Oh.'

'Yes, it's a difficult lesson to learn . . . For example, I trusted you too much. You'd catch me when I was busy, when I was preoccupied. – I'll bet you found that out from my clerk . . . You're a crafty one.'

'Sorry, Father.'

'It's over now. – But it wouldn't be over if I were to give you money again . . . Your mother would have more than a little to say on the subject . . . To me.'

'Yes, I'm beginning to regret ever asking her to visit me in the rehab . . . That trip turned my life around – but it turned hers around as well, in rather more ways than I'd bargained for.'

* * *

'Well fancy seeing you, Phoebe. I hadn't expected to see you just now – I thought you'd be flat out . . . revising for finals. Far too busy to visit your mother.'
'I am. – Flat out busy. – I'm on the first week of the one month refresher course. . . Ha! – I'm amazed I've forgotten so much.'
'We won't ask why.'
'No. . . That's a bit of a painful subject right now . . . I've . . . er . . . broken it off with my latest man, well sort-of man.'
'The one you told me about, that you . . . er . . . hadn't done anything with . . . umm . . . yet?'
'Yes. – The lecturer, Precious Ellington.'
'What went wrong?'
'Nothing . . . Nothing at all.'
'Huh?'
'He's absolutely the most wonderful man I've ever met.'
'I thought you said you'd broken it off.'
'I did.'
'Why, for heaven's sake? . . . Mr Right doesn't turn up all that often – and when he does he usually turns out to be gay or married already or something . . .'
'No . . . nothing like that.'
'So sorry, Phoebe . . . I didn't mean to pry into your . . . umm . . . affairs.'
'Ha! – That's still what it wasn't – an affair . . .'
'Oh. – Well I'm not going to ask.'
'Yes you are – silently – and I'm happy to tell you . . . I need to tell you anyway . . . My priorities have changed.'

'Well I suppose that might be a good thing – after the last . . . er . . . lover you had.'

'Oh him . . . No. – He's history.'

'I can't say I'm sorry . . . Is this one history too?'

'Umm . . . I don't know . . . I hope not . . . I . . .'

'Dear Phoebe. – What is it?'

'Umm . . . S'pose I've grown up . . . I've realised I have to establish my own values – and live by them . . .'

'Well . . . Yes – we all do . . . I married your father because of who *I* am.'

'Really?'

'He reflects my values, what I believe in . . .'

'Oh . . . It goes even further between me and Precious . . . er . . . He shows me values I didn't know I had – but they *are* mine . . . deep down.'

'That's good. Then *why* . . . don't answer if you don't want to . . . have you sent him packing?'

'I have to focus on what I really believe in most of all . . . It was something he said once – not in a lecture – about a hierarchy of values . . . something he learned from his mother in difficult times . . . struggling . . . what's really important and what's not.'

'So what came out on top?'

'You.'

'Me?'

'You and Dad.'

'What on earth for? – We'll look after ourselves . . . somehow. We always have – and we've looked after you and James.'

'Well the situation's the other way round now . . . You're not in a fit state – neither of you – to look after yourselves. You with that dreadful business of waking up during the operation to take out your gallbladder. And Dad with his neurological problems – whatever they are. He tries to make light of them but you and I, with our medical backgrounds, know just how serious they could be.'

'Yes.'

'Well I'm going to look after you . . . in whatever way I can. – It's payback time.'

'I won't hear of it.'

'You just did.'

'I don't have to play by your rules. Ha! – You never played by mine.'

'Well you're going to have to play by mine now. – You and Dad.'

'I can't answer for him.'

'I'm not asking you to – but I am asking you to accept that our roles are reversed . . . umm . . . Yours and mine.'

'Nobody's ever looked after me in my entire . . .'

'Well I'm doing so now. – And don't ever ask me where I get my stubbornness from.'

* * *

Getting a bit short of the readies . . . Plenty going out . . . not as much as before – a lot less than before – but nothing coming in from this bloody broking business. Not now. Not a squeak . . . Not enough to mount a camel – whatever that may mean – or mount anything at all . . . Can't afford any social life nowadays. And can't ask Mother or Father for anything. Not with their problems . . .

* * *

'We've got to sit down and have a serious talk, Roddy.'

'We had one not so long ago . . . I remember you waking me up for it.'

'That was about James . . . This one's about us.'

'Oh . . . Oh dear . . . I must be in serious trouble.'

'Roddy?'

'Yes, dear?'

'Don't you "Yes dear" me.'

'No, dear . . . Sorry dear.'

'Ahem . . . Ready now?'

'Y . . . er . . . Ahem.'

'Good . . . I'm not sure how I'm ever going to be able to get back to work . . . I can't get the image out of my head – of the possibility of the patient being awake when I plunge in the knife.'

'Nor can I when you put it like that.'

'Whoops! – My turn to say sorry . . . I always forget you're not medical. I s'pose we doctors take so many things for granted when we're talking to each other . . . We share so many brutalising experiences . . .

brutalising for other people, I mean . . . if they were to have them . . . without being medical, I mean.'

'Gosh, Lizzie, it's not like you to stumble over your words.'

'That's just it. – I stumble over everything . . . Not the furniture . . . Yet.'

'I don't imagine you ever will. – That'll be my party trick . . . if I really do have a neurological problem – which seems likely.'

'Whoops again. – I really don't mean to be insensitive today . . . I don't know what's come over me.'

'I would – if I had the energy.'

Later . . . Later . . . I'll guide you . . . But, seriously . . .'

'I am serious.'

'Later . . . umm . . . What in heaven's name – or anyone else's – are we going to do if we're both Krupp . . . umm . . . out of action.'

'I know what "Krupp" means – at least what I've always thought it to mean – to anyone in our generation or, even more, to our parents' generatiom . . . It's about the Krupp munitions factories not being able to work after they were bombed out – but I doubt it means much to anyone else.'

'I'm not talking to anyone else . . . So don't avoid the question. – We're not in court. We don't have to worry about what your jury might understand – or not.'

'They're not "my" jury . . . I wish they were.'

'What are we going to do?'

'I don't know.'

'Neither do I.'

'Survive somehow, I s'pose – like other people.'

'Dear Roddy . . . Ever the optimist.'

'Realist . . . mostly.'

'Well that's what we're going to have to be . . . Me too . . . Both of us.'

* * *

Yes . . . Father must be right. – I have to learn from my mistakes . . . But what were they? – Drinking, drugging? Yes . . . Commodity broking? Yes, probably – but what else can I do? I live by my wits . . . No qualifications . . .

* * *

Yes, the revision course in surgery is ok . . . Got that . . . I remember an orthopod saying his job's a cross between an art and a sport. Ha! – Not that remembering this is going to help me in finals . . . It's all the fluid balance stuff that gets me – making sure you put in at the top end of the patient what you lose from the sharp end – and at the bottom end . . . and through the skin. – Mustn't forget the skin . . .

o O o

You said I'd loved before . . . Not like this I haven't . . . You said I'd love again . . . I don't want to – not with anyone else, my sweetest Phoebe . . .

* * *

So . . . If it's square one time, whadoido? – What-do-I-bloody-do? – Right now? . . . Or ever? . . . Wanna build a rehab . . . Yup. Still do. Put my personal experience to good use. But how do I get from here to there? . . . Assets? – Bugger all . . . 'cept the gift of the gab . . . to some extent – not like father – no training . . . Dammit! Why didn't I work harder at school? – Had all the opportunities . . . Too much booze and whacky backy . . . Nah. – Don't go there, James . . . No point. – Gotta move on . . . Liabilities? Ha! – Addiction. – That just about covers the lot . . . Okay, okay, okay . . . Where does that leave me? Ha! – Up the proverbial creek . . . and with absolutely no proverbial paddle . . . And both the parents in poor shape. – No Bank of Mum and Dad any more . . . Best stick with what I've got . . . Broking . . . Hate it now . . . Unethical . . . Hmm . . . Can't all be unethical . . . Must be some straights in The Square Mile . . . one or two . . . Gotta try something . . . Hmm . . . Yeah . . . If you can't be with the one you love, then love the one you're with . . . Something like that . . .

* * *

'D'you s'pose Precious ever thinks of me, Mum?'
    'Course he does. – All relationships are mutual.'
    'Huh?'

'He'll think of you whatever you think of him.'

'You sure?'

'Yes – of course . . . A relationship is what happens in the middle . . . between two people.'

'Ha!'

'Oh dear . . . What have I said? – Aaargh! What have I said! – And me a gynaecologist!'

'Yes . . . One of the gynaecologists on the refresher course – talking about treatments for prolapse – said, "Anything that goes into the vagina is called a pessary" – and she wondered why we all laughed!'

'Umm . . . Yes . . . What I meant was that a one-sided relationship is just infatuation. Anything for real is mutual . . . You don't have to doubt it. – You feel it, trust it.'

'I hope so . . . I do hope so . . .'

* * *

Ah . . . That's good . . . Me balance seems to have come back a bit – not quite as good as new . . . Hope it stays that way – or gets a bit better . . . Lot of fuss over nothing really . . . Not like Lizzie, poor love . . .

* * *

S'pose I'd better try to dig myself out of this 'anaesthetic awareness' pit . . . somehow . . . But how? . . . Never known myself unable to cope before. Never failed at anything really – not anything I was interested in . . . Been on the antidepressant things a few weeks now . . . Nothing's changed. – I still can't take the thought of a patient being awake – as I was – just when I'm about to . . . umm . . . whatever. – Just feeling a bit dulled out . . . What was it? . . . Oh yes . . . "The lights are on but nobody's at home" . . .. And the Cognitive Behavioural Therapy is worse than useless . . . Very clever – but nothing to do with the price of fish . . . Not really . . .

* * *

Revision week for skins, eyes, ears, noses and throats. – Odd they bunch them all together this week . . . Still, if you've got only four weeks to cover the whole shebang, you've got to make some adjustments . . . come to terms with some uneasy bedfellows . . . Oh! . . . Oh, Precious . . . I wish . . .

o O o

What is it about fate? . . . So wonderful – and then so cruel . . . Can't go back. Can't go back . . . Must go forward – but where? . . . No point in going Stateside – running away . . . Committed to my lecture course – for now, for next year . . . And the research – back to the drawing board . . . Only one way to do it – one step at a time, one day at a time . . .

* * *

James Finch, Senior Account Executive . . . God, I can't say it any more – with a straight face . . . "Senior"? – I'm twenty one for fuck's sake . . . Twenty one – younger than their children . . . Most of them . . . "Executive"? – Executive what? . . . Wanker most likely, spiel merchant, con artist . . . showing mugs – silly, greedy mugs – how to lose everything they've built up in business – over years – how to lose it all in a few trades, a few weeks . . . if that . . . Where's the ethics in that? . . . How can I say anything ethical other than, "Listen, Cloth-

Ears, you're going to throw it all away" . . .

*　*　*

So here I am . . . back in Chambers, where I belong . . . Now let's see . . . Oh . . . Not much on . . . Well, might just be the end of term coming up. For us in the law and for school children. Holidays . . .

*　*　*

'I came to see you again – because nothing else seems to work . . . I'm becoming desperate.'

'Yes . . . I'm often the last port of call – after people look at every other possibility.'

'Isn't that rather frustrating?'

'Umm . . . Not really. – It means that people who *do* come back are the ones who really want to be here – who are prepared to try anything.'

'Isn't that rather risky . . . for them?'

'And for me to some extent.'

'Why?'

'It's risky for patients because they're desperate. – They'll believe anything and trust anybody by that time . . . As you yourself know only too well, the private sector isn't entirely whiter than white.'

'You've got that right! – I know that from the hormone people . . . People who are not doctors at all but talk in fancy terms and con a lot patients – even putting them off legitimate treatments . . . But why would it be risky for you . . . to see people who really want to get better?'

'Well, again I expect it's something you know well in your work . . . The more desperate they are, the more the patients expect a magic fix – especially if they're paying for it . . . They'll tolerate NHS people saying nothing can be done but they expect us in the private sector to be miracle workers. – Ha! – And without them having to commit themselves to doing anything at all . . . except paying the bill. – And sometimes they dispute even that . . . if things don't work out exactly according to their expectations – and demands.'

'Yes, I know . . . I know.'

'But here you are . . . with no expectations.'

'That's true . . . How did you know?'

'You're a professional . . . You'll have looked everything up in advance – and checked on me – and come back straight away, not after this delay, if you were fully confident, particularly bearing in mind who it was who referred you to me.'

'Well I'm here now . . . That must say something.'

'Yes it does . . . It means I have to work hard to justify my fee.'

'I wondered why it was so high – much the same as mine.'

'Yes – and for the same reasons . . . It reflects my training and experience . . . as it should . . . and it guarantees that you'll be very angry if I don't do everything meticulously professionally – particularly as AXA, BUPA and the other private medical insurance companies don't cover my fees'

'Yes . . . er . . . Why not?'

'Because they don't believe in what I do. They're very conservative – quite rightly, in my view.'

'You're doing your very best to put me off seeing you.'

'Yes.'

'Why?'

'Because I want you to know that I come with absolutely no guarantee of success . . . I've done a lot of EMDR . . . Eye Movement Desensitising and Reprocessing, the psychological process that helps the thinking brain to unblock the feeling brain. I'm confident in the process and in the way I do it – using sound and touch and muscular movement as well as eye movement . . .'

'Why?'

'Because it gives four inputs instead of one – which makes it more effective . . . and less expensive in the long run . . . And that's why I never charge for a preliminary discussion, like now. – I want you to be totally confident that I've done my homework and I'll do my very best for you.'

'Well I take that for granted, really – bearing in mind, as you said, who referred me to you.'

'But I haven't told you the most significant factor – for you.'

'What's that?'

'I've never previously treated a patient with anaesthetic awareness.'

'Oh God.'

*   *   *

Medicine . . . Yes, I'm ok on the diseases. I've read them up in the books – and mostly on the web nowadays – and seen them on the wards . . . But I just don't trust Big Pharma . . . I don't trust the pharmacology and therapeutics – and that's half the exam . . . or nearly . . . Ha! – Big Pharma isn't remotely interested in anything that doesn't give them a hefty financial return . . . Why else do their reps pester the doctors as much as they do? Why else do they pay for post-graduate lectures – and professorships? . . . It's not right . . . It's not right . . . I'm sure Precious would agree with me on that . . .

o O o

Wonder what Phoebe's up to? . . . Working, I guess. – Finals very soon . . . hmm . . . Anyone else in her life? . . . Doubt it . . . Hope not . . . No. – Sure not . . . Nobody in mine. Not interested . . .

* * *

'I can't do it, Roddy. I can't.'

'Gosh, dear sweet Lizzie. – I've never heard you say that . . . in your whole life . . . about anything.'

'Except the mouse.'

'Oh yes . . . except looking for the mouse in the kitchen – after it ran across the floor in front of us in the living room when we were reading one evening.'

'There's no need to spell it out for me – word for word . . . It's bad enough remembering it at all – without the graphic details.'

'Oh. Sorry, dear. – My insensitivity again.'

'No. – Don't give yourself a hard time over it . . . It's all due to my hypersensitivity in the first place.'

'So what's happened this time?'

'The EMDR thing . . . I went to see that counsellor again . . . He's very nice – and seems to be very careful and professional . . . my sort of professional.'

'So what went wrong? . . . I do hope he hasn't unsettled you even more.'

'No. – No, we haven't even started it . . . and I won't let him.'

'Not if you don't want it. – Of course not.'

'I couldn't . . . I . . . er . . . He . . . umm . . . hasn't done it before – with anaesthetic awareness, I mean.'

'How did you find that out?'

'He told me.'

'Had you asked him?'

'No . . . umm . . . No. – He volunteered it.'

'That was honest of him.'

'Yes . . . Yes it was . . . but . . . but – I know we all learn from our mistakes – but I dare not have another mistake . . . umm . . . done on me. – One's more than enough . . . Imagine what would happen if he made it even worse . . .'

'It doesn't bear thinking about . . . Nor the mouse.'

'Aaargh! . . . Roddy!'

'Whoops! . . . My turn to say, "Whoops" . . . Sorry, dear.'

'I dunno . . . It may be a woman thing . . . but I can't go through with it. I'll just have to live with it – and hope it goes away.'

'We got a cat.'

'That's not quite the same thing, Roddy. – Not a universal solution . . . Aaaaargh! You men!'

* * *

Let's face it . . . Not much choice . . . really. – No experience in anything else – It's sales of some kind . . . or nothing . . . er . . . What other kind? . . . Stocks and shares? – Too young. – Insurance? – Boring as fuck . . . Ha! . . . I'd rather top myself. – Selling advertising in programmes? – God! Gimme a break . . .

* * *

Poor Lizzie . . . Rotten luck – and I'm no help to her . . . er . . . It's not like my situation. – I've got The Garrick to go to – which she hasn't . . . Wonder why she doesn't join The Sloane Club – women only – Yes, that might suit . . . umm . . . No, probably not. – Lizzie likes it in a man's world . . . like The

Garrick . . . Ha! . . . Not going there. – Wouldn't do at all . . . Except in the reception room, with the pink-trousered Zophany . . . She likes him. Ha! . . . Tried to get me some! – Great sense of humour, my Lizzie . . . But it's not right for women to go into the bar . . . Wouldn't do at all . . . Whatever next? . . .

* * *

Week four . . . Psychiatry, geriatrics, pathology, radiology, industrial medicine and other odds and sods . . . No wonder hardly anyone's turned up. Not worth the time, really – with finals next week . . . Not as if Precious were here . . .

o O o

I'd love to see her . . . Just a glimpse . . . Oh dammit . . . Wouldn't be right . . . Ha! – Goodness gracious, Precious Ellington, you're a love-sick loon . . . Yeah that's right – love-sick loon . . . No harm in that – for now . . . P'raps for ever . . . Hope so . . . hmm . . . Maybe not . . . Oh God, I don't know . . .

* * *

'So what d'you think I should do now . . . er . . . if I don't have the EMDR?'

'You could ask the counsellor what other options there might be.'

'I suspect he'll bring it back to EMDR – and try to persuade me . . . I don't want that . . . It's difficult to explain how a rational person like me can be stuck with a totally irrational problem.'

'You're not alone. – James was.'

'James? . . . James? . . . Huh! – James was . . . James *is* . . . an addict . . . My problem's nothing at all like that.'

'No – of course not – except that they're both irrational processes in otherwise rational and sensible people. James is totally clear-headed now that he's off whatever it was he . . . Hmm . . . I never did find out.'

'Nor did I.'

'Not even when you visited him in rehab? On the family programme in Hazelden?'

'No . . . We looked . . . James looked in his group – and I looked in mine – towards the future.'

'But surely a clear vision of a future path has to be based on a thorough appraisal of the past.'

'Umm . . . Not really . . . Well, only in part.'

'Which part?'

'Acknowledging that our own way of seeing things – and doing things – wasn't helpful . . . didn't work . . . So we have to ask other people . . . work alongside other people with similar perception defects.'

'Hang on a bit . . . You're getting me all tied up here . . . That really is the blind leading the blind . . . What did these Hazelden people say you did wrong, Lizzie? . . . We both know what James did and . . . er . . . I did – by not confronting him – but you?'

'I was just like you . . . I didn't see the obvious evidence of what James was up to – until it was too late – because I didn't want to . . . He's my son . . . and I want to believe the best of him . . . and absolutely not believe he's an addict . . . by nature.'

'Well you saw it before I did – and I'm not sure I would go that far even now . . . He's just been a bit silly. – That's all.'

'Ask James.'

'I thought you said – implied – that Hazelden didn't approve of you asking James what he'd been up to.'

'No, they don't – but he and I can share the recognition that we neither of us see ourselves very well.'

'Well I see myself clearly enough . . . I think – when I'm steady on me pins.'

'We all think that . . . er . . . That's the problem with having a perception disorder – like James and I have – rather than a visual problem.'

'But what's this got to do with your anaesthetic thing?'

'Nothing directly . . . It's just that we're none of us as strictly rational as we might like to think we are.'

'Ha! – Try telling that to a judge!'

'I just did . . . well – the next best thing – a QC . . . P'raps now you can see why I asked you what I should do now . . . I . . . really don't know – for myself.'

'Well, if you don't know, I certainly don't.'

'Yes . . . umm . . . No . . . umm . . . Yes, I can see that . . . umm . . . I think.'

* * *

'I'm sorry you've been having such a bad time, Dad.'

'All over now. – Always look on the bright side.'

'That's what they said in the crucifixion scene – in *Monty Python*.'

'I thought they said, "Bring me sunshine.".'

'No. – That was Morecambe and Wise.'

'Umm . . . Same thing really – humour – in the days when it really was funny.'

'Well there's nothing funny about what you and Mum have been going through recently. I . . . er . . . I just wanted to say how sorry I am for both of you – and for being such a brat.'

'That's very thoughtful of you, Phoebe . . . er . . .Your

mother said you'd been in to see her . . . Very thoughtful – but shouldn't you be getting your head down? revising?'

'I am – but mustn't overdo it and give myself brain pain.'

'Is that a medical term?'

'Not yet. – Should be . . . maybe. – They dress it up with all sorts of fancy diagnostic labels . . . "Depression" mostly . . . Then they can prescribe drugs and think they're doing something helpful.'

'Oh.'

'And patients are just as bad. They like labels too. – "Nervous Breakdown" usually. – Then they can tell their friends, expect sympathy and do nothing for themselves.'

'Your mother and I haven't done that. – I hope.'

'No. – No you haven't. – You're the ideal patients . . . Looking for what you can do to improve your own situations.'

'This doesn't sound like you, Phoebe – not the Phoebe we used to know and love . . . Yes, your mother said you'd changed – for the better, of course.'

'Ha! – I could've gone the other way.'

'Gawd, that would be something!'

'Not likely now.'

'Oh . . . I thought you'd got a new man.'

'I wish.'

* * *

'Mother, I thought I'd pop in just to say, "Hi" . . . There's nothing I've come to ask for, nothing I want.'

'Gracious . . . You and Phoebe both turning over new leaves at the same time! . . . "Be grateful for small mercies", I say – big ones actually . . . You haven't got yourself a . . . er . . . partner as well, have you?'

'No such luck! . . . I tend to look in all the wrong places –

party girls, that sort of thing.'

'Oh.'

'Why "Oh"?'

'Just a natural parental instinct. Concerned for you.'

'Ha! – Grandparental more like! – Wanting us to breed. – Come on . . . Own up.'

'Well I . . . er . . .'

* * *

Gruesome . . . "Multiple guess" more than "multiple choice" . . . Why can't they give us essays – like in *Bugsy Malone* . . . Gives us the chance for a bit of waffle . . . S'pose it's easier for them to mark the answers nowadays – with those damn document readers. "No crossings out", as it says. – That's what all that's about . . . Confuses the poor little machines . . . Still, It's good training – for decision time on the wards . . . Wonder if I'm up to it . . . Maybe I'll find out in the personal interviews. – Always prefer practice to theory . . .

oOo

She's taken finals by now . . . No problem there – She's a bright one . . . Like in *Bugsy Malone* – great musical – she could be anything that she wanted to be . . . mine one day . . . Live in hope, Precious. – That's what Mom said – Live in hope . . .

* * *

Okay okay okay . . . Wakey wakey. James. – Time to get a grip . . . Sort myself out . . . Do what the American speaker, I.Clancy, said in that tape they played us at Hazelden . . . If I feel bad, get a job . . . If I feel terrible, get a terrible job . . .

* * *

'How did it go?'

'Dunno really . . . Should be ok – but I may be kidding myself.'

'Speaking as an examiner – for the membership, not just in finals – I always pass people if I possibly can . . . The people who fail are the ones we consider dangerous.'

'And the shaky ones, who just scrape through, eventually become locums?'

'Umm . . . Actually that's not at all funny. Locums are paid very well in the UK. But I don't know anything about the anaesthetist who did me . . . It could have been just a mistake – and the poor man will be cursing himself, having to live with that for the rest of his life . . .'

'He deserves to.'

'No he doesn't. He deserves to be given another chance . . . unless he was always a risk.'

'German, wasn't he?'

'Yes . . . Come to think of it, that's quite a point . . . Germany has an excellent medical system. – The diagnostic centre I saw in Wiesbaden was incredible . . . It takes three days to work your way right through it . . . as a patient.'

'That must cost a bit.'

'Yes, it does. – But you get what you pay for . . . Always do – infallible rule . . . And the doctors are brilliant – like the Israelis, who've won more Nobel prizes than are good for them.'

'That's a step too far for me – Gaza and that – at present.'

'I won't push it.'

'On that basis, I'll look it up – how much the Israelis have achieved in the medical and scientific world . . . and the Germans . . . Then what was your locum anaesthetist man doing over here?'

'That's what I'm asking myself . . . It's the EU open boundaries thing – but why would he *want* to work here? The NHS certainly isn't the envy of the world to Germans – doctors or patients.'

'Precious works here.'

'As a researcher and lecturer. – We're still in the top flight for that . . . so far. – It's in the practical world, when we try to put our brilliant ideas and inventions into practice – in industry and medicine and science in general. That's when we fall down.'

'Why's that?'

'We get lazy, complacent . . . Why – in the USA – should Henry Ford ever have created a car that wasn't black? He had the monopoly, more or less. And why should we create a new healthcare system when ours is already the best – and pretty well a monopoly?'

'I hope I'll be able to join *any* healthcare system.'

'Of course you will . . . Remember this. – If you're bright enough to get into medical school, you're probably bright enough to come through at the other end.'

'Thanks, Mum . . . Wish me luck . . . Oh no, you don't do "luck", do you?'

'No . . . I believe in the random distribution of chance – like my anaesthetic awareness – but not in luck . . . "Lady Luck" is a creation of the bookies. – She's a hooker, giving a corrupt service, taking all and giving nothing of lasting value.'

'Mum! – I've never heard you talk like that!'

'Start now, kiddo . . . I hope things have gone well for you in finals . . . In my opinion – totally unbiased of course – you'll make a wonderful doctor.'

'Thanks. – Thank you very much . . . Why don't all medical students – as bright as they have to be to begin – finish up becoming good doctors?'

'Well . . . This is just my opinion – and totally biased. – They don't love the work, love the patients.'

'Why not?'

'That's something you'll have to ask people who believe in the NHS . . . I left it for very good reasons – and I'm glad to clarify them for you without nowadays risking World War III. – I saw what it did to the young enthusiastic doctors – the ordinary ones, not the whizz kids who always do well. – It sapped their energy, their creativity, their life.'

* * *

There we are . . . They asked for a legal opinion . . . I read up the background papers. Calculated the pros and cons of various strategies. Looked at the potential costs – and benefits, of course. And now writing out the opinion – with the relevant case law references . . . That's the way. – Back in harness, where I belong . . .

* * *

God alive! – Look at that! . . . All those envelopes. On the tables, arranged by name . . . "Finch" should be in the middle somewhere . . . Yes that's it . . . But why's that creepy 'pastoral carer' hovering around? . . . Not for me I hope . . .

oOo

Yessss! – There's Phoebe's name – on the pass lists . . . hmm . . . She'll know I know . . . Send her an e-mail? . . . hmm . . .

Silly to do that. – Might upset her . . . hmm . . . Silly not to – Might upset her also . . . Aaaaargh . . .

Okay – Here goes . . . 'Well done, Dr Phoebe Finch!'

. . . Ah – and here's her reply . . . 'Thanks. Love you.' – Just that – no more . . . But that's enough – quite enough – to dream on . . .

* * *

'Well done, darling. We're so proud of you . . . And it's so considerate of you to allow Dad to bring you here to The Garrick . . . I know The Establishment isn't your thing. – You've made that very clear in the past – but it's generous of you to humour him, to share your glory with a bit of his.'

'Well he paid for it. You both did . . . my education, my success, I mean – and this place as well. It must cost a fortune to be a member here – at a prime location in the heart of theatre-land.'

'Yes it does – but you and lots of other young children subsidised it.'

'What?'

'This is *"The House at Pooh Corner"*, if you wish . . . AA Milne left one quarter of his estate to The Garrick.'

'Who got the rest?'

'His family, the Royal Literary Fund and Westminster School.'

'All very elitist.'

'Maybe – but all the product of a Bear with very little brain . . . You can't get more egalitarian than that.'

* * *

Well if Phoebe can come good so can I. We Finches are tough

little birds – nut crackers . . . Ha! – Roddy would enjoy that . . .
Not quite what I meant but never mind . . .

* * *

'Very proud of our Phoebe. – Aren't you?'
    'Yes. – Yes, of course . . . It was kind of you to take us to The
Garrick . . . It seemed to mean a lot to her – surprisingly.'
    'Why so?'
    'Why did it mean a lot? or why is it surprising?'
    'Both.'
    'I can't speak for her – I wouldn't dare, even now – but my
guess is that she was seduced by it.'
    'She's after one of the members? – After just one meeting?
Can't think that we met anyone in particular.'
    'No, idiot. – The place . . . You may be used to it but it's
dazzling to a young impressionable mind like Phoebe's . . .
and to other guests as well. – I remember when you first took
me there. Turned my head.'
    'Oh. – I'd hoped it was my conversation, my erudition.'
    'That was a turn off.'
    'Really? – Why?'
    'You spoke about the commercial bar . . . your work. You
were on better form last night with Phoebe.'
    'I'm not nervous with Phoebe.'
    'But you were with me? . . . then?'
    'And now sometimes.'
    'Why on earth?'
    'I'm always frightened you might leave me . . . find some-
one better – more exciting.'
    'Well bless your little cotton socks.'
    'Silk actually.'

*   *   *

'Congratulations, Dr Finch . . . Good marks, very creditable.'

'Thank you.'

'What made you apply to be on my firm?'

'I like neurology. The workings of the central nervous system fascinate me.'

'But I'm not a neurologist. – I'm a geriatrician, providing care for the elderly.'

'I know . . . But there's a lot of neurology in geriatrics – inevitably as people get older. I don't want to be a neurologist. I want to be a GP – and GPs spend most of their time with old people.'

'Why? I mean why would you want to be a GP?'

'I'm more interested in people than diseases . . . er . . . I've got to know the diseases of course – and in the elderly you see the whole lot . . . particularly the progressive damage to the central nervous system – and the peripheral nerves of course . . . from diabetes especially . . . But it's the people who've got the diseases who really fascinate me.'

'Why so?'

'It's their Health Service . . . They come to us . . . They define the work doctors do, I s'pose. – It's up to us to respond as best we can.'

'Yes . . . with whatever resources we can lay our hands on . . . We're not very high in the food chain – geriatricians.'

'Yes, as I've seen during my training . . . The financial prizes - merit awards and private practice - go to the clinical disciplines that are most likely to be needed by middle-aged middle-class males.'

'Like me?'

'Yes.'

'Umm . . . We'll let you know . . .'

o O o

No . . . Gotta find a way, gotta find a way somehow – to move on . . . My life has value – of its own, not just with Phoebe . . . God, I miss her! . . . Ronnie Scott's, Byron's, the conversations . . . the kisses – with or without onions on the side with the hamburgers . . .

* * *

'Yes, it really is unusual for an elective two week period to be taken in the USA. Most of my medical student contemporaries have gone to African countries. The Jews have gone to Israel – for safety and to high-profile posts arranged through their families. A fair number of my friends went to Australia – to keep that as a future option if the UK is in trouble, one way or another, in future. But I wanted to come here to see if an American friend of mine has been telling me the truth.'

'You're very welcome – but why would your friend not tell it how it is?'

'Maybe both our countries have an attitude problem – Uncle Sam telling the world how it should be run . . . And us saying you should be learning from us – about socialised medicine . . . Maybe we both get it wrong.'

'And maybe our nation is as divided as yours on this . . . The Democrats are passionate about ObamaCare and some of the Republicans – particularly the Tea Party Libertarians – want the Affordable Care Act repealed in full.'

'But what do the people want?'

'The mid-term elections showed a swing to the GOP – the Republicans.'

'But mid-terms always go against the president, don't they? – You've been stuck with one lame duck Commander-in-Chief after another in the final two years.'

'It depends how they play it – continue to make the country ungovernable in some respects – with the Senate, and maybe the House as well, controlled by one party and the president controlling the other – or maybe neither – but they somehow learn to cooperate . . . It's all worked out on how they reckon it'll play to the public in the media.'

'*Fox News?*'

'On the one side – and *The New York Times* and *The Washington Post* on the other . . . Hey, you seem to know quite a bit about us already.'

'I've read up on it – but I don't know if it's true . . . That's why I'm here – to see for myself.'

'But why did you come here, to Bangor, Maine, when you could've gone to Manhattan – and taken in a show and a baseball game?'

'I wanted to meet Dr Charles Burger.'

'You've missed him. – He's on vacation right now.'

'I know.'

'But you still came here?'

'Yes . . . If his ideas – and those of Dr Harold Cross and Dr John Bjorn who created this place – are any good, they'll work just as well when he's not around.'

'Yes . . . You really have done your homework . . . That's impressive.'

'Not in my home country, it isn't . . . When I tell people I want to be a GP, a family physician, they usually say, "But you're quite bright. – Why don't you become a specialist?".'

'And how do you answer?'

'I thank them for the "quite".'

'Ha! . . . It's the same here in most places – but these doctors here were the pioneers ... all influenced by Professor Lawrence Weed of the University of Vermont – the father of the Problem Oriented Medical Information System, the PROMIS system ... Today it's standard.'

'Yes – I use it. I particularly like the way it records the words of the patients. Their starting position.'

'Yes. If a patient says, "I'm tired", it's no answer to say, "All your test results are normal". The underlying cause of the tiredness may be emotional or social – and it's just as much part of the family physician's job – as we see it in this practice – to look into that. It has to be followed through.'

'Yes. I read that Dr Burger said he was happy to contribute to medical development in the community ... and that he'd been waiting for about thirty years to do that. I'm not prepared to wait that long.'

'That's good ... It's all good.'

'And I also read that Dr Burger was one of the first in Maine to use fully electronic medical records in primary care – not just putting in the diagnosis and the path results and the names of the drugs prescribed. That's all that tends to get recorded in the notes of GPs in the UK. Making a record of what the patient actually said makes the whole relationship patient-centred ... Dr Burger sounds like my sort of doctor.'

'Could be ... and you might like to read this report of something else he said. – It reminds all of us here what this is all about ... That's why we want him to put it on the wall in reception – for all the patients to see ... "The bottom line is you want to focus on the patient. Patients don't want to see you typing into a computer. They want us to be paying attention to them ... More work needs to be done defining new roles for nurses and medical assistants. The whole concept of Patient-Centered Medical Home is based on the idea that physicians can't do it all."

'That's the way.'

'Well I must say, Dr Finch, it's a pleasure to have you here with us. – And I'm sure we'll have a lot to learn from you.'

'I'm afraid it's more likely the other way round . . . I can tell already . . . My friend was right. – He told me – This is where it's at.'

'We'll see what you think at the end of your two weeks.'

o O o

Waiting . . . waiting . . . to know her professional future . . . Huh! – and mine . . . Wonder where she is – and what she's up to.

* * *

'James, I have to tell you that that your appointment as a Senior Account Executive in this firm has been terminated.'

'Oh . . . Did I do something wrong? Did I upset someone? Or fail to follow procedures?'

'Your absence – for such a long time – is unacceptable . . . for whatever reason.'

'I can explain . . .'

'No need . . . We've already appointed someone else in your place . . . This is the real world – the commercial sector – not the Welfare State.'

* * *

'Dear Dr Finch,

I have the honour and privilege of offering you the post of Foundation Year One doctor in the Department of Geriatrics – or Care for the Elderly, as we prefer to call it now . . . To be precise, no other candidate came close.

Please confirm in response to this e-mail that you will accept this offer. As you know, the appointment starts in two weeks' time on the first of next month and lasts for four months.

Before then you will need to check in with the employment office in this hospital, in order to ensure that all the formalities are in place.

You will also need to check in with your predecessor in order to familiarise yourself with the routines of this department to ensure smooth transfer of responsibility.

I congratulate you and I look forward to working with you alongside the other members of the team.'

Arthur Arbuthnot
Consultant in Care for the Elderly.

*   *   *

'Hello, Phoebe . . . Lovely talking to you. – How're things in America? . . . Anyway, your mother and I are just phoning to say what a clever girl you are! – And what a wonderful e-mail that is from the consultant. You certainly wowed him . . . No I don't need any reassurance that he's not black, like yer boyfriends . . . We're bursting proud of you. And you can write your own prescriptions now! . . . on the wards . . . No . . . umm . . . I'm not asking for one. – I'm on top form and you make me feel even better . . . umm . . . Love you . . . I'll just hand you over to Mum . . .'

'Hello little one. Who's a clever girl then! . . .More than I did – getting a job in my own teaching hospital . . . Yes, I've done pretty well since then – but you've made your mark already . . . Well yes, that goes without saying – of course we have to deliver . . . You will. You will . . . Lots of love, Byee . . .'

* * *

'That was a pretty dim phone call of mine – talking about black boyfriends . . . although I s'pose she mentioned it first . . . Must've given her the impression – at some point that it's important to me . . . Colour.'

'I didn't cover myself in glory either. – Almost getting her to feel sorry for me not doing as well as she has . . . stealing her thunder a bit.'

'And we both forgot to ask her about America.'

'Plenty of time for that later . . . hmm . . . Maybe not. – She'll be busy . . . On her way, I s'pose . . . Bit worried about James still.'

'He'll come good . . . Who'd have thought the Phebe would turn out as she has done?'

'I would.'

* * *

'James? – The Phebe . . . I've got a job . . . Oh, I'm sorry to hear that. – What happened . . . aha . . . aha . . . Just like that? . . . Oh . . . That's dreadful. – You were ill . . . Well they damn well should see it that way . . . They can't just turf you out like that . . . Oh, they can . . . Well they shouldn't be allowed to . . . Isn't there some law or other – Employment Protection Act or something? . . . Oh . . . So what are you going to do? . . . Well I wish you all the luck in the world for that – not that Mum would approve of luck . . . But what are you going to do in the meantime? – to put food on the table? . . . Well good luck with that as well . . . Umm . . . I've just told the parents that they matter more to me than anything – or anybody – else . . . Yes, including you – because you're perfectly capable of caring for yourself when you behave yourself, when you're well . . . No, I'm not coming all over the bossy elder sister now that I'm a doctor. – I'm just facing reality. Their reality.'

* * *

Precious, dear Precious, Are you proud of me? . . . Yours is the one opinion that really matters to me – even more than family . . . You're my family. Ha! . . . I still want your babies . . .

o O o

Yesss again! There's her name on a very special list. – Doctors given their first house appointment in their own teaching hospital . . . Geriatrics, that's good – shows she's a people person, not an egg-head . . . and trusted clinically – so much of it, so varied and so unpredictable . . . Not on the list of Prizewinners – no surprise there – Phoebe's a steady worker but not someone who's got the potential to change the face of clinical medicine through sheer brilliance . . . Hmm . . . but I wonder about that . . . Ha! Depends which face . . .

* * *

Dammit, dammit, dammit . . . I don't see myself getting rid of this anaesthesia nonsense very easily . . . God, what a terrible thought! – S'pose I never do . . . I'm in the wrong profession for this malarkey . . .

* * *

Wonder if I really do have a neurological illness . . . All very well putting on a brave face . . . Hmm . . . Got to really . . .

Only way I know . . . Hmm . . . Better see the consultant again sometime . . . if I have any more symptoms . . . Hope not . . . But I'm getting more cramps . . . and me balance isn't quite right after all . . .

* * *

The chips really are down now . . . Ha! . . . Getting to learn how the other half lives . . . Hmm . . . Not very comfortably . . . Hey ho! . . . Gotta sort myself out good and proper – The Phebe has. Why shouldn't I? . . . or the camels won't know who's been mounting them . . .

* * *

'So how was it? How did you find your two weeks with us?

'I've been conned.'

'By us?'

'No. No. – Sorry, that was careless of me . . . No – by the people who told me that the NHS is the envy of the world . . . I've never seen anything like this.'

'But you have to remember – this is an exceptional practice . . . even in the US of A . . . There are many people here – forty million of them – who had no medical insurance before President Obama came along . . . He gets a lot of stick – but he's actually achieved more than Clinton or LBJ or Kennedy – who was a great talker . . . and some.'

'What impresses me most here – in this medical practice – is the patients . . . They're actively committed to their health care. – It's something they're involved in, believe in . . . They *own* it.'

'But your NHS is owned by the state – the people.'

'Those are definitely not the same thing . . . That's what

I've realised . . . In the UK the state is distant from every-body. Nobody owns it. It's just a thing. It just is . . . People value it – the NHS – because they're frightened of being left without it . . . But they take it for granted. They don't really contribute to it . . . except in taxes – some of them – and in charity fun runs, that sort of thing . . . The NHS isn't really *theirs.* – It's the government's, The Department of Health's . . . Those people – the mandarins – do what they want with it . . . It's top down directed, even though they call it an "Arm's-Length Body" . . . I should've seen that before. – The NHS being a bureaucratic fiefdom. – My mother told me. My American friend told me . . . But I didn't listen . . . That was another thing my friend said . . . You can't put a new idea into your head until you make room for it by getting rid of an old one.'

'Ha! . . . Maybe you could say all that again – to my daughter . . . You know, nothing's clear cut – nothing's given to us. – We have to learn everything for ourselves . . . painfully sometimes.'

o O o

Another year of talks coming up . . . Ha!.. Be careful what I do with my money clip this time . . .

* * *

'Thank you, Dad. Thank you so much for paying for me to do my elective two weeks in America . . . It's given me a very great deal to think about . . . – And your congratulations on my first professional appointment mean a lot to me. You established your career from a zero base and I intend to do the same.'

47

'I have every confidence in you, Phoebe . . . You have an excellent independent mind and you use it well.'

'Sometimes too well . . . picking fights that don't need to be fought.'

'Ah well . . . I wish more vexatious litigants would say the same . . . Ha! – Even though lawyers like me do very well out of them, it's not rewarding work when people are just being silly . . . I like to fight a case on principle, on the law.'

'Yes, I respect that in you . . . and I want to fight for my patients' welfare – even when they're their own worst enemies . . . I s'pose that's one of the main differences between law and medicine, seeing people as idiots or unfortunates.'

'Oh I don't know . . . I feel very sorry for some of my clients – when they're being done over by big corporations or by the government.'

'But the government makes the law.'

'True – but the letter and the spirit of the law is what we fight over . . . and the letter has to win . . . If parliament makes bad law, it has to be referred back to the politicians to get them to re-draft it . . . We can't act – judges can't – on what they think the law was meant to say. They have to act on what it *does* say . . . Ha! – but I remember a letter in *The Times*, years ago, pleading with The Master of the Rolls not to make any new case law in the next six weeks before finals.'

'Yes, I sympathise . . . We get new ways of understanding illnesses and their mechanisms – Hughes Syndrome was an example . . . He's still very much alive, Dr Hughes, – at Tommy's and Guys.'

'Well I bet he was pretty unpopular with the final year students at the time of his discoveries – and with some of his contemporaries, who may have thought they knew every-thing – but had to start again.'

'Maybe . . . but I'm sure his patients were grateful – if it helped to get them better, relieve their symptoms . . . er . . . One of the reasons I've gone into geriatrics is so I can help you, people like you.'

'Ha! . . . Thanks for that! – I'm not a geriatric yet!'

'Any progressive illness finishes up on the geriatric ward . . . eventually.'

'You're a bundle of fun today! . . . And I'm not convinced that my future's going to be grim at all. – I'm fine right now.'

'Yes, you are – and that's great. I'm just letting you know – in my clumsy way – that I put caring for you and Mum above my own professional and personal life.'

'You mustn't do that . . . You have a life of your own to live.'

'You – and Mum – gave me everything I've got . . . I'll give you whatever I can . . . No argument.'

'Gracious, Phoebe . . . You'd never make a lawyer.'

'No . . . I wouldn't.'

* * *

'Mum, I'll tell you what I told Dad . . . umm . . . Thank you very much for enabling me to study in the States for a couple of weeks . . . I reckon it ought to be compulsory – for all of us . . . Still, the course of lectures Precious gives is the next best thing. And thank you also for your congratulations on getting my first job . . . But my very first responsibility is to the two of you . . . You've both been laid low by things that you couldn't possibly have avoided. The NHS should primarily be for people like you.'

'We're not that desperate . . . yet.'

'I hope you never will be . . . umm . . . I'm just letting you know that the Welfare State – in one way or another – might . . . probably will . . . let you down . . . because it does too many indiscriminate things for too many people. – But I won't.'

'Glory be! Is this my own personal revolutionary I'm hearing?'

'I haven't changed my commitment to revolution . . . just its direction.'

*   *   *

'Is there power in positive thinking?'

'Yes . . . It's well known in clinical practice – like mine in neurology – that there's considerable variation in outcome in patients who have similar conditions . . . illnesses or injuries . . .'

'I believe so . . . I've read about it.'

' . . . One possible explanation is that a positive attitude, a belief that all will be well, makes a positive outcome more likely . . . through the influence of endorphins – brain hormones.'

'D'you think that might apply to my neurological problem . . . er . . . if I have one?'

'Yes, it could do – but it's difficult to determine that in advance . . . or which individual will benefit.'

'Aren't there any tests?'

'We can test the structural competence of the physical brain – with an MRI scan, Magnetic Resonance Imaging, like you had . . .'

'What else can you see on an MRI scan?'

'In the spine we can see prolapsed intervertebral discs.'

'I thought discs "slipped".'

' . . . No, that's a common misconception, thinking they're like tiddlywinks, popping in and out . . .'

'Yes.'

'. . . They're soft centred . . . If the outer capsule is compromised, the nucleus can squeeze out – like firm toothpaste – and impinge on the spinal cord or on the root of one of the nerves . . . and cause symptoms – tinglings, numbness and disorder of function – in the area that's supplied by that nerve . . .'

'Is that what happened in my leg? . . . A doctor who saw me – not my regular private GP who referred me to you – said that was what had caused it.'

'No. In your case – on the Nerve Conduction Study, when little electric shocks are given to tags stuck on your skin and make your muscles jump . . . '

'I'm not likely to forget it! But it wasn't too bad.'

' . . . looking at the way your nerve impulses are transmitted, there's evidence of interference with the conduction mechanisms. The nerves are not fully up to speed . . .'

'Why does it go like that?'

'We don't know.'

'And why does it get better? . . . in some people? . . . some times?'

'We don't know that either – except that the body is constantly repairing itself and remodelling itself all the time . . .'

'And then it gives up?'

' . . . I wouldn't put it quite like that . . . It goes on trying . . . but in some illnesses the nervous system becomes progressively more defective.'

'Are there other illnesses that cause similar symptoms? The tinglings and numbness and so on?'

'Yes . . . In clinical practice one learns from experience to keep an open mind – diagnostically and therapeutically.'

'And in my case?'

'The probability is that you do have a neurological illness of one kind or another.'

'But you're not totally sure.'

'Ah well . . . There's an old saying – among doctors – that surgeons know nothing but do everything, physicians – like me – know everything but do nothing . . . and the only doctors who know everything and do everything are post-mortem pathologists – one day too late.'

'Ha!'

'That's the reality of the medical world.'

'My daughter's just qualified as a doctor . . . and got her first job – in her teaching hospital – in geriatrics.'

'There's a lot of neurology there.'

'Yes, that's what she said . . . It's why she wants to do it . . . before becoming a GP – eventually.'

'Congratulations . . . umm . . . Did she put you onto the idea of positive thinking?'

'No . . . It was a book – *The Power of Positive Thinking* – by Norman Vincent Peale.'

'Yes . . . There may be truth in it . . . There's certainly some evidence.'

'Will that help me?'

'It certainly won't do you any harm . . . unless you go completely "pie in the sky" and lose all your judgement.'

'That wouldn't do . . . I'm a lawyer.'

'There's no answer to that!'

'No . . . But I s'pose it's like what my wife – a gynaecologist – says ironically about some of her colleagues, "Trust me – I'm a doctor." '

* * *

Booted out on me ass . . . Just like that . . . Huh! . . . Don't s'pose that previous grievous client will mind. – Cotton bloody futures! . . . Hmm . . . What to do now? . . . Ha! . . . Live off me wits . . . Same as always . . . Nah . . . Gotta do better.

– No choice really . . . And bossy boots Phoebe's right . . .
Hate to say it . . . Yup, gotta face the parents' reality . . . and
mine. – Gotta put food on the table . . .

o O o

'Welcome to this course of lectures and seminars on healthcare and welfare systems. In this, your final year in med
school, you're getting progressively closer to having to make
clinical – and financial – decisions . . . My name is Precious
Ellington. Yes, it's a funky name for a guy . . . as they say in
the jazz world I come from . . .'

* * *

'Yeah, it's a demanding job, geriatrics. – Care for the Elderly
or whatever you call it – on this firm . . . The chief's a
stickler.'
'That's good . . . for the patients.'
'Oh God! . . . Another emancipated, politically correct
female! . . . Should've known. – They told me you did your
elective in the States.'
'Yes.'
'Funny choice.'
'Yes. – If you think so.'
'Well this job won't suit you . . . All these old crocks in
God's waiting room . . . Always complaining, calling out
"Nurse, nurse" all the time, forgetting what you just told
them . . . Let 'em die, I say – as in the USA.'
'Ever been there?'
'No . . . Don't want to. – Don't need to . . . Got a nice little
earner booked up in my father's practice in Devon . . . Nothing
too demanding – plenty of golf, sailing, bit of fly fishing – that

sort of thing . . . But Dad says the government stuff's getting tedious – always wanting GPs to do more work for less money – and these inspections and revalidations . . . Someone always on your back . . . Ha! . . . Good job we've got the British Medical Association – the medical politicians – on our side.'

* * *

'Now then Lizzie, me old fruit, what are we going to do about you?'

'I . . . er . . . I dunno . . . And you haven't called me that for ages . . . Which fruit did you have in mind?'

'Melons.'

'Roddy Finch, you're disgraceful! I'm not that large . . . umm . . . Am I?'

'"Do your boobs look large in this?" . . . That what you mean?'

'Yes.'

'I'll always love you – lust after you – whatever your shape.'

'Yes, well that's nice . . . but you haven't answered the question . . .

Do they?'

'Just a bit . . . Delicious.'

'Oh.'

'Have I said something wrong? . . . I was only trying to be nice to you.'

'You are nice . . . very nice – and very supportive.'

'Like your bra.'

'What has got into you, Roddy? Has some doctor given you Viagra or something?'

'No . . . umm . . . er . . . No. – I just thought how lovely you look . . . and we haven't had it for ages, what with all these worries.'

'S'pose not . . . Sorry about that . . . It's probably the anti-depressants causing me to put on weight – just a bit – and knocking me off my greens.'

'Ha! . . . And you haven't used that expression for ages.'

'Sorry.'

'Not your responsibility . . . Neither of us is up to it really. – Too much going on. Too many worries.'

'Oh we'll come through . . . somehow, I expect.'

'That's good – hearing you being optimistic . . . I certainly am.'

'What over?'

'Everything . . . Why not? . . . We're a long time dead.'

'I wish you wouldn't use that expression – or tell me I'm fat . . . Women are sensitive over that sort of thing.'

'I didn't say that. I . . .er . . . didn't mean it that way . . . I . . . er . . . fancy you . . . Only young once . . .'

'That's better . . . And what d'you think should be done about me?'

'Ha! . . . Right now?'

'Roddy Finch. You're extraordinary . . . At death's door one minute and then wanting to get your leg over.'

'Yes . . . and what are we going to do about it?'

'Make a girl feel loved . . . as you do . . . in your own special way . . . Come here, you lovely man.'

* * *

'Won't waste your valuable time, Mr Finch. Yer'll soon find out if yer can sell advertising space . . . On commission. – Yer'll sell – and make good money – or yer don't . . . Simple as that.'

'I've sold before . . . Commodities.'

'Mug's game – for punters and you.'

'Oh . . . er . . . Why? . . . If you don't mind me asking.'

'I don't mind. – Why would I mind? – Should have seen it fer yerself.'

'What?'

'With those punters yer're pushing at an open door.'

'Didn't feel like it.'

'They're greedy . . . Lost the plot . . . Lost their business judgement . . . or wherever . . . Throwing it at yer . . . And if yer can't catch a chunk of it, that's *yer* problem.'

'Oh.'

'Gotta be up front . . . Selling advertising space . . . No shite . . . Yer have to be straight wiv 'em. – No promises . . . Jus' tell 'em – Might work, might not.'

'You can't sell that.'

'I can, mate. – Made three hundred last year.'

'Three hundred grand?'

'Yep . . . five times the next highest earner . . . Still sixty grand's a good living, mind . . . er . . . for them . . . But nuffin' to spare – that's the point – for toys . . . Some of 'em made nuffin' . . . whole year thrown away, living off poncy Mum and Dad . . . Telling 'em a load a porkies . . . Stupid. – Wrong game for 'em.'

'Er . . . Yes . . . How do I learn from you? . . . if you're willing to show me.'

'No prob . . . No skin off my nose . . . If yer ain't got the basics – not a grafter – nobody can teach yer . . . It's a gift, see? . . . Fact of life.'

* * *

'That was nice . . . mmm . . . lovely . . . umm . . . Even though I didn't get anywhere . . . antidepressants again, I expect . . . umm . . . I've noticed something, Roddy . . . being on my own

... keeping the office open but nothing to do ... much ... Seeing occasional former patients wanting advice – no new ones, no cutting ... Alice won't stay indefinitely. – Paid ok but not enough to keep her busy ... interested.'

'So what is it you've noticed?'

'You and I tend to talk only about our problems – not so much nowadays about fun things.'

'Not surprising ... Hasn't been much fun – for either of us.'

'But if all we do is moan and groan to each other, we'll get bored, fed up.'

' ... "For better or worse, for richer or poorer, in sickness and in health" ...?'

'Yes – but not for lunch.'

'Oh ... I can always have lunch in chambers – times like now, when I'm back in form – or at the club.'

'No ... I'm very happy for you to have lunch here. – Course I am ... any time – It's just I don't want it imposed on us ... with no other choice.'

'Would you like me to take you to The Garrick some time?'

'No. That wouldn't be right ... on a side table by ourselves, taking you away from the long table and the snug ... umm ... with your chums.'

'So what would you like?'

'For things to be different ... like they used to be.'

'I don't remember a time when we had no troubles at all ... Look at Phoebe and James. – Everybody's got problems of one kind or another.'

'But they're the wrong sort of problems – for them ... and for us right now.'

'Like "leaves on the line" or the "wrong kind of snow" in the winter, causing the trains to be late?'

'Ha! Yes ... I remember that excuse ... And yes, I am

saying that, I s'pose. – I like problems I can get my teeth into
. . . well, hands anyway . . . er . . . gloved hands with a scal-
pel . . . not problems I can do nothing about.'

'Yes.'

'Ha! . . . And here I am, complaining about always talking
about problems – and I'm doing it again.'

'Married life.'

'No it isn't . . . I heard in a medical talk that couples – of all
ages and however long they've been together – tend to talk
about things they want to change . . . in the other person . . .
But a happily married life – or some other close relationship
– is the most important health factor of all . . . for physical
health – heart disease, diabetes – even more significant than
giving up smoking.'

'But it isn't always like that . . . happy, I mean . . . for
everybody.'

'How would you know?'

'Clients . . . potential litigants . . . They don't come to see
me – or your patients see you – if they haven't got problems.'

'But that's professional.'

'Yes . . . but personal also . . . Not my field – divorce – but
something like forty percent of all first marriages fail . . . and
it gets even worse with subsequent marriages.'

'Best stick with me, kid.'

'Yes . . . Yes, I certainly shall . . . umm . . . In the snug we
. . . aah . . . Sorry – can't tell you that – Chatham House rules.'

'Don't worry . . . I shan't pry – That's your safe haven . . .
It's just that I'd like us to have a safe haven all of our own . . .
here . . . at home . . . even more than we do already.'

'In splendid isolation? Ha! . . . A life with no problems is no
life at all. – You know that.'

'Umm . . . Yes I do . . . I s'pose.'

o O o

Yes . . . This is where I'm meant to be. – On the wards with patients who really need medical help . . . and with no chance of providing it for themselves . . . Hmm . . . Psychiatry and geriatrics – the two disciplines with greatest need for human interaction – and least likely to get it . . . Treated as the butt end of clinical practice – even in a teaching hospital . . . Look at that idiot who had the job before me! He's not worth asking the time of day, let alone a medical opinion . . . Just as Precious said about doctors who allow themselves to be mere units of healthcare – without thinking for themselves . . . Dear Precious . . .

*   *   *

'Father, I have a statement to make . . . and a request to ask.'

'I'd rather you ran them past your mother first . . . or maybe both of us at the same time.'

'I can understand that. – I've burned you too many times. – But would it be ok if I told them to you? . . . and then waited for a reply – from both of you?'

'That's ok – so long as you realise that I'm not the soft touch I used to be . . . and your mother never was.'

'Fair enough . . . I don't want to go back into commodity broking . . . Too shifty.'

'I could've told you that . . . The City itself is pretty shifty at the best of times but commodities take the prize – even above the money markets.'

'Yes . . . and I've taken a job selling advertising space – programmes for special events, that sort of caper.'

'If it's a "caper", it sounds like another scam.'

'Sorry. – Silly word – unless all selling's a scam . . . But it's the only thing I know I can do.'

'You could do lots of things . . . It's a question of motive and application.'

'Well my motive is to build a rehab . . . but I haven't got the money – and I'm not going to ask you for it.'

'Oh . . . But you are going to ask me . . . us . . . for *some* money?'

'Yes – just for now . . . to put food on my table . . . but . . .'

'But what, James? . . . What this time?'

'I don't need to stay living in the flat – in a smart part of town.'

'So where will you live?'

'Somewhere cheaper . . . renting, probably – no, definitely . . . obviously – and sharing.'

'Well I'm blowed! . . . er . . . How much d'you want?'

'Hopefully a lot less than you'll get from letting out the flat . . . and only until I'm earning my crust – rather than cadging it off the two of you.'

'And how long will that be? . . . er . . . Your mother's bound to ask.'

'I just don't know.'

'Well that's honest . . . Remarkable . . . remarkable.'

*   *   *

So what are my options? . . . Realistically? . . . Huh! . . . Not many . . . Can't go on as I am – getting nowhere . . . Try again in the operating theatre? . . . Hmm . . . Can't do that against the dictates of the contracts people. If something went wrong while I was operating, I'd be taken to the cleaners . . . And if I panicked again I'd lose the sympathy of . . . umm . . . everybody . . . EMDR? . . . No. – Too weird, too untried, untested . . . Not for me . . . Hypnotherapy . . . Might give it a try . . . I

dunno. – I don't fancy anything 'alternative' . . . Not my scene
. . . Stay with the antidepressants and CBT? – Not getting
anywhere . . . Counter-intuitive, really, CBT. – Trying to treat
an irrational problem with reason . . . I know what happened
to me . . . The anaesthetic awareness. I know it's extremely
rare and very unlikely indeed to happen to one of my patients.
I know I'm still alive . . . I know, I know, I know – but it doesn't
help . . . So . . . So . . . So . . . It looks like it'll have to be the
hypnotherapy . . . God help me . . .

o O o

No . . . It's not the same without Phoebe picking up my money
clip. The fire's gone out of it . . . But I owe it to this batch of
students to do my best for them . . . Keep my eye on the ball,
not let my mind wander . . . Ha! Yeah. I remember Joe Girardi,
the Yankees coach, saying, 'If you think too much, you fail –
because the game happens too quickly . . .

* * *

'It's lovely to see you, Phoebe, but I have to say it's such a
contrast to what it was like in my time. – We were on call
twenty four hours a day.'
'In some ways that might have been a good thing, Mum . . .
Even now – more or less – you've always been close to your
phone – until very recently . . . And I still am.'
'But the EU directive was meant to make junior doctors
less tired, safer.'
'Speaking from the vast experience of three weeks in the
job, I'd say that some doctors will never be safe . . . too full of
themselves and their entitlements, too political.'
'Gracious, Phoebe – to hear that from you!'

'Umm . . . I mean "political" as the BMA seems to mean it – *doctors'* rights rather than patients' rights.'

'Oh.'

'And another thing . . . How am I meant to learn? – if I'm not around? on the wards? . . . Anyway, I love the job, love the patients.'

'That's the way . . . So do I . . . er . . . So did I.'

* * *

'Yer problem, Mr Finch, is yer nervous . . . They sense that, see? . . . know yer trying ter sell.'

'But I *am* trying to sell.'

'Nah . . . Wrong attitude . . . Gotta give 'em value or virtue. – That's the way.'

'Sorry . . . I don't understand.'

'Either they thinks they're gettin' sumfink – and yer givin' 'em the best chance of gettin' a return . . .'

'Yes, I'd read up on it . . . Lord Nuffield said he was sure that half of all his adverting worked – but he didn't know which half.'

'Did 'ee now? . . . Nah . . . Gotta have instinct . . . nous . . . nose fer it . . . Know whaddi mean? – Can't get that from books. – Never read one in me life . . . 'cept sports stories.'

'Umm . . . What's the virtue?'

'Make 'em feel they're s'porting a good cause . . . Don't lay it on, mind . . . Leave 'em to tell yer themselves.'

'How do I do that?'

'All in the silences, mate . . . All in the silences – when yer keeps yer marf shut.'

* * *

'Really worried about you, Lizzie me love . . . Yer gotta look on the positive side – like I do.'

'For now."

'Huh?'

'Whoops! . . . Shouldn't have said that . . . Yes . . . You must be right . . . I've got to do that . . . umm . . . somehow . . . Just don't know how.'

'Well I'm still quiet at work . . . Possibly the lead-up to Christmas – but never like this before . . . More likely the word's got out. – Roddy Finch's off his game . . . Not reliable . . . Huh! Markets – mine as well as any other – don't like uncertainty.'

'So what do you do? . . . to keep your spirits up, fill up the time?'

'Read up the law reports . . . Chat to the others. – Keep meself sharp . . . Show them I'm back on form.'

'Well I go to lectures at the Royal Society of Medicine or the Royal College of Obs and Gynae . . . Problem is everyone puts on sympathetic faces and asks me how I'm getting along. – Counter-productive, really . . . for me. Makes me more depressed.'

'Go on the attack . . . Good principle in court – when you're in a tight fix.'

'But I don't want to "attack" anyone . . . I like to keep the peace, to be helpful to others.'

'Yes, it's difficult being on the receiving end of other people's concern all he time. – Isn't it? – At least until we're through all the tricky bits.'

'I wish I could be.'

* * *

'That's really shocking . . . the way you're looking after my mother . . . Call it a health service? – disease service more like.'

'She came in only last weekend . . . She was in a very poor state.'

'Plenty of time for you to sort her out . . . I mean look at those marks on her legs . . . I know she's difficult at times . . . drinks a bit . . . but have you been kicking her?'

'Certainly not . . . Those marks are due to Vitamin C deficiency. She doesn't eat sufficient fresh fruit – and her alcohol consumption won't help.'

'Vitamin deficiency! – In this day and age? . . . That's dreadful! . . . I'll certainly be making a complaint about that – write to my MP . . . What do the Social Services people – and the home helps – think they're doing?'

'The Social Services found her . . . following up routinely on their at-risk register of old people living alone – as most do.'

'Not following up well enough, it seems to me – and what about her GP? . . . God knows we pay enough in taxes to keep you lot in business.'

'It's a question of supply and demand . . . overwhelmed . . . Umm . . . Do you mind me asking when you last saw her yourself?'

'Six months ago, something like that . . . Look, it's not my job to look after her. – I've got work to do. – I mean that's why we have the Welfare State – isn't it? – to look after people like her . . . Disgraceful!'

* * *

'Make yourself perfectly comfortable . . . That's right . . . Sit with your feet flat on the floor and with the palms of your hands flat on your thighs . . . That's right . . . Now follow my finger with your eyes . . . gently up . . . and gently *down* . . . up . . . and *down* . . . in time with your breathing . . . in . . . and out . . . up . . . and *down* . . . and now, as your chest goes down, gently close your eyes . . . That's right . . . breathe in . . . and . . . out . . . That's right . . . Relax your facial muscles around your eyes . . . and at the corners of your mouth . . . Relax the muscles of your shoulders . . . and *down* your arms . . . Relax the muscles of your chest . . . and *down* to your tummy . . . Relax the muscles of your thighs . . . and *down* your legs . . . Feel that lovely sense of relaxation spreading from the top of your head . . . to your toes . . . Remember a happy time, a beautiful time, a lovely time . . . Step into that positive resource now . . . See what you saw . . . Hear what you heard . . . Feel what you felt . . . Take that lovely feeling and let it spread into your past . . . your present . . . and your future . . . Take that lovely relaxing feeling into the area of your life that you feel needs help . . .'

o O o

'So how's my real politician now?'

'Ha! . . . That's nice of you, Mum – That's exactly the way I see myself nowadays . . . Politics in practice on the wards. – Real life, not theory.'

'Marx wouldn't approve of that . . . Never did a job in his life. – Lived off Engels.'

'Good ideas, though . . . Some of them.'

'I'll need a lot of persuading.'

'Well how about, "To each according to his need."? . . . The old people I see on the wards every day have no chance, without someone – somehow – looking after them . . . But there's no votes in it. – That's the problem . . . Old people vote . . . but not when they get to this stage . . . Disenfranchised really . . .

Nobody's really interested in them. – Not like young people who may choose not to vote – and follow whichever current revolutionary is in fashion . . . mistaking banality for profundity.'

'I remember your Che Guevara t-shirt.'

'That was just to rebel against you . . . and Dad.'

'Very healthy.'

'Umm . . . Thank you, Mum . . . But, y'know, I do see one problem – my chief taught me this – and Precious said it in one of his sessions – with the elderly . . . really elderly, not like you and Dad . . .'

'Thank you, Phoebe.'

'They both said we have to define the needy, define the need and define the resources that can be shown specifically to alleviate each need.'

'Yes . . . That's right. – I saw so much waste when I worked in the NHS . . . Can't afford that in the private sector. – Got to be personally responsible . . . That was the idea of giving doctors budgets in the NHS.'

'Maybe . . . but it just leads to complaints of underfunding – and Tory cuts – when, as Precious said, there haven't been any cuts in real terms . . . only cuts in what the last government promised as bribes to the electorate.'

'Heavens, Phoebe . . . You sound just like your father! . . . And – in my professional lifetime – I've certainly seen the end product of universality in healthcare provision, promising everything to everybody.'

'Yes, that's what I'm learning . . . If politicians – and doctors – aren't prepared to define need . . . and take into account the capacity of patients to benefit . . . it shows their true interest isn't really in helping . . . Patients are just political pawns . . . It suits the political game – and medico-political game – to give them too much or too little . . . and the politicians – of all types – win both ways . . . They win votes – of a certain kind . . .'

'Yes . . . It's government by slogan.'

'I fear so . . . I'm even coming to see – from practical experience – that healthcare, in total, maybe *isn't* a birthright . . . You have to consider what it costs – and what the benefits might be – or not . . . Otherwise the care is wasted.'

'D'you think, Phoebe, we should have a two-tier system in healthcare? . . .the same as in everything else? . . . one tier for those who can afford it – like Dad and me . . . er . . . so far? – and one for those who genuinely can't?'

'Well . . . I wouldn't go that far . . . Yet . . . But something's got to change . . . Our Welfare Stare – that I've always believed in so passionately – isn't working in practice . . . as far as I can see generally . . . in the big picture.'

'Heavens again, Phoebe! . . . That man of yours – and your chief as well – seem to have had an immense influence on you.'

'I'm learning for myself – in practice.'

* * *

Oh no! . . . No, no, no . . . What now? . . . Why am I unsteady on me feet again? . . . Haven't drunk as much . . . Ha! Maybe not more than usual – but still more than you should, Ha! As the neurologist would say . . . Why do I find it difficult going up stairs or getting up off the loo seat? . . . Frightening . . .

* * *

Well that job didn't work. – Not as good as I thought I was at selling. – Still, better to find out now than after throwing another year away . . . Umm . . . What in God's name – Ha! . . .

Mother would approve of that! – Me calling on God! – do I do now? . . . Not a bloody clue . . . Frightening . . .

* * *

Hmm . . . I remember feeling relaxed – first time in a long time – since the . . . er . . . hypnosis thingy . . . Still do . . . Don't remember what happened after that . . . Must've worked, I s'pose . . . Cost enough . . . even without going to see that special man in America . . . Said he learned it from him. – Must be the same general process – hypnosis – anywhere, I s'pose – Huh! . . . I don't feel much different now . . . Still can't imagine going back to work . . . Can't risk it . . . Frightening . . .

o O o

'I've made my decision and that's that . . . Well, more or less.'

'Which one this time?'

'I'm considering not applying for another job after this one finishes at the end of the four months.'

'What on earth's that about?'

'Higher priorities.'

'Is that man, Precious, taking you off to America?'

'No. – I haven't seen him or heard from him . . . in person. – Just one text when I passed the exams. – That was the deal – well, my terms.'

'Dear little one, you always were impetuous . . . It's wonderful to be so decisive . . . in a sensible direction . . . You sure this is? . . . er . . . sensible?'

'It would be the most sensible thing I've ever done in my life . . . I'm planning to do something I really believe I should do – because it's the right thing to do.'

'But, if you leave before you've completed all the necessary house jobs for registration, the GMC won't let you practise . . . and you won't be able to earn your living.'

'I'm thinking of doing something else.'

'After all those years of study? – and after qualifying and getting a teaching hospital house job?'

'Yes . . . I've thought about it since I qualified . . . I've made some enquiries and I'm coming round to thinking it's the right thing to do.'

'Well all right then . . . I . . . er . . . I s'pose you can always go back to it . . . when you want to . . . They can't un-qualify you . . . just make you complete your foundation years of training.'

'Yes. They'll fill my present place easily enough.'

'Yes, I'm sure . . . Yes. But what are you thinking of doing?'

'Becoming a registered carer.'

'What? . . . for old people? . . . people who can't look after themselves properly?

'Yes.'

'But you're a doctor. – You could do so much more . . . Really helping.'

'I will be helping.'

'Shall. – Future tense, not imperative.'

'Ha! Dear Mum . . . Still correcting me.'

'Oh! . . . Sorry . . . Force of habit . . . So who are you thinking of caring for? . . . Some old person you met on the ward?'

'No.'

'Who then?'

'You . . . You and Dad.'

'What! . . . You'll do absolutely no such thing.'

'Future tense or imperative?'

'Umm . . . Both . . . Over my dead body!'

'Or Dad's.'

'Oh . . . Oh.'

'I've seen – on the ward – the way people go into a sharp decline . . . when they're not looked after properly . . . It's my responsibility to look after you.'

'It certainly is *not* . . . We're perfectly capable of looking after ourselves – and each other.'

'For now.'

'And what does that mean?'

'It means I'm being realistic . . . Neither of you are.'

'Is . . . Neither is singular . . . Whoops! . . . Sorry about that.'

'Gosh, Mum, here we are – having the most important conversation of our lives . . . well, mine anyway . . . umm . . . second most important . . . and you're still Grammarian-in-Chief!'

'I won't hear of it . . . Nor will Dad . . . I'm sure I can speak for him . . . er . . . just this once.'

'You can speak on behalf of the whole wide world if you want to . . . but it's what I've got to do . . . It's the same instinct that made me want to be a doctor in the first place.'

'You and your instincts!'

'And what's that meant to mean?'

'Oh . . . Sorry . . . Just slipped out.'

'Well it can slip back in again . . . I'm not doing this as a grand gesture – or as a headstrong crazy thing, like some of the things I've done in the past . . . It's what I want to do – for myself as well as for the two of you.'

'But why, Phoebe? . . . Why, little one? . . . Why? – You've got so much to lose.'

'I've lost Precious already.'

'Oh my God! . . . Is that why you let him go? For us?'

'Yes.'

*   *   *

Don't want to fail. Don't want to lose her . . . But mustn't hassle her. Ha! She'd hit my pitch right into the outfield . . . And my field of dreams would be over . . .

* * *

'It's meant to be the other way round.'

'What is?'

'Children are meant to learn from us – not us from them . . . After you told me what Phoebe said, I fear she may be right.'

'About us not living in reality?'

'Yes.'

'My reality – the anaesthetic awareness – is only too real . . . I'd get over it if I possibly could.'

'I want to avoid mine . . . for as long as possible.'

'Hmm . . . So what are we going to do about Phoebe's plan?'

'Respect it . . . and thwart it.'

'How?'

'Show her that we don't need her.'

'How? . . . We're neither of us fully functional . . . and it's a bit difficult changing careers at our age.'

'But it's possible . . . People do . . . You could. – Better chance than me.'

'So your Grand Plan is that I should change my career . . . Ha! . . . How very like a man! – But I don't want to do anything else . . . Surgery's in my bones, I s'pose.'

'Couldn't you be a different type of doctor? . . . I mean – at least you'd get your dignity back . . . umm . . . be back with your colleagues.'

'I doubt it . . . Everything's so specialised nowadays. – I'd have to start from scratch . . . and the truth is nobody would take me on . . . at any level. – I'm in a new category, "Poor old Lizzie".'

'Yes . . . and I s'pose I'm going to be "Poor old Roddy" . . . Well bugger that!'

'Roddy?'

'Ha! . . . Sorry, dear.'

'You're not a bit sorry.'

'No . . . I'm not . . . This whole thing's a right buggeration . . . for both of us . . . No idea where it'll end up. – On the scrap-heap, most likely.'

'You're a bundle of fun . . . and a vulgar one – even though Terry Pratchett would've called it an "embuggerance". – What would they say about you if you spoke like that in the club? . . .'

'Hmm.'

'Roddy, I said, "What would they say about you if you spoke like that in the club? . . ."'

'Yes . . . I heard you.'

'And what've you got to say?'

'Hmm . . .'

'Ah! – I'm getting really slow on the uptake . . . I s'pose that's why you lot – in the snug – are against women members.'

'We're not on duty in the club.'

'Oh that's how you see us. – And you're all real-life Rumpoles . . . "She who must be obeyed.".'

'Hmm.'

'Roddy? . . . Say something . . .'

'Hmm.'

'Ha! . . . The Queen's Counsel . . . at the commercial bar . . . subdued into silence . . . by his wife.'

* * *

'It's really kind of you both to say I could come back to live with you for a bit . . . while I look for a residential job – like The Phebe.'

'You've not got the same crackpot idea that y'sister's got? Have you?'

'Shh.'

'Oh . . . Sorry, dear.'

'What idea was that?'

'Oh you know Phoebe . . . the idea of the week . . . umm . . . So long as you keep your room tidy . . . And don't get under our feet – like the cat.'

'Actually I think we have a splendid relationship with Denning . . . Law unto himself but no trouble – provided we look after him.'

'You don't feed him.'

'He could feed himself if he had to . . . So can you, young James. – Y'mother's got more than enough to cope with.'

'Yes . . . Yes . . . I can . . . Don't know how – apart from the microwave or a takeaway – but that's ok.'

'What you need is a wife . . . a rich one preferably.'

'Roddy, you're impossible! . . . I don't suppose it ever occurs to either of you that I might like a wife of my own.'

'You?'

'You?'

'Yes me. – What's so odd about that? nowadays?'

'Hmm.'

'Hmm.'

'Yes. – Thought that'd shut you up . . . both of you.'

'Umm . . . Lizzie?'

'Yes, dear?'

'You don't really mean that . . . er . . . Do you?'

* * *

'Welcome back.'

'Thank you . . . I didn't have any other choice.'

'Really? . . . Why not?'

'My daughter's thinking of sacrificing her career – to care for me and my husband.'

'That's very noble of her – but, hopefully, unnecessary.'

'Yes . . . and my maternal instinct is to protect my child . . . I'll do anything to get well – even come to see you.'

'Ha! . . . Some might say that was a misjudgement.'

'Oh dear! . . . I didn't mean it rudely . . . I . . . er . . .'

'Don't worry about that. – I anticipate you meant that you're willing to take the risk of venturing into uncharted territory.'

'Yes.'

'As you will doubtless recall . . . so am I.'

'Yes.'

'I want you to be absolutely sure that this is what you want to do.'

'Yes. It is . . . umm . . .'

'What's the hesitation?'

'I don't want to be made worse.'

'My experience of things going wrong – when other people do things – is that it happens when they're *over*-confident.'

'Yes – the anaesthetist who did me was talking about football . . . not concentrating on my care.'

'I've made mistakes myself – of course I have – particularly when I was learning my trade.'

'Me as well.'

'Even now I have a supervisor – a consultant psychiatrist. – I run things past him . . . I'll ask him to see both of us together.'

'Not immediately. Let's get on with it. – I've got to take the chance some time . . . er . . . with somebody.'

'Well at least I hope I've learned the value of something Mark Twain said . . . "I was grateful to be able to answer promptly, and I did. I said I didn't know.".'

'Ha! – Yes, I like that. We seem to speak the same language – you and I.'

'Okay . . . Then let's see this as a very careful adventure that we're both involved in together. – After all . . . In the private sector we share one thing in common . . .'

'What's that?'

'If patients are happy with what we do, they might tell one other person. If they're not, they'll tell the whole world . . . and the press . . . and the regulatory bodies . . . and then demand the return of their fee . . . All in the name of lessons being learned – for the benefit of other patients.'

'Yes, I've seen professional colleagues destroyed in that way . . . over silly little things – mistakes that any of us might have made . . . That's the Shipman legacy . . . The General Medical Council nowadays has a majority of lay members – people who haven't had any clinical experience . . . not understanding that we doctors have so many decisions to make – all the time – in the heat of the moment.'

'But there's also the ground rule of the private sector . . . If we don't like the heat, we shouldn't be in this particular kitchen.'

'Agreed. Let's give it a go.'

'Yes . . . Here's the background paperwork – on EMDR and how I myself use it. – You can read it in your own time rather than when you're paying me for mine . . . a couple of questionnaires and an explanation of the process. Then there's an example of episodes from my own childhood and adult life – with it set out in a simple structure.'

'Yes . . . I like things being properly organised and clear –

not wishy-washy, caring and sharing.'

'Then there's a blank template for you to fill in your own experiences of traumatic events – of any kind . . . as many as you think had an effect on you.'

'I tried to bury some of that stuff . . . from childhood, I mean.'

'It'll still be there . . . and it'll have echoes in the present – over how you feel about certain things.'

'Do we really have to go over all that unpleasantness?'

'I would recommend it . . . Take the chance to look at it and – if I'm anticipating you correctly – say three things . . . "It did happen" . . . "It was wrong" . . . "It was then, not now". And then – after that's securely embedded – "I don't have to carry it with me any more, on the surface or buried deep down".'

'Hmm.'

'Don't worry . . . I won't rush you . . . Or take you where you don't want to go. – That would simply re-traumatise you.'

'Yes.'

'What I found, when I had EMDR myself after the death of my wife, was that it was almost surgical . . . It took away the bad bits and left me with the normal healthy parts – the natural response that anyone would have – and the EMDR enabled me to heal and get on with life.'

'I like that analogy a lot . . . surgical . . . without the medical risks.'

'Well there certainly are psychological risks – when people use EMDR as a party trick, showing how clever they are.'

* * *

Oh Precious, precious Precious, I do miss you . . . I so much want to see you, talk to you, hold you, kiss you – with or

without onions . . . And the rest . . . I can't, I can't, I can't . . .
Gotta look after the family. – Not James. He can look after
himself . . . Needs a kick. – But no fault of theirs – the parents
– they're in this mess . . . You'd understand, with your mother's difficulties when you were my age . . . and younger . . . I
must do what she did. – Give the care that many others don't
. . . Hmm . . . The Welfare State should – but on what I've seen
. . . on the wards, in real life, not in theory – it doesn't . . . Too
many people chasing too few resources and pushing each
other out of the way – like a January sale . . . So much waste
. . . and lack of thought . . . for each other . . . What are we
going to do? . . . Precious, you and me? . . . umm . . . you and
I? . . . to put the world to rights?'

o O o

'It's what I want to do. One day I want to build my own rehab.
I reckon this work, as a care assistant, is good experience for
me . . . starting at the sharp end, doing the thankless tasks.'
    'We'll see how long you last . . . Anyone can make a bed
and re-stock cupboards for one day – or even a week – as a
publicity stunt. Even politicians do that for one day or one
week.'
    'I want to do it for life . . . Well, work in a rehab – not make
beds and stock cupboards . . . I've seen how the other half
lives – and I didn't like what I saw.'
    'Take it from me, James, this job's a killer. We do the work
nobody else wants to do – certainly not the nurses, let alone
the counsellors, the demi-gods . . . and, as you say, we never
get any thanks. We're non-persons, phantoms. We don't exist
. . . "Lucy Who?" is the name I go by . . . People assume the
jobs we do just get done - "somehow".'
    'Well I want to learn precisely how they're done. – Then I'll

never take my staff for granted . . . umm . . . in the way you are – even by some of the patients . . . p'raps especially by some of the patients . . . '

'Yes, that's true for some of them . . . Just because they're paying to be here – or their parents, more like – they act as if they own the whole place and can order us around any way they want.'

'That's rough.'

'Yeah . . . It's all part of the entitlement mentality – the-something-for-nothing society.'

'Oh . . . I s'pose I've got to learn how to be taken for granted . . . umm . . . God knows I've done a lot of taking other people for granted in my time . . . parents, clients, girlfriends . . . umm . . . Is there any lunch anywhere?'

'Not if you didn't bring it in . . . You've certainly got a lot to learn, James . . . Here – have some of mine.'

* * *

Maybe I could work as a conciliator in divorce cases. Work to help couples sort things out sensibly . . . Judges are always suggesting it. Governments want it. – Stop people throwing their money away on litigation . . . Ha! – spending it on lawyers like me . . . "Not fair!", they say – always do . . . Favourite word of politicians . . . some of them . . . "The law's only for rich people" . . . Ha! – Politicians have only them-selves to blame . . . If they want less litigation – and less paid out in legal aid fees to criminal lawyers – they should make fewer laws . . .

* * *

'That's very sad . . . How long were you married?'

'Forty six years . . . She'd have been very cross – missing the big five oh.'

'But to stay together for that length of time is a wonderful achievement for both of you.'

'Thank you, doctor . . . Very kind of you . . . Are you married?'

'Not yet . . . Will be one day – I hope.'

'I hope you'll be as happy as we were . . . Plenty of cross words – they're healthy . . . kept me on my toes – but no resentments.'

'We did the best we could for her . . . but – at the end – she didn't have the strength.'

'Ha! – You'd never have said that in her younger days . . . She was a fighter, our Rose – "Rose of England" we called her.'

'That's wonderful . . . Did she do something special to earn that title?'

'Not particularly. – She wasn't the head of anything or the winner of anything . . . She just loved people – and we loved her. She had English values . . . kindness, thoughtfulness, nothing too much trouble for her.'

'Well that's very special . . . in my view.'

'You're very kind yourself, doctor . . . always ready to spend time with patients – or relatives, like me now – even though you're so busy.'

'Thank you . . . In some ways that's the part of my work I enjoy the most – getting to know the people, not just their illnesses.'

*   *   *

'I filled in the questionnaires . . . Nothing too exciting for you there.'

'Hmm ... Freud spent his whole life studying strange people and weird complexes ... but I like Professor Martin Seligman's ideas – from the University of Pennsylvania – "*Positive Psychology*", he calls it. – Looking at what people do well and copying that, enhancing that.'

'Sounds good to me.'

'He's a great man ... Wonderful ideas – and human.'

'How d'you know? ... Did you meet him?'

'Yes ... at a conference in California – just by Disney World. Ha! ... The founder and organiser, Dr Jeffrey Zeig, made a crack about that, saying that psychologists often watch mice going through a maze – in experiments – but there, in the Evolution of Psychotherapy conference, the Mouse watches the psychologists going through mental mazes.'

'Ha!'

'The answers to the questionnaires don't show anything unexpected ... At a glance.'

'Is that why you put us through them? your patients?'

'Yes ... I like to be fully prepared in advance. No surprises.'

'And the consent form?'

'So that you're sure you're really committed.'

'Not to protect yourself?'

'I can't protect myself in this work ... If I'm not vulnerable – emotionally – I can't sense what the patient is feeling. – I'd be all closed down ... Can't do my work like that.'

'You telepathic?'

'I think we all are – like animals and birds ... maybe all living creatures are – until it's trained out of us in childhood ... at home sometimes – and at school.'

'Yes ... I remember – so many times – being told, "You shouldn't feel that way" and "It's perfectly ok" when it obviously wasn't.'

'What wasn't?'

'The stuff with my father . . . I wrote it down on your forms – as you asked. This is all confidential, isn't it?'

'That's precisely why I work entirely on my own nowadays – no staff, nobody . . . Not like a residential rehab where everybody gets to know everything . . . Leaks like a sieve.'

'There must be some advantages.'

'Many – but I don't think counsellors can do one-to-one work until they've had all their training in group – and seen all the psychological games people play . . . They're easy to spot from the outside but not when you're actually involved in it, one-to-one.'

'Ah . . . I see . . . Well, I s'pose there's no point in coming to see you if I'm not open with you.'

'You'd be surprised how many people want to persuade me that black is white – such as saying they can drink sensibly when they obviously can't . . . Things like that.'

'Yes – Like my son . . . You met him.'

'Yes, I remember . . . How's he doing?'

'He's started work in a rehab . . .'

'Really?'

'. . . as a care assistant – helping out the nurses.'

'Good . . . That's the way. – Get the real feel of what it's all about . . . Now then – back to you.'

'Yes . . . Back to me . . . It's ok for me still to be nervous about this, isn't it?'

'I'd be worried about you if you weren't.'

'Oh . . . Good.'

'What we do now is to take all those events you've written about and put them into a clearly structured format – you and I together – on this new form . . . one after another and putting them into groups in which they all say the same thing – the same negative belief about yourself – "I'm stupid" or "I don't deserve better" or "I'm not worth loving" and so on.'

'I did feel all of those things . . . at times.'

'And maybe even now . . . when you think back to those events.'

'Umm . . . Yes.'

'And possibly you feel similar things over your anaesthetic awareness?'

'Yes . . . "I'm stupid. – I should've got over it". – Just like my mother used to say to me over silly little things that happened to me at school.'

'I doubt you felt they were "silly little things" at the time.'

'No, I didn't . . . They were huge . . . but I should've got over them by now.'

'Early childhood experiences go down deep. Freud – and the Jesuits – were right about that . . . although the Freudians, who follow the great man, sometimes make psychoanalysis into a religion. – Holy writ. – They can make a right performance out of it. In your case, as I said, we'll put all the similar negative beliefs into groups. Then they'll all go down in groups – like ninepins – and they simply become part of your history, but no longer unsettling, disturbing.'

'Saving time?'

'Yes – and money – but also being more effective, recognising the way the brain files things – not the way we think it ought to file . . . chronologically.'

'How d'you mean?'

'Sometimes the brain might file according to the colour blue – the blue curtains in your bedroom in childhood, the blue sky on a holiday, some blue china, a blue dress – memories all over the place from different times.'

'That isn't very rational.'

'We're not rational . . . we're intuitive . . . until it's trained out of us.'

'Surely – ideally – we should be both.'

'Yes, I think so . . . The significance today – for you and me – is that EMDR doesn't appear to be rational, even though there's a lot of evidence – from functional PET scans – of what's happening in the brain and why EMDR seems to work.'

'Oh . . . I must look that up.'

'It's more a matter of trust, really . . . Just let it happen, don't try to work it all out.'

'But that's against all my training.'

'Yes, that's why doctors can be very difficult to help . . . Our training – even in psychiatry and psychology, such as it is for most of us as medical students – tends to be all intellectual.'

'It has to be.'

'EMDR has more in common with the arts – although, as I say, it does have a scientific base . . . It's more like music or painting . . .'

'Or drama.'

'Yes.'

'I thought I'd had enough drama for one lifetime.'

'Yes you have . . . And this is the time to help you to leave the drama behind, retaining the appropriate sense of distress that such a thing could ever have happened to you but no longer re-living it in the present.'

'I do hope so.'

*   *   *

'James? . . . Yer father . . . How's things? . . . Well I didn't expect it to be a bunch of roses for you. – Being a gofer never is . . . Yes, that's right. – It's how we learn. – But are you enjoying it? . . . er . . . Are you in the right place? . . . er . . . Is this what you really want to do? . . . Good . . . Good . . .

Well good luck to you, son . . . Us? How are we getting on?
. . . umm . . . Talk about changes! – but we're ok really . . .
Good as can be expected, I s'pose . . . Yer mother's gone off
to try that EMDR thing after all . . . Yes . . . Yes, that's right
– Nothing else worked . . . umm . . . Hope it doesn't make her
worse . . . Oh nothing, no reason at all. – Just nervous on her
behalf. Wretched business, wretched business . . . Me?
– Fine, fine . . . Getting to the club every so often. – Must
take you there again some time. Decent people – kind, very
supportive . . . Well here we are – each of us moving on in
our own way – Phoebe too . . . No nothing in particular . . .
er . . . just yet.'

o O o

'Life's so unfair to some people . . . umm . . . Death is so
unfair.'

'That's the way it is in geriatrics. We do our best. That's all
we can do.'

'I mean . . . She wasn't a sun-worshipper or a compulsive
tanner. Why would this particular patient get a melanoma?'

'There isn't a "why". Some people just do . . . Could be a
genetic predisposition. – As you know, from your under-
graduate days, there are millions of cell divisions all the time.
And some of them go wrong all the time. The remarkable
thing is that we live as long as we do. What we're trying to
find out is how the body recognises – and removes – the
faulty cells and retains the good ones . . . Otherwise we'd all
get all sorts of cancers all the time.'

'But when I took her history, while she was still lucid –
before the cerebral secondaries destroyed her – she seemed
to have had a blameless life . . . She didn't smoke, hardly
drank, ate all the right things, happy relationship – every-

thing in her favour.'

'Well that's what we're trying to research on my firm . . . One of the things . . . Why some people get cancers and others don't. The immune system – in some people – the cellular environment, gets compromised and the cancer cells take root instead of being bumped off by the body's natural defences . . . It's a war. The wrong side wins sometimes – and we need to find out why.'

'I find it difficult to be so dispassionate . . . I got to know her well while we were still investigating the causes of her unsteadiness – and all the other symptoms and signs you pointed out on the teaching round . . . I hadn't realised that an amelanotic melanoma – particularly on the palms or soles – can be so dangerous.'

'Yes, being pink rather than black, they're often assumed to be benign – and in those particular parts of the body they're repeatedly traumatised.'

'Well at least I did know that they often metastasise before the primary lesion is noticed.'

'Yes, as in this lady's case, it had spread to the regional glands in the groin – and the post-mortem showed it had spread to the peritoneum as well, which accounts for her abdominal cramps.'

'I felt so dumb, so powerless to do anything of any value for her.'

'I didn't appoint you to be God.'

'Oh . . . I don't see myself that way – and my mother, who believes in these things, says that God's a man – because it says so in the Bible.'

'Ha! . . . I'm not sure that He exists at all – not an Old Testament retributive God . . . As you'll have observed on the wards . . . because you get to know the patients really well – seeing them every day – some rather unpleasant people do well and some lovely people, like this lady, get felled, chopped down like an old tree.'

'I spent some time with her husband yesterday, when I gave him the death certificate . . . He's lovely too. – It really is so unfair.'

'That's another thing . . . People who are calm and gentle . . . umm . . . accepting whatever comes their way and making the best of it, do well – usually – and people who put up a fight also tend to do well. It's the ones who give up, turn their faces to the wall, who go down . . . And we don't know why that is . . . not really. – Not at all, if we're honest.'

* * *

'Laundry day . . . Come on James, move yourself.'

'Where to?'

'Where d'you think? . . . Get the dirty sheets, pillowcases and towels from the men's bedrooms, put them into the wheelie thing and take it to the laundry room . . . I'll do the same for the women's bedrooms . . . Then we'll meet up in the laundry and I'll show you how to work the washing machines and dryers.'

'Surely that's common sense.'

'You're not allowed to use common sense nowadays . . . There has to be a written policy and a written procedure, a training programme and a monitoring system. – Health and Safety . . . And the Care Quality Commission . . . And probably the Employment Protection Act or something.'

'What if I just read the manufacturer's instructions?'

'No . . . We're not allowed to do that . . . umm . . . If someone hasn't trained you, and if you haven't been signed off for that, there'd be hell to pay – and the boss would probably be in trouble with the lawyers . . . fined . . . if something went wrong. – Like someone slipping on a wet patch or getting an electric shock – or both – with catastrophic consequences.'

'Ha! . . . You've got a vivid imagination, Lucy.'

'Not half as vivid as the regulator's . . . They never look at what's going right – not interested in that – only at what might go wrong . . . Not that they give a damn about anyone actually getting hurt. – It's all about making sure the regulators themselves never get blamed for missing something.'

* * *

I don't often talk to you, God. – More Lizzie's line than mine . . . But I reckon we've had a rough time . . . One way or another, just recently . . . What've we done to deserve that, I'd like to know? . . . I know justice on earth is a question of how the arguments are presented – and getting the right judge – but I'd imagined You played by better rules . . . fair ones . . . Otherwise what's Lizzie been doing? . . . praying to you all these years? . . .

* * *

'If you sit on the piano stool at the electronic keyboard, I'll sit on a chair opposite you so that we're facing each other . . . I rest my arm up on the top so that it doesn't get tired, reaching over . . . And your eyes won't get tired either – because you're looking down, rather than straight ahead . . . and also you're not getting distracted by what you could see elsewhere in the room or through the window.'

'That's good . . . umm . . . I was wondering how long it's going to take . . . in each go – keeping my eyes moving.'

'In my experience, a lot more time – effective time – than with you looking straight ahead . . . Customarily twenty four passes – from one side to the other and back again – are done in EMDR . . . I may do up to four hundred – until we both want a rest – or until you've said all you have to say on an issue . . . or when you get a bit stuck and I feel you'd benefit from a therapeutic interject.'

'What on earth's that?'

'Well, for example, it's when I ask you whether you'd have the same attitude towards someone else – in the same situation – as you do to yourself.'

'Oh.'

'Ready?'

'Yes.'

'You're going to play the middle of those three black notes with your left hand – there – and then the same note, three octaves higher – yes, that's the one – with your right hand . . . Now watch my signet ring as I touch first the back of your left hand and then the right . . . Keep your head still and just move your eyes.'

'I thought you said EMDR shouldn't be done as a party trick.'

'This is the real thing . . . well, my version of it.'

'What's so special about your version?'

'I give four inputs at the same time – first to one side of the body and then the other – with touch, sound, muscular movement and eye movement . . . Four times the input of eye movement alone.'

'What's the advantage?'

'Several . . . Four inputs – to one side of the brain and then the other – speeds up the process of communication between the thinking brain and the feeling brain.'

'Really?'

'Yes . . . As I mentioned previously, functional PET scans of people having EMDR confirm that both cerebral hemispheres are active, rather than one side or the other.'

'Remarkable.'

'What was remarkable was the intuitive sense of Dr Francine Shapiro, the Californian psychologist who created EMDR ... umm ... These particular scans – which didn't exist when she began – confirmed her belief ... It's one possible explanation of why it works in resolving the traumatic memories that get stuck in the feeling brain.'

'How did she discover it?'

'She tried it out on herself ... er ... That's not recommended, by the way ... until you've been formally trained – so that you don't hurt yourself even further.'

'Don't you worry ... I've no intention of doing this on myself – or anyone else ... I'm in trouble enough already.'

'Anyway, the patients Dr Shapiro worked on were people like war veterans and rape victims ... She got them fully functional again – emotionally ... behaviourally ... socially – and she received a lifetime achievement award from the State of California.'

'From Schwarzenegger – The Terminator? ... The Governor?'

'I don't know ... But I do know she's helped – and her staff have now trained – a huge number of people, all over the world ... Even the UK is beginning to catch on.'

'Why d'you say "even"?'

'We tend to be rather slow in taking on new ideas from anyone else ... I s'pose that's a good thing in some ways. – We had relatively few Thalidomide children.'

'Yes I know ... Thank God.'

'But perhaps there's also a bit of, "Why should we learn anything from anyone else? – We've got the NHS." ... EMDR has only just been accepted by NICE as a treatment for Post Traumatic Stress Disorder.'

'Yes, they're dead slow on new gynae ideas as well – such an incredible performance . . . Snails are quicker.'

'But not necessarily more effective – or safer . . . You yourself – understandably – were very cautious of starting this.'

'Well . . . best to get on with it now.'

'Good . . . Gently . . . Let's start with episode one – on the structured format we prepared . . . Remember to keep moving your eyes but not your head. Try to keep a steady rhythm . . . Event number one – Repeated childhood sexual abuse from father from age four to age thirteen . . . Most significant image. – Him opening my bedroom door . . . Negative belief about self. – I am responsible . . . Feelings. – Shame, self-loathing, fear . . . Subjective unit of disturbance or distress on a scale of zero to ten. – Ten . . . Body sensations. – Fast heart beat, tightness in chest, gagging.'

Plonk plink, plonk plink, plonk plink, plonk plink . . .

* * *

'Oh.'

'Oh . . . It's you.'

'What are you doing here?'

'It's lecture day . . . I come here to revel in happy memories. – Smoky hamburger . . .'

'With onions?'

'Of course . . . and courgette fries on the side.'

o O o

Part 2

'Now then, when we're doing all these bilateral inputs – eye movement, sound, touch and muscular movement – all four of them with you sitting at the piano and me facing you, please talk about that time with your father . . . Say what you see and hear and feel . . . Take your time. – Often it takes a full hour or more to process the first event. It tends to get quicker later on. – The brain gets the hang of it and you get more confident as the disturbance or distress level gradually reduces . . . as you'll discover for yourself.'

Plonk plink, plonk plink, plonk plink, plonk plink, plonk plink, plonk plink, plonk plink . . .

'I'm frightened of going to bed . . . I drag out supper for as long as I can . . . I cling to my mother – but she doesn't seem to notice . . . I've got that tight feeling in my chest . . .'

Plonk plink, plonk plink, plonk plink, plonk plink . . .

* * *

'Congratulations, Dr Finch.'

'Thank you, Precious. I've missed you . . . But I have to tell you straight away – the situation hasn't changed . . . I've already said that I'm not planning to do a second house job.'

'That's sad for you – and for future patients . . . er . . . and for me.'

'It's the way it has to be . . . Mum's still unable to work – gets the heebejeebs any time she thinks of going near an operating theatre. Dad's getting worse, poor man – but doesn't really acknowledge it . . . Probably the best thing for him.'

'Having a neurological problem?'

'No. – Fighting it.'

'Yeah . . . And James?'

'Working as a care assistant in a rehab.'

'Won't do him any harm. – If it's where his heart is. – Gotta follow his star.'

'You're mine. – My star.'

'And you're mine . . . Surely we can work something out?'

'No.'

'You're so sure of yourself, so precise – so brutal . . . almost . . . if I didn't know you.'

*   *   *

'How's the EMDR going?'

'We're only just beginning it – just now on the stuff with my father . . . when I was little.'

'Why has it taken so long? – And why aren't you working on the real issue . . . the anaesthetic whatsit?'

'Because there's a lot of preparation that has to be done first . . . Getting things sorted in the right order so that potentially re-traumatising episodes from the past can be resolved at the same time as present traumas – so as not to cause further echoes. – Then collecting them all into groups in the way the brain naturally works and selecting a particularly relevant image for each disturbing event, calculating what the principal negative belief is – and estimating the level of validity of a possible alternative positive belief

– determining what feelings are brought up, assessing the relative level of distressing emotional significance of each event and sensing what associated body sensations there might be . . .'

'Lizzie?'

'Yes, dear?'

'Would you mind speaking the same language as I do? . . . by any chance?'

* * *

'Well that's done – and nobody broke any bones or got electrocuted.'

'Not this time.'

'Huh?'

'That's the attitude the Care Quality Commission inspectors and the Health and Safety people have . . . Always looking for the worst possible outcomes, the biggest risks . . .'

'Oh.'

' . . . Seems to me they've got lawyers nagging at them all the time – and that makes our lives impossible . . . and makes mistakes more likely . . .'

'Oh.'

' . . . Huh! . . . There's no issue in life that a lawyer can't make more complex, more troublesome, more Godawful . . . more expensive.'

'My father's a lawyer.'

'Oh . . . So's mine.'

* * *

Me wonky walking's a bit better again . . . That's good . . .

Can't have people thinking I've been hitting the hooch – like that chap who hit the deck right outside one of the other clubs . . . lying on the pavement – face down . . . Not the best form . . . Word got round. – Club secretary had to have a word with him . . . Wouldn't do for that to happen to me . . . Wouldn't do at all . . .

o O o

'There now . . . All the previous events have been processed appropriately. – All disturbance levels down to zero and all positive beliefs up to seven.'

'Yes . . . They're just history. – They happened . . . but that's all . . . They don't say anything about me – that I'm unloveable . . . or stupid . . . or self-destructive . . . Like they used to.'

'It's extraordinary, isn't it? – As I said, almost surgical. – These negative beliefs about yourself can't go back in . . . Just like a bad appendix – or gall bladder – can't go back in again.'

'Ha! – I'm glad of that . . . umm . . . Seeing me every day this week was a great help. No point in hanging on to any of this stuff . . . Get it all out – once and for all – and, as you said, it got quicker. Got momentum.'

'It's one of the only three therapeutic processes I know that are really healing.'

'Remind me . . .What are the others?'

'Psychodrama and NLP.'

'Oh yes . . . umm . . . Why don't more people do them – and EMDR?'

'They're practical skills . . . You have to have natural talent – like hand/eye coordination in many sports – and then you have to go to the gym or out on the practice court, day after day after day.'

'Surgery's the same . . . Medicine – being a physician

– seems to me to be just a matter of being clever . . . One day computers will put those doctors out of work . . . and robots will take over most surgical procedures . . . More reliable.'

'The same may be true for some forms of teaching – at school and university – and some therapies.'

'Such as?'

'Anything that involves simply learning facts. – Computers are better at that . . . More accurate, more dependable . . . They don't get tired or preoccupied with personal things . . . umm . . . CBT's really an educational process rather than a therapy. – They've already developed an on-line form of CBT. – No surprise to me . . . That's why doctors like it. – Anyone can do it.'

'That's what used to be said about giving anaesthetics.'

'True . . . And that's also why therapists have such a vast potential for causing harm . . . So many of them . . . all believing that anyone can do it on minimal training sometimes . . . Ha! In the UK there are now more therapists than doctors.'

'That's frightening . . . They can't all be skilled . . . umm . . . Same's true for surgeons . . . Believe it or not, some of them don't have basic practical skills.'

'Yes . . . maybe . . . You would know . . . But at least surgeons are trained – and the bad one's weeded out . . . umm . . . Mostly.'

'Some still get through the net . . . They may have the technical skill but lack the judgement . . . And the same's true for some physicians and psychiatrists – putting everyone on pills . . . No sense of the norm . . . of natural variation . . . Everything's pathological – Got to be fixed.'

'That's the same with some therapists . . . umm . . . lots of them . . . And some of them have had only a couple of weeks' so-called "training" before they set themselves up as experts . . . It's just plain wrong. – It takes twelve years to train a brain surgeon but therapists, who mess around with people's brains just as much – in their way – may get by simply on charisma . . . which can be very dangerous.'

'Yes . . . And that's also true for some surgeons . . . Hmm . . . Hopefully further developments in robotics will put paid to that lot.'

'But nothing will ever displace sheer talent . . . or insight . . . or human kindness. – Look at the Robin Williams teacher in *Dead Poets' Society*.'

'Yes . . . God love him.'

'Yes, I think He did . . . It's like what Segovia, the guitarist, said of the young John Williams . . . "God has laid a finger on his brow." '

'I hope He lays a finger on mine.'

* * *

Need to be careful here, James . . . Getting very fond of Lucy. Don't want to lose her . . . Mustn't go too fast . . . Hmm . . . Interesting – talking to a girl and really enjoying it when I'm not trashed . . . A new experience for me . . . a great new experience . . .

* * *

'Progress?'

'Dear Roddy. These things can't be rushed . . . After all, it took me long enough to get to him – so I wasted a lot of time before even seeing him.'

'I know. I know . . . Forgive my impatience . . . You raised my hopes last time.'

'I thought you were worried that I'd bought into a load of psychobabble.'

'Well you know me . . .'

'Should do by now.'

' . . . always wanting things neatly cut and dried.'

'And tied up in plain brown paper with string and sealing wax. – Yes that's my man . . . But what raised your hopes?'

'You were so intense, so keen, so committed.'

'So would you be if you saw light at the end of the tunnel . . . Whoops! I didn't mean to say that. – Very insensitive of me.'

'Not a bit. Not a bit. – I can see my way forward now . . . But do you? . . . er . . . Do you see light at the end of your tunnel?'

'Yes.'

'Are you actually working? . . . on the anaesthetic business now?'

'We've done all the preparation.'

'I thought you did that last time.'

'That was on everything else. – On all the other . . . umm . . . events.'

'So where's the . . . umm . . . light coming from?'

'From those events . . . They don't trouble me any more.'

'They must do . . . umm . . . your father . . . er . . . and so on.'

'It doesn't . . . umm . . . he doesn't. – He was a sick man.'

'Very sick.'

'I mean medically.'

'I mean criminally.'

'That as well – but only because he was medically unwell.'

'Oh my Gawd . . . If you only knew how many times people use that excuse in court – even in the commercial bar, let alone criminal.'

'How so? . . . In the commercial bar?'

'When things don't look good . . . umm . . . on the way the case is going . . . you can guarantee that a sickness certificate will be produced. Doctors – and their certificates – are all part of the entitlement culture.'

'Well I'm not . . . umm . . . part of my own or anyone else's.'

'Indeed not.'

'Me lud.'

'Huh?'

'You sound as if you're in court.'

'Oh . . . umm . . . Sorry about that . . . umm . . . But I still don't understand what's given you hope.'

'Case law.'

'Huh?'

'If this EMDR thingy has worked on all the other stuff – particularly on something as significant as my father's behaviour . . . umm . . . from so long ago . . . it should work on the anaesthetic awareness . . . Why not?'

'Why not? . . . because it seems to me like one of your "holy mysteries".'

'Perhaps it is.'

'Oh Gawd.'

'Roddy, do stop saying that – in that silly tone of voice.'

'Sorry dear.'

'Me lud.'

'Oh . . . I didn't mean to be disrespectful – to you or the Almighty – I . . . er . . . I mean it's so very different from my world . . . so esoteric . . . umm . . . ephemeral.'

'Dictionaries aren't good for you, Roddy.'

'Huh?'

'You lawyers bandy words about all day . . . I'm sure you practise with your dictionaries – in the robing room . . . or in the club.'

'In the loo, if you must know. – That's where all the best speeches are prepared.'

'Oh my Gawd.'

'Lizzie?'

* * *

So sure of myself, so precise – so brutal . . . Am I really?
– Oh Precious, my precious Precious, if only you knew . . .

* * *

Well this is the big one. – Make or break day coming up. –
Hmm . . . I wonder if he's as nervous as I am . . . So much
depends on it . . . All my eggs in this one basket. – For now. – I
get better or I don't . . . Holy Mary, Mother of God, Pray for us
now and at the time of our death . . .

* * *

"When you wish upon a star
  Makes no difference who you are
  Anything your heart desires
  Will come to you."

Oh Disney. Oh Satchmo . . . I wish, I wish, I wish . . .

o O o

'I'll run through the format – the same as we did for all the
other events we've already covered. -
  Event fourteen: Anaesthetic Awareness.
  Most Significant Image: Eyelids taped shut. Intubated.
Hearing the discussion on football.
  Negative belief about self: I am silly, making a fuss. I should
have got over it.

Preferred positive belief: It was an accident that says something about the anaesthetist but nothing about me.

Validity of that cognition on a scale of one (not true) to seven (totally true): four.

Feelings: Trapped, terror, shame, embarrassment, unreality.

Subjective Unit of Disturbance on a scale of zero – not disturbing – to ten – worst imaginable: ten.

Body sensations: Paralysed, drowsy, pressure on stomach.'

'Yes. That's right . . . It brings it all back – as if it's happening right now . . . umm . . . I'm glad I don't have to close my eyes.'

'It will all be straightforward – same as the ones we've already processed.'

'Really?'

'Yes . . . Dealing with the very first episode – with your father – was very challenging for you. And you came through that brilliantly.'

'It's strange . . . That's haunted me all my life. – I've had nightmares about it – right up until now.'

'But not in the last ten days or so, since we processed that event?'

'No. – But I don't get them all the time anyway . . . Only at times when I feel powerless to change something.'

'Between a rock and a hard place?'

'Yes. – Like trying to get a CQC inspector to have a bit of common sense.'

'Ha! No chance of that . . . They're not paid to think. – Only to tick boxes. – Everything has to tick the right boxes . . . Otherwise they themselves get grief from their supervisors . . . And the supervisors get grief from the Director . . . And she gets it in the neck from the Minister – and the press.'

'Hmm. That's exactly right.'

'And that's how you feel over this event?'

'This is much worse . . . I had no option when I was unconscious . . . umm . . . I was paralysed and blind . . . No option at all but to lie there, knowing everything that was going on but unable to communicate – in any way at all.'

'Nope.'

'But the sense of impotence is the same . . . "Talking to a brick wall" doesn't come close to describing it . . . It's like trying to talk under water – or in outer space . . . without a helmet or any breathing apparatus . . . An anaesthetic mask would have become a hindrance – in some bizarre way – not a help.'

'Yes.'

'I doubt it . . . I doubt you can imagine it . . . I've never known anything like this – in any experience in my entire life . . . I . . . er . . . prayed to die . . .'

'Yes.'

' . . . And that's a sin . . . er . . . in my religious belief. – It's not up to us to determine our days. – That's in God's hands.'

'Well He . . . She . . . seems to want you to stick around. – Maybe to do more significant things in your life than you've ever done.'

'It would be nice to do anything at all.'

'Yes . . . umm . . . Ready now?'

'Yes.'

Plonk plink, plonk plink, plonk plink, plonk plink, plonk plink, plonk plink, plonk plink . . .

'I remember talking to Miss Thorneycroft – the surgeon – the day before. Nice lady. Very professional. And the anaesthetist. Affable enough. Seemed competent . . . Being collected from my room and transferred to the trolley. Very skilled, those orderlies. Wouldn't do to drop the patient on the deck . . . In the prep room. Don't remember him putting in the cannula. Drowsy from the premed . . . Urhhh . . . Aaaaargh! . . . No. No. No . . . NO! . . . Umm I . . . er . . . I don't know if I can go through with this.'

'We don't have to. – It's up to you. – We can stop at any time you wish . . . Just like now.'

'Thank you.'

'But what would you suggest to another patient – who just happens to have the same name as you? . . . and the same . . . umm . . . difficulty?'

'I'd tell her to pull herself together.'

'That's a bit harsh . . . umm . . . Maybe you'd say that to yourself . . . But would you really say it to the other Lizzie?'

'I . . . er . . . s'pose not.'

'What would you say?'

'Umm . . . "Come on girl . . . You've done great so far . . . Don't chicken out now." '

'Whose voice was that?'

'Umm . . . Ha! . . . My hockey mistress at school . . . How did you know?'

'I've done this before.'

'I thought you said you hadn't treated anaesthetic awareness before.'

'No – I meant I've done a lot of EMDR before and I'm used to people getting emotional echoes – and sometimes physical echoes – from past events.'

'What's a physical echo?'

'A somatic memory – as if the body keeps the score of events . . . as time goes along . . . umm . . . An emotional event – say, a divorce – might produce physical symptoms such as "heart" pain, even though the physical heart is in good shape.'

'Psychosomatic?'

'Yes – of a kind . . . umm . . . What happens is that any

further separation – of any type – leads to similar symptoms . . . That's why I asked about body sensations associated with each event . . . umm . . . Psychologically-based symptoms should resolve entirely.'

'That's all very "touchy feely" . . . sensitive . . . I didn't think that you were into that sort of thing.'

'I'm not . . umm . . . I think there are two different meanings for the word "sensitive" – easily hurt, quick to take offence and, on the other hand, sympathetic, empathic.'

'Yes. In my book the first lot are just plain wet. Two women with identical physical problems will behave very differently – one stoic and the other pathetic.'

'As it happens, I treat both groups with equal care and concern. Over the years – in my work – I've learned that I don't know enough about other people's emotional backgrounds to be able to judge them . . . umm . . . For example, other people may judge you – but I certainly don't – and I'm hoping that you'll learn not to be so hard on yourself.'

'I dread being thought "wet".'

'Only you would think that – about yourself but perhaps not about the other Lizzie.'

'Oh.'

'What now? What would suit you best? Would you like to stop now? . . . Or continue?'

'I'll give it a go.'

'Event fourteen: Anaesthetic Awareness.

Most Significant Image: Eyelids taped shut. Intubated. Hearing the discussion on football.

Negative belief about self: I am silly, making a fuss. I should have got over it.

Body sensations: Paralysed, drowsy, pressure on stomach.'

Plonk plink, plonk plink, plonk plink, plonk plink, plonk

plink, plonk plink, plonk plink . . .

'. . . Can't open my eyes. Can't move a muscle. Hearing them talking – something about four two, a famous score line evidently . . . World Cup years ago or something. Wonder where I am. Then I hear the familiar sounds of any operating theatre. – The clanks and hisses and murmurings . . . and the occasional spoken command – "Down a bit", "Not too far", "That's it. – Hold it." . . . Suddenly I know exactly where I am . . . I want to scream. – I can't. – I want to touch someone's arm. – I can't. – Move my head. – Can't . . . Fear . . . Gripping me . . . Pay attention! – You silly man. – Do the job you're paid for! – Aaaaargh . . .'

'Good . . . Good.'

'No smell . . . No mask over my mouth and nose . . . Intubated . . . No gas. – Nothing smelly . . . Just oxygen . . . presumably . . . God, God, God . . . What if the oxygen runs out too? . . . Can't take it, can't take it. Got to scream, scream, scream. – SCREAM! – Nothing, nothing, nothing happening. Nothing going out and nothing coming back. – The world's ended . . . I'm dead. Wish I am. Wish I'm dead . . . Dear God. Kill me! Kill me! Kill me! Let me go. Please let me go. Holy Mary, mother of God, intercede for me. – Sinner that I am. Miserable wretch that I am. Oh Roddy, Roddy, dear Roddy. Aaaaargh!'

'That's right . . . Let it go now.'

'Aaaaargh! Tell them I'm awake! Tell them I'm awake! Do something. Do something. DO SOMETHING!'

'That's right.'

'Let me die now. No more. No more. Safe in the arms of Christ. Sleep. Sleep. Sleep.'

'Hmm.'

'Gently. Gently. Gently.'

'Hmm.'

'No! No! No! Still here. Still the same! PAY ATTENTION! Oh Lord – love us. Love me. Lizzie. Your Lizzie.'

'Mmm.'

'I can do this. I can do this. Fight it, Lizzie, Fight it, girl. Up school! Up school!'

'Mmm.'

'No good. No good. Exhausted. Done for. Finished. Lizzie's done for. Lizzie's finished.'

Plonk plink, plonk plink, plonk plink, plonk plink . . .

'Just rest for a bit.'

'Aah . . . Aah . . . Aah.'

'. . . On we go . . . Event fourteen: Anaesthetic Awareness. Most Significant Image: Eyelids taped shut. Intubated. Hearing the discussion on football.

Negative belief about self: I am silly, making a fuss. I should have got over it.

Body sensations: Paralysed, drowsy, pressure on stomach.

How disturbing is that event now, on a scale of zero to ten, where zero is just an event – an understandably distressing event for anybody – and ten says, "I. – I, Lizzie – I'm silly. I'm making a fuss. I should have got over it."?'

'Umm . . . Seven or eight.'

Plonk plink, plonk plink, plonk plink, plonk plink, plonk plink, plonk plink, plonk plink . . .

'I'm lying there, fully aware of what's going on, fully conscious. Praying that I'll drift off – never wake up – die, die, die – but I don't. Praying that they'll stop talking about football – blessed football! – Nothing I can do. Nothing I can do to attract anyone's attention – the anaesthetist, the assistant, Petra Thorneycroft, the theatre sister. – Nobody. – Nothing I can do. NOTHING I CAN DO!'

Plonk plink, plonk plink, plonk plink, plonk plink . . .

'Trapped. Trapped. Can't get away. Oh God. Oh God. Oh God. Can't get away.'

Plonk plink, plonk plink, plonk plink, plonk plink . . .

'Like my father . . . No escape . . . Nothing I can do. Nothing. Nothing.'

Plonk plink, plonk plink, plonk plink, plonk plink . . .

'CONCENTRATE YOU SILLY MAN! Look at the gauges on the machine! LOOK AT THEM!'

Plonk plink, plonk plink, plonk plink, plonk plink . . .

'Look at me! . . . Yes, look at me. Lying here. Helpless. Helpless. HELPLESS! Helpless. – Just like the patients I operate on. Aaaaargh! No! No! No! No! NO!'

Plonk plink, plonk plink, plonk plink, plonk plink . . .

'Whaa, pfwaa, pfwaa, whaa, ooh . . .'

Plonk plink, plonk plink, plonk plink, plonk plink . . .

'Please see me. Please notice me. – Just like when I was a child. – Please notice something . . . Anything. Anything . . . I'm helpless. Helpless. – Totally dependent on you . . .'

Plonk plink, plonk plink, plonk plink . . .

'STOP TALKING! Whaa, pfwaa, whaa . . . Please stop talking. Look at the gauges. Look at me. Lizzie. Me, Lizzie. Little Lizzie. Unable to do anything. Can't get away. Can't get away. Trapped. Trapped . . .'

Plonk plink, plonk plink, plonk plink . . .

'Holy Mary, Mother of God, pray for us now. Pray for me now. Lizzie. Lizzie. Little Lizzie . . .'

Plonk plink, plonk plink, plonk plink . . .

'Got to end sometime. Got to. Can't go on for ever. – Another case to do. Another case. – Bound to stop sometime. Sometime soon . . .'

Plonk plink, plonk plink, plonk plink . . .

'Pfwaa. Whaa. Ooh.'

Plonk plink, plonk plink, plonk plink . . .

'Just rest a bit.'

'Ooh. Oooh. Ooooh . . . Yes.'

'Right . . . On we go.'

'Yes.'

Plonk plink, plonk plink, plonk plink . . .

'Event fourteen: Anaesthetic Awareness.

Most Significant Image: Eyelids taped shut. Intubated. Hearing the discussion on football.

Negative belief about self: I am silly, making a fuss. I should have got over it.

Body sensations: Paralysed, drowsy, pressure on stomach.

How disturbing is that event now, on a scale of zero to ten, where zero is something that happened to you – a dreadful event for you, for anybody – and ten says,"I'm silly. This isn't about anyone else. It's about me. I'm silly. I'm making a fuss. I should have got over it."?'

'Umm . . . Three.'

'Do you think it could go lower? – to two or one? or even to zero?'

'I don't know.'

'Or d'you think this is as far as it can go? – Down to an ecological level? A natural level for this event? . . . for anybody?'

'I don't know.'

Plonk plink, plonk plink, plonk plink, plonk plink . . .

'Got to stop sometime. Got to stop sometime. – This operation, this terror . . . umm . . . Does stop sometime. Does stop. Sometime . . .'

Plonk plink, plonk plink, plonk plink . . .

'How disturbing is this event now? The anaesthetic awareness? – Where zero says, "It's nothing about me. It's just something – a dreadful something – that happened to me".

And ten says, "No. It's all about me. Me, Lizzie. I'm silly. This isn't about anyone else. It's about me. I'm silly. I'm making a fuss. I should have got over it."?'

'Umm . . . Three.'

'Could it go lower?'

'No. – I don't think so.'

'I think that's right. You gave it your best shot. You really did.'

'Phew! . . . Ooh.'

'Yes. – That's right. It's hard work. Very hard work. And you've done very well. Very well. – Up school!'

'Ha! Yes . . . Yes. – Up school.'

'Now then . . . Put in the positive belief, "It was an accident that says something about the anaesthetist but nothing about me". How true is that belief now? – On a scale of one to seven, where one says, "No, it's rubbish" and seven says, "Yes, that's totally true."?'

'Umm . . . Four.'

'Put in that positive belief. Say it now, "It was an accident that says something about the anaesthetist but nothing about me.".'

Plonk plink, plonk plink, plonk plink, plonk plink . . .

'It was an accident that says something about the anaesthetist but nothing about me.'

Plonk plink, plonk plink, plonk plink . . .

'Yes. It was just an accident. Could have happened to any patient. Anywhere. Any time. – One of mine. Aaaaargh!'

Plonk plink, plonk plink, plonk plink . . .

'Aaaargh.'

Plonk plink, plonk plink, plonk plink . . .

'Aaargh.'

'How true is that belief now? – On a scale of one to seven? – Where one says, "It's all about me, my fault, my silliness" and seven says, "It was an accident that says something about the anaesthetist but nothing about me."?'

'Three.'

'Three? – Just checking. – Less true than before?'

'Yes . . . Less true.'

Plonk plink, plonk plink, plonk plink . . .

'Put in the positive belief again, "It was an accident that says something about the anaesthetist but nothing about me.".'

Plonk plink, plonk plink, plonk plink . . .

'It was an accident that says something about the anaesthetist but nothing about me . . . Hmm. Yes, I s'pose it was . . . umm . . . nothing to do with me. – Can't have been. Can't have been.'

Plonk plink, plonk plink, plonk plink . . .

'Put in the positive belief again.'

Plonk plink, plonk plink, plonk plink . . .

'It was an accident that says something about the anaesthetist but nothing about me . . . It really wasn't. Wasn't anything about me . . .'

Plonk plink, plonk plink, plonk plink . . .

'Again.'

'It was an accident that says something about the anaesthetist but nothing about me.'

Plonk plink, plonk plink, plonk plink . . .

'Can't have been. Can't be anything to do with me.'

Plonk plink, plonk plink . . .

'Not me. Not me at all.'

Plonk plink, plonk plink . . .

'And how true is that now? – "It was an accident that says something about the anaesthetist but nothing about me." – On a scale of one to seven?'

'Seven.'

'Totally true?'

'Yes. – Totally true . . . umm . . . Eight or nine.'

'Nope. – Seven's the top.'

'Just joking . . . Ooh. Ooh. Ooooh. I feel so free.'

'Not finished yet. – Body sensations . . .'

'Oh yes, I forgot.'

'You said, "Paralysed – physically and mentally, drowsy, pressure on stomach.".'

'Yes I did . . . umm . . . Paralysed obviously . . . umm . . . No – wait – I . . . umm . . . I don't feel that paralysed sensation any more.'

'Physically or mentally?'

'No. Not physically. Not mentally . . . I'm up and running again . . . Thank God. Thank you, Jesus.'

'Huh?'

'Not you . . . Well, I mean thank you to you, obviously, but that's the thing about this, isn't it? – Patients get ourselves better.'

'Yes. That's precisely what I like about EMDR – in the way I do it and in the way I believe everyone should do it . . . Remember the way I was trained . . . Stay out of the way. – It isn't a talking therapy . . . Let the process itself – the bilateral stimulation – work its magic.'

'Yes . . . It is magic . . . As you said, "almost surgical".'

'And the body sensations? – The drowsiness, the pressure feeling in the stomach?'

'Oh . . . umm . . . Oh. – Still there . . . Not drowsy. – Wide awake, fully aware, no terror, no symptoms like before. – Aah . . . still the pressure feeling on my tummy . . . and right leg.'

Plonk plink, plonk plink, plonk plink . . .

'Yes . . . Miss Thorneycroft doing her thing – and the theatre sister . . . and a medical student, leaning on me.'

Plonk plink, plonk plink, plonk plink . . .

'Ah well . . . Not the worst thing that could've happened to me.'

Plonk plink, plonk plink, plonk plink . . .

'Feelings now?'

'Fine . . . umm . . . free . . . umm . . . Nothing negative.'

'Body sensations?'

'None.'

'Done. All done.'

'Yes. All done . . . Up school! . . . Phew! I'm so tired! – and exhilarated at the same time.'

'You did come by cab, didn't you? – As I suggested?'

'Yes.'

'Well let yourself settle a bit before you go off into the big wide world.'

'But I want to tell the whole wide world. – I'm free . . . I'm free. – Lizzie's free!'

'Yes, free to walk straight into a bus if you don't look where you're going.'

'D'you mind if I call my husband?'

'I wouldn't just yet.'

'Why? . . . umm . . . Why not?'

'Because – as you remember from the work we did on your father's . . . umm . . . behaviour, we have to check to see if the process sticks.'

'Oh yes . . . Not a "dead cat bounce".'

'What on earth's that?'

'Oh, sorry . . . It's one of my son's expressions – from commodity broking – prices sometimes bounce a bit after a crash . . . umm . . . for no good reason. – Just like a cat that was already dead would bounce a bit if you threw it off a tall building.'

'Yes . . . umm . . . I s'pose so.'

'Oh, sorry . . . It really isn't a nice expression at all, is it?

– I suppose I got used to it . . . immune . . . With all the things I hear – at home and at work.'

'Yes . . . umm . . . Be careful about that . . . There's an expression we have in our line of work, "The good thing about recovery is we get our feelings back. The bad thing is . . . we get our feelings back.".'

'Oh.'

'It's probably a good idea just to let things settle. Don't say anything to anybody – or do anything wild – until we've had the follow-up session, just to make sure that it's all in the past now.'

'No "Up school!"?.'

'Not yet . . . Later. – When we've checked that the whole process has worked effectively.'

'Ha! Delayed gratification . . . I hear enough about that from my daughter.'

'Good . . . Settled now . . . Be careful with the traffic.'

'Yes. – Oh . . . Thank you . . . Bye.'

* * *

'Dr Finch, I'd like you to put in my notes, in the computer, "Do not
resuscitate". In capitals maybe.'

'Please tell me why. – Only if you want to, of course.'

'I . . . I don't feel it's worth the bother, the struggle, any more . . . Diabetes, heart disease, prostate problems – not cancer but it's humiliating . . . dribbling, suddenly having to go – and then again – not getting much sleep, not continuous, repeatedly having to get up to have a pee . . . Oh – and digestion troubles . . . Constipation or diarrhoea. One or the other . . . Said it's why they sent me in. Can't see the point really . . . If it's not one thing it's another . . . In every way . . .

And constant back pain – some days better than others but no real respite. You don't get better from osteoporosis. Shrinking, four inches shorter now, stooping, looking old – stooping – and feeling it . . . What's the point? – When I can't see so well? . . . And no real friends in the old people's home. – You don't knock on other people's doors. In an old people's home. Or telephone. Don't want to disturb anyone. Probably watching TV – game shows probably. Interrupting. – Nothing else to do. – No visitors. Family's too busy nowadays. Except Christmas. And my birthday. Ha! Why would I want another birthday? At my age? Nice to see the grandchildren. Occasionally. Some of them – and even the ones who do come can't wait to go home . . . Social media. That's all they live for. – No use to me. Social media. Not social at all . . . "Friends"? What friends? Not like my day. No friends nowadays. Moved away. Dead. Forgotten. No real community. Common room's empty. Except for Sunday lunch . . . Only time you see the others. Really. Not much to say. Said it all before. Heard it before. Family news. – What news? – "Woman has baby", "Boy breaks bone", "Daughter in Thailand. Gap year" . . . "Lose weight", they say, "Good for your blood pressure, back pain, diabetes", they say. "What for?", I say . . . to meself . . . "What's it all for?" '

'Hmm . . . It's difficult for you.'

'Yes it is . . . Getting older . . . "Care for the Elderly". Ha! – What's "Care for the elderly"? . . . Who really cares? About the elderly?'

'I do.'

'I'll say this for you, doctor. – You're a good listener . . . umm . . . Don't bother about the notice.'

* * *

'That's interesting . . . If my father's a QC and your father's also a lawyer – and we're both care assistants . . . What d'you s'pose went wrong? . . . Why aren't we running the place? – Well you anyway. – Or at least
shareholders . . . if there are such things in private rehabs like this one?'

'Not as far as I know.'

'My father . . . more my mother really – ever since she came over to see me in Hazelden, the rehab I went to in the USA . . . decided that the best thing for me was to give me nothing . . . make me work for it . . . whatever I wanted.'

'Yes. My parents said the same, did the same – although I never went to rehab.'

'What did you do?'

'In what way?'

'Why didn't you go to rehab?'

'I didn't need to.'

'That's impressive – doing it all on your own.'

'Sorry. I seem to have given you the wrong impression. Somehow . . . I didn't go to rehab because I'm not an addict.'

'That's even more impressive – avoiding taking stuff when it's everywhere . . . Can't avoid it.'

'I can. – I didn't want it. After a short time in uni.'

'Oh.'

'And I don't work in a rehab because I want to save the world . . . right now . . . It just seemed like an interesting job . . . not much else around, to be frank.'

'Oh . . . Why not?'

'Why not? God! – You've led a sheltered life . . . No austerity . . . None of my graduate friends can find a job – except lawyers and accountants. Even the doctors don't take it for granted nowadays.'

'My mother's a doctor, a gynaecologist . . . She's not working. – But that's rather different.'

'Oh?'

'Some idiot of an anaesthetist didn't see she was awake.'

'I would hope she was.'

'Huh?'

'If she was operating.'

'Ah . . . No . . . She was the patient. – Gall bladder something . . . Done by keyhole surgery.'

'Laparascopically?'

'Yes, that's it . . . er . . . How do you know?'

'Most of them are nowadays . . . But . . . but that's terrible . . . Not seeing that. – The gas man. – No wonder she can't work . . . Terrifying.'

'You seem very familiar with medical things.'

'I was a nurse . . . umm . . . Didn't like it.'

'Oh. – Why not?'

'Too much bossing around by doctors.'

'So now you're a care assistant? – Bossed around by nurses.'

'Yes. Doesn't make sense, does it?'

'So why d'you do it? This job?'

'Nobody expects anything of me . . . So they can't criticise me, can't get at me.'

'Oh . . . umm . . . Oh . . . I'm . . . er . . . trying to work that one out.'

'My mother's an inspector . . . for the CQC . . . always finding fault . . . one way or another. Nursing's too close to home.'

'Oh . . . Oh I see. – But isn't this work? In this rehab? . . . umm . . . Also too close?'

'I want to help people. Somehow. I . . . er . . . wanted to be a doctor.'

'Why aren't you?'

'Didn't get a place. – My chemistry grade wasn't good enough. – Didn't believe in it . . . All that theory . . . I saw what drugs did in practice to my grandmother. – Mum's mother – pharmaceutical drugs . . . She rattled, she was on so many. One drug interaction after another. – All in the name of "helping".

'So your mother became an inspector to get back at the doctors?'

'S'pose so.'

'And you became a care assistant to get away from being bossed about as a nurse by doctors . . . and by your mother as well. – And now you're bossed about even more?'

'Yup . . . I'm on strike . . . from what I could be doing if I really used my mind . . . I want time to think things through for myself . . . Doesn't make sense, does it? If you put it your way. – Not really.'

'Makes perfect sense to me . . . My older sister's a doctor. – Just qualified. On her first job.'

'What's that about? for you?'

'She was always the clever one. At school . . . I lost interest.'

'Oh . . . What about your younger sister?'

'Haven't got one.'

'I thought you said your "older sister".'

'Oh, yes I did . . . I meant "older than me".'

'Ah.'

'My mother was always picking me up on things like that. – Grammar.'

'Funny things. Parents.'

'Yes.'

* * *

Still wishing on my star. – And why not? Phoebe's great . . .
Hmm . . . Nobody like her on this year's course. – Not that I
want anyone else . . . More women this time. No fight. No fun
. . . Any of them. Men or women. Far too like American
students this year. Soft. Respectful. No bite . . . Won't learn
anything for themselves that way. Not about human things
that really matter . . . Not involved . . .

* * *

'Any progress, me love?'
   'I think so . . . But I won't know until I test myself at work
– and I'm not ready for that yet. As I've said before, the risks
would be too great – to my patients, to my credibility and to
my own self-confidence.'
   'So what are you going to do?'
   'Wait.'
   'Wait for what?'
   'Wait for two things really. – To see if I get any more nightmares and to see what I feel when I even consider going back
to work . . . Oh – and of course to see what happens in my
follow-up appointment next week.'
   'Why not tomorrow?'
   'EMDR bounces my head about a bit. – I was warned about
that in advance. – Memories come up . . . umm . . . some I
didn't even know I had . . . umm . . . Unsettling thoughts come
in from nowhere . . . All sorts of things – from the past . . .
and also from the present . . . and fears for the future as well
– from everywhere, come to think of it . . . er . . . I need a bit
of time to stop spinning around, get back onto terra firma.'
   'Are you sure you were safe . . . er . . . having that EMDR
treatment at all?'
   'What choice did I have? . . . The CBT was worse than

useless, the effect of antidepressants is always primarily a placebo effect – and I don't need that sort of con trick – and my life wasn't going anywhere ... Nor was the thought of Phoebe sacrificing her personal and professional life for us – you and me – being prepared to do whatever she could to help us regardless of the cost to herself.'

'That's the pious pelican in reverse – the chick sacrificing herself to feed her mother.'

'Yes – and I won't allow it ... Gotta get it the right way round. – She's my chick ... I'm the mother.'

'What am I? – An optional extra? ... Like the feminists would have us believe?'

'You know perfectly well I haven't got a feminist ... er ... feminist ... umm ... What do feminists have?'

'I ... umm ... I think it might be wise for me to pass on that question.'

'You'd never allow a witness to get away with that.'

'I'm not in court.'

'Nor am I ... I'm simply saying that ... umm ... It may be a woman thing ... umm ... I'm prepared to risk my life for my family – just like Phoebe.'

'So am I ... I'd fight to the death for you – and the children.'

'I know you would, my love ... You're my wonderful alpha male ... But maybe that's not quite the same thing as fighting a battle on one's own, in the calm stillness of personal decision, rather than alongside all the other troops in the full heat of battle.'

'Gosh, Lizzie. – That's one of your speeches ... just a little one – like James said ... er ... when you were in America, in New York ... But nine-eleven wasn't that kind of battle ... Somewhat one-sided.'

'No ... I was thinking about the EMDR ... It's a lonely

business,
    working on myself. – I'll let you know how things go after
my next session.'

o O o

'I'd love you to meet my family some time . . . Mum isn't really
the dragon I make her out to be – just because she works for
the CQC . . . Her heart's in the right place.'
    'I'm sure it is. – You're lovely . . . Why wouldn't she be? . . .
I'd like you to meet mine . . . Sometime. – Possibly not the best
time just now, with both the parents out of action and Phoebe
so busy.'
    'Don't you want me to meet them? . . . Aren't I good enough
– as a care assistant?'
    'As far as I'm concerned, you're wonderful – just as you are
– whatever you do . . . We speak the same language.'
    'But your parents are so posh . . . And your sister's doing
what I failed to do.'
    'Doesn't feel posh to me – from the inside . . . S'pose The
Garrick's posh – Father's club – posh as they come. And
Mum's a bit posh when she's all "Consultant specialist" annat
. . . But Phoebe would be furious . . . Nobody calls her "posh"
– and lives.'
    'She sounds fun.'
    'I'm her brother. Not for me to judge.'
    'Well my sister's a problem all on her own. – She could pick
a fight with herself . . . and still lose.'
    'Ha! – My sister does the same . . . er . . . used to . . . and
wins – every time..'
    'How does she do that?'
    'She's the brainy one.'
    'You're not so stupid . . . Commodity brokers can't be

totally dumb – Gotta think on your feet.'

'How would you know?'

'Thought about doing it once . . . Not for me. – Some women in it but it's a man's world really.'

'Not very nice men . . . Too sharp, dishonest.'

'The whole commercial world's like that . . . Look at the banks, what they've been up to. – Oh! . . . Sorry . . . Your father's a financial lawyer.'

'Straight as the proverbial die.'

'What is the proverbial die?'

'Umm . . . Don't know – but it's gotta be straight . . . it's in the proverbs.'

'And here you are now . . . proving that a leopard can change its spots.'

* * *

Dammit. I don't seem to be getting over these silly symptoms quite as quickly as I did earlier. – And I haven't been drinking. Much . . .

* * *

Not much point, me thinking of a future career – of any kind – just yet . . . Dad's on a lonely road to nowhere. Mum's unfit for purpose. James is nuts – as much use as a bright idea in an idiot. Ha! – That's exactly right, come to think of it . . . He's always full of bright ideas – and they're always idiotic . . . Still, I s'pose he'd say the same about me. Now. – But that's the difference between us. He does what he feels like – always has done . . . all addicts do, far as I can see . . . and I do what I believe in, what I think is right. – And that brings me a lot of pain . . . Hmm . . . Probably even more pain than if I did the opposite. – So it's a choice . . . for me . . . Pain this way or pain that way . . . And no Precious either way . . . Still, no point in moping. – And no time. – Patients to see . . .

* * *

What is it with this new batch of students? – No originality. No spark. – Gotta wake 'em up somehow . . . Phoebe would show 'em. Ha! – And how! . . .

* * *

'So how have you been since last week?'
  'No nightmares.'
  'That's good.'
  'But not good enough – yet.'
  'How d'you mean?'
  'I'm not back at work.'
  'I would suggest you don't try that just yet.'
  'Why not? – Surely that was the whole point.'
  'It is – but this is like piano practice.'
  'I've only been playing two notes.'
  'No, I mean when you're learning a new piece – you take it slowly. Otherwise you may embed a mistake . . . and then repeat it later. Again and again.'
  'Oh. That's a bit of a disappointment . . . My husband's itching and scratching to see me get well.'
  'So am I – although I wouldn't use quite that expression . . . keen, eager, hopeful.'
  'Yes, I am too.'
  'Then let's take it gently to make it stick . . . First of all we have to see if the negative belief has stayed at three – or gone up or down – and the positive belief stayed at seven.

'Or eight or nine.'

'Ha! No – Sorry. – Still not allowed.'

'You're a spoilsport.'

'Yes . . . I'm a professional – like you – I follow strict protocols. That way research into the effectiveness of a procedure can be meaningful, capable of replication independently by someone else, rather than anecdotal.'

'Yes, I understand that – and I accept it . . . It's funny how I've forgotten simple things like academic discipline after being out of action for only a short time.'

'The brain, the memory, the ingraining of habits . . . They all like routine – structure and repetition. – That's how we learn new things . . . Poetry, for example . . . if it scans and rhymes like it used to.'

'Seamus Heany's ok.'

'He certainly is . . . He's got a beat – if you listen for it – and very clear images.'

'Yes . . . and I've got to be more disciplined, rather than rushing ahead?'

'Yes, 'fraid so.'

'Ha! – It's just what I used to say to the children.'

'I'm sure they benefited.'

'Yes. They certainly did – but they didn't always appreciate it.'

'Expecting appreciation from children is . . . umm . . . like . . . umm . . .'

'Herding cats?'

'Not quite.'

'Hoping a cat will say thank you?'

'Yes. That's it.'

'Or patients sometimes.'

'You fishing?'

'Ha! – Maybe I was . . . subconsciously.'

'D'you believe in all that stuff? . . . Ids, Egos, Superegos, complexes and that sort of thing?'

'To a degree.'

'What degree?'

'I don't think we should make too big a thing of it.'

'Tie ourselves in knots? – like RD Laing?'

'Or Lewis Carol.'

'Alice?'

'Not specifically . . . I was thinking of Charles Dodgson – his real name – *'Examples of Symbolic Logic.'*

'I don't know them . . . What happens there?'

'He gives you a set of statements – and you have to work out the next one.'

'That sounds fun.'

'Not when he gives you ten and you have to work out the eleventh.'

'Oh, I see . . . said the blind man.'

'Huh?'

'Ha! – Force of habit . . . A joke my daughter brought back from school – years ago. – Still stuck in the family folklore.'

'An anchor . . . a way of doing things, habit, mannerism.'

'Yes . . . We have some.'

'All families do . . . The most remarkable example is in identical twins, separated at birth. They can have similar specific idiosyncrasies – special ways of saying things and doing things – they discover 50 years later, when they eventually meet.'

'That's weird.'

'Carl Jung didn't think so . . . He reckoned there's a common pool of knowledge – subconscious – that we can tap into.'

'Yes, I heard that from my daughter. Her new boyfriend – a lecturer in healthcare ideas – mentioned it.'

'That's good . . . I heard about Karl Popper – *The Philosophy of Science* – in Cambridge but I didn't know medical schools taught students about ideas.'

'They don't generally. This man's very special, seems to me. – Teaches them to think . . . er . . . for themselves. Not parrot learning.'

'I s'pose that's something we can thank computers for – the opportunity to look something up, google it, if we don't know . . . Gives us time to do more adventurous, rewarding, things with our minds.'

'But what's all this got to do with my EMDR follow-up assessment?'

'I'm confirming – to you yourself as well as to me – that you think very clearly. There's absolutely no impairment in your intellect or in your reasoning.'

'That's what I found so odd about CBT . . . I felt patronised, belittled.'

'That may have been just that individual therapist. Some big-name people swear by it.'

'But do they get patients better?'

'I don't know . . . er . . . I assume so. They'd go out of business

otherwise – because they'd get no new patients, no referrals. Most of mine come from previous patients – or GPs who've been happy with the outcome for their patients.'

'Yes. – Same for me.'

'Each to his or her own, I s'pose . . . umm . . . Let's see how you've done with the EMDR we did together . . .

Event fourteen: Anaesthetic Awareness.

Most Significant Image: Eyelids taped shut. Intubated. Hearing the discussion on football.

Negative belief about self: I am silly, making a fuss. I should have got over it.

Body sensations: Paralysed, drowsy, pressure on stomach.

How disturbing is that event now, on a scale of zero to ten, where zero is just an event – an understandably distressing event for anybody – and ten says, "I'm silly, I'm making a fuss. – I should have got over it."?'

Plonk plink, plonk plink, plonk plink, plonk plink, plonk plink . . .

'Umm . . . Two.'

'Not three?'

'No – just two.'

'Or four?'

'A dead cat bounce? – Oops, sorry . . . I don't think you like that expression.'

'No, I don't – but I expect it's just one of those little verbal anchors stuck in your mind.'

'Are there other sorts of anchors?'

'All sorts – physical . . . umm . . . tactile, visual, auditory, behavioural . . . all sorts.'

'Yes, I see . . . said the blind man.'

'Ha! – So two is where it is? – Interesting that it's gone down during the week, even though we've done no work on it.'

'Yes . . . Two feels right'

'Could it go lower?'

'No. I don't think so . . . It feels the right level, acceptable for what I went through . . . And I do think, just a little bit, that I should've got over it.'

'But does it say, "I am silly. I'm making a fuss."?'

'No. Not at all.'

'Give me a number.'

'Zero.'

'Really zero? – Not just saying it?'

'Just to please you? – and keep the fee down? Certainly not . . . Zero it is.'

Plonk plink, plonk plink, plonk plink, plonk plink, plonk plink . . .

'Where now?'

'Still zero.'

'Good.'

'And the positive belief? – "It was an accident that says something about the anaesthetist but nothing about me"?'

Plonk plink, plonk plink, plonk plink, plonk plink, plonk plink . . .

'Seven – Very positive.'

'Body sensations?'

'None.'

'Anything else – to do with this incident? Any echoes anywhere?'

'No.'

'Excellent.'

'Does this mean we're finished?'

'Yes.'

'And can . . . er . . . may I go back to work now?'

'Take it gently. Don't charge in. The experience you've had – of being out of work, not just the traumatic episode itself – will have created an anchor, a new familiar.'

'Oh.'

'Best to do a gradual de-sensitisation . . . a sort of behavioural therapy approach. Go to the hospital one day, then to an empty operating theatre, then to a prep room – I think you called it – or whatever it is you have . . . and so on.'

'And then get back to work? – I so want to prove to everyone that I'm back, I can do it.'

'That's not a good motive . . . It might work for Paul Newman – in that gambling film, *The Hustler* – but I don't want you taking any gambles at all . . . Gently gently, one step at a time.'

'Ha! That's exactly what they taught my son in rehab.'

'Yes. – It's the way any behavioural change works best . . . Physical too sometimes.'

'Umm . . . Would you see my husband? – for the neurological problem we talked about in one of the EMDR sessions? for his reaction to it?'

'I wouldn't be able to help him with the neurological problem itself, with the physical progression . . . But I could help him, possibly re-framing things through NLP – *Neuro Linguistic Programming* – if he wants me to. With his emotional . . . er . . . spiritual reaction.'

'I thought you weren't a religious person.'

'I'm not – but we all have a spirit . . . and a spiritual journey of some kind . . . in our own way . . .'

'Yes.'

' . . . and miracles do occur. – You're one yourself.'

'With your help.'

'Yes, there is that. I do the work I was trained to do – and add a bit – but you did the real work, taking on the emotional challenge . . . You deserve the credit for that.'

'Thank you . . . umm . . . Goodbye . . . er . . . That's it, is it?'

'Yes. – Goodbye.'

o O o

'You were saying that your symptoms fluctuate – get better or worse unpredictably.'

'Yes – and not to do with me alcohol consumption . . . Hardly drink nowadays . . . I go to the club for the company, conviviality. – Whoops! – Not that there's anything wrong at home . . . me wife's been seeing this chap for therapy for her "anaesthetic awareness" – whatever it's called . . . Gone very well.'

'Good . . . That's very good . . . umm . . . but – in your case, from the examination I made just now and from the blood tests you had done last week – you're not so good . . . not as you were.'

'Oh . . . I feared not . . . Any diagnosis yet?'

'Not a precise one – no . . . But it's looking more like a progressive neurological illness, something physically wrong with the way your brain and nerves do their work.'

'Oh . . . "Buggrit", as my wife says.'

'Your wife?'

'Terry Pratchett really – his *"Discworld"* novels. – She loves them.'

'Yes . . . buggrit . . . But we'll see . . .'

*   *   *

'What would you say is the most important thing we give our patients on this ward? – and why?'

Silence apart from a few shuffles.

'Don't worry. This isn't an exam. You're not going to be judged . . . A teaching round shouldn't be an ordeal. – It's an opportunity to examine ideas as well as patients.'

More shuffles.

'As medical students you don't yet have the power of doctors to cause significant damage . . . But you can damage yourselves – intellectually and philosophically – if your minds are stuck in ruts . . . That mental inertia – of yours – will also damage your patients in due course, when you're qualified, if you fail to give them the best clinical options and protect them from the worst.'

Murmurs.

'. . . Now then. What d'you think? . . . What's the most

130

important thing we give our patients on this ward? ...
Anybody?'

'Intravenous bisphosphanate infusions and high doses of
Vitamin D.'

'Yes. That's a good suggestion – although those treatments
are usually given in the Medical Day Unit, not on the wards
... And why would that be?'

'To save money and un-block beds.'

'You're absolutely right – but I was looking for an answer
to my first question ... Why is that treatment an important
thing to give to patients?'

'To counter the effects of osteoporosis ... Common in the
elderly.'

'And what are those effects?'

'Fractures – from falls – but spontaneously sometimes,
when the bones are so depleted of calcium that they become
brittle.'

'Yes indeed ... And which bones are commonly affected?'

'Hip and spine.'

'What makes you say that?'

'That's where they look ... on the bone density scans.'

'Yes ... They do ... But *all* bones are affected. Patients
may fracture all their metatarsals – in one foot – in one go if
they trip on a paving stone ... But what's the trap? ... in the
bone density scan? – for the spine at any rate?'

Silence.

'Work it out ... What are they looking for?'

'Thinning of the bones.'

'Yes ... And what sort of fracture commonly affects the
spine? – often spontaneously, as you say?'

'A collapse fracture.'

'Which is ... ?'

'When the vertebral bodies collapse ... and the patient

131

can't carry things – or walk comfortably.'

'Yes. I like the way you're thinking – on the practical end results for the patient ... But what's the trap? – with the scan?'

Silence.

'If the vertebral body collapses into itself, what happens to its density?'

'It increases.'

'Yes ... Think about that for a moment.'

'Oh!'

'Oh what?'

'The scan will be normal.'

'That's right ... And what's the clinical implication? – that we've just been discussing a few moments ago over patients we saw earlier on this round – with respect to any clinical condition?'

'Oh ... "Treat the patient, not the test result".'

'Good. Got it ... And what's the major issue with hip fractures in the elderly?'

'They can't play football.'

Laughter.

'Actually he's right. – Mr ... er?'

'Dombell.'

'Mr Dombell's right – at one level ... on one consideration. What's that?'

Silence.

'You see, we tend to think – as medical people – in clinical terms ... about disease and decay, tests and treatments. But what's on the patient's mind?'

Silence.

'Go on ... What's on the patient's mind?'

'Television.'

'Yes ... Too true ... The one-eyed companion ... What

else?'

'Sex.'

Laughter.

'Careful ... Careful ... That's actually a serious point. Sexual activity – for comfort if not for procreation – is very important in the elderly ... indefinitely for some ... What else?'

Silence.

'Take your white coats off ... umm ... No, Mr Dombell, I meant figuratively ... Think as the patient thinks – not as doctors think.'

Silence.

'What do elderly people talk about – most frequently?'

'Illnesses.'

'Back pain.'

'Mobility allowance.'

'"I'm a celebrity. – Get me out of here!".'

Laughter.

'Grandchildren.'

'That's the one ... So what's the social consequence of the vertebral collapse?'

'Ah.'

'Yes – you've understood it now, haven't you? ... And this may be the most significant consideration – from the patient's perspective ... not being able to kick a ball around with the grandchildren.'

Shuffles.

'Now then ... What are the clinical consequences of a fractured hip? – in this age group?'

'Wheelchairs.'

'Yes. – One in three adults who lived independently before their hip fracture remains in a nursing home for at least a year after the injury ... And what's even worse?'

Silence.

'Twenty percent die within one year . . . even though they had previously been in good health – other than having osteoporosis.'

Silence.

'And what's the most significant risk in prescribing bisphosphonates?'

'Bisphosphonate related osteo-necrosis of the jaw.'

'Yes – all medical students tend to know that . . . BRONJ, as a memorable acronym . . . It's savagely important – a dreadful side-effect – We should always remember that the Hippocratic Oath includes the promise "to abstain from doing harm". – But the chances of anyone getting osteo-necrosis of the jaw from oral bisphosphonates are about the same as the chances of chickens growing teeth.'

Polite laughter (from those who hoped to ingratiate themselves and get a house job in due course).

'But intravenous bisphosphonates – given by infusion once a year – are more risky, in terms of BRONJ . . . So how would you reduce the risk?'

'Take all the teeth out before you start the treatment.'

Laughter.

'Well you're on the right lines . . . Do a thorough dental check.'

Shuffles.

'Also we have to remember that common things occur commonly . . . That's where we should focus our attention – in a state healthcare system or anywhere else – not on rarities . . . although my job, as a specialist, is to consider all possibilities.'

Shuffles again.

'But what's the other risk resulting from dental disasters when you prescribe bisphosphonates?'

'Haemolytic anaemia?'

'I don't see the connection . . . I think that idea might have come out of the back of your head.'

'It's a lonely place in there for him, Sir.'

Laughter.

'What other consideration do you have to bear in mind – at your own peril – if things go wrong?'

Silence.

' . . . You'll be sued out of existence and hauled before the GMC . . . And that prospect tends to lead to defensive medical practice. – Doctors doing too much, or sometimes too little, purely to protect themselves.'

Throat clearings.

'Now think again about what you're going to do for the patient with osteoporosis.'

'Home help?'

'You're on the right lines . . . Try again . . . Think more about preventive measures.'

'Recommend daily exercise?'

'Yes . . . Good . . . What else?'

Silence.

'Yes. It's difficult when our whole medical educational system, for five or six years, is hospital based – apart from a couple of weeks in a general practice somewhere.'

Silence.

'Two "C"s . . . That's how I remember them.'

Silence.

'Don't make wild guesses . . . That would just embed the wrong answers in your minds . . . Try this – carpets and cataracts.'

Silence.

'The most likely place for people to fall is at home – as a result of tripping on carpets . . . Nail them down or take them out altogether . . . The carpets, not the patients.'

Awkward laughter.

' . . . And cataracts?'

'Impaired vision . . . Can't see where they're going.'

'That's the one . . . A simple operation, costs little, done as an out-patient, safe, takes twenty minutes each eye . . . Some surgeons prefer to do each eye separately at different times. – Why?'

'Double the fee.'

Laughter.

'Umm . . . Yes . . . umm . . . We'll pass over that . . . Any other thoughts?'

Silence.

'It cuts the risk of infection spreading from one eye to the other . . . and causing total blindness.'

Shuffles.

'The operation – when it's done successfully – dramatically improves quality of life and reduces the risk of falls – with all the fearful and expensive consequences we've talked about.'

Shuffles.

'Yes, I know it's not dramatic modern-day intervention – the sort of glamourous stuff that interests newspapers . . . and some medical students and doctors.'

More shuffles.

'It's straightforward common sense – an increasingly rare commodity at times . . . in these days of high tech medicine . . . And what else do we have to consider for our patient with osteoporosis? . . . Two "P"s.'

'Polypharmacy?'

'Yes, well done . . . Not what I had in mind but very important in the elderly. – They tend to be on multiple medications, forget to take them in the right dose or at the right time and get all sorts of side effects . . . And then doctors tend to treat the side effects with more medications – rather than stopping as many as possible.'

'Yes. I've seen that – on my GP stint.'

'What other "P" can you think of?'

Stage whisper of 'Relief'.

Laughter.

'Sorry . . . I missed that.'

Silence.

'Okay ... The two I'm thinking of are pain and paracetamol.'

Mutterings.

'Yes . . . Patients benefit hugely from pain relief. It's one of the most important things we doctors can ever do for our patients – but we have to keep it simple . . . use the least risky and most effective drug, avoiding stimulating addiction but providing peace of mind and improved sleep.'

'Why paracetamol?'

'It's effective, inexpensive are relatively safe.'

'Why "relatively"?'

'Compared with aspirin and ibuprofen causing gastro-intestinal haemorrhage – and opiates and other strong pain-killers being addictive.'

'But I've seen paracetamol overdoses in A and E.'

'Yes. – Paracetamol overdose can cause fatal liver damage . . . Intravenous acetylcysteine is an effective antidote if it's given within eight hours . . . Incidentally, what's the MLD of paracetamol?'

'The what, Sir?'

'Come on, that's something you should know ... The minimal lethal dose – the smallest number of tablets that might kill you.'

'One hundred.'

'You're guessing again. That's not a good scientific – or clinical – principle when it's so easy to look things up on the web . . . Anyone know?'

'Thirty.'

'Yes. That's nearer the mark . . . A total of twelve grams – twenty four of the five hundred milligram tablets – is potentially fatal, depending on body weight.'

'Doesn't that information – on the web – encourage potential suicides to take more?'

'How would we ever know? . . . There are certainly more guaranteed ways of self-harming or of killing yourself – and other people – and all that's on the web as well . . . Perhaps there's no answer to the conundrum of the risks in letting people have too little or too much information.'

Shuffles.

'And there's another thing about paracetamol . . . What's the cost to the NHS each year for this simple drug? – that people could buy over the counter from the chemist?'

Silence.

'As budget holders, you need to know these things . . . Whatever is spent on one thing cannot be spent on another – however much politicians might believe in "creative accounting" when they work out budgets . . . counting things two or three times over. – We're not politicians . . . We have to live in the real world.'

Mutterings.

'The answer is that last year the NHS spent *eighty million pounds* on paracetamol . . . Incidentally, that cost is twenty times what would be spent buying it over the counter in a pharmacy or supermarket. Doctors wrote twenty two million prescriptions for it . . . Imagine what else might have been done with that money.'

Groans.

'Umm . . . Dr Finch . . . Back to the top . . . From your experience of being just over halfway through your appointment as my Foundation Year One doctor, what's the most important thing we give to our patients on this ward?'

'Hope.'

'Yes indeed . . . You might all benefit – and so might our patients – from seeing a *YouTube* clip on Alice Somer Herz, a Holocaust survivor, at the age of one hundred and eight. In this remarkably lucid interview she says that the secret of a long and happy life is optimism.'

* * *

'What does the counsellor say now?'

'He says we're finished.'

'Who's "we"? – You and me?'

'No, nitwit. – Him and me . . . No need for any more EMDR . . . and I assume that means no more treatment of any kind. I'd already stopped taking the antidepressants – after what they did to me – and they didn't help anyway . . . I don't need them – or anything else.'

'That's wonderful . . . I'm so thrilled for you. – Oh! and for Phoebe.'

'Yes . . . I don't know I'd have gone through with all that without feeling I needed to get better for Phoebe's sake.'

'Not for your own?'

'Well yes . . . I do want to get back to work . . . and just feel "normal" . . . Ha! – I'd forgotten what that feels like.'

'Until now? . . . er . . . You really do feel better?'

'Yes . . . I think so . . . Got to take it easy to begin with, he says . . . One small step at a time.'

'That's sensible . . . Christmas coming up. Don't want to overdo things.'

'Glory! . . . I'd forgotten about Christmas. – I've been in a different world. – Not sure I can get everything sorted in a week . . . Gotta get organised . . . Maybe we should just go away somewhere. Just the two of us . . . Would you think of going anywhere? . . . Would you like to?'

'Bit of sun would be nice.'

'What d'you fancy?'

'Bit of you.'

'Roderick Finch, QC, You're impossible . . . I'll let Phoebe know where we'll be. No chance of her getting any time off duty. – Busy time, Christmas . . . In hospitals. – Specially for junior staff covering for each other . . . Same's probably true for James . . . Junior staff carry the can everywhere. – Tidying up the damage from other people's parties. – Last in, first to be on duty on Bank Holidays . . . Not a good time to get ill. Christmas . . . with all the juniors on duty.'

* * *

Would've been nice seeing Phoebe over Christmas . . . Put a bit of spark back into my life – a lot – brighten me up again . . . Dammit, I do so miss her – talking seriously with me, teasing me, sharing onions with me. Ha! – So silly that. Me a quarterback, gone soft. Me, sacked by a woman – again . . . Hmm . . . Better than linebackers I s'pose – solid as rocks – No chance of them feeling anything . . .

* * *

'Got any plans for Christmas? – Going home?'

'Hadn't thought . . . Mother's still not right. – Don't wanna put too much on her. – The Phebe's probably working. Always is these days . . . Always was . . . Hard worker, that one. I'll

140

give her that. Plays hard too . . . Anyway, I'm on the roster for the day itself.'

'Like to come to my place? . . . Sometime . . . Have some leftover turkey . . . Meet Mum.'

'Whooa, Lucy. D'you really mean that? . . . The dragon in her den?'

'I really have given you the wrong impression there . . . Sometimes she finds it difficult to take off her professional coat. – With me. When she's at home. – Not always . . . Sweet as pie otherwise.'

'A CQC inspector "sweet as pie"?'

'Course she is. – We're all human.'

o O o

'Is the room ok for you? Is the hotel good enough?'

'It's amazing. What a clever girl you are for choosing it . . . umm . . . How did you find it?'

'I've had a lot of time on my hands. Dreaming of what I'd do – where I'd go – when I was better.'

'Remarkable. Did you always believe you'd get better?'

'Yes. In a way. One way or another.'

'Even when you were right down? . . . Despairing?'

'Yes.'

'How?'

'The worse it got, the more determined I became . . . You should know that. – You married me . . . I'm your wife.'

'Yes . . . Yes I know. I just wish I could do that. Was it the power of positive thinking?'

'No . . . Sheer bloody mindedness. – The Michael Mates principle.'

'Huh?'

'Surely you remember. – The MP under pressure. Given a

watch with "Don't let the buggers get you down" engraved on the back.'

'Oh yes . . . Wonder what happened to him.'

'Dunno . . . S'pose it would be interesting to find out.'

'Not really.'

'Why not?'

'We're all different . . . What works for him might also work for me. Or it might not.'

'I think you said that the wrong way round . . . You put the negative option second. That's the one that'll stay with you. – The second one.'

'Really? Where did you get that from?'

'The counsellor. He said it to me once.'

'Oh . . . umm . . . I must try that on a jury . . . if I get back to work.'

'You're making the same mistake . . . Well, similar. I think.'

'Huh?'

'Try, "*When* I get back to work.".'

'Ah . . . P'raps I should see him meself.'

'I mentioned that to him . . . He said he obviously couldn't help you with your physical state but, if you wanted it some-time, he might be able to help you to see things differently. "Re-frame them", I think he said.'

'Isn't that what's called, "the power of positive thinking"?'

'He said it was NLP. – *Neuro Linguistic Programming.*'

'What's the difference?'

'Dunno . . . You'll have to ask him. If you want to . . . But I must say you're doing wonderfully on your own. Most of the time . . . I mean that joke of yours at Gatwick was very funny. – In the long check-in queue, winding round and round. With all the Spaniards . . . And you calling out "Maria" just to see how many people looked up.'

'Just a but of fun.'

'That's my Roddy . . . Anyway I hope you enjoy it here. In this hotel.'

'What's not to enjoy? Our private balcony overlooking the pool. And with the sun in the afternoon like now . . . And with live classical music. – Not canned rubbish. How did the island get the reputation for being . . . for . . . er . . .'

'For what?'

'Plebs. Boozers. Blow jobs to pay for cocaine.'

'Roddy! Really!'

'Sorry, dear.'

'Parts of any island – or any resort anywhere – are like that. But the rest is lovely . . . Look at Mallorca.'

'I'd rather not . . . I'm very happy here . . . Just with you . . . Although, come to think of it . . .'

'Roddy!'

* * *

'What's the surprise you've got for me? . . . To what do I owe the privilege of an invitation to meet Dr Phoebe Finch in the bistro? . . . at her expense?'

'It's good news and bad news . . . Which d'you want first?'

'Bad news . . . Get it over with.'

'Ok . . . I'll tell you the good news . . .'

'Ha! – Then why did you give me a choice? . . . Only to make your own decision?'

'To tease you . . . Tee hee.'

'I should've known . . . My oh my, have I missed you! . . . Go on then. What's the good news?'

'Mum's better . . . the EMDR fixed her anaesthetic aware-ness . . . er . . . So she says . . . She tried it out – went into a prep room and theatre. – She felt like she did before it happened . . . Just a bit battered . . . more than a bit . . . but functional. She's going back to work as soon as she can . . . when the contracts people allow it . . . That's the plan.'

'That really is super . . . I'm so glad for her and for all your family. It's been a dreadful time for her – and for all of you. – But especially for her . . . umm . . . What's the bad news?'

'You're stuck with me . . . if you still want me.'

'I want you for ever and ever . . . as I told you before . . . till the sun goes out.

o O o

'And have you had any better ideas? . . . while you've been on strike?'

'Yes . . . Lots.'

'Want to tell me some?'

'I'd love to . . . when they're better formed. But at the moment I keep finding that each new idea leads to more questions.'

'Yes. I find that in my recovery. I was told in Hazelden that it's a never-ending process . . . There's always more to learn. – We're never "recovered" from addiction. Only "recovering" . . . But it's an action programme. I have to *do* things to get better, not just think about them.'

'Yes. I can see that . . . But how can you know what to do? . . . If you don't know where to start? . . . or where you're going?'

'They said, "Work the Twelve Steps. The recovery programme. Continuingly. – It works if you work it".'

'And what's the goal? . . . apart from abstinence?'

'Yes. That's the precise point, isn't it? . . . I can't see the purpose of recovery if all I can say is, "I haven't had a drink or a drug in twenty years" . . . I've seen some people like that in meetings . . . Stuck in a rut . . . Miserable buggers.'

'What about the other people?'

'Getting on with life . . . Following the suggestion that recovery's a bridge to normal living . . . whatever that is.'

'Don't you know? . . . normal living? . . . where you're heading?'

'Yes I do . . . I want a better life . . . more constructive life. More useful than before.'

'But that's running away from something, rather than towards something.'

'Bit of both.'

'But if you haven't got a clear goal for the future you'll be all over the place.'

'I *have* got a clear goal . . . I want to run a rehab.'

'That's fine, wonderful . . . But what for? What's going to be the end result?'

'To help addicts – of all kinds – to get well . . . Understand what they've got – what addiction is – and deal with it . . . each day, one day at a time.'

'Towards what end?'

'Wellness.'

'What's "wellness"?'

'I thought you knew . . . umm . . . abstinence for a start – for those of us who don't have the gift, the genes maybe, to use mood-altering substances sensibly . . . Nancy Reagan said, "Just say no". They said that in the Mental Health Unit . . . But I can't "just say no" . . . once I've started. – And even before I start I go up the wall if I don't go to AA and work the Steps . . . I know that now.'

'That's good . . . if that's what you want . . . what's good for you, helps you. And your relationships . . . But what then? What's the "wellness" you talk about? . . . What are you aiming for?'

'To be grateful rather than resentful. . . . Not like that guy on television the other night – fancies himself despite saying he doesn't use drugs any more – attacking bankers and everybody. Wanting revolution but no idea what to do afterwards . . . umm . . . I want to learn enough so I don't make too many mistakes . . . in my rehab.'

'And what d'you want the rehab to do? . . . apart from help the people in it?'

'Challenge the ideas . . . the system that leads to the hell hole I was in first of all . . . Over here.'

'And how are you going to do that?'

'I've been told in the rooms – the places where AA holds its meetings – that it's a programme of attraction rather than promotion . . . a selfish programme.'

'And what does that mean? . . . To them? Or you? . . . Selfish?'

'Doing what works for me . . . Keeping what I give away.'

'Ha! Yes, that's right. – The opposite of what people usually mean by "selfish" . . . If you're kind to other people, considerate, you yourself feel good, have a happier life, better life.'

'Yes . . . That's how one counsellor explained it to me . . . over here . . . in the rooms.'

'I thought people were meant to be anonymous in those meetings. That doesn't sound very anonymous – if you know what he does.'

'That was coincidence. He was the counsellor my mother saw . . . I saw him when I wanted to find out how to set up a rehab . . . but I met him again at an AA meeting . . . He told me there – after the meeting – his take on "a selfish programme" . . . when I asked him.'

'Why not before? Why not in the meeting . . . It might help people.'

'But it might upset others. If he goes on to talk about the

Church and the State being against individuals . . . as he said to me later . . . away from the meeting . . . That's politics . . . They're "outside issues", as far as AA's concerned.'

'Why?'

'Because Tradition One says, "Our common welfare should come first. We keep what we have only with AA unity".'

'But that won't go very far . . . It's very inward looking.'

'It's helping over two million people right now . . . all as a result of two men – Dr Bob and Bill W – getting together eighty years ago . . . It's a programme of attraction rather than promotion. As I said.'

'Yes ok . . . But why don't they set up rehabs?'

'Outside issues . . . Not their skill. Too much politics . . . Like your mother.'

'She means well.'

'I'm sure she does . . . from what you say . . . But her work is necessarily divisive. Separating the sheep from the goats . . . AA isn't like that. Takes in all comers . . . The ideas work by osmosis . . . Oh, sorry . . . Chemistry.'

'And biology . . . Then why doesn't your counsellor man set up a rehab?'

'He did once . . . Loved it, he said.'

'Why not now?'

'Doesn't want the grief. The hassle. The constant grind of regulations getting in the way of ideas.'

'Ha! – He's on strike.'

o O o

'This island is remarkable. Who would ever have imagined Tenerife it would be so lush – on a volcano – and so beautiful?'

'I would. I read a guidebook to build up my anticipation –

celebration – after this wretched time.'

'Oh yes. Of course. – You always were one for doubling your pleasure.'

'Roddy! We'll pass over that remark very quickly. – The staff speak perfect English, half the guests are English and the other half, the Germans, may well do.'

'Then they'll be envious . . . My Lizzie's back on form.'

'And not putting on any more weight – Let's get a sense of relative significance here – despite the fabulous food.'

'And supper under the stars . . . Could've been in shirt sleeves.'

'What's that got to do with not putting on any more weight?'

'Huh?'

'I said, "What's that got to do . . ." '

'I heard you . . . I was just being romantic . . . Anyway, I like you cuddly.'

'Love handles.'

'Pfwooar!'

'Roddy! . . . That's the same in any language . . . and it's not nice to point it out to a girl. Now I'll have to go on a diet.'

'Don't do that. *Please* don't do that.'

'But other women will notice.'

'I don't care about them.'

'Well I do . . . All women do.'

'Good job I've got the club . . . Something better to talk about.'

'Ha! Politics, cutting other lawyers down to size, the Six Nations cup, booze . . . What else?'

'It's not "booze". They're very fine wines . . . The club has an excellent cellar.'

'It may do . . . Has, I'm sure . . . But if I've got you right – on the conversation you men have in the snug. – I'm surprised any women would want to become members.'

'Groucho Marx.'

'Huh?'

'Didn't want to belong to any club that would have him as a member.'

'Oh . . . Let's look at the stars, shall we? . . . And I've got an idyllic drive planned for tomorrow.'

'Can't we stay here? It's one of the top hotels in the world. It says so in the brochure.'

'It said the same in Cyprus last year – and that hotel was awful . . . But the wild orchids on the drive up into the mountains were very lovely.'

'The chef was on holiday most likely.'

'Yes . . . You said that at the time . . . Anyway it'll do you good to get out and about a bit.'

'Must you doctors always think about what's good for people? fussing and bothering over us all the time? bending us to your medical will?'

'Aargh! – You men!'

'Umm . . . Happy Christmas.'

'Oh yes . . . Happy Christmas . . . Sorry. Bit preoccupied by being free at last.'

'That's fully understandable . . . And I'm very happy for you . . . More wine?'

'I've had sufficient, thank you.'

'Never enough of a first-rate claret.'

'There is for me . . . Oh . . . I told Alice to tell the regular referrers – the GPs – that I'm going to be back in business. Real soon. Gotta get back into shape for that.'

'That's good. Give you something to look forward to . . . Although, I must say, I'm very happy here . . . Away from it all.'

'I'll enjoy every minute of my time here . . . But I can't wait to get back and get on with life.'

* * *

'D'you really mean that? – That you'll love me till the sun goes out?'

'Course I do. – Or I wouldn't have said it.'

'No. You wouldn't. What if there's an eclipse?'

'Partial or total?'

'Oh Precious. That's such a silly thing to say. – So academic.'

'It was such a silly question . . . Anyway, the sun doesn't go out in an eclipse. It's only hiding.'

'Feels like it. Feels like it's gone out.'

'Yeah. The birds think so . . . In a total eclipse.'

'Are you calling me a bird?'

'Wouldn't dare. Why are you so nervous? I've given you my word. I'll stick to that.'

'Yes . . . Yes, I'm sure you will . . . It's just that I don't deserve it . . . I've treated you so badly.'

'Aah. That's it. – No you haven't. You did what you believed was right. When two of your values clashed. That makes you a more moral – ethical – person. Not less.'

'Umm . . . Has there been anyone else?'

'S'pose there might have been eventually . . . Gotta move on eventually. We all do . . . Got to. – Or stay stuck . . . And that's not fair to the other person.'

'Huh?'

'Same as in any form of bereavement. Keeps the other person – the dead person – tied in. Not free. Not free to move on . . . To wherever . . . whatever . . . whoever.'

'You make it sound like a dance . . . Relationships.'

'It is.'

'Who plays the tune?'

'All of us together ... The music of the spheres. The infinite. – Where we came from, where we're going. All of us ... Eventually ... This is just the rehearsal ... Or maybe it's the full deal.'

'What is?'

'This life ... whatever it is.'

'D'you believe in an afterlife? ... Where your mother is now?'

'God rest her mortal soul.'

'What do you actually *mean* by that? ... God? ... Soul?'

'The part of us ... of everything ... that can't be destroyed ... The essence. The part of us that existed a hundred years ago and will exist in a hundred years from now. – Not the body. That's just the car that drives us around. For a bit.'

'Were we destined to meet? ... you and me? ... to be together?'

'Who knows? ... I don't think so. – But I'm glad we did. One miracle's occurred already ... that we're alive ... Let's create another. Let's make the best of life while we can ... The life we've got. We know about.'

'But what's that bit about trapping each other? ... alive or dead?'

'We do ... Tend to ... If we give someone headroom there's a mutual attraction – electro-magnetic ... er ... quantum. – Yes, quantum more like. – Draws spirits together. Could be warmly. Could be destructively ... Like you see in mass rallies. – Potential for good or evil ... To create or destroy.'

'But I don't want to destroy anyone ... Nor do you.'

'But we all have the potential ... And the power. Depends how we use it.'

'So what happens? ... when two spirits interact?'

'They're like magnets, I s'pose ... Of variable strengths.'

151

'Why variable?'

'Circumstances . . . Depends what else is going on.'

'And what's the stuckness?'

'When one magnet stays on . . . all by itself . . . The other one's caught . . . Not free to move on. Entirely . . . Quantum again. Maybe.'

'Huh?'

'Maybe there are multiple universes. All at the same time – whatever that is . . . Time . . . And we're all in all of them.'

'You've lost me.'

'Never again. I'll never lose you again . . . Phebes you is mah woman now. You is. You is. You is. You is. You is.'

* * *

'Your mother's very nice.'

'Course she is . . . She's got half my genes.'

'Huh? . . . I thought you had half hers.'

'Work it out, James. Work it out. – Not at your brightest this afternoon.'

'Huh?'

'A half is a half – whichever way round it is.'

'Umm . . .'

'Aargh . . . Half my genes came from my mother. The other half from my father.'

'Yes. I know that . . . But your mother's genes came from her parents before you were even born. How can half her genes come from you?'

'They didn't.'

'But you said . . .'

'I said she's got half my genes.'

'But that's what I said . . . You can't give her your genes backwards . . . Anyway, half your genes came from your father – and she can't have any of his. Hadn't even met him when you were conceived . . . Well, after a time.'

'Leave him out of it.'

'Isn't he your father? . . . Really?'

'No, I mean yes of course he is. Where else did I get my blue eyes from?'

'The milkman?'

'There aren't any milkmen nowadays . . . Not many . . . All supermarkets . . . But he's my dad all right.'

'But you said, "Leave him out of it".'

'Out of the equation.'

'What equation?'

'The consideration.'

'I'm sure he wouldn't like that . . . or your mother . . . They seem very happy.'

'They are.'

'Then why split them up?'

'Huh?'

'Why leave him out of the . . . er . . . equation? – or whatever?'

'Because he can't give his genes to my mother.'

'That's what I told you.'

'James, James, James . . . Slow down a bit . . . Ahem . . . Half of my genes came from my mother.'

'Yes . . . And the other half didn't.'

'That's right . . . Yes . . . No they didn't.'

'Yes . . . no. – Which?'

'What I said.'

'What did you say?'

'Aaaaaargh!'

* * *

'It's been a lovely break . . . and lovely being here with you.

Just the two of us on our own. Like old times.'

'Romance is not yet dead.'

'I'll say . . . It's understandable that I should feel on top of the world after the EMDR – but you're incredible . . . Meant to be falling to bits . . . with your neurological business . . . And you're not.'

'Unsteady on me pins occasionally.'

'Yes, poor love . . . Anyway, as far as I'm concerned, you're great. – You're the husband I always wanted and I gotcha!'

'Wooooaaah!'

'No. – You can't frighten me like that. Not after what I've been through . . . Can't wait to start work again some time soon . . . Yes . . . Might just as well check on my e-mails now. See if there's anything I need to catch up on . . . Ha! . . . I feel like Phoebe . . . Dead keen. Doing her first job . . . umm . . . Hello, what's this? . . . Odd to be getting an e-mail from the hospital staff contracts department . . . What? . . . What? . . . WHAT?'

'What's up? . . . Sweetheart?'

'They . . . They won't let me work.'

'Huh? . . . Why on earth not?'

'Listen to this . . . er . . . Here's the crucial bit . . . "The advice of our lawyers is that the hospital would be held liable if any untoward surgical event were to occur . . ." . . . Yes, here we are . . . "Accordingly I am instructed to tell you that your contract with this hospital is suspended forthwith while . . . Yeah, yeah . . ." . . . Aaargh! Lawyers!'

'Umm . . .'

'Oh, sorry love. – not you.'

'What's their concern?'

'Well the gist of it is the bit I read out to you . . . I can't work. – Not allowed to . . . I'm being punished for what that

anaesthetist did to me . . . As if I hadn't suffered enough! –
And without them knowing what I'm like now.'

'Sweetest, Lizzie . . . I'm afraid that's the crucial point. –
Not my subject. Litigation. Suing people. – But everyone
knows you've been off work . . . Patients – and their lawyers
– will soon dig that up if . . . umm . . . anything did . . . er . . .
happen '

'But it's so unfair! . . . I'm being punished in advance for
something I haven't even done.'

'Yes . . . Yes, I can see how you would think that. – And it's
true . . . It *is* unfair. But you know how doctors think and I
know how lawyers think.'

'How do they think?'

'They couldn't defend you . . . umm . . . the hospital . . . er
. . . Even the slightest thing that went off course, some minor
little thing – let alone the major ones, can happen. – It would
be indefensible . . . They'd have to pay a very great deal of
money – megabucks – if there were any suggestion that they
sent you into bat with a duff head on your shoulders – and
knew they were doing so – or couldn't prove they didn't . . .
Impossible . . . and hadn't done all the checks and so on . . . In
advance . . . Hell to pay.'

'Oh . . . But it's so unfair.'

'Medical things *are* unfair. – You know that . . . Legal
things *are* unfair. – I know that . . . Life's unfair.'

Lizzie cried.

o O o

That's wonderful . . . Mum being helped so much by EMDR
. . . Odd that I wasn't taught about it in med school . . .

* * *

'I've decided to put my toe in the water.'

'Was it dirty?'

'Roddy, you really are impossible! You've developed a new lease of life . . . and now you're deliberately winding me up, just for fun . . . What's got into you these days?'

'Seeing *The Rite of Spring* at the Royal Ballet.'

'I should've known . . . The Christmas break put even more life into you. By the spring, particularly with global warming, you'll be absolutely insufferable.'

'Hope so.'

'Which? . . . Global warming or you being all over me?'

'Both . . . Bad news for some, good news for us . . . er . . . Global warming, I mean.'

'I'm sure we're not meant to think like that.'

'Why not? – It's true.'

'But we're not meant to say so. What will they say in The Maldives?'

'Glug.'

'Roddy! Stop that at once. You and your mates in The Garrick might get away with remarks like that – to each other – but you can't get away with them with me.'

'Why not?'

'Because we're all God's children.'

'Can't they build an ark?'

'It's not funny.'

'I thought it was . . . And couldn't you ask Moses to part the waters?'

'Roddy, that's quite enough.'

'All right . . . all right . . . but it was good fun while it lasted.'

'Don't you even want to know what I've decided?'

'Oh. So sorry . . . Forgot about you.'

'Yes, you did . . . Except when you . . . umm . . . I'm going into the hospital to see how I react.'

'To the psychiatrist to whom the private GP referred you?'

'Certainly not. I don't want to see him ever again . . . He's a one-trick pony. – Against EMDR when he'd never seen it . . . Just because it isn't CBT or drugs.'

'Hmm.'

'No. – I'll go up to the operating theatres and into a prep room to see how I feel.'

'Don't push yourself too far.'

'I'm not going to do anything . . . surgical . . . Not with the contracts department playing up – Just see if I still react the way I did last time . . . I'm sure it'll be ok. I feel fine now.'

'Maybe I should say a prayer.'

'You? Ha! That'll be the day. – God would get such a surprise.'

'Well I hope neither of us meets Him just yet . . . but maybe there's no harm in opening a line of communication.'

'Now I don't know if you're winding me up again or if you're being serious.'

'I'll be serious. – Just for you.'

'And Him.'

* * *

'What's the most troublesome issue for this patient? Miss . . . er . . . Amin?'

'Varicose ulcers, Sir.'

'Yes. That's the precipitant cause for her being here. What's the contributory cause?'

'Obesity . . . Leading to incompetent valves in the long saphenous veins. Also there are perforating veins connecting the deep system to the superficial system. They will need to be tied off surgically to prevent a recurrence of the ulcers.

These should be treated initially with *Viscopaste* bandages.'

'Excellent . . . Anything further to say about her obesity?'

'She should lose weight.'

'D'you imagine that doctors have told her that before?'

'Umm . . . Yes.'

'D'you think it will help if you tell her again?'

'We could recommend gastric banding.'

'What does that achieve?'

'It makes the stomach smaller so that she feels full even after a small amount of food.'

'And what happens then?'

'She gets thinner.'

'So with various surgical interventions her problems are sorted.'

'Yes, Sir.'

'No . . . I'm afraid not, Miss Amin. – That's a hospital perspective . . . "An interesting case – maybe for some doctors not a particularly interesting case – in bed four." D'you think she sees herself that way?'

'Umm . . . I don't know, Sir.'

'What do you know about her? . . . on a personal basis . . . on her social history? . . . *Who* is she?'

'She's a fifty four year old divorced female with two grown up children, living in a Council estate. She works as a shop assistant. She smokes twenty cigarettes a day.'

'Very good – but that's still a hospital doctor's viewpoint, rather than her own. – You've asked her for important clinical and social information as you see it . . . But she may have different priorities in her life as she sees it.'

'Oh.'

'On the information you have provided, I'm sure you would pass your finals – and I don't want to detract from that – but there's more to her than being a demonstration case.'

'Yes, Sir.'

'Lets ask Dr Finch what information she has on this lady – who came in yesterday so there hasn't been much time . . . It's all a question of asking ourselves, "Whose Health Service is this? – The doctors' or the patients'?" – and "How do we define the responsibility of doctors? How far does it go?" . . . Dr Finch?'

'Mrs Rosemary Smith divorced her husband when he left her for a colleague at work. They'd been having a relationship – those two – for some years so there was little chance of reconciliation. Mrs Smith is lonely. Her children tell her that they couldn't wait to get away from home – from the moodiness and tantrums. She eats for comfort. She began smoking again, after five years of abstinence, because it reduces her appetite. She took a job because she had to . . . Her husband, despite court orders, fails to support her . . .. Standing all day, exacerbates her varicose veins . . . Her Council flat is on the fourth floor, which is difficult for her when the lifts break down, as they frequently do.'

'Thank you, Dr Finch . . . Now then – Miss Amin, d'you have any comments on what Dr Finch has told us?'

'It's a social commentary, Sir – and very interesting to some people – but it's not medical . . . It won't help me to pass my examinations . . . My family want me to be a specialist . . . And so do I.'

* * *

'Done it!'

'Done what?'

'I've been to the hospital, met up with Joan Prendle, my regular anaesthetist, changed into greens, gone with her into the prep room and the operating theatre – and it was all ok.'

'That's wonderful, sweetheart. Well done! . . . umm . . . I'm a bit taken aback you didn't tell me in advance.'

'You'd have worried about me – and I'd have worried about you worrying about me . . . I wanted to do this just for me . . . After all, it's my own crazy head that'd gone wonky and there's nothing you could do to settle it down again.'

'Never was.'

'Roddy?'

'Oh . . . Sorry . . . Wasn't thinking. – So delighted for you.'

'Hmm . . . On that basis I'll let you off with a caution, just this once.'

'Ha! You sound like a magistrate, dealing with a young offender.'

'I am.'

'Ah . . . Tell me about it. – The hospital.'

'There's nothing more to say, really . . . I was back in the old routine – apprehensive at first, of course – but the system took over.'

'What system?'

'The regular well established pattern . . . The way we always do things.'

'No hiccoughs?'

'Course not . . . You know I never drink on the day – or the night – before I go into an operating theatre . . . I need a still hand . . . clear mind . . . Don't want other people to smell it on me. – Damage my reputation.'

'I meant "blips".'

'Oh. – No, no blips at all.'

'That's good . . . And what's your reputation? . . . Now?'

'Same as it was, I s'pose . . . Still me . . . The gang – the theatre sister and co, the porters . . . theatre operatives or whatever they like to call themselves nowadays. – They're the ones who control who does what . . . when the patients come and go, how long the list lasts, who's on it even . . . All very supportive.'

'That's nice . . . In my trade the other barristers can't wait for each other to drop off their perches. – More work for them. Mortgages to pay . . . School fees.'

'The NHS just gets in locums . . . Spends a fortune on them.'

'Germans? East Europeans? Africans?'

'Anybody they can get – from anywhere.'

'Any check on them? Reliable? Properly qualified? Experienced?'

'Not in the way we regulars have to go through the hoops all the time . . . No time for that. – S'long as the paperwork's ok, that's it . . . On you go . . . And then the locum agency gets it if there's anything . . . umm, what's the word? . . . "untoward".'

'Like your chap.'

'S'pose so . . . Didn't ask.'

'Why not?'

'Nothing to gain . . . Past history.'

'That really is remarkable. – This EM . . . whatever.'

'Yes.'

'Just "Yes"? . . . Nothing more to say?'

'No . . . Past history. – Got to look forward.'

'Remarkable.'

'Oh . . . I'm so glad we went to Tenerife. I feel so refreshed.'

'I'd always thought the Canary Islands were for plebs.'

'Roddy! You really can't use that word nowadays . . . Just as we can't call the porters "Trogs" – troglodytes living in caves in the basement of the hospital – or even "porters".'

'Why not?'

'It's not politically correct. – Might upset someone.'

'Sod that for a bowl of raspberries.'

'Roddy! . . . Behave yourself. – You may be able to get away
with that sort of guff in The Garrick but nowhere else . . . and
not with me.'

'No, Sir.'

'Roddy?'

'Sorry, Sir . . . er . . . Madam.'

*   *   *

'Don't get me wrong, Lucy. – I'm not trying to run before I can
walk . . .'

'I expect you are.'

'How can you say that when you haven't yet heard what I'm
going to say?'

'Go on then. – Say it.'

'I want to be a counsellor.'

'Ha! Gotcha!'

'Whadd'you mean?'

'You've been a care assistant for less than three months
and already you want to move on . . . Another three months
and you'll want to run the place.'

'And why not?'

'Because my mother – or other people in her job – would eat
you for breakfast . . . and eat the rehab for employing you.'

Why? . . . the rehab?'

'Because they have to show that staff have the proper
qualifications, training and experience for the job they do . . .
Otherwise, if something goes wrong, they'll get taken apart
. . . There'll be an enquiry. And negative publicity. And the
rehab'll get a bad name. – Look what happened to that one on
an island in the Thames estuary . . . Gave all rehabs a bad
name. Possibly . . .'

'Oh yes.'

'. . . And no new patients will come here if something goes wrong when the paperwork isn't right . . . It's like ten pin bowling. – One pin knocks down the next . . . if the ball is aimed well . . . which it always is in the private sector.'

'What d'you mean?'

'There are always plenty of people who want to do it down . . . find fault in any way they can . . . just because it *is* the private sector.'

'Why?'

'Because they believe in the NHS . . . They want it to be the *only* system.'

'Where are they going to get their new ideas? . . . like those I learned in America.'

'That's the last thing they'll want.'

'Why?'

'America's the Great Satan – and not only in the eyes of the Ayatollahs.'

'Why? – When their rehabs work so well . . . or the one I was in did . . . compared with the pit I was in over here?'

'They close their eyes – and their minds – as soon as money's involved . . . They hate it.'

'Doesn't stop them wanting it for themselves . . . Marching, protesting – even going on strike nowadays – always for more money . . . That's what my sister was always banging on about – in one-sided conversations and on the drums. – They make out it's to improve the services to patients but it always comes down to the same thing . . . "More pay for me".'

'Yes . . . That's what happened with the last government. They gave in to all the demands from the unions . . . Paid the GPs a huge amount of money – and got worse services for the patients . . . Then they brought in targets for this and that and everything so you couldn't move for paperwork . . . I saw that in my nursing work . . .'

'Oh.'

'. . . This government's no better – in the opposite direction – wanting a market economy . . . And everyone – every government – wants to reorganise everything from top to bottom.'

'So what's the solution?'

'There isn't one.'

'Huh?'

'The NHS – and the private sector – are political footballs. The only thing that matters is politicians scoring goals against the other side.'

'But there's *got* to be a solution . . . That's what I believe. That's what I want to work towards . . . umm . . . do with my life.'

'That's what I really like about you – your enthusiasm – but don't go too fast. Walk first. Run later.'

'Yeah . . . You said that before . . . P'raps I should just set myself up – in Harley Street or somewhere – as a counsellor.'

'My mother was talking about that.'

'About me?'

'No . . . about people being able to set themselves up as counsellors in this and that – even in early childhood sexual abuse – without anyone being able to stop them.'

'So she wants more regulation?'

'Either that or the private sector gets more litigation . . . It's all or nothing . . . one way or the other.'

'And the NHS gets away with appalling services – to the people who need the most help.'

'Yes. I've seen that myself.'

'So what are we going to do about it?'

'Walk before we run.'

'Is that what you're doing?'

'Yes . . . I'm walking very slowly, thinking, thinking a lot. I

can do plenty of that on this job in the laundry . . . As I see it
– as I told you before – I'm on strike . . . in my own way.'

*   *   *

Giving these talks is what I do . . . Mustn't forget that . . . No
good dreaming about Phoebe all the time. – No reason to
think she'll change her mind . . . No evidence . . .

o O o

'This lady has multiple pathology – a common problem in the
elderly . . . One that makes my work challenging and
stimulating . . . She presents an interesting challenge on
clinical and personal priorities . . . So what are they? the
priorities? . . . We know she has carcinoma of the breast,
thyroid deficiency and pernicious anaemia – as well as
various personal and social issues that I'm sure Dr Finch can
tell you about . . . and, after last week's session, I hope you'll
have found out for yourself . . . Whose patient is this?'

'Mine, Sir . . . John Fotheringay.'

'Fotheringay? . . . Unusual name . . . Do I know your father?
. . . One of my contemporaries. – One of the brighter ones. –
GP now, I think.'

Yes, Sir.'

'Do give him my good wishes . . . I remember the time we
. . . aah . . . Maybe not . . . umm . . . What would be your
priorities? . . . for this lady?'

'Treat the cancer.'

'Why?'

'She'll die of it.'

'Anyone else have any thoughts on that? . . . treating the
carcinoma first?'

Silence.

'Dr Finch?'

'What you taught me – on the clinical round – was that she's more likely to die *with* it than *of* it.'

'Yes . . . At her age, with a slow growing tumour of low malignancy, we might recommend a simple "lumpectomy" – to remove the primary lesion if it causes her discomfort or fear – but not do anything more dramatic . . . Why not, Mr Fotheringay?'

'Too costly?'

'No . . . Not really. – Occupying a hospital bed is costly . . . before we do anything at all . . . The extra costs of investigating and treating this problem wouldn't be prohibitive . . . Other reasons?'

'Need the beds?'

'We always need the beds . . . Demand always exceeds supply . . . The potential need is unending . . . It depends on where we doctors and patients – Ha! and administrators nowadays – draw the line . . . What is "need"?'

Silence.

'How about the other issues – the myxoedoema and the PA?'

'Treat the PA first.'

'Why?'

'Because there could be dreadful consequences – sub-acute combined degeneration of the spinal cord – if we don't.'

'Very good . . . Did your father tell you about that? . . . Does he show you clinical things sometimes?'

'No, Sir . . . I looked it up. – On the web.'

'Excellent . . . That's the way. – And if you don't look it up the patients or their families will. – Got to stay one step ahead . . . Yes . . . And what about the thyroid deficiency, the myxoedoema? What about that?'

'It develops slowly ... My father told me that it's often diagnosed by locums – because the regular GP hadn't noticed the gradual change in the patient.'

'True ... But, as I'm sure your father will also have told you, it's so easy nowadays simply to do a thyroid screen as a routine blood test. What's the possible snag with that?'

'Cost?'

'Yes ... Even though one thyroid screen doesn't cost all that much, the cost of doing one every year for every patient in the land would be very considerable – and reduce the amount of money available for other things.'

'But they do that on a BUPA check-up.'

'Yes ... In the private sector you get what you pay for ... But what's the disadvantage in that? – for those patients?'

Silence.

'They may get into the habit of believing themselves to be ill until proved otherwise ... They're called "the worried well" ... It may be good business for the private doctor but it's not a happy state for the patients.'

Shuffles.

'And what's another disadvantage of relying on test results?'

'They could be inaccurate.'

'Yes, that's true – hopefully not very often. – So what do you do about that?'

Silence.

'Yes. How would you know if the test is likely to be inaccurate? – And what do you do if you think it is?'

'Phone the lab?'

'Yes, you could – but that won't make you very popular if you do that all the time ... What else might you do?'

'Repeat the test?'

'That's right ... It's much less trouble – clinically for us and personally for the patient – and less expensive for the NHS – if we simply repeat the original test . . . if the result doesn't fit with the clinical picture . . . rather than instigate a vast number of further tests.'

Mutterings.

'But what would make you think the initial test result might be inaccurate?'

Silence.

'Ha! Yes . . . That's the problem with high tech medicine . . . We may become so dependent on test results of one kind or another that we lose our basic clinical skills – like knowing what questions to ask the patients . . . and ourselves.'

* * *

Can't go wrong in the Garrick . . . That's the great thing about a club. Members choosing members. No silly buggers . . . Plenty of variety. All sorts. Politicians of all colours. Journos. The odd bishop . . . Hmm . . . Not really odd – just a bit eccentric. – Writers, actors, singers, thesps of all kinds . . . And then doctors and lawyers of course. All clubs have them . . . But The Garrick has the fun ones, distinguished in their own way – gotta be – but with that extra dash of individuality, something of the maverick . . . My sort of people . . .

* * *

'Hello, Mum. It's unusual for you to make a special time to see me in the hospital . . . What's up? . . . er . . . Something happened to Dad?'

'No . . .Up and down but generally he's in fine form. – Gone off to the club . . . I just hope he doesn't celebrate the new year too much . . . Not good for him . . . The specialist told him that – but I don't want to take away all his fun.'

'It won't be fun at all if his neurological problem takes off.'

'He's mostly been very positive recently . . . Oh . . . Ha! That's what he's up to . . . I've just realised . . . He's got a new idea into his head. – The power of positive thinking. – That explains it.'

'Explains what?'

'His attitude, his behaviour. Despite recent wobbles . . . er . . . physical ones . . . It's like when we were undergraduates together.'

'Careful, Mum . . . Careful of giving too much information. – I'm your daughter, remember?'

'Ha! We're both very fortunate . . . umm . . . Dad and me.'

'Dad and I.'

'Ha! . . . You're on form . . . Pedant!'

'I'm loving my job. I love being a doctor . . . My kind of doctor.'

'I remember . . . And so do I. – And it's all going to happen again.'

'What is?'

'Being my kind of doctor again . . . I'm in great shape. – I'm going back to work as soon as I can sort out a little local difficulty with the hospital.'

'Wow! That's wonderful! . . . Is that the power of positive thinking as well?'

'No . . . I tried that right at the start. Trying to pull myself together. Telling myself that it's all in my head . . . and that I was in charge of it. – Of what I put into it.'

'So what did it? What turned you round? . . . Whatever you're having, I'd like some.'

'Ha! Careful of too much information, Phoebe.'

'For my patients.'

'Too much for them as well . . . Whatever next!'

'So what happened?'

'EMDR happened . . . It got me better. It was surgical . . . It took out the bad bits. From my memory. And threw them away. And gently sewed up the wound and put me together again.'

'Nothing left?'

'Just a sense of having been through the mill. A grinding mill. – But I'm ok now. I'm not there any more. I got out.'

'Wow! That really is wonderful . . . and I really do want some of that for my patients.'

'Yes . . . The thing I like about it is that I got myself better really . . . I mean the counsellor was very nice – but the healing was from the inside.'

'Magic.'

'Yes, magic it is . . . So I came in specially to thank you.'

'Me?'

'Yes . . . You goaded me into it.'

'Goaded you?'

'Well . . . Made me an offer I couldn't refuse . . . No, that's not quite right . . . Put me in a situation that gave me the motive to go through with it.'

'Huh?'

'Sacrificing your own happiness, your own career, for Dad and me . . . I wasn't going to let you do that. So I went through with it. – And I've got you to thank for it.'

'Yes . . .But him as well. The counsellor.'

'Yes . . . Doing his job properly. That's what I try to do.'

'Me too.'

'Yes I know . . . You always have thought for yourself, done things your way. – And good for you.'

'Not good for me all the time . . . Sometimes I hurt myself – and other people . . . when I go too far.'

'You mean well.'

'Thank you, Mum . . . er . . . Thinking of an offer you can't refuse – Just to make you smile. – My chief, a lovely man, told me a great joke the other day.'

'Go on then.'

'What d'you get when you cross a Mafia member with an existentialist.'

'No . . . What?'

'An offer you can't understand.'

'Ha! That's good. Very good . . . I must tell your father.'

'Yes . . . and I'll tell Precious.'

'Happy new year, darling.'

'Yes . . . Yes, it will be . . . Happy new year to you too. And Dad – if possible.'

* * *

'I was thinking about what you said about being on strike . . . I mean, you're working – very hard . . . Not as if you'd downed tools or anything.'

'There are many ways of going on strike – not just the trade union way.'

'Such as?'

'I work with my brain, my mind . . . That's what I'm good at – except chemistry. – And I won't. I refuse.'

'Refuse what?'

'I told you. – Well, inferred it. – I refuse to work with my brain.'

'Huh?'

'I could use my degree, my nursing degree, and use that part of my brain – the intellectual part – but I don't want to.'

'Why not?'

'Umm . . . It probably sounds as if I've got a very high opinion of myself . . . S'pose I have in some ways . . . I don't

171

want to use my skills – such as they are – in support of a system I disagree with.'

'What system?'

'Statism.'

'State what?'

'State-ism. – The belief that the state is central, has all the answers, the solutions to all life's problems.'

'But my sister says . . . or used to before she met Precious . . . that the fault lies with capitalism.'

'We haven't got capitalism.'

'Ha! Try telling her that! . . . umm . . . What have we got?'

'A mixed economy . . . very mixed. Part statist, part capitalist. – But not much capitalist, not real free-market capitalism . . .'

'Oh.'

'. . .The government keeps stepping in. – Saying this industry is vital. Or that bank's too big to fail. Or the north of England – and all of Scotland, Wales and Northern Ireland – have special needs . . . and need special arrangements . . . Always more need . . . and more money . . . from the state. Well, from the productive sector that pays taxes.'

'Well they do need more.'

'No they don't. – That's a very patronising attitude . . . Look at Scotland – the land of Adam Smith, James Mill and David Hume, James Boswell, Robert Burns, Thomas Carlisle, Sir Walter Scott, Alexander Fleming, James Logie Baird – God knows how many brilliant minds . . .'

'How on earth d'you know all those names?'

'I made a point of finding out about them at the time of the Scottish referendum on independence. – Try googling "Famous Scots" and see who comes up . . . There's nothing wrong with their genes.'

'So why do they live off the City of London now?'

'The Nationalists say we stole their oil.'

'Ha! We give them their welfare . . . They live off us. We pay for their privileges – many that we ourselves don't have . . . free prescriptions, no tuition fees at university . . . But they make out we're the cause of all their hardships.'

'Some of them . . . Some of the Scots – Not all.'

'But why?'

'Politics . . . The entitlement culture.'

'Well I lived off my Mum and Dad for far too long. Took them for granted.'

'But not now.'

'No.'

'I respect you for that.'

'Thank you . . . But what's all this business about you being on strike?'

'I've withdrawn my labour – I don't do what I could really do.'

'Why? . . . er . . . Why not?'

'Precisely because it contributes to an entitlement culture . . . creates dependency, not in those who genuinely need – and deserve – public support in some way or other . . . not necessarily through the state . . . but in people who would otherwise be perfectly capable of providing for themselves.'

'So you're a one-girl revolutionary?'

'Individualist.'

'What's that?'

'The opposite of statist . . . I believe that only individuals create . . . The state – for all its good intentions – destroys . . . Look at Scotland and see what's become of that magnificent country and their fabulous heritage.'

'They've got an excellent tennis player . . . better than any of ours.'

'They've got lots of wonderful people . . . individuals . . .

But statism sucks the life blood out of the country . . . the creative people – in industry and commerce, not the arts. The arts people always do well . . . if they're any good. – But then the state subsidises the ones who aren't! . . . And it's going that way here as well.'

'But you're not achieving anything – all on your own . . . And if everybody followed your example there'd be nothing at all – for anybody.'

'P'raps the prospect of that is exactly what everybody needs to see.'

'But you're just one person.'

'One person's enough – for an idea . . . Look at the Scots I mentioned earlier. They were each revolutionaries. – In their way.'

'Or that English Leftie who keep talking about revolution,'

'He's a very skilled talker – and he has an immense number of social media followers. He's very influential.'

'He's just plain wrong.'

'That's been said about every individual thinker in history . . . and look what they did to Socrates . . . and Galileo,'

'Hmm . . . So what's to be done? . . . Now? . . . How do we stop the lunatics taking over the asylum?'

'Only by having better ideas,'

'And you going "on strike", as you call it, is a better idea?'

'Yes . . . It gives me time to work out even better ideas.'

* * *

'Why did you insist on coming here, rather than Byron's?

'To mark a new phase in our relationship . . . Byron's was the warm-up. This is the real thing – a French bistro that the local French people go to . . . That's the way to judge a restaurant. See who goes there.'

'I can't imagine anything worse than counting off the toffs
– at Le Gavroche or Chiltern Firehouse or places like that.'

'How d'you know about them?'

'My father took James and me to Le Gavroche when he
was trying to educate us . . . And show us off, I think.'

'I've never been to either of them. But I gather the food's
excellent . . . to match the price . . . And I'm showing you off
here.'

'Who to? . . . There's nobody here . . . not famous people
. . . Far as I know.'

'I don't know either – and I don't care. I'm showing off my
Phoebe to the whole wide world, saying "Look what I got! –
La creme de la creme!".'

'Now you're just showing off your French.'

'It's the language of love . . . and I love you.'

'I love you too . . . I think . . .'

'Don't you know?'

'Umm . . . I've never felt this way before. It seems so
natural.'

'Sounds good to me . . . So does the sound of the special –
lobster with pappardelle in a cream sauce . . . Want some?'

'Do they do onions?'

'Sure . . . But onions are off today.'

'No they're not . . . Look. – They're on the menu . . . as a
side.'

'They're off. – I said so.'

'That's very dominating of you. Why?'

'Because this is better . . . more delicate.'

'Oh . . . Imagine that . . .'

'I do.'

'It's a new experience for me . . . being dominated . . .
delicately.'

'Nah. I'm not into that sort of thing . . . Just loving you.'

'In that case I'll have the special . . . It doesn't seem too pricey here. – Not like those other places.'

'Then let's keep it special . . . Just for us.'

'Suits me . . . umm . . . Happy new year.'

'Yes . . . A very happy new year – to us.'

'To us.'

* * *

Part 3

'I've been to see the hospital contracts department . . . and I'm in danger of using one of your favourite expressions.'

'Which one?'

'Oh Gawd.'

'Hmm . . . That's serious.'

'Yes it is. They won't let me work at all at present. They say that my suspension means that I can't even go into the hospital.'

'Not even as a patient?'

'It's not funny, Roddy.'

'I didn't mean it to be funny. I was just wondering how far they intend to take this . . . You know you're better now – You're over it. I know you're better . . . How can anyone else judge?'

'The hospital malpractice insurers make their own judgement . . . on the advice of the consultant psychiatrist who saw me initially.'

'Well he's not been supportive so far . . . Have you even seen him since that first time when he gave you CBT and drugs?'

'No.'

'Ha! He simply wants you to do things his way.'

'That's the way it always goes . . . with psychiatrists.'

'Why not with other specialists?'

'They're not so defensive with patients . . . Only with each
other. – Turf wars. – That sort of thing.'

'I've never heard you talk about "turf wars" before. What
on earth are they? . . . and why haven't you mentioned them
before?'

'Well obs and gobs is really a hospital within a hospital . . .
So are some other specialist departments like skins and eyes
. . . In these departments we all muck in together – all the
consultants . . . and the staff as well, really.'

'But that doesn't apply in the rest of the hospital? Why
not?'

'Because of competition for beds . . . er . . . influence . . .
and money – getting the biggest slice of the budget for their
own department – and more prestige and money for
themselves.'

'But hospital doctors are salaried in the NHS.'

'Yes, that's true, but merit awards – clinical excellence
awards – come on top of that. They can be very substantial –
far more than the basic salary . . . They're awarded as a
distinction, an incentive to stay in the NHS rather than go
fully private . . . a bribe, I s'pose.'

'So who awards them?'

'Specialists put themselves up to the Awards Committee
that decides who's done exceptional work, published papers,
invented new approaches – brought distinction to the hospital and the profession – and the NHS, of course.'

'Why, "of course"?'

'It's all spelt out by the pundits who are on the committee
. . . They represent the employers – the Department of Health,
the state.'

'How do they spell it out?'

'Among other things on their website, they say quite
specifically that they want to see day-to-day commitment to

the values and goals of the NHS.'

'How?'

'Looking at job planning, service objectives, clinical governance, service organisation and delivery, policy making, planning . . . That sort of thing.'

'Sounds commendable.'

'It is – for bureaucrats . . . But for clinicians it all takes time away from looking after patients . . . The committee doctors rule the roost . . . It's a cat fight.'

'Why? – Surely they all want to work together to improve the status of the hospital? It must be a win/win situation to cooperate with each other.'

'They don't see it that way. There's nothing to win apart from the merit awards I mentioned. What happens in America is that consultant posts have limited tenure – three years usually. So they're always competing with each other to get higher qualifications and get admitting privileges to more prestigious hospitals. Then they can charge higher fees . . . The profit motive works to everyone's advantage – especially the patients'.'

'But not here?'

'You dear sweet innocent man . . . "Profit" is a very ugly word in the UK – generally, not just in healthcare. – You know that.'

'So what's the snag? . . . with merit awards?'

'The contrast in the motives of doctors who work for themselves or for the state . . . Private doctors in the UK work on the same principle as doctors in America. – Do good work, get a good reputation, make more money.'

'But isn't that just what you said about merit awards in the NHS?'

'It's not quite the same thing . . . Merit awards – they come at several levels – are lump sums . . . They're awarded and that's that – you got 'em . . . Patients aren't involved at all. The quality of care given to the patient is not the determining factor – because the patient isn't paying . . . The taxpayer is.'

'Oh.'

'It's all very invidious . . . mutual back-scratching by the cognoscenti – those who truly believe in the NHS as a political idea and system of healthcare . . . But then the NHS consultant specialists fight each other over the number of beds they have under their command . . . More beds equals more status – and, for those who have private practice on the side, more referrals from GPs.'

'Gawd! – and I thought the bar was a jungle!'

'You ain't seen nuffink – in the way of the law of the jungle – until you see doctors scratching each other's eyes out.'

'But how does any of this affect you? You're fully private – and so are the hospitals you work in.'

'The beliefs and attitudes of the NHS have all seeped into the general culture . . . We're all educated alongside each other and we do our training jobs – like Phoebe's now – alongside each other . . . The ideas of the Welfare State are ingrained in each and every one of us . . . It's very hard work digging them out – as I had to do when I went fully private.'

'Then why, if it's so wonderful, do doctors like you leave the NHS – or emigrate to Australia, as I read in *The Times*, many are doing now?'

'Partly for better working conditions, partly for more money, but mainly to find an environment where they're appreciated, rather than harassed . . . Ask yourself why lawyers don't all do legal aid work for the state.'

'Ahem.'

'Yes, "Ahem".'

'But why are you caught up with the hospital contracts department now? – in a private hospital? It seems to me that what we've been talking about is completely off the point.'

'Ah well . . . It's because of the basic culture of clinical practice in the UK . . . The General Medical Council – with a majority of lay members – oversees and rules everything . . . Nowadays the GMC is really an arm of the state. – It has a statist mentality . . . We're closer to Moscow than Washington – geographically and ideologically . . . The state – the NHS – is sacrosanct, inviolable.'

'Gosh, Lizzie. – Where did you find those words? . . . in a private loo somewhere?'

'Stop it. – I'm making a serious point . . . The doctors – and the insurers – in a private hospital have to follow the same ethical and clinical guidelines as those in the state sector . . . Initially that looks like like a good thing. – Getting rid of the cowboys. – But the end result is they're all frightened of being hauled up in front of somebody . . . They dare not be outside the loop – and be told they're not doing things the way they're generally done.'

'So how do people innovate? . . . do something that isn't part of "the system"?'

'With difficulty.'

'Ah . . . At last I see what you're saying . . . Your consultant psychiatrist – and your hospital – are playing safe . . . regardless of your actual clinical state.'

'Yes.'

* * *

'So there you are – this is my decision. I'm fully committed to you . . . and for once I'll make the running . . . How's about we move in together? . . . somewhere?'

'Oh, Precious, that would be wonderful . . . umm . . .'

'There's a "but" coming. – I can hear it.'

'Yes . . . umm . . . I must focus on my work . . . It's my long-term security – for me and my family. Mum's come through – so far – but she's not back at work yet . . . and Dad's only going to get worse . . . I don't want to pick you up and then put you down again.'

'Then we'll both have to look after your family . . . if it comes to that.'

'You can't do that.'

'We've discussed that before – or, to be more accurate, you've made your opinion clear before. But now I've had time to reflect . . . I'm telling you that I mean what I just said. – I looked after my mother, God rest her mortal soul, and I'd like to be involved in the care of your family, if they need it . . . and if they want me.'

'You've never met them.'

'Ha! Are they that bad?'

'No, I mean you're making a blind commitment.'

'No I'm not . . . I'm committed to you.'

'Oh.'

* * *

Why would me work dry up when me mind's still in top gear? That's what QCs are for. – Thinking clearly. Arguing a point. Me problem with weak legs is a nuisance at times. But it isn't as if I fall over in court, as I saw a judge do once when he was drunk . . . Trying a case in the Bailey . . . Funny thing. – That didn't do his career any harm after he sobered up . . . I've never drunk like that . . . get a bit light-headed now and then but not drunk drunk . . . Nobody's been worried about me legal judgement until now. Knowing what's what. Nothing wrong with it. No connection with me physical state – and that's not really bad . . . umm . . . Not yet . . . Hopefully never

... Hmm ... But me work isn't coming in like it used to. 'Roddy's off his game', I s'pose is what they're saying ... Not much I can do about that ... Hmm ... Maybe the other lawyers in the Garrick will see I'm in good shape – mentally – and put the word round ... Hope so ...

* * *

'Fascinating ... I've been reading a book called, *Games People Play* by Eric Berne. He created *Transactional Analysis* – TA. It's fabulous – so true to life – and very funny.'

'Careful. – You'll be fully trained and ready to take over the centre by next month.'

'No I won't. Why should I wait that long?'

'Ha! Here I am – on strike – and you want to charge ahead and rule the world.'

'I s'pose I've always been like that ... "Wants to run before he can walk" – just like you said – was one of my earliest reports at school ... and others said much the same.'

'There's nothing wrong with being an enthusiast.'

'Yeah ... Thanks for that. But I trip myself up sometimes ... get too far ahead of myself. Ha! – That was in another report.'

'Maybe the teachers simply wanted you to do things their way ... Some people – teachers, doctors, lawyers, any professionals really – tend to be like that ... Want to put us all into properly labeled boxes.'

'Hey! I'm not dead yet.'

'Ha! I didn't mean that sort of box ... umm ... I meant "category" ... Something clear and understandable ... No threat to anyone.'

'How d'you mean?'

'Well ... I remember one of my school reports saying, "It

would be good if Lucy could hold just one idea in her head for as long as a week".'

'What was that meant to do? . . . Stop you thinking at all?'

'Maybe . . . Thinking for ourselves threatens people – all sorts of people – teachers, politicians, the clergy . . . Not all of them, of course – but anyone with fixed ideas.'

'Yes . . . I remember reading a comment – I think by Dr William Glasser, the American psychiatrist creator of *Choice Theory*. – "Universities exist to *prevent* the spread of human knowledge".'

'He said that? A doctor, a psychiatrist, said that?'

'Yes . . . He did . . . or someone very like him did. He certainly thought for himself . . . Wonderful man . . . Hardly ever prescribed anything. Didn't think tablets ever cured unhappiness – which was just about the only diagnosis he ever made.'

'Oh.'

'If you're really excited by the first psychology books you've ever read, you probably *are* in the right slot, professionally . . . umm . . . People either take to it – as a subject, concept . . . er . . . wanting to find out more about how the mind works – or they get frightened off.'

'How do you know?'

'I saw it at uni – in some of the other students . . . Either they wanted to see where new ideas might lead. Wanted to unsettle themselves, I s'pose . . . or they wanted to stick to one solid idea – complacent, self-assuring way of seeing things – and push everything else out of the way.'

'Well I certainly know which group you belong to . . . and I want to join.'

'It's not a club you have to join – or can join. You're either in it from birth or you're not.'

Part 3

o O o

'Do sit down, Mrs Finch. I have been instructed by the hospital authorities to make an assessment of your fitness to practice.'

'That's good. I'd like that. I want to get back to work.'

'It is my function . . . er . . . responsibility . . . to assess your capacity . . . er . . . and your awareness of potential risks to patients – and to the hospital – of you returning to work in your former capacity as a consultant in obstetrics and gynae-cology . . . We cannot afford any "untoward incidents". I'm sure you understand.'

'Yes, I do . . . I'm totally committed to that myself . . . After all, I've suffered one.'

'Yes indeed. Very unfortunate . . . Very unfortunate.'

'Thank you.'

'Indeed . . . I have to be assured that you yourself are now taking responsible action before you can be given a position of responsibility for others.'

'I accept that.'

'And how do you propose to demonstrate that?'

'I've submitted myself to appropriate treatment for post traumatic stress disorder.'

'And who gave you that diagnosis?'

'I . . . er . . . thought it was obvious . . . umm . . . Anaesthetic awareness is dreadfully traumatic.'

'I'm sure it is . . . and I have every sympathy with you.'

'Thank you.'

'But . . . umm . . . you know . . . Different traumas and phobias of one kind or another require different treatments.'

'Yes . . . This is your discipline rather than mine.'

'Good . . . Good, I'm glad you recognise that point. It's very difficult, isn't it? . . . when doctors become patients. Always a tendency to treat themselves.'

'I tried that, tried pulling myself together, using all the determination and will power that got me where I am today professionally.'

'I have to remind you, Mrs Finch, that your professional position today is that you are not permitted to practise . . . or even to enter the hospital . . . We can't have you judging your own fitness to practise when patients' lives could be at risk . . . Otherwise all doctors . . . including some very dangerous ones – Shipman, for example – would be judge and jury for themselves.'

'I'm not a Shipman – a potential mass murderer. – I was the victim . . . well not of murder, of course . . . but of careless inattention.'

'Very unfortunate . . . Very unfortunate . . . But not germane to the current state of your fitness to practise.'

'How d'you mean?'

'Precisely how you came to be traumatised – a road accident, an assault, an anaesthetic awareness – is not the issue in question . . . It's how you are *now*.'

'Yes . . . I fully accept that.'

'Ah . . . I'm glad we're agreed on that point.'

'Yes.'

'Umm . . . You say that you "submitted yourself to appropriate treatment" . . . Please tell me who was it – precisely – who recommended you to have this treatment? Who referred you? . . . and in whose opinion was it "appropriate"?'

'I saw a counsellor.'

'Who was it who recommended you to see this . . . er . . . counsellor?'

'A friend of my husband . . . in his club.'

'A medical man?'

'I don't know . . . Possibly . . . I didn't ask.'

'I see . . . And what did this counsellor do?'

'He referred me on to another counsellor . . .

'No fee-splitting, I trust . . . Can't be sure of the ethics of non-medical people.'

'I don't know. It didn't occur to me.'

'Indeed not. – You took them on trust?'

'Yes.'

'Didn't check their qualifications . . . and professional indemnity?'

'One of them – the one who actually treated me . . . cared for me . . . with EMDR – used to be a doctor.'

'But not now?'

'No . . . He told me he took himself off the GMC register . . . He didn't want to prescribe.'

'Did you check that with the GMC?'

'No.'

'You . . . ah . . . took him on trust?'

'Yes.'

'On an issue where the lives of your patients could be at risk.'

'On the issue where my own life was going completely to pieces . . . I couldn't work . . . Merely going into an operating theatre re-traumatised me.'

'Yes indeed . . . and you took your own life – and the lives of future patients – into your own hands and trusted yourself to be . . . ah . . . "cared for" by someone who has medical qualifications but chooses not to use them. Does that not strike you as being rather strange?'

'As I said, he doesn't want to prescribe. So he works as a counsellor.'

'But avoids assessment by the GMC – and answerability to

its ethical and clinical guidelines?'

'Yes, I s'pose so.'

'You "suppose" so – but it hadn't occurred to you that you were putting yourself – and therefore future patients – at risk?'

'Naturally I made my own judgement on his personal and professional behaviour . . . I was desperate.'

'And desperate people need desperate remedies?'

'Yes.'

'And trust to the . . . ah . . . care of a non-medical . . . ah . . . an ex-medical . . . person?'

'Yes.'

'And not check with professionals who are supervised regularly by the GMC . . . giving you and other patients vital protection?'

'The CBT was no help and the antidepressants made me put on weight . . . and they reduced my libido.'

'So your view of yourself in the mirror – and your . . . ah . . . personal pleasure – took precedence in your mind over due diligence and clinical safety?'

'I wouldn't put it that way.'

'Just how would you put it, Mrs Finch?'

'I . . . er . . . wanted help . . . any help that would get me functional again.'

'But you didn't see fit to consult your own – practising and properly registered and regularly assessed – professional colleagues?'

'That was my first port of call . . . of course . . . That's why I came to see you after seeing a private GP. . . but the treatment he and you prescribed hadn't worked, hadn't got me better.'

'There are other clinical approaches . . . and other medications that are tried and tested – with gold-standard double-blind controlled clinical trials – that could be effective.'

'Yes, I'm sure . . . but I felt I might benefit from an alternative approach.'

'So you sought . . . ah . . . "benefit" from "alternative" methods?'

'EMDR is mainstream in many countries – and is now supported here by NICE.'

'For some clinical conditions . . . but they're cautious – appropriately cautious, if I may say so – over giving EMDR blanket approval. The science isn't there.

'But it worked on me.'

I'll be the judge of that, Mrs Finch.'

* * *

'I give you credit. You behaved impeccably with my mother – and over the cold turkey.'

'I was well brought up . . . Going off the rails was my own stupid fault – and I haven't forgotten the example Mother and Father set me.'

'Why do you call them "Mother" and "Father" instead of "Mum" and "Dad"?'

'Dunno . . . S'pose I thought it sounded posh . . . when I was little, when I wanted to impress people.'

'Didn't you tell me that the worst thing you could ever call your sister is "posh"?'

'Yes.'

'But that's what you wanted to be?'

'Yes.'

'Why?'

'She had the brains . . . I had to have something.'

'Ha! . . . Not your best choice. – Any buffoon can be "posh".'

'Yeah . . . I've met a few . . . Brokers . . . Couldn't do

anything else. Being "posh" was all they'd got . . . All I'd got, really.'

'James Finch, you're a nutter . . . You're a lot more than "posh" . . . on your good days.'

'Well thanks for that! . . . And whad'you mean "on my good days"?'

'I'm teasing you . . . I think you're bright enough to do anything you want to do. – It's just that you might not have been good at school subjects . . . People mature – intellectually and emotionally – at different ages.'

'So I'm a "slow developer" eh?'

'Hey . . . Hey, James . . . I'm only teasing you – and pontificating a bit.'

'No prob . . . No offence.'

'Anyway, what I said was I really appreciated how you behaved towards my mother . . . You were very polite to her.'

'Well she was to me . . . and I was in her home.'

'Why would that make a difference?'

'It doesn't really, I s'pose. I just felt I ought to be on best behaviour . . . Didn't want to let you down.'

'Oh.'

'I mean your mother's part of the medical establishment . . . and I'm a laundry boy and prescription fetcher.'

'You were invited by me as James Finch, someone who has a sense of commitment to doing something that matters. – Mum would appreciate that. So do I.'

'But we never even talked about it . . . I didn't want to appear naive, stupid, running before I can walk.'

'You've got to get over that school report some day . . . develop more self-confidence.'

'All I've ever done is sales.'

'That's a skill . . . a real skill . . . I couldn't do it . . . I don't think I could.'

'I s'pect you could . . . You're bright.'

'Ha! . . . And you've got to get over your sister complex as well . . . Sibling rivalry, the success of the first-born . . . That sort of thing.'

'Oh.'

'Let yourself acknowledge that I was proud to take you to my home . . . and introduce you to my mother.'

'Oh.'

'Oh what?'

'Oh it feels strange not having to put on an act . . . a performance, make a speech.'

'Aah, I see . . .'

'See what?'

'The effect on you of having three high achievers in your family.'

'It's the same for you in your family . . . umm . . . You never did say what your sister does.'

'Judith? . . . She's a psychiatrist . . . Sorts everyone out and puts the world to rights . . . But I never doubted my own place in the world . . . in the way you seem to have done . . . I'm just taking my time finding it.'

'Well I hope I've found mine now. – In a rehab.'

'Oh.'

* * *

'So what happens now? Does he write a report or something? Did he say?'

'No, not really . . . He just said that it was up to him to decide whether the EMDR had worked for me.'

'How would he know?'

'He makes up his own mind.'

'How?'

'Heaven knows.'

'That wouldn't do in a court of law.'

'It isn't a court of law . . . He's been asked for a clinical opinion.'

'A hunch?'

'I don't suppose he'd call it that.'

'Maybe not – but, without tests of some kind, that's what it is.'

'All diagnosis is guesswork – psychiatric diagnosis most of all.'

'But your whole career – livelihood – depends on it.'

'Yes it does – and that's the way it goes with medical opinion . . . We try to narrow down the element of guesswork . . . er – reduce the risk of getting it wrong - but ultimately we have to take a punt.'

'Ha! – You sound like James.'

'Yes, I do I s'pose . . . Funny thing, really . . . My professional life

hanging by a thread – and dependent on the opinion of someone who doesn't believe in miracles.'

'Nor do I.'

'I didn't mean holy miracles . . . I mean a clinical technique that's effective even though he's unfamiliar with it – especially when he's unfamiliar with it. – Ha! Not even interested in finding out about it. Didn't ask me a thing about it. At any time'

'That won't stand up in a court of law.'

'But, as I told you, medical things don't work on the same principles as legal things.'

'Oh yes they do – when things go wrong . . . as they have with you.'

'Oh dear . . . Oh Roddy, please don't go all legal on me.'

'You might be glad of my legal background one day.'

'Oh Gawd.'

*   *   *

'I realise now I've got to get on with my work . . . get myself on the register, whatever happens to either Mum or Dad – or both of them.'

'Why so? . . . All of a sudden?'

'Because, if money's going to be tight, I can earn more as a doctor than as a registered care assistant. – I'll be able to employ one . . . if necessary – and still have some cash left over to invest in my relationship with you . . . And have a long-term career if that's the way it goes.'

'What a wonderful hierarchy of values . . . er . . . priorities . . . My Mom would be proud of you.'

'That's nice . . . I feel there's a chance now . . . of things working out ok . . . Well not for Dad, poor man, but for the rest of us. – Now that Mum's back in action.'

'At work?'

'Not yet . . . But she'll be able to do something . . . umm . . . somehow – and not get the screaming abdabs.'

'That's good . . . Well, half good . . . er . . . one third good . . . No. Maybe half.'

'Huh? Where's your clinical research head gone now?'

'Umm . . . Not good for your father, possibly good – hope-fully – for your mother . . . better for you and me . . . better than it looked before . . . Seems to me.'

'Yes. And to me . . . umm . . .'

'Umm what?'

'Umm I still don't know what to do with you . . . Ha! – Listen to me! – I've known what I want to do with you since I first set eyes on you . . . and heard you . . . I love you, Precious. I really do.'

'So where's the catch? I love you too. – Does that help?'

'Course it does – but it doesn't change the facts.'

'Now you've got a research head on. Can't we just . . . ?'

'Just what?'

'Umm . . . Live together anyway? . . . Give ourselves the best chance of a long-term relationship.'

'That would do the opposite. – You should know that. That's what the figures show. – Living together reduces the chance of a long-term relationship.'

'Ha! You really have taken over the role of the lecturer! Where does that leave me?'

'As the love of my life . . . Where else?'

'Oh . . . That's good.'

'Poor Precious . . . I forget how shy you are . . . Inconsiderate of me . . . Now then . . . Let's start from first principles . . .'

'Glory be! – Is this what I sound like? . . . when I'm in "research" mode?'

'I don't know how I sound now. I'm just trying to get it right . . . Don't want to mess things up again.'

'You didn't mess things up first time round.'

'Well I don't want there to be a third time.'

'Okay, okay, okay . . . Let's go to my place and . . . umm . . .'

'Precious Ellington! What has come over you?'

'You have . . . or will . . . I hope.'

o O o

Dear Mrs Finch,

I recognise that you have been severely traumatised by the episode of anaesthetic awareness that you unfortunately suffered. You have my sincere understanding and sympathy over this distressing incident.

I attach a copy of the formal report that I prepared for the hospital authorities as a result of our recent meeting.

You will note in particular that I contacted the General Medical Council to ask for their guidance on assessing the effects of clinical treatments that do not follow the specific guidelines of the National Institute for Health and Care Excellence. I was informed that precedent has established the principle that doctors are free to seek whatever therapy they wish for their clinical conditions. However, where medico-legal and possibly ethical issues are involved as in your case, it would be expected for the doctor to accept the need for care by a registered medical practitioner. He or she, in turn, would be expected to follow the NICE guidelines or make a specific case for an exception.

The alternative practitioner from whom you sought assistance is not a registered medical practitioner and the treatment you received from him is not supported by NICE for the condition from which you suffered.

Accordingly, the recommendation of the GMC is that, if you wish to resume clinal care for patients, you should seek the opinion of a registered medical practitioner who would follow the appropriate guidelines – or make a formally argued case for a specific exception – or risk being held responsible for subsequent mishaps. Therefore, on precedent, the recommendation of the GMC is that you should follow the NICE guideline and have cognitive behavioural therapy and be prescribed antidepressants under the supervision of an appropriately qualified, registered and trained consultant specialist.

As you will doubtless recall, this concurs with my own clinical recommendation to you when you first consulted me.

You yourself, without referring to me, chose to discontinue that tried and tested treatment. You sought the opinion of an alternative practitioner and you underwent a form of treatment that is outside the NICE guidelines.

Accordingly, as I am sure you appreciate, you and the hospital would be uninsurable against the possibility of future untoward events affecting patients under your care.

I can understand that this opinion may well be distressing to you but as you see, our hands are tied.

Accordingly, I shall be obliged, if you so wish, if you would make an appointment through my secretary so that appropriate clinical care can be resumed.

My hope – and that of the hospital authorities – is that you will shortly be able to resume your duties, under supervision, as a valued member of the consultant staff of this hospital.

With good wishes for your personal and professional future,

* * *

'Mmmmmmm.'

  'Mmm.'

  'Mmmmmmm.'

  'Mmmm.'

  'Mmmmmmmm.'

  'Mm. Mm. Mmm . . . Mm.'

  'Mmmm.'

  'Mm. Mm. Mmm . . . Mm. Mm. Mm.'

  'Mmmmm.'

  'Yah . . . Mmm . . . Mm . . . Ooh . . . Uh . . .'

  'Ooh.'

  'Uh . . . Uh . . . Uh . . . Mmmm . . . Ooh.'

  'Mmmmm.'

  'Uh. Uh. Uh. Uh.'

  'Mmmmm.'

'Uh. Uh. Uh. Uh. Uh. Uh. Uh. Uh.'
'Uh. Uh. Uh. Yah . . . Mmm . . . Yah.'
'Uh. Uh. Uh. Uh. Uh. Uh.'
'Mmmmm.'
'Uh. Uh. Uh. Uh.'
'Mmmm. Uh. Uh. Uh.'
'Uh. Uh. Uh. Uh. Uh. Uh.'
'Yah. Yah. Yah. Uh. Uh. Uh. Ooh.'
'Uh. Uh. Uh. Uh. Uh. Uh. Uh. Uh.'
'Err . . . Errrr . . . Errrrr.'
'Uh. Uh. Uh. Uh. Uh. Uh. Uh. Uh.'
'Yah. Yah. Yah. Yah. Whrrrr. Whrrrr.'
'Uh. Uh. Uh. Mmm. Uh. Uh. Uh.'
'Yeee! . . . Yeee! . . . Umm . . . Yeeee!'
'Uh. Uh. Mmm. Uh. Uh. Mmm. Uh.'
'Sssss. Sssss. Yah. Yah. Yah. Yah.'
'Uh. Uh. Uh. Uh. Uh..Uh. Uh. Uh.'
'Mmm . . . Mmm . . . Ssss . . . Mm. Mm.'
'Uh. Uh. Mmm. Uh. Uh. Mmm. Uh.'
'Yah. Yah. Yah. Yah. Yayayaya!'
'Uh. Uh. Uh. Uh. Uh. Uh. Mmm.'
'Yayayaya! Yayayaya! Yayayaya!'
'Uh. Uh. Uh. Uh. Uh. Uh. Ooh.'
'Ya. Mmm. Mmm. Ya. Yayayaya!"
'Uh. Uh. Ooh. Uh. Uh. Ooh. Uh'
'Mmm. Mmm. Ah. Ah. Ah.'
'Uh. Uh. Uh. Uh. Ooh. Uh. Ooh.'
'Ssss. Ssss. Ssss . . . Yayayaya!'
'Uh. Uh. Uh. Ooh. Uh. Ooh. Uh.'
'Whrrrrrr. Yee . . . Yee . . . Whrrrrr.'
'Uhuhuhuhuh. Yaaaaa! Yaaaaa!'
'Yesss! Yesss! Yesssss!'
'Ooof . . . Ooooof . . .. Ooooof . . . . . .'

'Ah! Ah! Yah! Yah! Yah! Yah! Yeeee!'
'Ooof.'
'Yeeeeeee!'
'Oof.'
'Yeeee!'
'Oof.'
'Yeeeeee!'
'Oof.'
'Mmmm.'
'Mmmmm.'
'Mmmm.'
'Mmmmmm.'
'Mmm . . . Yeeehah!'

*   *   *

'So what's happened to you with the shrink? . . . er . . . in his report?'

'I shrunk.'

'Huh?'

'I was insignificant to him . . . He was stuck in his own particular mindset . . . in a trance.'

'Was he hypnotising you? . . . when you saw him?'

'No. – He was hypnotising himself . . . Seeing only what he expected to see, wanted to see.'

'How so?'

'His ideas are set solid . . . He doesn't want to look at anything new . . . unless it's no more than an extension of the "tried and trusted" approaches that he – and the GMC and the rest of them – believe in.'

'But surely that's sensible . . . umm . . . to some degree . . . umm . . . to a lot of degrees really?'

'That's true. We can't have any crackpot idea being given

free rein.'

'Homeopathy?'

'Yup ... That's an interesting example ... No scientific basis whatever but some people swear by it.'

'What d'you think of it?'

'Not much ... Placebo effect probably.'

'But your mind's open.'

'Umm ... Not really ... I don't want to stop other people doing whatever they believe in ... provided they don't damage themselves – and then expect us to pick up the pieces afterwards ... at state expense.'

'So what was your psychiatrist's attitude to the EMDR you had?'

'He never even asked about it.'

'What?'

'He was totally fixed on CBT and drugs and that's that ... and he quoted NICE and the GMC in support.'

'Well surely they should know.'

'You'd think so ... umm ... probably they do on physical things ... er ... treatments that can be assessed on blood tests or scans and things.'

'But not on mental things? ... umm ... emotional things?'

'No ... not really ... There's a basic inertia ... in the thinking behind all the treatments ... They have to make sense.'

'But surely that's reasonable.'

'It depends who defines "sense" ... umm ... and "sanity".'

'Isn't that obvious?'

'No ... Very distressingly no ... I once saw a DVD – made by the Scientologists of all people – on the history of psychiatry ... It was

terrifying ... One doctor used to do frontal lobotomies in the back of his van – with an ice pick stuck up the nose of the patients ... children sometimes – all in the name of "science"

. . . in the treatment of depression", whatever that may be.'

'Don't you know? – You of all people?'

'I'm not depressed as such. As a clinical diagnosis. Never have been . . . Downhearted at not being able to move on – and do my work – but not depressed.'

'Then why does he prescribe antidepressants for you?'

'That's the whole point . . . He doesn't know what else to do . . . And he doesn't want to know, dares not know – doesn't even want to look.'

'Why not?'

'They stick together . . . the psychiatrists . . . and the GMC backs them up.'

'Why?'

'It's all smoke and mirrors . . . The Scientologists have a point.'

'I thought Scientologists set people off against their families . . . that sort of thing . . . umm . . . You're not going over to their side, are you?'

'Gracious no . . . My enemy's enemy is not necessarily my friend.'

'Why this talk about "enemies"?'

'It certainly felt like that when I was with the psychiatrist.'

'Why? . . . Surely he only wants to help?'

'You'd have thought so . . . But I fear his prime motive is to protect himself . . . That's what they all do . . . stick together . . . support each other . . . protect themselves.'

'But why?'

'They call their approaches "best evidence" . . . "gold standard" . . .'

'That's a good thing . . . What's wrong with it?'

'They're euphemisms for "the way we do it".'

'And what's wrong with that?'

'It means they're stuck . . . can't look at new ideas – only at new drugs.'

'CBT isn't a drug.'

'Ha! – Don't be too sure about that . . . It's a virtual tranquilliser, hypnotic – sends the therapists off into la-la-land, trying to prove they're brighter than their patients.'

'How can you be brighter if you're asleep?'

'Autopilot.'

'Oh . . . but it can't be true about trying to prove that they're brighter . . . umm . . . I mean they may be brighter but that can't be their motive.'

'Oh yes it can . . . CBT's an intellectual approach, not an emotional one – like the EMDR that got me better.'

'But it's extraordinary – to me, as a layman – that these people . . . umm . . . the psychiatrists, the doctors on the GMC . . . don't start from a position of seeing what works and then wondering why.'

'Ha! . . . They do it the other way round . . . They decide what works – even if it doesn't.'

'But why? why? why?'

'Because they'd have to make a quantum shift in their whole understanding, their whole approach. – And they'd be frightened of being sued out of existence if they acknowledge that their way of doing things has been ineffective . . . umm . . . wrong . . . in the past.'

'And the Scientologists are right? . . . I'm not at all comfortable with that idea.'

'You know perfectly well I don't believe that stuff . . . but I can't get that DVD out of my mind . . . They're right on that – on the dangers of psychiatry – even if they're wrong on everything else.'

'But it's very unsettling, starting again, thinking things out from scratch when everything is nice and settled . . . It's much easier in the law . . . with case law precedents.'

'Yes . . . It was fine for us in obs and gynae until Hughes syndrome turned up.'

'What's that?'

'Antiphospholipid syndrome.'

'Huh?'

'Oh, sorry . . . That's what it is technically . . . umm . . . In pregnancy it's the most common – and potentially treatable – cause of recurrent miscarriage . . . it's associated with pre-eclampsia, premature birth and stillbirth.'

'You're still baffling me with science . . . I'm a humble lawyer.'

'Well get this . . . It's estimated to affect more than one percent of the population – a huge number of women – but it was only described in full in the nineteen eighties . . . The previous generation of obs and gynae people to mine had to re-think what they thought they knew for certain.'

'Good for them . . . Keeps them on their toes.'

'Yes, I agree . . . but that's exactly what *doesn't* happen in psychiatry.'

'Oh.'

'And, what's more, psychiatrists, doctors of the mind, treat patients with drugs but also with ECT – electro-convulsive therapy – insulin shock therapy and frontal lobotomy . . . Those barbaric treatments are used even now occasionally . . . But psychiatrists are taught very little about psychology – studying how the mind works.'

'But surely they have to know how it works before they can treat it when it goes off beam.'

'You'd have thought so – but that's not the way it works.'

'What works?'

'The system . . . It's the system. – The way doctors, psychiatrists see things and run things their own way. – that needs to be challenged . . . The same as Hughes did in obs and gynae.'

'You seem to know a lot about all this psychology stuff . . . On top of what you know in your own field.'

'Of course I do . . . now . . . What else was I going to do with my time? . . . That's what upsets me . . . By now, from a standing start, I probably know more about psychology – how the mind works – than many psychiatrists. They're taught about mental illness and how to prescribe and prescribe and prescribe – which psychologists can't do because they're not doctors. In medical school we – all of us – were taught pretty well nothing about psychology . . . But this man is determined to treat me in the only way he knows – with drugs and CBT . . . Huh!'

'Why? . . . Why doesn't he want to learn more about psychology?'

'He's frightened of breaking ranks . . . They must know – all of them – that the emperor has no clothes.'

'Huh?'

'That their whole discipline is internally self-validating but built on a false premise . . . Their basic ideas are rotten and therefore the treatment is rotten.'

*   *   *

'The Gestalt book I read at the weekend was very exciting . . . *Gestalt Therapy Integrated* by Erving and Myriam Polster . . . I loved the practical applications . . . umm . . . makes me want to read Fritz Perls. – He created it.'

'I didn't realise you read so much.'

'Never have until now.'

'You were panting with excitement over TA last week.'

'Well . . . umm . . . I . . . er . . . No, James, young fella . . . Don't go there.'

'Go where?'

'Going to say something I thought I shouldn't.'

'All the more reason for saying it.'

'Huh?'

'If something we say doesn't rattle a cage or two, it probably wasn't worth saying.'

'Umm . . .'

'It's the same with medical advances and ethics.'

'Really?'

'Yes . . . If a medical advance doesn't challenge the existing code of ethics, it probably isn't an advance.'

'Oh.'

'Come on, James. Use your head . . . What was it you were going to say?'

'Umm . . . I . . . er . . .'

'About TA and Gestalt?'

'Umm . . . I wasn't.'

'But you said you were excited . . . and then you said, "Don't go there" . . . or something. '

'Yes.'

'And I said, "Go where?" . . . and you said . . .'

'I know what I said.'

'But I want to know what you *didn't* say . . . umm . . . stopped yourself saying . . . umm . . . What was it that excited you about TA or Gestalt?'

'No . . . That wasn't it.'

'Really?'

'Umm . . .'

'Well I said you'd been panting with excitement and you said . . .'

'Yes . . . umm . . .'

'James, for heaven's sake. – What were you panting with excitement about?'

'Umm . . .'
'Yes?'
'Umm . . . You.'
'Oh!'

* * *

'Would you like to meet my family some time? Mum and Dad and my brother James?'
   'Yes.'
   'No "if"s or "but"s or other qualification?'
   'I hope I qualified earlier on . . . before we fell off to sleep.'
   'Ha! – You sure did qualify! . . . Never known anything like it.'
   'That's good . . . Me too.'
   'Makes me shiver – just remembering it.'
   'Mmmm . . .'
   'Umm . . . Precious?'
   'Mmm . . . Yeah?'
   'Wanna go round again?'
   'Mmmm.'
   'Mmmmmmmm.'
   'Mm. Mm. Mmm . . . Mm . . .'

* * *

'So what was it that made you go on strike?'
   'Nothing made me . . . I chose to.'
   'Okay . . . What was the stimulus?'
   'A book.'
   'A book?'
   'Yes, a book.'
   'Someone hit you over the head with it?'

'Yes.'

'Really . . . for real?'

'Yes . . . The author.'

'Why would he do that?'

'She.'

'Okay . . . Why would she do that? . . . Did you say something that upset her?'

'Ha! – No . . . but I was living a life that would have upset her.'

'And she hit you over the head with a book?'

'Yes. – She wrote it . . . I read it.'

'Oh.'

'D'you want to know about it?'

'Yes . . . if it's that important a book to you.'

'After the Bible, it's the most read book in America . . . and it's the book – more than any other – that Americans would take to a desert island.'

'Do Americans read that much?'

'Course they do . . . It's we Brits who're dropping down the literacy tables . . . And a previous Australian prime minister – John Howard – got all his cabinet to read this book . . . right at the start – after they'd just won the election.'

'Oh . . . Must be quite a book.'

'Changed my life . . . Changed my whole way of thinking.'

'And made you go on strike?'

'Nothing *makes* me do anything . . . I choose my actions – and reactions.'

'Should I read it? I don't read much . . . Too many books around when I was young.'

'It's up to you.'

'You wouldn't tell me to read it?'

'Certainly not . . . You're free in this country – so far – to read what you want.'

'But you think it would be good for me to read it?'

'I don't know what "good for you" means.'

'Improves my mind.'

'It depends what you take into it . . . If you have a closed mind on ideas – political ideas, philosophical ideas – then it won't improve anything . . . your mind, other people's minds, the world in general, anything or anybody.'

'But why would people read a book with closed minds?'

'To rubbish it . . . if they can.'

'Why would they do that?'

'I told you . . . It's a political book, philosophical book, challenging people's ideas . . . The word gets round and people rubbish it without even reading it . . . And if they can't rubbish the ideas – she writes very tight, no waffle, nothing in it that doesn't have to be in it – they rubbish the author.'

'How?'

'Pointing out inadequacies . . . inconsistencies . . . in her personal life.'

'Yes . . . I was told – by one of the counsellors – that Albert Ellis, who created *Rational Emotive Behaviour Therapy*, had the reputation of being a foul-mouthed unpleasant man . . . but he had a good idea.'

'That's the way.'

'The way of what?'

'Keeping your mind open . . . open to new ideas that might work better in practice than our existing ideas.'

'Father was always trying to get me to read books . . . Mother too.'

'And did you?'

'Left it to The Phebe. – She's the clever one.'

'You're clever enough to do anything you want to do. – I told you that before. – But you won't do anything really worthwhile in life, as I see it, if you don't read books with ideas in them . . . You'll be stuck – talking about people and events – not ideas that can lead to actions that could change the world.'

'That's what I want to do . . . change the world.'

'Then read.'

'But I can't read politics . . . or philosophy or whatever you call it.'

'Why not?'

'Too boring.'

'Not in the way Ayn Rand wrote *Atlas Shrugged*.'

'That's a philosophical textbook? . . . with a title like that?'

'Yes.'

'But I couldn't read that.'

'Not with a closed mind you won't . . . Here you are now . . . just like the people who rubbish it – and rubbish the author – without even reading it.'

'But I'm no good at textbooks . . . They're not my thing.'

'It's only a "textbook" because it's full of ideas . . . but she wrote it as a novel . . . a very exciting story.'

'Why?'

'Because people read novels . . . They like stories.'

o O o

Dammit . . . That won't do. – Me leg giving way – and I haven't touched a drop . . .

* * *

I'm so fortunate to be on the Foundation Programme . . . Some of the top jobs might have been earmarked already and others taken up with people from minority groups . . . Just to show political correctness. Ha! – Not my best chance, white and with a private school background ... Ha! ... And to think that less than a year ago I was arguing the toss – politically – with Precious ...

* * *

Golly Golly, Miss Molly! ... That was some riff ... She's the one ... Phoebe's the one for me ... Ha! – Imagine that! ... I have to cross the Atlantic to find Miss Right, my Miss Molly ... Little Richard will have to sing to her for me ...

'I am going to the corner, gonna buy a diamond ring.

When she hugs me and kiss me make me ting-a-ling-a-ling.

Good golly, miss Molly, sure like to ball.

When you're rockin' and a rollin' can't hear your momma call.'

Hmm ... Wonder what her momma would call if she met me ... Ha! – Diamond ring? ... That'd be the day! ...

* * *

'I like you too ... a lot.'

'Thank God for that ... You kept me waiting a long time before telling me. – I was worried it might have been better to keep my trap shut ... as I originally intended.'

'I was thinking through what I know about you – that you've been in rehab.'

'And out the other side.'

'Yes ... but that's not a guarantee, is it?

'No ... I go to AA meetings – two or three a week – and I work the Twelve Step programme as a prevention against relapse.'

'But why pay all that money to a rehab if it doesn't work?'

'It did work . . . It showed me that I'm an addict . . . showed me that I'm like the others.'

'But you knew that didn't you? before you went in?'

'Well . . . Being an addict isn't just a result of using – or doing – addictive things . . . It's how we're made – some of us – since birth, possibly.'

'You asked the midwife for a joint?'

'Ha! – Nice one.'

'Well . . . did you?'

'Some people – like me – have an addictive potential. Others don't . . . Well they don't appear to.'

'Oh . . . an addictive personality.'

'No . . . That's a mistake lots of people make . . . We each have our own personality – our ways of saying and doing things, what we like or dislike, our sense of humour – but some of us have an addictive nature . . . possibly genetic.'

'That's just an excuse.'

'No . . . It's a responsibility.'

'Huh?'

'If I know I've got something, it's my responsibility to treat it . . . And that's the catch. – We have to be shown that we're addicts . . . We don't see it for ourselves.'

'Why not? – It should be obvious.'

'You'd think so . . . but the winos on the park bench think they have a problem with housing . . . or with Social Services . . . They see alcohol as their friend and comforter.'

'That's insane.'

'Yes.'

'And that's what you're like?'

'Yes . . . That's my potential . . . I go to AA and work the Steps to avoid going down that slope.'

'But you don't need to go that way if you know you have that . . . er . . . potential . . .'

'I forget.'

'Forget what . . . umm . . . birthdays? . . . the day of the week?'

'That I'm an addict and can't risk doing addictive things.'

'But that's insane . . . forgetting that.'

'That's what I said.'

'But AA can't cure that.'

'No it can't . . . Nothing can *cure* it . . . but AA does remind me – temporarily – what I'm like . . . because I see other people like me . . . So then I work the Steps to keep me sane day by day.'

'Sounds spooky to me . . . And isn't AA a religious cult of some kind? like Scientology?'

'No . . . I haven't got any religious belief.'

'Just willpower?'

'No. – That's what got me into trouble . . . doing things my way.'

'What other way is there?'

'God's way.'

'But you said you're not religious.'

'I'm not.'

'You're getting me confused here . . . How can you talk about "God's way" and then say you're not religious?'

'In AA I can have any God I like – as long as it's not me myself on the golden throne. – My God is the Twelve Steps . . . They work for me.'

'I don't know them. – I'll google them. – But surely all you need is common sense . . . Just say, "no" – Do sensible things and don't do stupid things.'

'I do that anyway – or don't . . . but it's not enough to keep me sober and sane . . . My addictive head will always want to find an easier way – and tell me I'm not really an addict.'

'But surely all you have to do is look at the evidence.'

'I can see the evidence but still not believe it . . . and then I find some other explanation for it – like childhood trauma or other people

upsetting me or things going wrong in my life.'

'That's insane.'

'Yes . . . I acknowledge that. It's my natural state . . . I work the Steps in order to be the person I want to be. – It's like wearing specs or lenses so I can see . . . But that doesn't change my eyes . . . I'm still short-sighted and I can't afford to forget that – or forget I'm an addict by nature . . . I need reminding . . . umm . . . With short sight there isn't an inner voice telling me I haven't got it. But with addiction there is.'

'That's frightening.'

'Yes. I hope so.'

'You *want* to be frightened?'

'I want to be cautious . . . I don't want to forget that I'm an addict. That would be frightening . . . I've had enough pain.'

'So where does this leave me? . . . umm . . . in our relationship? – if we have one?'

'With an informed choice.'

'Ha! – That's what I was saying to you earlier . . . about me choosing to be on strike.'

'I heard you.'

* * *

'Roddy?'

'Mm?'

'What d'you think – legally – I should do about the psychiatrist's report?'

'You're asking me to "go legal" on you?'

'Yes.'

'Er . . . ah, me lud . . .'

'Stop faffing about.'

'Just trying to keep your spirits up . . . umm . . . I haven't read it.'

'But you know the gist of it – that I've got to have anti-depressants and CBT . . . and be under supervision . . . or continue being unemployed.'

'Sweet Lizzie . . . It's so sad for you – and annoying – particularly now you're back to your former self.'

'Yes . . . but what's your legal opinion?'

'I haven't got one . . . for a member of my family.'

'Hunch? . . . Please.'

'Fight them and you'll lose.'

'Why?'

'They're the Establishment . . . They make the rules.'

*   *   *

'So what happens in *Atlas Shrugged*?'

'Read it for yourself . . . It's an adventure story – in the book and for the reader.'

'But what does the title mean?'

'Well that's the core statement . . . One character asks another what he would advise Atlas to do when he's stagger-ing under the load of carrying the world on his shoulders . . . He tells him to shrug.'

'Drop it? . . . Let it shatter?'

'Yes.'

'That's terrible . . . So unfeeling.'

'No . . . The present state system – the entitlement culture – is un-feeling . . . expecting Atlas to carry everyone else's burden, regardless of what he suffers and regardless of what other people do – or don't do – to help themselves if they're capable of doing so.'

'So who is "Atlas" in present-day life?'

'Creative people.'

'The Luvvies?'

'No. – They're only creative in a very narrow sense . . . and they're always clamouring for state subsidies – as special cases.'

'So do lots of other people . . . the Scots, the Welsh, the Northern Irish – and even some regions of England . . . minority groups of one kind or another – racial groups, the disabled in various ways . . . even women, who are actually in the majority . . . and some business people and even bankers – saying that they're special cases or too big to be allowed to fail.'

'That's exactly what Ayn Rand was pointing out.'

'And she was suggesting they should be dropped?'

'Yes.'

'But that really *is* terrible . . . How can you possibly support those ideas? . . . They're so cruel.'

'That's the challenge of the book . . . Are they really cruel?'

'Of course they are.'

'No they're not . . . That's the journey she takes us on – seeing which system is really cruel . . . a statist system or free-market capitalism.'

'Where dog eats dog and the weakest go to the wall.'

'Yes, that's the starting position of the book . . . That's what happens in a statist system.'

'Surely you've got that the wrong way round . . . It's the capitalist system that neglects those most in need and feathers the nests of those who've already got it cushy. – I've seen that with my own eyes in the City.'

'And you've seen – with your own eyes – what happens in a state-run Mental Health Unit . . . The two extremes are as bad as each other.'

'Then what's the solution?'

'Individualism.'

'But that's selfish.'

'Think about that for a minute . . . "Selfish" has come to mean "at other people's expense". The Church and the State deliberately create that misconception – for their own benefit. – "Selfish" really means "in my own self-interest".'

'That's the same thing.'

'No it *isn't* . . . It's in my self-interest to care for people, to create a kind and compassionate society . . . to give rather than take.'

'But that's what the state does . . . gives . . . through the NHS and welfare systems and so on.'

'And look at the end result . . . The people in power take from productive individuals by force and then – expensively to the extent of profligacy – throw away the proceeds of their theft . . . on their own pet projects.'

'But in the City they give "jobs for the boys".'

'They do exactly that in the local Councils . . . closing down the libraries and reducing street cleaning and other services people want – so they can blame government "cuts" – while paying themselves fat salaries . . . and giving grants – bribes – to groups of people to vote for them.'

'But, in the City, they really don't care for anyone else . . . The Freemasons and the Livery Companies do charitable work – but even they are really self-serving . . . You scratch my back and I'll scratch yours – and I'll put you up to be an alderman and vote you onto boards so you get a nice little earner . . . er . . . a big earner . . . as a non-executive director of several companies . . . and then you can do the same for me.'

'Yes . . . That's how it works . . . and it's wrong.'

'But you said the solution is individualism.'

'Yes.'

'But that's what I've just described in the City.'

'No . . . That's another form of corporatism . . . manipulating the system – whichever system it is, state or so-called private.'

'Why d'you say, "so-called"?'

'Because anything that expects special treatment from the state – demanding special privileges and bailouts and all sorts of allowances for one thing or another – is really an extension of the state system . . . not truly private.'

'In which the weakest go to the wall.'

'In which the weakest are cared for by the strongest.'

'Don't make me laugh . . . They wouldn't do that.'

'Look at the evidence . . . from previous generations . . . They *did* do it – building charitable schools and hospitals – and they also do it now – in many ways, supporting charities and giving personal donations even though we have a welfare state.'

'But you can't *rely* on that.'

'You mean you can't *enforce* it.'

'Yes . . . I s'pose I do mean that.'

'So you want a compassionate society enforced by the barrel of a gun? . . . That's what Hitler was voted in to do – establish National Socialism as a welfare state . . . Stalin and all the other despots took direct control through the barrel of a gun – saying there was no need for the triviality of elections when the best form of government had already been established.'

'I've got no time for any of them . . . You must know that.'

'I do . . . but maybe – as Ayn Rand points out – you haven't seen that the first compromise always leads to the next.'

'Hmm . . . So, if the Luvvies aren't the really creative people, who are?'

'People running their own lives and creating their own

businesses for their own benefit – not expecting, and certainly not demanding, anything from anyone else.'

'A nation of shopkeepers?'

'Yes . . . with some "shops" bigger than others, employing more staff than others, creating and selling more goods and services than others, contributing more to society at large than others.'

'Utopia.'

'Galt's Gulch.'

'Huh?'

'That's where you go if you're on strike. – Read the book.'

o O o

'I'm caught . . . If I trust my own judgement – I know I'm well now and perfectly capable of doing my work responsibly – I'll be banned from the hospital for ever . . . and I'll be in trouble with the GMC as well if I go against any of their recommendations . . . er . . . diktats. But if I do as the psychiatrist insists, I'll be fuddled by the CBT – which I don't need at all. – And taking the antidepressants – which I also don't need – will result in me putting on weight and going off my greens.'

'My poor Lizzie . . . That's a rock and a hard place if ever there was one.'

'It feels more like a soft head and a soft . . . umm . . . wherever.'

'Ha! – at least you haven't lost your sense of humour.'

'Not yet.'

* * *

'Where's Mr Dombell today?'

'He's got shingles, Sir.'

219

'Where?'

'At home, Sir.'

'Ha! . . . I meant where on his body?'

'Haven't seen him, Sir.'

'No, I suppose not . . . umm . . . Why would my question be significant?'

'Might give it to other people – through body contact.'

'Anyone have any thoughts on that?'

'You can't catch shingles.'

'Thank you, Miss Patel. – You're absolutely right . . . Now let's ask the others . . . Anybody?'

'You can catch chicken pox through direct contact with the blisters.'

'I don't want to discourage you, Miss Patel . . . You are absolutely right again – but I want to exercise the brains of the others, rather than allow them to piggy-back on yours.'

'Even though I come from a Hindu background, I'm a Muslim.'

'I beg your pardon . . . I apologise . . . Insensitive of me . . . Just an English expression.'

'I know what it means . . . like I know what "brownie" means as well.'

'Indeed . . . I . . . er . . . wouldn't use that expression – ever – except for a chocolate fudge biscuit, of course.'

Hesitant laughter.

'It's not funny . . . being a victim of prejudice.'

'No . . . Absolutely not.'

'How would you know?'

'Umm . . . I think it would be best for us to discuss this matter – in private after the teaching round is over.'

'Why not now? . . . It's an important issue – for some of us.'

'Yes – and for me . . . I'll be glad to discuss it later.'

'I won't be staying.'

* * *

'But why would *Atlas Shrugged* cause you . . . lead you towards going on strike?'

'Because I don't give permission for my mind – such as it is – to be the property of someone else.'

'But that's a bit extreme, isn't it. cutting off your nose to spite your face?'

'I've no intention of cutting off my nose . . . or anything else . . . I'm not into self-harming.'

'I mean . . . How can going on strike influence anything? . . . It's like the tube train drivers going on strike – at the most inconvenient time for passengers and at great expense to the City economy – when one of their mates is caught being drunk when driving a train . . . They don't influence anyone – just annoy them.'

'It's not like that at all . . . The driver would be risking the lives of others . . . The only person I hurt is myself – earning less money than I might otherwise.'

'Self-harming.'

No . . . Self-enhancing . . . giving myself time – and a clear head – to think things through.'

* * *

'Now that Miss Patel has left us . . . er . . . You might wish to make a note of what you heard. – I fear this might go further. – Let's get back to discussing the significance of shingles . . . If you can't catch it from someone else, where does it come from?'

'The chicken pox virus . . . Varicella.'

'That's true – but where is it?'

'In the air.'

'Yes, it might be – and you could catch chicken pox if you haven't had it before or if you haven't been vaccinated against it . . . which is presumably true for Mr Dombell, who may have had a sheltered childhood somewhere . . . either not being exposed to the virus in an isolated community or not being immunised against it.'

'South Africa, Sir. – In the bush.'

Laughter.

' . . . but you can't get shingles that way . . . Any ideas?'

'Unsafe sex?'

'You can catch other viruses in the herpes group that way . . . but not the chicken pox virus. Well, not very likely. Body contact would be too painful. Any other ideas?'

Silence.

'Dr Finch?'

'It lives inside the dorsal root ganglion of a peripheral nerve root – ever since the time the patient had chicken pox.'

'And what wakes it up? . . . and causes the characteristic rash in the dermatome supplied by that nerve?'

'Anything that disturbs the immune system.'

'That's right. Thank you . . . Now back to you students . . . Why would this be particularly relevant in old people?'

'Pain?'

'Yes . . . In which parts of the body in particular?'

'Genitalia?'

'Yes . . . You certainly got that right . . . Where else?'

'Face?'

'Yes . . . Ophthalmic shingles, affecting the eye, is a major emergency – and anywhere on the face is dreadfully debilitating . . . I recall a patient saying to me, "I feared one day that I should die . . . The next day I feared that I should not.".'

Hesitant laughter.

'Where else would you really not want to get shingles? . . . in old age?'

Shuffles.

'No?' – The chest wall. – And why would that be so fearful in old people?'

'Too painful to take a deep breath.'

'Got it! . . . and with what result?'

'Pneumonia.'

'Got it again! . . . Pneumonia used to be called "The old man's friend" – carried him off gently. – Nowadays it's treatable and people have much longer active lives . . . worth fighting for . . . What would you say to that, Dr Finch?'

'All patients are worth fighting for – provided they have quality of life.'

'And who decides that?'

'They do . . . or should do . . . but sometimes doctors decide for them – on the Liverpool Care Pathway . . . that gradually withdraws all sustenance.'

'Yes. I fear so . . . Ladies and gentlemen, this is the clinical, financial – and even administrative – world we now live in.'

* * *

'My mother says she approves of you.'

'I hadn't realised I was up for an interview.'

'Of course you were . . . All mothers are like that – wondering when they're going to have grandchildren – and be able to tell their daughters everything they're doing wrong.'

'You can count me out on that score . . . for the time being.'

'And what makes you believe it will be exclusively your decision?'

'I didn't mean it that way . . . umm . . . I want to earn my living and support my wife and children.'

'That's good . . . I like nuclear families – although sometimes mine has nuclear explosions.'

'Why?'

'I told you . . . My sister can have a fight with herself and still lose.'

'Then she must also win.'

'Ha! – I hadn't thought of it that way.'

'You mean I thought of something before you did? . . . Gosh! . . . Can I live with that knowledge . . . that huge responsibility?'

'James?'

'Yes?'

'Umm . . . Good for you! – I like a man who stands up for himself . . . My sister's like that . . . Or she would be if she could.'

'Huh?'

'She's a lesbian.'

'So what? – And you're being vulgar and judgemental.'

'Yes.'

'What d'you mean "Yes"?.'

'I'm not politically correct. My sister is. My mother is a bit . . . has to be in her job.'

'I don't mind you being politically incorrect but I don't think it's necessary to be vulgar and judgmental . . . I've been that myself – many times . . . before I got into recovery. I don't want to be like that any more – and I'm uncomfortable when you are.'

'You haven't met my sister.'

'Some other time . . . umm . . . What about your father?'

'Stays well outside the danger zone.'

'Sensible man.'

'Yes . . . but he won't set the world on fire with new ideas.'

'And you will?'

'Yes . . . when I'm ready.'

'Will the world be ready for you?'

'I don't care.'

*   *   *

'You said you'd been "a bit weaker in the legs" on and off since we last met.'

'Yes . . . Had a bit of a fall last week – bit embarrassing really.'

'Would your wife say the same?'

'I always embarrass her.'

'Ha! . . . No. I meant would she describe it as "a bit of a fall"?'

'Don't know really . . . I try not to bother her . . . She's got problems enough of her own at the moment – not physical ones . . . umm . . . employment issues – difficult proving that she's fit for work again after time off.'

'Yes . . . umm . . . What I'm looking for is independent evidence on how you've been . . . I admire your bravery and determination but the clinical signs – when I examined you just now – are markedly more extensive, in comparison with what I recorded in my previous notes . . . Your muscles are more stiff and your tendon reflexes are more brisk, your limbs are thinner and you've got more fasciculations – the spontaneous flickering in your muscles . . . You'll have noticed them.'

'Mustn't make a fuss.'

'Indeed not . . . But, at the same time, we've got to get an accurate assessment of this and other things – how you manage various aspects of your life – in order to give you the best advice.'

'I'm a croquet player. – I can take hard knocks. – Bound to peg out some time . . . maybe not in the way I would wish.'

'It hasn't come to that yet.'

'"Yet"?'

'Not by a long chalk.'

'What's the score?'

'The signs of deterioration in your neurological state would tend to indicate a progressive disease.'

'Hmm.'

'I mentioned previously that I think it would be a good thing if your GP refers you to my NHS hospital . . . These neurological conditions can be fearfully complex – and expensive – to manage.'

'I value my independence.'

'I respect that . . . but let me put it this way – your family might also value theirs.'

'Meaning?'

'You might require progressively more care – with all sorts of people providing support of one kind or another – and that can be progressively more time-consuming and expensive.'

* * *

'This new bunch of final year students are so meek and mild . . . They want it all given to them on a plate. – All the answers . . . Not keen on being told to think for themselves.'

'We spoiled you last year.'

'I'll say.'

o O o

'I don't see that I have any other choice but to do as the

GMC and the psychiatrist insist.'

'There are always choices – for both of us . . . even in our present states – but some of them seem very uncomfortable . . . for now.'

'All right, let's spell them out – purely as a theoretical exercise . . . to keep our minds open to any possibility . . . One . . . I submit to their demands, get depressed, put on weight . . . er . . . and have other problems . . . but I'll be able to resume my work – under supervision . . . Don't like that but it's probably the only way – and hope that these conditions will be lifted in time.'

'What time?'

'Umm . . . maybe a year or so.'

'What would be the criterion? . . . the observation? . . . that leads to them . . . er . . . whoever "they" are by that time . . . making that decision?'

'That I had done my work well . . . No complaints, no untoward events . . . compliant in every respect.'

'Sweet love, that's not you – compliant. – Never has been.'

'I could do it . . . determinedly . . . with a strong motive . . . and with your understanding and support . . . and be as full of beans as I can.'

'As a devil's advocate, I suggest that strategy might play into "their" hands.'

'How so?'

'They will give credit to their treatment . . . not to you.'

'Oh . . . and then what?'

'Keep you on that regime . . . p'raps without the supervision and the CBT after a time.'

'What time?'

'Whatever time they decide . . . whatever time is usual.'

'Usual for what?'

'Usual in other cases. – How long are people usually supervised? . . . in disciplinary cases?'

'Mine isn't a disciplinary case.'

'But that may be their only practical precedent, guideline . . . How many cases of anaesthetic awareness d'you s'pose they've ever seen? . . . in senior clinical staff?'

'Oh . . . er . . . none.'

'In which case they'll probably use disciplinary cases as their benchmark . . . How long would that be?'

'I don't know . . . A year would be my guess.'

'And CBT?'

'Less than that . . . probably 20 weeks, she said . . . I . . . er . . . could "play their game" on that one.'

'Through gritted teeth.'

'I'd just have to grin and bear it.'

'That's not your style . . . It's more mine – in a case where I really dislike the client . . . or the judge.'

'You'll have to train me . . . as a pupil.'

'That'll be fun.'

'No it won't . . . That's nothing to do with you – it's just the sheer frustration – being subjected to playing games . . . on their terms.'

'We could make up our own rules.'

'Okay . . . I could survive that . . . It's the antidepressants I'm worried about.'

'Yes . . . me too.'

'But I'm not on them right now . . . What's the issue?'

'I'm looking at the situation from their perspective.'

'Which is?'

'The same situation as now . . . You may be fine – in your own mind – but *they* have to make the judgement . . . take the risk of anything going wrong . . . You would have to stop work if it did – but *they'd* get the blame . . . and there'd be hell to pay.'

'Oh . . . I'd be on them for ever.'

'Is that what happens now? . . . in some patients?'

'Yes . . . Their doctors say they need them.'

'But do they?'

'Who knows?'

'Yes. That's my point . . . The person making the judgement has a lot to lose.'

'So has the patient.'

'That . . . er . . . might be a secondary consideration.'

'Oh God. On God. Oh God.'

'My poor darling Lizzie . . . I'm just being a devil's advocate.'

'A very good one.'

'It's the way I'm trained to think.

'Me too – in terms of looking at the worst possibility first.'

'Right then . . . That's the first option. – What's the next?'

'Die.'

'Don't you dare.'

'No . . . I wouldn't. – Haven't got the courage for that.'

'I thought suicide was a sign of weakness . . . Running away.'

'Possibly it's a sign of strength . . . Who knows?'

* * *

Dear Dr Arbuthnot,

I have to inform you that a formal complaint of racism has been made by a student, Miss Urvashi Patel, about comments made by you in a teaching round.

The complainant said that you humiliated her in front of her peers and your House Officer, Dr Phoebe Finch, and that you referred to "brownies" as biscuits.

This teaching hospital has a strict policy on racism and

other forms of prejudice. It is considered to be totally unacceptable.

It should not be necessary for me to emphasise that students are under a great deal of academic and financial stress in these days of great competition for a limited number of places at the university and in times of general financial austerity.

It is perhaps particularly distressing that the complainant is one of our most talented students. No concern has previously been voiced by any consultant on her academic ability or on her personal behaviour.

Within the next seven days you are required to supply this office with a clear account of the incident.

*   *   *

'You were very sharp with me – saying I was vulgar and judgemental.'

'You were.'

'Hang on . . . Hang on . . . I've come to tell you that you were right. – And I apologise.'

'You haven't hurt me. – But it did show me a side of your character that I haven't seen before.'

'Family stuff . . . Yes . . . As I said – more or less – I've won prizes for being judgemental . . . usually about the people closest to me . . . Sorry.'

'No prob . . . It shows we're normal human beings . . . not fictional black and white characters.'

'That's one of the justifiable criticisms of *Atlas Shrugged* . . . The characters are larger than life . . . caricatures really.'

'So why are you so keen on it?'

'It's a book about ideas . . . not simply about people and events.'

'That's good.'

'And what really interests me is whether ideas work in practice.'

'Why wouldn't they?'

'I mean they always work – one way or another. – That's obvious . . . But sometimes they have the opposite effect from the one that was intended . . . That's why we have to see what actually happens and then backtrack to re-assess the idea.'

'Sounds like hard work to me.'

'It is . . . That's why people generally aren't too keen to think for themselves. They expect teachers and politicians – God help us! – to do their thinking for them.'

* * *

'Alice, I've come to talk to you.'

'Thank you . . . It's been a difficult time without any real work. I like being busy.'

'And I like keeping you busy.'

'I know . . . I feel very sad for you. It's all so unfair.'

'It gets worse . . . I really don't know whether I want to work – under the conditions that are being imposed on me.'

'Where does that leave me? . . . and your patients?'

'That's why I came in to see you specially . . . umm . . . There really hasn't been enough work to keep you interested. I recognise that . . . I'm so grateful to you for your loyalty and support . . . More than I've had from the hospital people. – They're more concerned for themselves than they are for me. – Ha! – It's as if I've done something wrong and I'm threatening to damage them . . . or as if I were a superbug – contaminating them.'

'Yes . . . That's how their behaviour struck me . . . Obviously everybody knows about your . . . er . . . difficulty. Everybody talks about it . . . But they look after number one, seems to me.'

'Thank you . . . But in your case you've got to look after number one yourself some time . . . You'll lose your skills – same as I've done, I'm sure – if you don't keep in practice.'

'I'll survive.'

'No doubt – but I want a lot more for you – Ha! and me – than that . . . I'm just letting you know that I would fully understand if you decided to move on.'

'I don't quit when the going's tough . . . I dig in.'

'Great! . . . So do I – but sometimes I hurt myself . . . damage myself . . . doing that . . . I don't want that to happen to you.'

'It won't . . . I want to do the decent thing for a decent woman.'

'Thank you.'

* * *

'My mother's been telling me that she's begun to question the value of her work in the new political climate . . . being just a number in someone else's Grand Design.'

'Your mother? – I thought she played for the other team.'

'No . . . She still misses her work as a nursing sister – seeing patients, having responsibility for their care.'

'Why doesn't she go back to it?

'You must be joking! . . . She earns vastly more as an inspector for the CQC – making sure that all the boxes are ticked and nobody in officialdom gets blamed for anything – than she would on the wards.'

'That doesn't sound right.'

'It isn't right – in any sensible world. – But this is the NHS, the so-called envy of the world.'

'But money isn't everything . . . You and I both know that.'

'Yes, we do . . . because we can afford that opinion . . .

We're like students – full of opinions on how the world should be run – with their ideas and for their benefit but with absolutely no responsibility.'

'Ha! . . . Did you see that survey of one hundred thousand students, that showed that one in twenty in the UK – more men than women – sell sex to cover university costs? . . . Two-thirds say they do it to fund a lifestyle but just under half admit they do it primarily for sexual pleasure.'

'Well that's honest . . . better than saying it's all because they have to pay tuition fees . . . umm . . . I wonder what the situation is in Scotland, where they don't pay any fees.'

'They didn't report that.'

'No . . . They wouldn't. – It doesn't suit the political agenda on wicked Tory cuts.'

'So how are you going to put the world to rights? . . . You can't stay on strike for ever.'

'I could – but I don't want to . . . I want to earn my living through my creative work – whatever I decide to do – and pay my way, asking for nothing . . . And not allowing myself to be emotionally blackmailed either.'

'Over sex?'

'Ha! . . . That'd be the day . . . No. – Over feeling guilty for having a brain and using it.'

'But you're *not* using it.'

'Yes I am . . . I'm using it very well – thinking.'

'That sounds like an excuse a student would make . . . before getting on with some serious shagging.'

'Well that certainly was true in my day . . . We believed the purpose of uni was to get drunk, experiment with drugs and screw around – and do just a little bit of work of course . . . just enough to get through.'

'Sounds like my life as a broker.'

'Same for all – well most – young people everywhere . . .

But we've got to grow up sometime.'

'Is that what you're doing now?'

'Yes.'

'Funny way of doing it.'

'Yes . . . My way.'

'Let me know when you've worked it all out . . . Wouldn't mind joining you.'

'Generous of you, James . . . But you'll have to read the book first.'

'Aaaaaargh! – Women! . . . You're so demanding.'

'Yes. – We have to be . . . We've been pushed around by you men for too long.'

'Did you learn that from your sister?'

'No . . . I look at the world that's mostly run by men and I don't like what I see.'

'There was a time when I'd have said, "Tough!".'

'One day I might find a reason to say that to you . . . You're more of a dreamer than a thinker . . . So far.'

o O o

Hmm . . . Got to do a bit of belt-tightening one of these days . . . Doesn't look as if Lizzie will make it back to work any time soon . . . and not sure how much work there'll be for her after all this time off. – GPs establish new referral patterns . . . And the insurance money won't go on forever . . . They'll find a clause somewhere . . . Always do. Ha! – bloody lawyers! . . . If she'd still been in the NHS she'd have no worries . . . Get paid for life. – The taxpayer takes the hit . . . Now it feels as if she's got a life sentence . . . So have I . . .

* * *

'What's so odd about lumps and bumps?'

Silence.

'This lady says she's had the lump in her thyroid gland for 20 years . . . Why d'you s'pose she hasn't asked for treatment before now? . . . That's odd, isn't it?'

'She's been treating it herself, Sir – with arnica.'

'Your name, please?'

'Pulcherios.'

'Yes, Mr Pulcherios . . . And what is arnica?'

'I don't know, Sir.'

'Good man . . . Always a good principle to say when we don't know . . . Anyone?'

'A homeopathic remedy – commonly used to treat bruising, muscular strains, wounds and swellings . . . Good stuff, Sir, after a hard game of rugby.'

'Yes . . . Yes, I'm sure. – But why has she suddenly asked for conventional assessment and treatment now?'

Silence.

'Dr Finch?'

'Pain in the neck.'

'Umm . . . Be careful of the expressions you use, Dr Finch . . . Sensitive subject – for some of us just at the moment.'

'I meant she's suddenly developed pain in the lump in her neck.'

'Yes . . . Ah, yes . . . She wasn't worried about a disfiguring lump – had it for ages . . . got used to it . . . But now it's painful – and along she comes . . . Odd that. – Isn't it?'

Silence.

'You, Sir – the rugby player – tell me your name please.'

'Jones, Sir.'

'Yes, of course . . . It would be – straight from the Welsh valleys.'

'Yes, Sir . . . but sad to say the English beat us this year –

not by much . . . but enough.'

'Not enough arnica at half time perhaps?'

'Sore point, Sir.'

'Umm . . . Tell me what *you* know about arnica.'

'Works wonders, Sir.'

'But what's it made of . . . Where does it come from?'

'Little white tablets, Sir.'

Laughter.

'And what's in them?'

'Arnica.'

Laughter.

'Anyone?'

'Nothing.'

'Who said that?'

'Me, Sir . . . Chen.'

'And what did you mean, Mr Chen?'

'It's an extract of the European plant, *Arnica montana*. It's watered down hundreds of times to form a homeopathic "ultra-dilution" – which means there's actually nothing in it . . . No active principle.'

'But Mr Jones says it works – and this lady swears by it . . . umm . . . Is that true, Dr Finch?'

'Yes, Sir. – She gives it credit for keeping the pain away until now.'

'Ah . . . Yes . . . and what do you students think?'

'Worth a try.'

'Thank you, Mr Jones . . . But what would be the risk . . . umm . . . in this lady's case?'

'None, Sir . . . The lump's benign – a cyst.'

'But when did we know that?'

'Yesterday, Sir – on an ultrasound scan.'

'But supposing – right at the start – the swelling had been a carcinoma?'

'She'd be dead by now.'

'Possibly – but maybe surgical excision would have cured her . . . And if she'd taken arnica for a carcinoma?'

'Not the best treatment, Sir.'

'No . . . umm . . . What would you suggest would be the best treatment, Mr Chen?'

'Chinese herbal remedies, Sir.'

'Are there risks? . . . er . . . Are they effective?'

'Thyroid disease is common in China, Sir. It's frequently treated with herbal medicine or with a combination of herbs and drugs.'

'Do they work?'

'A positive response is common . . . The aggregate "cure" rate for hyperthyroidism, reported in more than a dozen studies involving more than seven hundred patients, is forty two percent . . . and with most other patients the condition is well-managed even after cessation of the therapy.'

'Yes . . . Yes, I see . . . You've obviously looked it up, done your homework. Well done . . . But we're dealing here with a benign cyst – that may have become painful as a result of a bleed into it. – We'll find out. – We're not dealing with hyper-thyroidism or Grave's disease.'

'No, Sir.'

'And how shall we treat this lady? . . . What shall we suggest to her?'

Silence.

'Dr Finch?'

She's not keen to have any treatment at all, Sir. Now that she knows that the swelling is probably benign, as she thought all along . . . She wants nothing – apart from arnica of course.'

* * *

I'm such a fortunate man, to live in this world. Not the fantasy world John Berger dreamed up – for his version of a Utopian state . . . in his Communist paradise where nobody worries about money and we all care for each other – but I'm so lucky to have found Phoebe . . . Pfwooar! . . . Gives me a spinal tingle just thinking about her . . . Hmm . . . But John Berger nearly caught her mind – caught a brilliant mind like hers . . . What is it with this country? – We Americans rescue the Brits from Hitler and they fall for Stalin . . . Well, Marx anyway. Ha! Same thing really. – One thing leads to another . . . The ideas of Marx lead to the gulags of Stalin . . . And what's the future now? – here or Stateside? . . . with fantasists just like Berger being so influential in the young? . . . Yeah – Must remember what Prof Weed said . . . 'Maturity is fatigue . . . When you're getting old and tired – and can't fight the battles any more – you turn to those who're still fighting and you say, "You're immature!" ' . . . Well Phoebe isn't . . . and I'm not. – We're still young . . . and still fighting . . .

* * *

'I found that a very challenging teaching round, Phoebe.'
　'Yes, it was, Sir.'
　'Why d'you think that was? . . . Have I gone off my game?'
　'No, Sir . . . It's just the way it went.'
　'Huh.'
　'And maybe there was an elephant in the room.'
　'I beg your pardon?'
　'Someone we were all aware of but nobody was talking about.'
　'Mmm? . . . And who might that be?'
　'Miss Patel.'

* * *

'You were saying that people expect teachers and politicians to do their thinking for them.'

'Yes . . . Mostly.'

'But people are always telling politicians what to do.'

'That's true – but they do so without thought . . . No thought for the bigger picture . . . the knock-on effects – financially and socially – of their particular demand.'

'Seems to me some politicians are like that.'

'It's even worse . . . Political parties – and trade unions – are like that . . . whipped into line – answerable to the Party or the Cause, rather than to the whole electorate or membership.'

'So what's the answer?'

'I told you before . . . Individualism.'

'But that's anarchy.'

'Yes. – Peace-loving anarchy.'

'That's a contradiction in terms.'

'No it isn't . . . It's in my individual interest – and everyone else's – to cooperate with other people, get along with them.'

'But groups have more power – street gangs, professional groups, political parties.'

'You're dead right they do.'

'So how d'you stop them? keep control of them?'

'By encouraging individualism – right from school . . . and at home even before that.'

'Elitism?'

'Yes of course . . . Each individual should be encouraged to develop his or her particular skills.'

'And lord it over everyone else?'

'Absolutely not – appreciate everybody else for *their* individual skills.'

'But some people have none.'

'That's not true ... except in extreme cases – extreme cerebral palsy ... things like that – and even some extremes can be overcome in remarkable ways ... Read *The Diving Bell and the Butterfly* about someone with locked-in syndrome communicating through blinking.'

'You're as bad as my parents – getting me to read books all the time.'

'As *good* as – not as bad as.'

'Oh.'

'And look at what Professor Stephen Hawking has done despite his ALS ... He's an inspiration to us all on the power of individual achievement.'

'But he's dependent on state care.'

'Yes ... There's a place for a minimum state.'

'What's that?'

'Providing basics – defence, police, contract law, health-care and welfare for the *truly* incapable and destitute.'

'Means tests?'

'Yes, of course ... They're hated precisely because they treat people as individuals ... and reduce the power of corpo-ratists to call the shots.'

'Hmm ... I'll have to think about that.'

'Yes ... so should every individual. Otherwise, as Ayn Rand says, the difference between a welfare state and a totalitarian state is merely a matter of time.'

'That's a bit sweeping.'

'I should hope so ... There's a whole culture – the entitle-ment culture – of rotten ideas leading to rotten practice ... It desperately needs to be swept away.'

'How?'

'First of all by opening our eyes and seeing what's

happening ... Ayn Rand finished writing *Atlas Shrugged* in 1956 as a warning, not a prediction ... Look at the individual freedoms that've been lost in the USA – and even more over here in Europe – since then ... All as a result of the state progressively being thought to be indispensable.'

'It protects the weak against the strong, the infirm and needy against the fit and healthy, the poor against the rich.'

'No it *doesn't* ... Those are false alternatives, paper tigers – made to look frightening precisely in order to protect powerful interest groups ... Look at your own experience in that so-called Mental Health Unit ... Look at the street people in a welfare state that prides itself on universal provision – the curse of individual compassion and commitment.'

'And look at the fat cats in industry and commerce ... I've seen them, met some of them. – Not a pretty sight ... or smell. – You can't disguise the stench of greed with cologne.'

'That's the whole point ... They're getting the consequences of their behaviour ... They betrayed capitalism and they're bringing it down – from within.'

'And it will be replaced by ...?'

'Fascism – of the Left or Right. – The two extremes are as bad as each other ... The common enemies of Individualism ... And the start of that process is Health Fascism ... Promising healthcare and welfare – "for free" at other people's expense – but at a terrible, terrible cost to individual freedom ... "Ve haf vays of making you compassionate!"

* * *

I'm worried about Dr Arbuthnot ... Worried for him. – He's a sacrificial lamb, waiting to be eviscerated ... on the altar of political correctness ...

* * *

I'm still not there. – Still can't see the alternative to Galt's Gulch . . . Running away from the world . . . Letting it drop – and leaving it to find its own solution – but what *is* it?'

o O o

'We've heard your evidence, Dr Arbuthnot, in which you say you were not the first to use the word "brownie" but did use the word "biscuit" – which we consider to be tantamount to the same thing. We've heard from Dr Finch, who confirmed your account . . . er . . . as one might expect from a loyal House Officer . . . We've also heard from Miss Patel, who said that you humiliated her – belittling her intelligence – in front of her peers . . . You deny this . . . And we heard from two of the other students on your firm . . . They are also women of Indian sub-continent racial origin . . . They confirm the account given by Miss Patel and they say that they felt equally shamed . . . We find that the evidence points to you being insensitive towards Miss Patel . . . on racial grounds . . . A formal reprimand will be recorded against your name, Dr Arbuthnot, and you will be required to make a formal apology to Miss Patel.'

* * *

'I've come to see you for another consultation because I'm stuck . . . Nothing to do with the anaesthetic awareness. – That's history.'
    'Well done.'
    'Well done to you too.'
    'Thank you . . . But what is it that you're stuck on now?'

'The reaction – by the hospital, the insurers, the consultant psychiatrist . . . even the GMC . . . to me being better.'

'Surely they'd be very pleased?'

'You'd have thought so . . . but they're frightened and angry – it seems to me.'

'Mmm . . . I would've hoped for better from them . . . umm . . . for you.'

'Yes . . . So did I – but that's not the way it's turned out.'

'What were they frightened about?'

'A form of treatment – the EMDR – they didn't understand . . . It got me better – and that scared the living daylights out of them.'

'Yes . . . They'd have to re-examine all their ideas on effective interventions . . . as well as having another look at the therapeutic approaches they're using now and seeing if they really *do* work.'

'Yes . . . I s'pose that's it . . . And they're angry because I've rattled their cages . . . their assumptions on how things should be done.'

'So what are you stuck on?'

'Their specific reaction . . . They're insisting that I have CBT and go back on antidepressants.'

'Oh . . . or else what?'

'Or else I can't work at all . . . And even when . . . er . . . if . . . I go back to work, they're insisting that it has to be under supervision . . . But, as I see it, the longer I stay out of work the more de-skilled I'll become.'

'Got it . . . Do what they require and you'll sacrifice your integrity by being belittled. And a lot else . . . umm . . . physically . . . But do it the way you believe is best for you and you're out of a job.'

'Yes . . . That's right . . . umm . . . What would you advise?'

'I'd advise you to do what you believe is best for you.'

'Are you avoiding giving me a specific opinion?'

'Yes.'

'Why?'

'Because I don't know enough about you . . . I could never know enough about you or any other person – not even a wife – to advise on that kind of decision . . . It has to be personal.'

'But I thought that's what counsellors do. – Give advice.'

'Not if they've got any sense – and experience of where giving advice can go catastrophically wrong.'

'Oh.'

'I see my counselling work as helping people to see their *own* way through their difficulties . . . I tend to ask questions rather than make statements.'

'What questions would you ask me?'

'Umm . . . What really matters to you in life?'

'My religious belief . . . my family . . . my work . . . my health . . . umm . . . kindness . . . umm . . . justice . . .

'In that order of significance?'

'Something like that.'

'Okay . . . Stand over there, by the door where you came in, and look into the full length mirror . . . There you are – at the end of your life – being questioned by St Peter . . . You can see – by looking into your eyes – if you're telling the truth . . . St Peter is asking you what you've done in your life with the talents God gave you . . . What have you done?'

'I became a doctor.'

'Did you enjoy being a doctor?'

'Yes – very much so . . . until now.'

'That was your enthusiasm?'

'Yes.'

'But not now?'

'No . . . Not unless I get back to being like I used to be . . . in my work.'

'So if you do what is being required of you now, how would you feel?'

'Certainly not enthusiastic . . . At least not to begin with.'

'And how long is "to begin with"?'

'That's not for me to decide . . . The authorities – the consultant psychiatrist – decides.'

'So your enthusiasm is going to be based on his perceptions? . . . and his timetable?'

'Yes, I s'pose so.'

'Are you comfortable with that?'

'No.'

'No enthusiasm for that prospect?'

'No . . . er . . . Why all this emphasis on enthusiasm?'

'D'you know what the word means?

'Must be from the Greek . . . I know that "Theos" is "God" . . .'

'And "en"?'

'"In".'

'Try again.'

'Umm . . .'

'What happens when people are enthusiastic?'

'Their eyes light up . . . Oh! . . . *"within"*!'

'Yes, that's right . . . "enthusiasm" means "God within" . . . I don't know if God lives in a church or mosque or synagogue or somewhere else . . . but I've seen God come alive in people's eyes.'

'Oh.'

'And I've seen the light go out in people's eyes . . . like it has done in yours since I last saw you.'

'Oh . . . So what should I do?'

'Come to sit down again . . . That's it . . . Now . . . You know I'm not going to answer your question on what you should do. So what d'you think I'll do now?'

'Ask me another question.'

'Yes . . . And what d'you think that question's likely to be? . . . for you to ask yourself?'

'Umm . . . "Where could I find my enthusiasm again?".'

'Yes . . . If you want to . . . Or you can stay as you are . . . It's your choice.'

*　*　*

'How're y'doing, Roddy? . . . Haven't seen you in the Club fera bit.'

'Bit weak in the legs . . . Hope I don't have to use a wheel-chair . . . eventually . . . like that accountant chap.'

'He gets about all right . . . Uses the lift at the side.'

'Misses the best moving view – of the pictures round the staircase . . . and looking down into the snug to see the regulars like us getting a bit . . .'

'Gently plastered?'

'Not for me nowadays . . . On the wagon – 'cos of this neurological nonsense.'

'Yer not alone in here, Roddy . . . You know that . . . "Dead men's shoes" is the only way ter get in.'

'I'm worried about how I'm going to get out . . . or stay in.'

'In a fire?'

'No . . . I'd like to stay a member until they put a notice up to say I've popped me clogs – but I'm not sure I can afford the annual fee . . . if me medical problems become more trouble-some or the cost of the meals – at the rate I've been going – particularly now that me wife's not at all sure if she's going to be able to get back to work.'

'Yes . . . I see . . . umm . . . Yer know the Club's loaded . . . The A A Milne bequest . . . er . . . Yer must know some of it goes towards supporting long-term members who've fallen on hard times.'

'Yes . . . but I'd never think of asking for it . . . charity.'

'Yer clown . . . The Garrick's a club. – Difficult to get in . . . Got ter be invited . . . and difficult to get out – unless yer pushed.'

'I don't want to be pushed. Or be pushy.'

'Yer not . . . Yer one of us . . . I'll talk to the Secretary.'

'I . . .'

'Too late now . . . It's a done deal.'

* * *

'Precious?'

'Yes?'

'We're going out.'

'Are we? . . . Where?'

'Pizza Express jazz club . . . Dean Street, Soho.'

'I know where it is . . . Been there many times . . . Down the spiral staircase to the basement . . . Through the blackout door . . . Waiters and waitresses coming in and out all the time. – Trying to make the place pay. – So many tables there's no room to move . . . Basic food – Pizzas obviously but some other stuff . . . decent fish last time I was there . . . Good music . . . Well, good enough. But still trying to live off the name of Amy Winehouse . . . She did some gigs there.'

'Have you quite done? . . . done spoiling it for me? . . . I've never been there. I bought a couple of tickets – to surprise you.'

'Oh . . . Sorry. – Got carried away.'

'Yes . . . You did.'

'Well it suits me just fine . . . mighty fine.'

'Don't want to go now.'

* * *

Down to earth again . . . Well, in the drains – in the laundry room . . . Can't get much lower than this . . . Ha! – Pond life . . . And like it says at the beginning of *Atlas Shrugged* – difficult book to get into at the beginning, "Our days are numbered" . . . Hmm . . . Are they really? . . . Is time running out for all of us? . . . unless we wake up and do something? . . . But Lucy doesn't want to do anything . . . yet . . . Wonder what she'll come up with . . . Oh whoops! – Mustn't forget Mother . . . Wonder what's happening to her . . . and Father . . . Must go 'n see them some time . . . Can't spend all my time reading books or going on courses or wrapped up with Lucy . . . Hmm . . . That'd be a nice idea . . .

*   *   *

'Sorry I screwed up the Pizza Express jazz evening.'

'My fault for having a lot on my mind . . . My chief's just been

crucified, thrown to the lions, whatever – for being racist . . . And he's not. He's a decent man, a kind man . . . and a very good doctor.'

'So what happened?'

'Some Indian girl got her knickers in a twist . . . if she wears any.'

'Come on, Phoebe . . . That's not worthy of you.'

'Aaaaargh! I don't know what's the matter with me . . . umm . . . Yes I do. – It's over what's been done to the poor man . . . The prejudice – if any – was directed at *him* . . . And I can't think why.'

'That's the way it is with prejudice . . . There is no "why" . . . Never was – as far as I could see – when I was on the receiving end.'

'Yeah . . . Maybe it's payback time for us whiteys . . . and straights . . . and the fit and healthies . . . Our whole world seems to be going upside-down in this country . . . politically, financially, socially . . .'

'But it doesn't have to go upside-down for you and me.'

'Oh I don't know . . . Might be fun to try all sorts of things we haven't tried so far.'

'What I meant was that we're both at turning points . . . deciding where we go from here – professionally and personally.'

'So?'

'So that's an adventure . . . but it's unpredictable, insecure.'

'No, it isn't . . . Just varied.'

'So I would hope . . . Imagine what life would be like if it were totally predictable – boring as . . . er . . .'

'Fuck?'

'Not with you . . . My mother – God rest her mortal soul – said she didn't want me to swear.'

'I didn't give my mother a choice . . . er . . . Why is a soul "mortal"? . . . I thought souls were meant to be immortal.'

'Just an expression.'

'So's "fuck"'

'Yeah . . . S'pose it is really . . . nowadays . . . Pity really.'

'Why?'

'There are other words.'

'Now you sound just like my mother . . . always correcting me when I was young.'

'Well I'd like to keep that word just for us . . . special.'

'How about "fornication"?'

'You really are in a funny mood today.'

'Yes I am . . . Poor Dr Arbuthnot . . . He doesn't deserve any of that stuff.'

'No. He doesn't . . . umm . . . As we didn't go out to Pizza Express, would you like to see the film on Martin Luther King?'

o O o

The counsellor was right . . . I have to make my own decisions – on my own values . . . priorities. No time to be self-pitying . . . Time to buck myself up . . . Ha! – 'Up school!' . . . Difficult to make a decision like this . . . Deciding to enter a profession's easy enough – did what I was good at . . . But considering staying in it – almost under duress – or leaving it altogether is very very difficult . . . And with Roddy not well . . . Oh Lizzie, Lizzie, Lizzie, this really is a bummer . . . Ha! Haven't used that expression for yonks . . . or that one . . . Now then . . . What's the 'start from scratch' option? . . . Stay at home and look after Roddy? . . . Could do . . . Not the end of the world . . . Why would I want to start another career right now? . . . with Roddy likely to get worse and become progressively more dependent? . . . Hmm . . . That's a thought . . . Be the best wife I can be . . . That's a profession in itself . . . I'd miss the hospital and the staff and the cutting – but I'm getting quite used to being without it even now . . . Do I really have to be a doctor? . . . Do I really want to be a member of a profession – alongside the psychiatrist and the doctors on the GMC – when they treat people the way I've been treated? . . .

* * *

'No students today? . . . for the teaching round?'
 'No, Sir.'
 'Important rugby match?'
 'No, Sir . . . a boycott – at the insistence of the Students'

Union after an emergency meeting last night.'

'Oh . . . Oh . . . I can see where this will lead . . . umm . . . Will you be all right? . . . manage on your own? . . . do all the clerking and all the blood tests?'

'Yes, Sir . . . umm . . . May I say something . . . er . . . personal, Sir?'

'Yes, of course.'

'I feel very sad that this should have happened to you . . . It's completely unjustified and totally unfair.'

'Well . . . It's the way it goes, sometimes – like the way patients get illnesses they don't deserve.'

'Yes.'

'Hmm . . . I hadn't anticipated that my professional career would end quite like this . . . in such an undignified way.'

'You're ahead of me . . . Will it really come to that?'

'Yes.'

'And you'll give up without a fight?'

'I learned long ago. Never fight a battle you're bound to lose, can not win.'

'Why not? Why can't you win? – What you said was the truth . . . You and I both know that . . . and Miss Patel and the others must know it too.'

'Yes.'

'And that's all you have to say about it . . . just "Yes"?'

'Yes.'

'Why . . . when I'm screaming for justice? . . . for you . . . for the truth.'

'Pontius Pilate had something to say about that.'

'Sorry. – That's more *my* mother's line of business than mine. What did he say?'

'He asked, "What is truth?".'

'What did he mean by that?'

'I s'pose he meant, "We each see the truth in our own

way".'

* * *

'Just taking a rain check, Father . . . No – nothing to do with the weather – I meant "How are you? and Mother?" . . . It's a baseball term I picked up in Hazelden. – If a game gets cancelled because it's raining, the ticket holder can use the ticket again for another game . . . You're right. I did use it incorrectly. – I'm not an American. Yet . . . No. – No intention just at the moment, Father. Just a bit dispirited over how much I learned over there and how little I learn here . . . No. Not about baseball. – It was winter, the football season, if you remember. – But I learned lots of other useful things about addiction . . . No. Not just from my room-mate, the New York cop. From all the patients . . . No. I don't remember much of what the staff said in lectures or group . . . No it wasn't a waste of money. – Not a bit. – That's how it works . . . learning to stay clean alongside each other in AA . . . Well it's worked for me so far . . . Don't you worry about it. I've got every intention of staying clean and sober. – My life's too good to mess it up again . . . Yes, even in the laundry . . . er . . . Nothing to report right now. – I was just asking how you both are . . . Well there's always a first time . . . Good. Good. – Doing okay . . . Learning a lot about laundry . . . No, father, it was a joke . . . I do the laundry of course. – It's part of the job as a care assistant . . . No, not on my own. There's a girl called Lucy usually does it with me. – Nice girl. – Her father's a solicitor . . . Dunno. – General, I think, not commercial for sure . . . umm . . . Not much. – Spend most of my days off reading up on psychology or occasionally going on a day-release train-ing day. No. That'll be the day! – In the private sector. I get the sense the NHS isn't really interested in anything other than pills and harm reduction. Making sure people know about "sensible drinking" – keep a drinking diary and things. Load of rubbish. – Wouldn't have stopped me. – And telling addicts not to overdose or get HIV . . . Yes it really is a good idea – but it doesn't do anything positive to help them . . . Bit of CBT, that's all . . . Cognitive Behavioural Therapy. – Helping people to think better so they can behave better . . . Well, not really. – I reckon it doesn't work at all for addicts. We think too well at times. We always have an answer for everything . . . Oh! – You noticed. – Yes, I s'pose you would . . . I reckon we have a "feeling" illness and need a "feeling" treatment . . . No – not "touchy-feely". – Need to learn how to acknowledge our feelings and express them appropriately . . . No – with anybody, not just with Lucy in the laundry . . . Oh, that was your little joke. – Okay, got it now. – No need to repeat it . . . umm . . . It'd be nice to have a family get-together some time . . . Yes, all four of us . . . Five? – Has . . . er . . . Mother . . . umm . . .? Ha! Of course. – Denning. – Silly me.'

* * *

'I came to tell you that Precious and I are getting together.'

'That's nice. – Do we get to meet him some time?'

'Yes. I'd love that – if there's a time that suits you and Dad and that we can both manage.'

'Bound to be. – Nothing much in our diaries nowadays. – Let me know what suits you and I'll organise your father.'

'Ha! – As always.'

'Well you can't expect men to organise themselves, can you?'

'That's true. – My last man couldn't . . . No. Best not go down that dark alleyway.'

'He wasn't that bad, was he?'

'Yes . . . He was.'

'Oh . . . Then why did you choose to be with him?'

'No. – I'm not going down that dark alleyway either.'

'But this one's black as well, isn't he?'

'Yes – of course – but I was referring to my emotional state at that time . . . which reminds me . . . How's your emotional state? . . . now that you've completed the EMDR?'

'I'm in a dark alleyway.'

'Didn't it work?

'It worked beautifully . . . I still remember the event – Of course I do. – but it's just an event . . . It doesn't terrify me any more. Or say anything about me.'

'What could it possibly say about you?'

'That I'm silly, making a fuss, should've got over it.'

'Nobody in their right mind would believe that of you.'

'I did. I . . . er . . . wasn't in my right mind. – But I am now.'

'So what's the dark alleyway? . . . Nothing between you and Dad, I hope.'

'No, no. Absolutely not – although I am worried about him . . . medically.'

'Yes. – So'm I . . . So what's your "dark alleyway"?'

'Best not to go down it.'

'Come on. You can't tantalise me like that – open it up so that I'm curious . . . and then leave me hanging out to dry.'

'Oh. – Fair enough. – I . . . er . . . It's the hospital authorities . . . being tiresome.'

'The same's happened to my chief . . . He's been sent to the wall, poor man, over something that wasn't even true . . . I know it wasn't . . . I was there . . . Probably ended his career . . . he thinks.'

'Yes . . . My hospital authorities may be ending mine.'

'But that's terrible . . . What's got into these people?'

'They see us as liabilities . . . to their own security.'

* * *

'I've got to be frank with you, Mr Finch . . . I'm simply not getting sufficient practical experience – court time, discussion time, 'what if?' time – with you being laid up . . . partially . . . er . . . not at your peak.'

'Yes, I understand that.'

'It's been a great privilege being your pupil . . . but I've got to move on.'

'Yes, I understand that as well.'

'I . . . er . . . hope you'll be able to give me a good reference.'

'Yes, of course . . . I understand.'

Thank you, Mr Finch . . . Goodbye – and good luck.'

Thank you . . . and I wish the best for you . . . Goodbye.'

Hmmm . . . S'pose there'll be a few more of those on the way – from one person or another . . . Can't blame them . . .

* * *

'I've read another book . . . *Choice Theory.* – William Glasser. I mentioned him before.'

'You building a library after all?'

'And why not?'

'Yes . . . Why not? . . . er . . . What could be theoretical about a choice? . . . You either take one or another.'

'Why not do both? . . . or something altogether different?'

'Yes – if that's possible. – It's an excellent idea . . . I never like being forced into making choices. – I've made too many wrong ones.'

'That was the only snag I could see in Dr Glasser's ideas

... They're a bit cut and dried. No "if"s or "but's" or "maybe's".

'So what *are* his ideas?'

'He had lots ... but the simple ones that I read about this week were on the four primary needs – apart from survival, of course.'

'Okay ... Sex and what else?'

'Don't be so sure about that ... I saw a study – by a Cambridge professor, no less – on sexual behaviour ... The average couple has less sexual activity nowadays than people did thirty years ago – and people in their twenties today are less sexually active than those in their fifties.'

'Something to look forward to then.'

'Ha! ... But what surprised me was how few times young people – between the ages of sixteen and thirty four – get it away ... Three times a month is the average for all couples and young people may have it even less.'

'Wow! ... Why not more?'

'Maybe it's because many of them live on their own and they're more attached to social media than real people ... totally hooked into their virtual lives and their computers, smart phones and the rest of it ... and there's a lot of stress of one kind or another.'

'And less stress in their fifties?'

'Yes – once their children are off their hands, I s'pose.'

'Well, we're both earning our livings ... Sort of.'

'Yeah ... I hope I've given my parents all the grief I'm going to give them ... Got to sort myself out now. They're not in the best shape themselves at present ... Must give Father a ring some time.'

'So what else was there – apart from survival and sex – in *Choice Theory*?'

'The starting point was asking why we answer the phone.'

'That's obvious – because it rings.'

'That's the same trap I fell into . . . Have you ever just let it ring? . . . or turned it off?'

'Oh . . . I see. – That's clever . . . I answer it because I choose to answer it.'

'And we do lots of other things because we choose to do them.'

'Open a door, boil an egg . . .'

'Yes – but we also choose our reactions to things . . . Nobody can *make* us angry or sad or happy . . . or anything.'

'Yes they can . . . If someone ran off with my boyfriend, I'd be very angry with her . . . and him.'

'But only because that conflicts with your values . . . If you were to change your value to being promiscuous, you might ask to join in . . . for a threesome.'

'That's not going to happen.'

'No . . . and that's your choice.'

'I hope it's yours as well.'

'Yes . . . umm . . . Why so? I . . . er . . . I thought you said just now you've got a boyfriend.'

'He was a theoretical one . . . a virtual one.'

'That's good . . . umm . . . In *Choice Theory*, as I said, even our feelings are choices . . . Nothing and nobody can *make* someone depressed.'

'Would you miss me if I told you I didn't want to have anything to do with you?'

'I'm in with a chance?'

'Stick to the point, James . . . for now.'

'I take that as a "yes".'

'Stick to the point . . . or I'll make a choice you might not like.'

'I'll choose my response . . . Dr Glasser said that depression is a choice. He likes to use it as a verb. – I depress, you depress, he or she depresses – and so on.'

'That's interesting ... But surely there are some people who simply can't pull themselves out of their pit of despair.'

'He believes they can – when they allow themselves to think in terms of choices ... When his wife, Naomi, died, he took out the mental picture he had of her in his "how life is" world but left it in his "how life ought to be" world. The two worlds didn't match – so he felt sad ... Later on he married Carlene – and his two worlds matched again so he felt good.'

'But what about people who feel really down? Surely they need medication.'

'He didn't think so ... Remember, he was a consultant psychiatrist – until he took his name off the medical register because he didn't value his license to prescribe ... He still saw patients just the same – but not in the hospital.'

'He chose to be his sort of doctor.'

'Yes ... He saw too many people who were in mental health units who didn't need to be there – or take medication ... umm ... You might like to look at Byron Katie's "work" – as she calls it – on *YouTube*. She's phenomenal ... Goes all over the world demonstrating how people can pull themselves out of their pits – out of their faulty thinking – without using medicines of any kind ... She tells her own story of being severely depressed for nearly ten years – spiralling down into paranoia, rage, self-loathing and constant thoughts of suicide ... For a whole two years she was often unable to leave her bedroom ... Then, as she said, she "woke up to reality" when she discovered that she didn't suffer if she didn't believe her own thoughts.'

'Incredible!'

'It would be if it were in a storybook – but she's very real ... Very like Dr Glasser in many of her ideas.'

'So what else is there in *Choice Theory*?'

'Lots ... I really want to study it in greater depth ... But for starters the primary needs – after survival – are fun, power, love and freedom.'

'Where's the sex?'

'It can be part of all of them, I s'pose.'

'I wish.'

'Oh . . . So I *am* in with a chance!'

'I've been let down . . . and chosen to be hurt . . . before. Now I choose not to take that risk. Not yet. – But I might change my mind . . . One day.'

'That'll be nice.'

'For me too . . . if that's the response you choose.'

* * *

'Ah here you are, Mrs Finch. I was glad to note that you had made a follow-up appointment . . . Very good of you. – Wise, if I may say so . . . even after some delay . . . although, clearly, you received my e-mail and the copy of my report.'

'Yes.'

'That's good. Very good . . . Now then. Let's see what we can do to help you to put this whole wretched business behind you . . . How are you? . . . in yourself?'

'I was feeling very relieved – not on top of the world, but in a really positive frame of mind . . . until I read your e-mail.'

'Yes . . . Yes, I can see that it might be a disappointment to you . . . Still, there's a clear way forward now.'

'It appears that I have no choice.'

'Ah well, Mrs Finch, we all have choices, don't we?'

'I can't see mine . . . if I want to get back to my surgical work.'

'Ahem . . . There is also the issue of supervision . . . working initially as an assistant . . . We have to take things gradually. – Make sure that we take things in simple steps . . .

so that there are no false dawns.'

'What are these simple steps?'

'Well, initially, we have to ensure that you are taking the most effective medication – for you.'

'I've been feeling fine without any at all.'

'Yes . . . Yes, you might do so in the comfort of your home – and with the support of your family . . . er . . . I assume they are supportive?'

'Is that a statement or a question?'

'Ahem . . . I do hope you're not going to be . . . er . . . difficult about this, Mrs Finch.'

'As I said, I don't see that I have any choice . . . other than to do what I'm told – by the GMC and by you.'

'Well that is the long and short of it, isn't it?'

'And is that a statement or a question?'

'Ahem . . . I'm trying to help you, Mrs Finch . . . Please ensure that you help yourself . . . er . . . I'm on your side, y'know.'

'Against whom? I wasn't aware that I have any enemies.'

'Against litigious patients . . . opportunists . . . like the ambulance-chasing lawyers. That sort of thing.'

'But what I had wasn't that sort of accident . . . It isn't as if there's any doubt about what happened – or about me being anything other than a totally innocent party.'

'You're missing the point, Mrs Finch . . . The past is not the issue in question . . . It's the future . . . er . . . The possibility of mishaps occurring as a result of your own actions, not of unfortunate things happening to you.'

'This is an "unfortunate thing" happening to me right now . . . I'm being prevented from doing my work . . . when no assessment has been made on the effectiveness of the treatment I received.'

'Ahem . . . I understand your feelings of frustration and

irritation. – I'm merely the messenger of bad tidings, not the instigator . . . Again I would ask you . . . er . . . advise you not to be difficult about the necessary precautions that the authorities – the GMC, the hospital lawyers, your own colleagues . . .'

'There's never been any suggestion of concern by my consultant peers or anyone else over the quality of my professional work . . . or my care for patients.'

'Ahem . . . There was the issue of you being about to operate . . . umm . . . "scrubbed up" is, I believe the term that you surgeons would use . . . and then finding that you were not in a fit state to proceed.'

'You make it sound as if I were drunk.'

'Not a bit. Not a bit . . . Just not able to continue your work in a responsible manner.'

'I made the decision myself . . . er . . . not to proceed with the planned operating list.'

'Indeed – and caused concern in other members of the surgical team.'

'Ah . . . That's it. – A whistleblower.'

'Ahem . . . People are concerned – correctly concerned – that no harm . . . avoidable harm . . . should come to patients.'

'But I'm fine now . . . I've been into a theatre and I had none of the previous symptoms, no traumatic flashbacks.'

'Yes . . . I heard about that . . . Do you think it wise, Mrs Finch, that impaired physicians should be the arbiters of their own fitness to practice?'

'No – obviously not . . . But it was I who made the judgement not to proceed.'

'Yes indeed, but who's to say that – in a distressed state – you might make a different judgement some other time?'

'I understand that – but I'm not distressed now.'

'I have to say, Mrs Finch, that my professional assessment

at this very minute is than you are stressed . . . Ahem . . . I would not consider you currently to be in a fit . . . er . . . emotional state to undertake clinical responsibilities . . . er . . . of any kind.'

'That's only because I can see my whole professional future collapsing around my ears – when I've done nothing wrong . . . I'm the victim.'

'I am well aware of that, Mrs Finch, and I have expressed . . . er . . . in writing . . . my understanding and sympathy for you . . . And I mean that in all sincerity.'

'But you haven't expressed any interest in how I am now . . . emotionally.'

'I make my own observation.'

'Before I came here to see you I was in great shape.'

'I have no reason to question that statement . . . except that it is not germane to the issue in question – your fitness to practice as a consultant surgeon, with all the stressful demands that entails.'

'Aren't you interested in finding out more about the treatment that helped me? Are you going to ask for a report from the counsellor?'

'Forgive me, Mrs Finch . . . As you will understand, I'm a busy man . . . Here's the prescription for the same antidepressant as last time. Make an appointment to see me again in one month and we'll check the blood levels. In the meantime, please confer with my secretary to re-establish the CBT . . . We'll soon have you back where you belong.'

o O o

Part 4

It's such a difficult decision – hardest in my life – knowing what to do now . . . How can I think of *not* being a doctor? – *I am* a doctor. – But what else could I do? . . . to keep my mind alive? Would looking after Roddy be enough? I dunno . . . And what if we run out of money? . . .

* * *

'If the medico-political situation in the UK gets hot – with politicians, bureaucrats and the medical establishment ordering doctors about even more – we could always try our hands in America. I'm still on the staff at Columbia . . . and you could come with me . . . er . . . in some capacity.'

'Concubine?'

'Sounds good to me.'

'And to me . . . That might be a longer-term plan. – Going to America – but I need to stay here to finish my pre-registration jobs . . . and stay in touch with my parents – to support them, if they need me.'

'And where do I . . .? . . . umm . . . It's difficult to find the right word.'

'Wherever – with your concubine.'

* * *

'It's not possible to be a consultant in a teaching hospital and have no students . . . I accept that . . . I've handed in my resignation. – It was demanded – more or less.'

'Who by, Sir? . . . The student union?'

'Their boycott began the pressure . . . but it built up very rapidly – developed a momentum of its own.'

'Yes . . . I saw the online petition. – An online lynch mob.'

'They see themselves as being like *WikiLeaks* and those masked crusaders, *Anonymous*. But the Establishment's on their side . . . That's what I can't fight.'

'Won't it blow over? . . . in time?'

'No . . . It's even becoming a party political issue . . . I mean "Arthur Arbuthnot" isn't exactly a common name in council estates.'

'Probably not . . . but I know you haven't got a prejudiced bone in your body – or prejudiced thought in your head.'

'But I can't fight perceptions . . . I can survive being called a "Tory toff" . . . It was the personal threats to my family that put the nail in my professional coffin . . . although I could see it all coming – right from the start.'

'How?'

'I was a student activist myself . . . in my time.'

'Oh . . . It's grossly unfair, Sir.'

'Life *is* unfair, Phoebe . . . You know that.'

'Yes, Sir . . . I do . . . You taught me that – and I've learned it at home.'

'You've learned well . . . You're a good doctor.'

'If you'll allow me to say so, Sir, you are as well – and a good man.'

'Thank you, Phoebe . . . But there'll be another good man – or woman – to take my place . . . You'll see.'

* * *

'Poor love ... Poor Lizzie. I'm so angry – on your behalf – with these people.'

'Thank you. It's lovely having your understanding.'

'What else would I do? ... Of course you have my understanding and support. But they don't seem to have any sympathy for you at all ... It's as if you were the cause of all this trouble, rather than the victim.'

'From the stories I read in the newspapers, rape victims sometimes get abused again – verbally, emotionally, in court – by defence lawyers ... And then there's all this stuff about the so-called "human rights" of out-and-out criminals.'

'Yes ... The law does appear at times to be "a ass, a idiot" but it has to go by the rules. – So does the medical profession.'

'Ha! – So you and I get let down by our own professions and also by each other's.'

'Oh I don't know ... You've been doubly clobbered but nobody's let me down ... yet.'

'The lawyers who advise the medical insurance companies?'

'Just doing their job.'

'You didn't see it that way at the time the insurance people refused to pay.'

'Yes I did. – But I didn't like it ... And in your case the consultant psychiatrist's just doing his job ... And the GMC is doing its.'

'But I think he's letting me down – and the GMC's letting me down ... They're all doing their jobs I s'pose ... But they're all of them protecting themselves rather than caring for me.'

'Can't let the heart rule the head.'

'Tell that to Phoebe! . . . and I thought you were on my side . . . really supportive.'

'I am . . . same as you might be for a patient – but you still have to operate on her . . . cut her open.'

'That's different . . . That's technical . . . professional detachment . . . I'm being cut open emotionally by the psychiatrist and the GMC. – They should be helping me . . . emotionally.'

'They think they are.'

'Funny way of showing it.'

'In court I have to present evidence . . . It's the judge's function to give an opinion.'

'So?'

'I have to be dispassionate – in court but not at home. – And y'know what my clients tell me when I explain that I really am defending them, presenting the case with the best chance of success?'

'No . . . What?'

'"Funny way of showing it".'

'Oh . . . Buggrit.'

* * *

'This rehab we're in seems to work ok . . . but nothing like Hazelden of course.'

'That's an unfair comparison . . . You told me Hazelden's been going for fifty years longer than this place.'

'Fair enough – but at least this rehab exists right here in the UK . . . so people who really are interested in finding out more about Minnesota Method ideas don't have to flog all the way over to America nowadays.'

'And how many people – doctors and counsellors – d'you imagine are interested?'

'Lots . . . They just don't know about it . . . umm . . . Twelve Step rehab.'

'Everyone knows about the Betty Ford . . . Even I knew about that – and I don't have a problem with addiction. My guess is most of them – the doctors and counsellors – don't *want* to know about Twelve Step ideas.'

'Why not?'

'They'd have to change too many of their existing ideas . . . And the God bit.'

'There isn't a "God bit".'

'You know that – and I know it now . . . from working here . . . but they don't.'

'Why not?'

'It's laziness really – and lack of any fundamental self-esteem on the quality of their own minds. – They're clever and they know lots of things but they may get stuck in one particular mind-set and hang onto it like grim death.'

'Ha! What they're doing in the NHS – in their treatment of mental illness – particularly addiction – *is* "grim death" . . . I've experienced it in the Mental Health Unit. Remember?'

'Yes of course I do . . . Horrid for you.'

'But why don't they want to do something better?'

'Precious gave me the answer to that. – Something The Phebe said he told her – It's very difficult to take in a new idea until you make room for it by taking out an old one.'

'But that's all the fun.'

'For you and me – but maybe not for them.'

'But why not, for God's sake?'

'Too threatening . . . mmm . . . There are lots of ideas in *Atlas Shrugged* . . . How are you getting on with it?'

'Very well . . . I've just read Francisco's speech about people's attitude to money being a reflection of their personal attitudes . . . on the value they put on their own and other people's lives

... Staggering! – And absolutely right. – It rings true with my experience in the City . . . Ha! – experience of the wrong kind.'

'And what d'you remember of the response of the people who heard Francisco?'

'They were shocked by it.'

'Did that surprise you?'

'No. – It's what I would've expected . . . generally . . . from people who don't earn their livings in the private sector.'

'So it wasn't too difficult to take on those ideas? . . . for you as someone working in the private sector – even now, not just previously in the City?'

'No – but what I've realised is that some people in the private sector – even in the City . . . Ha! – p'raps especially in the City – cheat and steal . . . They've betrayed capitalism as an ideal.'

'Yes, they certainly have . . . What Francisco emphasised is that money is an honest tool of exchange . . . to give value for value. That's a moral principle. So is the belief that man's mind is the provider of all goods and all wealth . . . And we ourselves are the owners of our own minds . . . and our labour.'

'Wow! You really have studied it . . . that speech.'

'Yes. I want to make sure that the ideas I put into my head really are better than those I had before . . . That's why I'm on strike. I own my mind. I own my work. I own my time.'

'Is that really why you're on strike? . . . You're not just ducking out of taking responsibility?'

'I want to do something special . . . So I have to make sure I've got my ideas sorted out first of all.'

'How long will that take?'

'Ayn Rand took twelve years to write *Atlas Shrugged*".'

'Are you going to take that long? . . . twelve years?'

'No. She's done the basic work on the subject . . . I have to see where it applies in my life.'

'In this rehab?'

'Anywhere . . . in healthcare and welfare systems, same as anywhere else . . . P'raps *particularly* in healthcare and welfare.'

'Why?'

'Because that's where politicians make their unachievable promises and then gain power over an unthinking electorate . . . and all the rest of us. They have to be stopped – not with guns but with better ideas.'

'Hmm . . . You're as bad as my father. – As I said earlier, he's always trying to get me to read more books.'

'Well that's where you find ideas . . . and then you create some of your own . . . and make a difference.'

* * *

So this is it . . . Backed up by me friends in the Club but losing out in me professional work . . . Certainly know who me friends are! Got to support Lizzie as best I can. – What a performance those medical authorities make of all this! . . . Gotta think it through, talk it through . . . like a case. – Same principle. – And fer me? fer my problem? . . . God knows. – Ha! – He probably does . . .

* * *

'I need to introduce myself formally to you, Dr Finch. I am Dr Sadiq Patel, locum consultant geriatrician. I shall be covering the work previously done by Dr . . . er . . . Dr Arbuthnot . . . From now on you will be answerable to me . . . I hear from my niece, Miss Amin, that you gave some sort of evidence in support of Dr Arbuthnot.'

'Yes, Dr Patel, I did. – I gave an account of what I heard . . . and observed.'

'And precisely what did you observe, Dr Finch?'

'That he meant no offence whatever.'

'That doesn't fit with the findings, the outcome.'

'No.'

'Do you have any thoughts on that, Dr Finch? . . . I consider that it's important for us to see eye-to-eye on this issue – right from the start. – Don't you?'

'Yes, Dr Patel . . . That's my only thought right now.'

'Good . . . Good . . . What benefit do you hope to gain from working on my firm?'

'To learn whatever I can.'

'"Dr Patel".'

'Dr Patel.'

'I believe it's very important to pay proper respect . . . Don't you, Dr Finch?

'Yes, Dr Patel.'

'And what branch of the profession do you hope to enter . . . er . . . if and when you are admitted to the Medical Register?'

'I hope, Dr Patel, to become a GP.'

'GPs are social workers with prescription pads . . . Don't you consider that the position of Foundation Year One doctor in a teaching hospital – a very distinguished position – is . . . ah . . . rather wasted on someone who wishes to enter . . . ah . . . general medical practice?'

'No, Dr Patel, I consider myself honoured to be on this firm . . . I like the patients and I enjoy the work. I'm very stimulated by it – clinically and personally – and I shall consider myself honoured to be a GP.'

'Yes . . . Yes . . . I understand that it pays very well nowadays . . . er . . . I shall of course expect you to cancel whatever arrangements you may have made for your holidays over the next two weeks before your four month contract with this hospital expires and you start your next appointment elsewhere ... I appreciate that this may be some minor inconvenience for you but I'm sure you will consider it a privilege to continue in your current post for this time of transition. It would be such a shame – would it not? – for you to leave ... er ... desert your first hospital staff position ... following the unfortunate circumstances caused as a result of the ... er ... betrayal by Dr Arbuthnot.'

o O o

'Hello, little one ... Yes. – S'me ... How are you? ... Oh ... That's tricky – changing chiefs in mid job ... A locum? Well, you know my feelings on that subject ... Anyway, I was calling you to suggest that we all meet up here for supper some time ... Yes, when you and Precious can both make it ... All right ... Yes, of course ... Thought we might invite James at the same time. – Dad tells me he's got a laundry girl in tow ... No, of course I wouldn't – and I'll make sure Dad doesn't. Aaaargh! – That man of mine! ... Yes, if you let me know what suits the two of you – give me some dates – I'll call James ... umm ... Is there anything Precious doesn't eat? ... He eats absolutely everything? ... Oh yes, silly me, he would – wouldn't he? ... He's American. – Brought up on hamburgers probably ... Oh. Sorry. – Just my little joke ... Fine. Fine. – *Boeuf en croute* it is.'

* * *

'I was thinking of going on a course sometime on addiction psychology.'

273

'To teach or to learn?'

'Ha! . . . To get a Master's.'

'And precisely what would a Master's be for?'

'What for? . . . Surely you know the answer to that? – To get letters after my name, to show I'm the real business, that I've had proper training.'

'And to bore yourself rigid with statistics, to get yourself further away from actually helping patients. To get a piece of paper – a certificate – that employers, health authorities and government inspectors can hide behind.'

'Why would they want to do that?'

'In case something goes wrong . . . If you make a mistake they won't get the blame . . . They can point to your certificate and say, "I made all the right checks . . . It's nothing to do with me.'

'Oh . . . That's dreadful. – I want to learn how to look after patients.'

'That's not the first priority of bureaucrats in any health-care and welfare system.'

'What is?'

'Not to get dropped on from a great height.'

'And what's the motive of the professors who run the courses?'

'Same as in any university – to reproduce themselves.'

'Making their chairs into beds?'

'That as well.'

'Huh?'

'Primarily they want to ensure the continuity of high table . . . They take on staff who are like them, share their values and ideas.'

'What's wrong with that?'

'The inertia.'

'The what?'

'Inertia . . . umm . . . stuckness, resistance to any new ideas or new ways of doing things.'

* * *

Got to look after me wife. That's m'number one priority . . . If she can't work as a doctor, what can she do? And how can I support her – personally If not financially – in whatever she decides to do? . . . And if she does stay on as a doctor, how can I care for her – in whatever way I can – when things are difficult for her, as they're bound to be? . . . The plain fact is I just do not know . . . And not in the best of shape meself . . . Dammit . . .

* * *

'James? – Your mother . . . Feeling good. – Thank you for asking. – Very good of you . . . Father and I were thinking it'd be nice to have a family get-together . . . No. Not charades. – Supper for six . . . Precious for one – We've heard quite a bit about him – certainly a great improvement on the last one – but we've never met him . . . Yes. – And your . . . er . . . squeeze, is it? . . . Oh, it's not . . . er . . . Sorry about that . . . to make up the numbers – and if you'd like that . . . And if she'd like it, of course . . . That's good . . . Yes, do ask her. – And we want to catch up on all your news . . . Fascinating!'

* * *

Has to happen some time . . . Gotta be paraded – like a cheer leader. – Yes, that's it . . . Twirling pom-poms between the acts of Phoebe's life . . . Ha! I guess I'm dead lucky to be in the game at all! . . .

* * *

'Students, you're here to learn. – I'm here to teach you . . . Who clerked this patient?'

'I did, Dr Patel . . . Smith.'

'Yes, Mr Smith . . . And what were your clinical findings?'

'A right-sided hemiparesis.'

'Caused by?'

'The scan showed a subarachnoid haemorrhage.'

'Tell me six possible presentations of subarachnoid haemorrhage.'

'Umm . . . I don't know them, Sir.'

'Come along, Mr Smith . . . You have to know these things . . . with your final examinations coming soon . . . er . . . Dr Finch?'

'Yes, Dr Patel?'

'Make sure he knows them by next week, will you?'

'Yes, Dr Patel.'

o O o

'That was delicious . . . The *Boeuf en croute* was worthy of the Waldorf Astoria – with US prime provided by Gallagher's.'

'Thank you, Precious . . . James and I were in New York fairly recently – seeing the nine-eleven memorial and the Frick – but we didn't have time to try any restaurants other than the Carnegie Deli, which was great fun . . . Incredible salt beef sandwiches – impossibly big.'

'Yes . . . I remember – near Carnegie Hall . . . I've been to some jazz gigs there . . . in the Hall.'

'On the rare occasions I've been to Manhattan – on a case

– I've always been surprised how good the food is . . . I always assumed it's Big Macs with processed cheese and fries – or nothing.'

'It's the cosmopolitan influence in a capital city . . . Same for Paris . . . and London.'

'Yes . . . Precious and I have been exploring the influence of the French chefs in London.'

'Yeah – fabulous! . . . But Byron's hamburgers are pretty damn good – especially with crispy onion bits and deep-fried onions on the side.'

'AchAhem.'

'Our chef's English – at the Club – and he's pretty damn good too.'

'And the celebrity chefs on TV make it look good – and so easy . . . Not that I can afford that sort of meal nowadays – after moving from commodities to commodes.'

'Ha! – Don't you believe him, Mrs Finch . . . We don't have commodes in the rehab. It's quite sophisticated really – including the kitchen . . . although the staff have to bring our own sandwiches.'

'That's a bit mean, isn't it? . . . of the management?'

'You can't talk, Phebe . . . You told me the food in the doctors' restaurant is vile.'

'You expect that in NHS hospitals . . . It goes with the territory. But the one time I was in a private unit the food w–
. . . – Just visiting a friend – er . . . was amazing but the nurses wouldn't have noticed. – All foreign.'

'Same with us . . . How about in America, in Columbia?'

'Fine, just fine – but not like tonight.'

'You charmer, you . . . I must say – our daughter's made a very good choice this time.'

'D'you have to say that, Dad? . . . Now Precious will be wondering who else I've dragged round here.'

'I wasn't dragged.'

'And I wasn't . . . I'm delighted to be here.'

'Oh! . . . Are we an item then?'

'Must you, Phebe? . . . There are limits to brotherly tolerance.'

'Payback time, kid, for all the . . .'

'Ahem, I was wondering . . . er . . . Precious, what the medico-legal situation is in the States . . . Phoebe may have told you about the problems m'wife's been having . . .'

'Yes, she did . . . umm . . . If I may say so, Mrs Finch . . .'

'Do call me Lizzie.'

'Er . . . Lizzie . . . You've had a dreadful time.'

'Yes . . . James was telling me too . . . Dreadful.'

'Well not much. – I couldn't say much . . . I don't know much.'

'Well it's all over now, anyway.'

'Not the medico-legal side, it isn't . . . No idea where it might finish up . . . eventually.'

'You're so pessimistic, dear . . . I'm in good shape.'

'You certainly seem it, Mother.'

'I am.'

'Ahem . . . I was asking Precious about the medico-legal situation in America – not about medical things as such.'

'It all comes down to the same thing really . . . Doesn't it? . . . I mean some idiot locum cocks things up and the hospital treats Mum worse than they treat him – 'sfar as we know.'

'I shall certainly want to know – in full . . . in due course.'

'Must you talk over me like this? – I feel great . . . It'll all sort out.'

'To answer your question . . . er . . . Roddy, we certainly are a litigious society. Stateside . . . Our lawyers would have a field day on your case . . . er . . . Lizzie.'

'I'm sure my dad wouldn't let it go, either.'

'Gosh . . . I've never asked you . . . what sort of legal work does he do?'

'Litigation.'

'Oh.'

'Oh.'

'Oh.'

'Oh.'

'Oh.'

* * *

'I don't know that I can do this – working as an assistant – after so many years as a consultant running my own show . . . It was ghastly, humiliating.'

'You poor love.'

'It was good to be back at work . . . and meet the team again – although half of them have changed already – but it's very unpleasant . . . I feel I'm being watched, scrutinised, all the time . . . like an accident waiting to happen.'

'I'd go nuts working as a pupil again . . . Though I s'pose every time I'm in front of a judge – Ha! . . . Those were the days! - I'm being assessed on whether I know me stuff.'

'Well we have to get revalidated with the GMC periodically – making sure we're up to scratch.'

'Don't you mean "up to date"?'

'Both really . . . Up to date with all the research stuff and with the latest resuscitation techniques. – I don't mind that at all.'

'What *do* you mind?'

'The back-scratching . . . Giving the assessors – and the GMC – credibility they don't deserve . . . The doctors who do the assessments – and who sit on councils and committees here, there and everywhere – are place men and women . . .

People who have time on their hands because they haven't got sufficient patients to keep themselves busy.'

'And the GMC?'

'Self-important nobodies.'

'That's a bit severe . . . although I'd probably say the same for the Bar Council.'

'Really? . . . How does that work?'

'There are five non-lawyers and four barristers on the tribunal panel that hears disciplinary cases. Usually two of the non-lawyers and one barrister from the panel actually hear the complaint . . . The non-lawyers come from all sorts of back-grounds – trade unions, business, voluntary organisations.'

'Yes . . . The Great and the Good – going from one well paid sinecure to another . . .The GMC works on similar lines – transparency, accountability . . . that sort of thing . . . judged by Joe Public.'

'It goes even further with us. – The Lord Chancellor – the top legal officer in the land – is a layman.'

'Ha! – The lunatics are already running the asylum! . . . all in the name of answerability . . . Huh! – But to whom? . . . What chance for us nowadays? . . . either of us? – The foot-soldiers – the "Poor Bloody Infantry"?'

* * *

'No . . . Don't ask me what sort of a time I had on the day release course – from the rehab – today.'

'What sort of a time did you have on the course?'

'Hey! – What's your game?'

'I'm playing your game . . . Check your books on TA and Gestalt. – You wouldn't have drawn my attention to it if you really didn't want me to ask. Why else would you bring it into the foreground? But what did you learn?'

'Sweet FA . . . Absolutely nothing.'

'Okay . . . Try it the other way round . . . What were they trying to teach you?'

'Methadone maintenance, safe sex, harm minimisation and lifestyle choice.'

'Stuff you know already?'

'Stuff that has nothing whatever to do with helping addicts to get well . . . to see a beautiful future for themselves – like mine.'

'They're not going to have a beautiful future if they're dead.'

'They might just as well be dead – if that's the best "training" there is on offer . . . I want them to have a life that's totally drug free – no alcohol, no drugs, no mood-altering prescription drugs . . . Nothing that plays into their addictive nature.'

'How can the course organisers justify teaching this stuff?'

'Because it's the backbone of all NHS treatment for addicts. – Your sister would know that. – Their approach all comes down to believing in "lifestyle choice" – and not believing that addiction is an illness . . . umm . . . Not seeing that people like me are accountable for our behaviour towards other people but not responsible for being addicts in the first place.'

'How d'you split that?'

'I'd give people the full consequences of all their actions . . . That would've stopped me dead in my tracks ages ago . . . But I kept being bailed out – by father in particular but also by the whole system. – A and E and everything . . . But they say you can't turn people away from A and E or stop their benefits.'

'And what d'you say?'

'Of course you can . . . if it saves lives.'

'Just one death and litigation lawyers – like my dad – would be in clover.'

'But more people die from overdoses of methadone than ever died on heroin. – Addicts sell their scrips or spit their prescribed methadone into a bottle and sell that.'

'Yes, I know . . . Yuck! . . . Some people prefer methadone to heroin – and it's fearfully difficult to get off it . . . Seems to me to be more addictive than heroin.'

'It's a funny thing . . . Well, not at all funny really . . . Some doctors still believe cocaine isn't an addictive drug because it has no immediate withdrawal effects . . . And very few doctors indeed believe antidepressants are addictive – because patients usually don't increase the dose or crave for more . . . until the withdrawal effects kick in two weeks after stopping them. – And then the doctors misdiagnose the symptoms – and say they prove that the patients needed the drugs in the first place . . . Jesus wept! It makes me so angry.'

'You make yourself angry.'

'And so I fucking well should!'

'James, James . . . Listen to me . . . If you're going to work in this field, you can't afford to have a hissy fit, a meltdown, like this every time something upsets you . . . You'll burn out in no time.'

'Well fuck that! . . . and fuck you too!'

* * *

'That was a lovely evening . . . We can be proud of ourselves for producing two lovely children – and for them making such sensible choices in . . . umm . . . er . . . What word is there? – other than "partners"?'

'I can think of several – but I doubt you'd approve of them.'

'Thank you, Roddy. Thank you . . . It's interesting, though,

– Isn't it? – that we tend to follow where America leads – in so many things.'

'Such as?'

'Previous permissiveness and now restraint . . . The youngsters of today have much more settled heads on their shoulders than the last generation.'

'Precious isn't a "youngster" – other than in comparison with us, of course.'

'Well he seems to be an exception in his generation – a thoroughly decent and moral man.'

'And a perfect match – Ah! There's the right word – for Phoebe.'

'You're calling Phoebe a "match"? . . . What type of match? – "Safety"?

'Well yes . . . nowadays . . . That's the effect Precious is having on her.'

'Isn't it just the effect of moving out of her student days and into real life?'

'The "baby-boomers" – in America – never grew up . . . Clinton, Woody Allen, Warren Beatty – old goats the lot of 'em.'

'I'm not sure that those three are "baby boomers" . . . Woody Allen's ageless . . . and I'm not sure he would classify as an "old goat".'

'Mia Farrow wouldn't agree. – Still trying to nail him. – But he wears well . . . Comes from having a young wife.'

'I don't want to get into that territory about him. Not one bit.'

'Well I certainly wouldn't want to use Clinton or Beatty as role models . . . umm . . . Lizzie?'

'Mmm?'

'How on earth did we get onto this subject?'

'I said "match" was a good word in place of "partner" –

and you went off on a tangent.'

'No I didn't . . . I can't be expected to understand an inference like that . . . I'm not trained to think your way. – I have to spell it all out in front of a judge and jury . . . Anyway, you can't call Phoebe and Precious "matchers" . . . It doesn't fly.'

'What doesn't?'

'The word.'

'Which word?'

'"Matcher".'

'Fly where?'

'Ahem . . . Oh Gawd."

'Aaaaaargh . . . umm . . . Roddy?'

'Mmm?'

'We're not getting past it, are we? . . . losing the thread like that.'

'Lot on our minds, I s'pect.'

'Hmm . . . Well I've got something on my mind . . . before the antidepressants knock me off.'

'Oh . . . umm . . .'

'Come on, Roddy . . . Don't leave a girl hanging around . . . Pull your silk socks up.'

'Yes . . . before I get too . . . umm . . .'

'Get on with it, man . . . No time like the present.'

'S'pose so . . . er . . . We're not dead yet.'

'Move your sweet ass . . . And that isn't an inference, by the way . . . It's a statement, a command.'

'Oh . . . umm . . . Yes . . . umm . . . No . . . umm . . . Yes, of course.'

* * *

'Mr Jones?'

'Smith, Sir.'

'Dr Patel.'

'Smith, Dr Patel.'

'"Sir" might be confused with an honour – a knighthood
– In some unworthy people.'

'Yes, Dr Patel.'

'In a previous teaching round – an important occasion
when you are so close to your final examinations – I asked Dr
Finch to tell you about six possible presentations of a subarachnoid haemorrhage . . . Ahem . . . Did she do so?'

'Yes, Dr Patel.'

'And what are they?'

'I . . . er . . . I don't remember, Dr Patel.'

'I see . . . Clearly Dr Finch did not teach you well enough
. . . When it comes to preparation for the viva-voce part of
your clinical assessments, the personal interview in your
final examination. You have to see that it's a very important
component of the total number of marks awarded. If I were to
be one of the examiners and you gave me that answer, I would
have to fail you . . . You understand that?'

'Yes, Dr Patel.'

'And you would know who to blame for that . . . er . . .
debacle . . . Would you not?'

'Myself, Dr Patel.'

'I think not . . . er . . . only in part. Dr Finch, I need to make
it totally clear to you that I consider the primary function of a
teaching hospital is to teach . . . This should be obvious
– tautologous.'

'Yes, Dr Patel.'

'We have to prepare the students for a lifetime of clinical
responsibility.'

'Yes, Dr Patel.'

'And what do you believe to be the epitome of clinical
responsibility? . . . where it is seen in its highest

attainment?'

'When patients feel they have been well cared for, clinically and personally.'

'I need to correct you on this, Dr Finch . . . In a teaching hospital, patients are clinical material – for research and training purposes. They should be seen as our opportunity to push back the frontiers of medicine.'

'Yes, Dr Patel.'

'I would not want us to be at cross purposes on this . . . I know that you have intimated that . . . er . . . life as a general medical practitioner would satisfy you.'

'Yes, Dr Patel.'

'And what do you see as the function of a general medical practitioner?'

'To care for patients in their own community, to provide early diagnosis of significant clinical conditions and to treat – as considerately as possible – the emotional problems of today so they don't become the physical problems of tomorrow.'

'That's all very esoteric, Dr Finch.'

'Yes, Dr Patel.'

'It is not adequate to respond, '"Yes, Dr Patel" in that manner. Automatically. You need to understand the meaning of the word "esoteric" . . . and what is it, Dr Finch?'

'Umm . . . "airy-fairy".'

'Do you imagine that the term "airy fairy" appears in the Oxford English Dictionary as the proper meaning of the word "esoteric"?'

'No, Dr Patel.'

'But you consider it appropriate to give me – your consultant – such a trivial definition?'

'Er . . . No, Dr Patel.'

'Then why did you do it? '

'It was the first definition – a colloquial expression – that came into my head.'

'Yes . . . clearly – as it would for a doctor whose sights are set no higher than to be a . . . er . . . GP.'

'Yes, Dr Patel.'

'The function of a GP is to be a sorting office . . . dealing with minor ailments and social problems so that they are distinct from the important clinical conditions that must be referred to consultant specialists . . . That should be obvious . . . Isn't it?'

'Yes, Dr Patel.'

* * *

Tripped again – even with me stick . . . Didn't hurt meself – but I feel so old . . . Old people have falls . . . Come on, Roddy, sort yerself out. Old people lose their minds. Mine's still sharp as a tack . . . Hmm . . . S'one good thing about this illness . . .

* * *

'Dr Patel told me today that the function of a GP is to deal with minor issues and be a sorting office for consultant specialists.'

'Ha! – He's not unique . . . Often the great men – and women – go further in saying that GPs should know precisely which specialist is particularly interested in which sub-specialty . . . It's up to the GP to read all their websites.'

'Yeah – as if they haven't got anything else to do . . . The GPs I mean.'

'I did a survey once – as part of my research for the lecture course – on the number of specialists and hospitals used by one group practice in central London in a year . . . They couldn't possibly know all the specialists in all the eighteen hospitals they used. Very often it was the patients who said where they wanted to go. They may have been there before and then moved home . . . or had a recommendation from a friend . . . Administrators and accountants may not like that but patients do.'

'Yes . . . and the specialists – in the conjoint clinical meetings in the hospital – also get a bit grandiose when they tell us about things most of us will rarely see in the rest of our clinical lives . . . if ever. – They pride themselves on their knowledge of minutiae.'

'Someone has to know that stuff . . . The most important thing for patients is to be told precisely what they've got and then be treated appropriately for it . . . After all, the only diagnosis they're interested in is their own.'

'That's what I saw in America on my two week stint . . . a fully computerised medical record used as an active resource for the patient as well as the doctors and staff . . . The patients carry a disc of their own medical records wherever they go. – That certainly sorts out any communication problems.'

'Quite right.'

'But here, in the UK, the records may be just a dumping ground . . . Garbage in, garbage out.'

'That's true for any computerised system . . . Don't I know it! . . . I spend my life trying to get worthwhile research data out of worthless records . . . Medical records have been hijacked by administrators – and by the Department of Health – for the limited number of things that interest them . . . Cost mainly.'

'And then the data's sold on – or unofficially leaked – to private medical insurance companies . . . in return for favours of one kind or another. It's also shared with social workers – non-medical people – and probably then with schools and the police and God knows who else.'

'Yes . . . It's worrying . . . the loss of confidentiality.'

'But I've just remembered something else I was told in America . . . Professor Lawrence Weed said – evidently – that patients have to choose between confidentiality and accurate medical care.'

'Yes, like it or not, that's true.'

'I *don't* like it . . . Patients trust individual doctors – not health authorities or the whole stupid system.'

'A lock can be put on access.'

'Yeah . . . like children being locked out of porn on their home computers . . . What a success that's been! – Children are far more computer savvy than their parents – Ha! – This would be laughable if it weren't so serious . . . Anyway, if hackers can get into the CIA they can certainly get into medical computers.'

'The CIA were hacked from the inside . . . by the hero – or traitor – Snowden . . . and then published on *Wikileaks* by Assange – another hero or traitor.'

'But nobody's interested in my medical records . . . or the records of the vast majority of people.'

'You bet your sweet life they are.'

'Who are?'

'The drug companies, the private insurance companies . . . Same as the supermarkets want to know what's in your fridge, bathroom and wardrobe.'

'My secrets are trivial – except for some things I'd rather forget – and my purchases are mundane.'

'But mundane purchases every week add up to a great deal . . . and we all have things we'd rather forget – or didn't want blasted on the net . . . Sometimes big things . . . in some people . . . They might be blackmailed on the threat of publication . . . sometimes.'

'Yes . . . And *Hacked Off* want the *Leveson Report*

implemented in full . . . to stop journalists prying into private lives.'

'At the expense of freedom of the press . . . It's heroes or traitors again . . . There's as much divisiveness here as in America . . . We're severely divided societies.'

'My mum says we always were . . . but Dad says he's never known anything like it . . . The run up to the general election's giving him a new lease of life.'

'Well that's one good thing . . . but I'm very disturbed about the possible result – whichever way it goes.'

'Maybe I've got you wrong – in the way I thought you'd vote – if you have a vote, which I guess you don't.'

'No . . . Not here . . . My vote's in the States . . . But I can cast my vote here in the UK – or wherever I am in the world – for American elections.'

'That's good . . . for democracy. – Ha! – Come to think of it . . . I'm not sure which way *I'll* vote. There's only one thing I really am convinced about – politically.'

'What's that?'

'We can hear the ice cracking underneath our society . . . Huh! . . . Even Dr Patel might agree with that . . . for reasons of his own.'

'Some people want it to crack . . . right now . . . here and in America . . . without any idea of what they're destroying – or what they want to put in its place . . . They just talk or shout or write in slogans.'

'Oh.'

'Oh what?'

'Sounds like me . . . before I met you – and started to think for myself.'

'That's good.'

'But I think I know how you would vote.'

'Do you now? . . . I'm a Libertarian.'

'Huh? We don't have that – Libertari-whatsit – over here.'

'It's never really taken off in America. We have the same divisions – big government or small government – as there are over here. But few people – maybe progressively fewer – are interested in minimal government. The ice is cracking on both sides of the Atlantic – and on both sides of the political divide.'

'Yes. I'm beginning to see what worried you – in Ayn Rand's warning ... We could finish up with a totalitarian state either way – Left or Right.'

* * *

'Oh hello, Judith ... Wasn't expecting you home.'

'Why not? ... I pop in every so often – same as you do – just to see Mum and Dad.'

'Well I'm glad to see you ... I ... er ... wanted to run something past you.'

'Yes?'

'I've got a new man ... er ... potential one.'

'They always are with you.'

'Take me seriously for a bit ... I can't be your "little sister" indefinitely ... He has a problem ...'

'Bisexual?'

'Huh? ... You've been having too many Freud eggs for breakfast ... always having sex on your mind,'

'And why not?'

'Because that isn't his problem ... 'sfar as I know.'

'Huh? ... You've got a new man and you don't know his sexuality? ... Careful, sister ... He might be one of us ... not come out yet.'

'Why does every conversation I have with you always finish up talking about gay and lesbian stuff? ... and this conversation hasn't even begun.'

'They're important issues to me ... should be to everyone.'

'Why? ... er No ... No – Don't answer that.'

'Why not?'

'We'd never get round to talking about what I want to talk about.'

'Which is . . .?'

'He's an addict.'

'Get rid of him.'

'Hang about . . . He's in recovery.'

'He's what?'

'He doesn't use drugs – or alcohol – any more.'

'Then he's not an addict.'

'Oh ... umm ... Anyway ... umm ... What I wanted to ask you was whether an addict who abstains – and goes to AA – can lose it a bit occasionally.'

'Lose what?'

'His judgement, his temper – for no reason other than he's had a bad day.'

'No idea ... Strikes me they're all bad news – addicts, alcoholics – the lot of them.'

'You don't seem to enjoy your work very much.'

'It's a job . . . It pays the rent.'

'Is that all?'

'No ... A fair number of gays and lesbians are addicts of one kind or another . . . I enjoy caring for them . . . Seems to me addiction is their reaction to living in a heterosexual community – since birth.'

'Well gays and lesbians can adopt nowadays ... That should make you happy.'

'It's the children who matter ... giving them an opportunity to grow up in a really loving household. – Even if they're straight. – Give them an understanding of humanity.'

'There was nothing wrong with ours – yours and mine.'

'Nothing wrong? Nothing wrong? – You've got no idea . . . what it's like . . . being a stranger in your own home . . . and in a judgemental – sexist – community like ours.'

'Well I don't think any of this applies to James.'

'Get rid of him – before it's too late. – Addicts can put you into the ground.'

o O o

'Ah . . . Dr Finch . . . Good to meet you again . . . You interviewed very well and you had an excellent reference from Dr Arbuthnot . . . I telephoned him. – We were at medical school together. – He told me he's not

working as a consultant in Care for the Elderly any more . . . and he's not sure what he's going to do next . . . Didn't say why . . . er . . . why not.'

'Politics, I believe.'

'Oh . . . I understand . . . Gets into everything – one way or another – nowadays.'

'He was an excellent physician and a good man . . . Still is.'

'That was certainly my impression of him . . . all those years ago. I s'pose none of us changes all that much . . . once the die is cast –

medicine, surgery, general practice, whatever . . . We each develop the mind-set of our particular discipline but the clinical and personal attitudes go with the individual . . . So who took over from him?'

'A locum . . . Dr Patel.'

'There's no need to call me "Dr Patel" . . . "Mukund" is fine.'

'Thank you . . . What I mean is *his* name is Dr Patel.'

'Oh . . . My mistake . . . It's the most common family name

in India . . . in Gujarat . . . like Smith in England . . . Patel's also an occupational name originally – landowners, farmers, village leaders – members of the village committee, taking the views of the whole village to the council and resolving problems and implementing ideas.'

'Sounds like the Chinese "barefoot doctors" I learned about in med school.'

'They taught you that? . . . in med school? . . . That's very enlightened – a long way from an ivory tower.'

'Yes I took to the ideas. – And as a future GP, I want to deliver care to people in the community in which they live . . . Get to know the whole family.'

'If they have one . . . This is something we Gujaratis are very committed to – family . . . The indigenous English don't seem to be so keen . . . Why d'you think that is?'

'Politics. Finance. It's not worth it, getting married. – Not on Benefits Street.'

* * *

This can't be right . . . giving a surgeon antidepressants – or anyone. – I need a clear head, not a foggy one . . . I had a clear head after the EMDR. Now my poor brain's in hock to the pharmaceutical companies . . . Got to be sharp . . . They've got it the wrong way round. – The GMC and that wretched man, the psychiatrist. – They think they're being supportive. My God! – They really *believe* that! . . . How can drugging the delicate cells and synapses of the brain, interfering with the endorphins and neurotransmitters – and everything else in that highly refined chemical soup – possibly help? . . . How could it *possibly*? . . . Change one bit and everything else is affected . . . That's what I understand . . . Ha! – I'm no endo-crinologist but 'homeostasis' means 'leave well alone' to me

... The arrogance of mankind knows no bounds in the minds of these people ...

* * *

Come on Roddy, sort it ... Sort it or die ... *Blade Runner* – great film – knew that ... but this is reality ... Gawd awful reality. My reality. My very own reality, dammit ... And I just don't know what to do ... How can I be any use to Lizzie – when she really needs me for once in her life – if I can't function? ... Huh! – Can't even earn me own living. And can't be much support to her ... Ha! How are the mighty fallen! ...

* * *

'I'm so sorry I behaved as badly as I did ... It was totally unprovoked by you and totally foul of me.'

'Yes it was. – And there won't be any more occasions like that if you want any sort of relationship with me ... What on earth got into you?'

'I checked that with my sponsor – my guide in AA – and he said I'd forgotten the warning.'

'What warning?'

'In the *Big Book of AA* ... HALT!'

'Halt what?'

'Stop rushing into behaviour that I'll subsequently regret – as a result of being Hungry, Angry, Lonely or Tired ... and I was all four.'

'Really? – Even lonely? ... when you were with me?'

'No, Soppy, lonely when I was on the day release course – all on my own, with my Twelve Step ideas.'

'Probably best to keep them to yourself ... in that environment.'

'I do – but it makes . . . er . . . I make myself so angry when I hear those people blathering on about ideas that I know don't work . . . They're counter-productive for addicts like me.'

'Would they work for addicts not like you?'

'There are no addicts not like me.'

'That's a bit – very – high-handed of you, James.'

'Umm . . . Yes. – Sorry again. – Grandiosity . . . We're warned about that as well . . . And there's something else I forgot.'

'What was that?'

'That even the Twelve Steps are only suggestions. It actually says that . . . in the Big Book itself – Chapter five, "How it works".'

'My God. – D'you know it from memory?'

'That bit, yes . . . It's read out in every meeting.'

'Why *every* meeting? – Are you all stupid or something?'

'No, not stupid . . . Well, that as well, I s'pose . . . Many of us are too bright for our own good . . . But we have a natural forgetting mechanism – selectively over our addiction . . . That's why we go to meetings – to remind ourselves that we're addicts . . . see ourselves by seeing each other.'

'I notice you included yourself in the those who are "too bright" . . . That's good. – Not running down your intelligence any more.'

'S'pose not.'

'Well give yourself credit for something you got right . . . Otherwise it's too one-sided. – Beating yourself up . . . That can't be good for you . . . And what were the other things in HALT? – You've done "lonely" and "angry".'

'"Hungry" – I hadn't had supper . . . Too busy nursing my resentments . . . And I was tired . . . All that wasted emotional energy.'

'Seems like there's an awful lot to remember . . . in this Twelve Step business.'

'Yes . . . That's why so many people relapse . . . But many people – doctors specially – think we have it cushy – when we say we have an illness . . . We use the programme as a reminder to ourselves, not an excuse for our behaviour . . . umm . . . I'm sorry again for mine.'

'Yeah well . . . Just don't do it again . . . Oh – by the way – please don't call me "Soppy".'

'Well I noticed you used the word "God".'

'Ha! – Well spotted. – It . . . umm . . . slipped out . . . Just an expression.'

'Ah! – You make mistakes as well!'

'Course I do . . . but I don't dwell on them – like you do on yours – letting them fester.'

'Damn! . . . and here's another mistake I'm making . . . We call it "taking your inventory" – looking at your mistakes – instead of my own.'

'Seems like an awful lot of hard work you have to do . . . in AA . . . Almost an obsession.'

'Yes . . . and there's no improvement at all if all we do is to change an obsession for doing something into an obsession for *not* doing it . . . Easy does it . . . Oh. – That's one of the AA slogans – "Easy does it" – like "One day at a time", "Let go and let God" and all the others.'

'But you're an atheist, like me.'

'Mine isn't a religious god . . . Just "Good Orderly Direction" – or "Group Of Drunks" . . . and the Twelve Steps.'

'Phew! – I get tired just listening to you.'

'It's hard work – recovery. – Hardest thing I've ever done.'

'No wonder – as you say – so many people relapse . . . And no wonder people on psychology training courses are so reluctant to teach all this. – The students would riot.'

'Nah. – Far too placid . . . Not like The Phebe.'

'She was delightful.'

'On her good days – but you're not her brother.'

'Ha! – And you're not my sister.'

* * *

'There's an opera I'd like to see – and take you with me . . . After seeing it at English National Opera a few years ago, I want to see the new production at Covent Garden.'

'What opera? . . . You don't do opera.'

'Yes I do . . . I do anything that's well done . . . Tra la! . . . "*Rise and Fall of the City of Mahagonny*".'

'The what?'

'It's a sardonic parody of life in a capitalist society.'

'Who by?'

'Kurt Weil did the music. – It's good. – Berthold Brecht wrote the libretto.'

'Brecht's a Marxist.'

'That's why we should see it.'

'You want to see something by a Marxist? . . . You know what it'll say . . . It'll be like a Harold Pinter play – without the silences . . . What did the critics say about it?'

'The *Daily Mail* – that bastion of Right-wing prejudice – said we should walk out.'

'Okay . . . We'll go . . . It'll be fun.'

o O o

'How are you coping with the work?'

'Loving it.'

'That's the way ... Dr Arbuthnot said you were an enthusiast.'

'It's strange not having students around – and so few people on the clinical team.'

'Ha! – This is where the *real* work's done . . . Out in the sticks.'

'Yes . . . I can see that . . . experience it. – And I'm learning so much . . . from the patients.'

'Yes . . . If you listen to them – and examine them properly – they pretty well tell you . . . and show you . . . the diagnosis.'

'I imagined ENT would be Ts and As and hearing aids . . . and, of course, the head and neck cancers.'

'Tonsillectomies – with or without adenoidectomies – are rare . . . er . . . should be . . . I remember being taught that in the UK – years ago in the NHS – seven children a year bled to death . . . from an unnecessary operation.'

'What changed? – Antibiotics?'

'Attitudes . . . Specialists – some of us – becoming more aware of people – and not trying to establish individual fiefdoms.'

'But you're a top specialist.'

'I'm a jobbing worker . . . That suits me . . . I told you. – I'm a Gujerati – through and through.'

'But this country is your home now.'

'Yes – and to a large extent my culture . . . umm . . . In America many Gujeratis become doctors . . . Maybe my sort of doctor.'

'I like the sound of that a lot.'

* * *

'I gather you've had some CBT before.'

'Yes . . . er . . . It was helpful.'

'But you discontinued it?'

'Yes. – I had family difficulties . . . Too much on my mind.'

'CBT could've helped you.'

'Me or my family?'

'All of you.'

'I must remember that for the future.'

'And also in the here and now . . . CBT focuses on the here and now . . . We shall not be digging over the past too much – except to hear about your specific trauma . . . Trauma-focussed CBT can be very helpful in resolving post-traumatic stress disorders – PTSD – and phobias.'

'It seems to be a remarkable therapy, helping so many clinical – and personal – conditions.'

'It certainly is . . . There's no real need to use any other therapeutic approach for anything . . . Dr Aaron Beck, who created the Beck

depression inventory, which you can fill in at home and then you and I can go through it together next week . . . Dr Beck also created CBT. What he says about other therapies is that – if they work at all – they must be based on the principles of CBT.'

'What a remarkable man.'

'Yes he is . . . American – still working at ninety three. – But he comes over here sometimes, cooperating with other researchers in applying CBT to psychoses – as well as neuroses . . . After all, they're all thought disorders.'

'That's admirable – having such an open mind.'

'Yes . . . Despite being from the USA, he collaborates with NHS colleagues over here. – Has done since long before ObamaCare came in . . . Clearly he recognised – as Obama did – that the NHS has a great deal to teach America.'

'I'm sure.'

'Well . . . Back to the here and now . . . Do tell me – in your own way – about what you would like to achieve in therapy

. . . what you would expect . . . what you would hope to gain from our collaborative sessions – probably twenty in all . . . CBT is goal-orientated.'

'I want to be able to get back to where I was before . . . running my independent practice . . . before the . . . er . . . unfortunate incident.'

'Yes . . . It must have been very distressing for you . . . Perhaps that's the risk – in the private sector – never knowing what might happen when you're outside the secure protection of the NHS . . . where everyone works together for the common good.'

'Umm . . . I . . . er . . . Yes.'

'Anyway, we won't be spending too much time on that – or on childhood issues, you'll be glad to know.'

'Good.'

'Yes . . . The past is over.'

'Thank God for that.'

'Well I wouldn't say that a deity is a necessary invocation . . . Would you?'

'I . . . er . . . No, of course not . . . umm . . . Just an expression.'

'Yes, I understand . . . It's very important that you see me as a colleague in our journey together . . . I'm right alongside you . . . so that we work on this together . . . always keeping an eye on your goal – *our* common goal.'

'Thank you.'

'What events relate to your particular difficulty?'

'There was only one event . . . the . . . umm . . . what they call "anaesthetic awareness".

'Yes . . . Yes . . . What treatment have you had?'

'I had some EMDR.'

'Ah . . . Not familiar with it myself – no need to be – but I know that NICE recommends it sometimes for PTSD . . . in carefully selected cases presumably . . . Now then . . . Tell me about yourself.'

'There's not much to say really . . . Came from an average middle class family . . .'

'Oh.'

' . . . Always wanted to be a doctor . . . Got into medical school, worked hard – and the rest you know.'

'Just out of interest – in our common quest – why did you leave the NHS?'

'Inadequate resources . . . for the work I was dedicated to doing.'

'Yes . . . Much the same now – particularly with all the cuts.'

'I s'pose so . . . Very difficult for you all.'

'And your home situation now?'

'My husband's a lawyer, my daughter's on her second medical training job – ENT after doing geriatrics – and my son's . . . er . . . working as a care assistant . . . previously he worked as a commodity broker.'

'Very courageous of him . . . to make the jump – and lose the income.'

'Yes . . . We're very proud of him.'

'Any grandchildren?'

'Not yet.'

'It's so problematic nowadays, helping youngsters to get properly paid jobs . . . so they can get on the property ladder – in any form – and start a family.'

'Yes . . . It'll certainly be nice when that happens.'

'Do any aspects of your life – and your background and current problems – interfere with your family life, your work or your social life?'

'Yes they do . . . All of that . . . The . . . umm . . . trauma, the unfortunate incident. – Nothing else. – I need to get back to work . . . As my consultant psychiatrist – such a helpful man

– said, I need to be back where I belong.'

'Any provision for your old age?'

'I'm sure we'll be all right.'

'I imagine . . . Now then . . . Let me tell you how we're going to go about this . . . There are various aspects of CBT that mark it out from other therapies . . . make it more effective . . . I'll go through them with you . . . Do stop me and ask questions at any time.'

'Thank you.'

'CBT differs from other therapies firstly because it's pragmatic – helping to identify and solve specific problems.'

'Ah.'

'It's highly structured, rather than have you talking freely about your life.'

'No need to tell stories?'

'No . . . We'll work together, setting goals for you to achieve and focussing on current problems.'

'That's encouraging.'

'You see, we're concerned primarily with how you think and act *now*, rather than with attempting to resolve past issues.'

'I see.'

'We'll work together . . . I won't be telling you what to do. – I'll work with you to find solutions to your current difficulties.'

'Excellent.'

'Well that's about it for today . . . except for a bit of homework for you . . . There'll always be little projects for you to do between sessions – trying things out in practice. Then, at the beginning of each subsequent session, we'll discuss how you got on . . . It's all very methodical.'

'Good . . . I like that . . . It's like being back at sch . . . er . . . university.'

'Your homework for this week is to see where some of your existing thought processes might get in the way of your progress – and then try out a different thought and observe the results.'

'I'll do that.'

'It's such a pleasure – if I may say so – working with such a willing client on this collaborative venture.'

* * *

It's dreadful – disgusting. – The NHS writes off the prostituting addicts – putting them on methadone for life – whatever short lives they have . . . Hmm . . . like those poor sods I saw in the Mental Health Unit – but protects the punters . . . *They're* the ones who should be brought to book . . . And HIV really is a gay plague – but nobody talks about that. – There's such a strong pro-gay lobby in the Department of Health . . . Wonder why . . .

* * *

'Hey man! That opera was terrific! . . . particularly the sets . . . Brilliant production . . . Didn't agree with a single line of the political stuff.'

'Well that's the whole point of seeing it . . . We might get a new idea from Brecht . . . You never know. – Not much point in seeing only the stuff we know we'll agree with. – No possibility of movement, no innovation unless we stretch our own mental experience.'

'Yeah, that's what I found so incredible in a play I saw in America when I was last there . . . *The Nether* . . . Who would've thought such a thoughtful and imaginative play – and beautifully produced and directed and with an amazing set – could be

built on the subject of sexual abuse of children?'
'Bit strong on your adjectives, aren't you?'
'Not strong enough . . . "superlative" should do it . . . And obviously I'm fundamentally against childhood sexual abuse – but the play, making it all happen in a virtual world – like a computer game – makes it possible to look at ideas and – and human beings and their . . . umm . . . predilections . . . er . . . foibles, Idiosyncrasies . . . umm . . . whatevers – in a dispassionate way . . . keeping our judgement but not being judgemental.'
'I've not seen it.'
'Would you like to? It's on in London now.'
'Not sure that "like" is the right word . . . But it sounds as if I've got to – not just to follow your suggestion but to keep my own mind open and active . . . alive.'

* * *

A bit worrying . . . James going off on one like that – even though he came back with an apology. Ha! – Addicts and their apologies . . . Heard them a thousand times in here . . . And their explanations and excuses. And heard all their psychological games . . . Do I really *want* to take that on board in my personal life – possibly with James – as well as at work? . . .

* * *

'So how did it go? . . . with the CBT?'
'I'll have to ask for God's forgiveness.'
'Did you kill someone?'
'Could've.'
'Heavens! . . . You of all people – with your peaceful and

forgiving nature – even towards that locum idiot . . . What happened?'

'Nothing'

'Huh?'

'Nothing happened . . . Like the psychiatrist, she wasn't interested in EMDR . . . very dismissive . . . She talked, I listened.'

'Isn't all therapy like that?'

'I always assumed so – most people do . . . I s'pose . . . But I experienced something different . . . when I had the EMDR.'

'Didn't you tell her that?'

'More than my life's worth.'

'So what d'you need God's forgiveness for?'

'For being totally single-minded – working towards my own goal . . . but making it look as if I was cooperating.'

'I doubt you'll roast in hell fire for that.'

'What would you know?'

'Whoops!'

o O o

'I must say, you're an excellent teacher, Precious. I remember your lectures like they were yesterday . . . They were fun.'

'Thank you . . . I'll grant that I know how to put things over – and how to liven things up a bit.'

'I'll say.'

'But I'm not unique . . . I'm sure you could do it.'

'I hope I never have to . . . My heart's in clinical medicine. – I like patients.'

'In which case they'll like you . . . All relationships are mutual.'

'Are they?'

'Of course . . . Take one at random.'

'All right. – Dr Patel – my previous chief, the locum . . . Can't stand the man.'

'Then he won't be able to stand you either.'

'Why? . . . I've given him no cause.'

'He won't need one . . . It's instinctive . . . We make up our minds about other people within 30 seconds of meeting them.'

'That's a bit severe.'

'Yes it is – and it's why it's not a good idea to rush into relationships – or dismiss them out of hand, giving them no chance to develop.'

'Is that why you took your time with me?'

'No. – I told you. – I'm shy.'

'You certainly made up for that the other night.'

'Well, there's an old saying . . . When the pupil is ready the teacher appears.'

'And how!'

'And some things can't be taught . . . They're instinctive.. That's possibly at the back of your mutual hostility with Dr Patel . . . You're a natural clinician . . . You know your stuff clinically, as he does even more so, but you're a people person.'

'Yes.'

'And I guess he's not . . . and he'll hate you for that.'

'But why? . . . I'm very respectful to him – even though he demands it.'

'Ha! . . . That's a contradiction in terms . . . You can't demand respect – It has to be earned.'

'But he's got plenty of skills of his own . . . Why does he want mine?'

'If he feels inadequate – for any reason – he'll always want more of things "out there" to fill up the emptiness he feels "in here".'

'Oh.'

'But it won't work . . . It never does. – And he'll have a wretched life . . . emotionally.'

'Why?'

'Because people are consistent in the way they make relationships . . . If he's a shit at work with you, he'll also be a shit with his consultant colleagues. That makes it unlikely that he'll ever get a full time post. He'll go from one locum job to another – with a permanent chip on his shoulder – and he'll probably be a shit at home.'

'Oh.'

'And what d'you s'pose that means?'

'I don't have to pay him back . . . His family will give him the full treatment when he gets home.'

'Yeah, that's right . . . umm . . . Tell you what . . . umm . . . You can give me the full treatment right now.'

'That's different.'

'No it's not . . . It's mutual just the same . . . between you and me . . . in a different way. – Come on. – The pupil's ready.'

'S'pose I say no?'

'You won't . . . I sense it – right here.'

'Ya filthy beast . . . You sure learn fast.'

'Good teacher.'

* * *

Wish I had more responsibility . . . I'm ready for it now . . . Grown up a bit since broking . . . I know my place – Lucy showed me that – in the laundry room until I 'm settled . . . in my head . . . Hmm . . . She's showing me that I needed to go on strike – just like her – sort my ideas out . . . It's like Step Seven in *Drop the Rock*. – Get a bit of humility – not feeling meek or humiliated but worthwhile . . . Huh! – and only as humble as we're grateful in our recovery . . .

* * *

'Here you are again . . . How nice to see you, Mrs Finch.'

'And it's nice to see you.'

'How did you get on with your homework? – On seeing where some of your existing thought processes might get in the way of your progress – and then trying out a different thought and observing the new results.'

'Very well, I think.'

'Tell me – if you would.'

'I looked at the idea of it being silly of me to make a fuss . . . Would I think that about another patient? . . . in the situation I was in? . . . No I would not.'

'What would you think?'

'That it was an unfortunate accident – could've happened to anybody . . . but certainly not my fault.'

'Good . . . That's very good . . . CBT works! . . . Now tell me about the precise time when you became aware that you were awake under the anaesthetic.'

'Interestingly, I became aware of it some time later . . . I was already at home – with my husband.'

'What happened?'

'I kicked him in the back.'

'Really?'

'Yes . . . in a nightmare.'

'Oh . . . I see . . . A flashback – in a dream . . . and how did you feel about that?'

'I felt guilty – for making a fuss – and I felt isolated . . . Nobody, apart from my husband, would understand that, I s'pose.'

'I understand it very well . . . These feelings of isolation are common in PTSD . . . I empathise with you.'

'Thank you . . . It's nice having you on my side.'

'Against the world?'

'It seemed like that at times . . . But it's so silly. – It can't be true.'

'That's what we call a "negative thought" . . . They're common as well. We'll be working – together – to help you to deal with your problems by changing the way you think and behave . . . That will influence how you feel.'

'That's good . . . I feel very irritable at times.'

'That's yet another feature of PTSD . . . I give you full marks for being so honest with me. Your commitment to the therapeutic process – and to me – is impressive . . . A therapist can help but cannot make your problems go away without your full cooperation.'

'I'm with you . . . confident that you're the right person to help me.'

'That's what's called a "therapeutic alliance".

'I believe that.'

'These negative thoughts can be very troublesome . . . They can get trapped – along with actions – in a vicious cycle . . . Thoughts, feelings, physical sensations and actions are all interconnected – and round we go.'

'On and on . . . It disturbed my sleep – obviously with the nightmares – and I lost my ability to concentrate . . . The worst time was when I tried to go back to work . . . I looked at the patient – lying there, helpless on the operating table – and I suddenly thought she might be awake . . . I remembered being in that position – totally powerless . . . Frightening.'

'Yes . . . Yes . . . I understand.'

'Thank you.'

'What we'll do is to help you to look for practical ways to improve your state of mind . . . That will help you to cope better with your symptoms.'

'It's strange . . . Isn't it? . . . I'm such a practical person. – Have to be as a surgeon . . . Why couldn't I think – and act – my own way through this?'

'That's the eternal problem for people in the helping professions – not knowing when to ask for help from someone else.'

'I know it now.'

'Good . . . Good.'

'You mentioned that CBT – with your help – would help me to "cope better" with my symptoms . . . I'd hoped they would go away altogether.'

'Hopefully they will – in time – or at least you'll be more functional . . . in practice . . . It's not a universal panacea – but there'll be a reduced risk of recurrence – of your depression.'

'What a relief that will be!'

'That's the advantage of working to a highly structured format – learning to face your fears in a methodical way . . . Well – Time's up now – for the discussion part of the session . . . Now for the homework assignment – the behavioural experiment. – Which negative belief do you think it would be helpful for you to challenge this week? . . . at home?'

'Umm . . . That it was all my fault, not being able to get through this on my own.'

'Excellent . . . Excellent . . . It would be a good idea to keep a diary of situations, thoughts, physical feelings, emotions and behaviour patterns . . . We can observe how they change – with the therapy – as time goes on.'

'I'll do that. I like structure . . . Maybe that's why I became a surgeon.'

'You really are getting the hang of this very well . . . It's a pleasure working with you.'

'And with you . . . I look forward to seeing you again next

week – and telling you about my homework.'

* * *

Wonder if Lizzie can square her conscience . . . after what she told me last week about manipulating the therapist . . . umm . . . Will she salve her conscience ever? . . . Ha! – Good job she's not a lawyer, defending someone she's absolutely sure is guilty. – But has to act on behalf of her client . . . Wouldn't suit her at all . . .

* * *

Wonder how long I'll be on these antidepressant things . . . Never needed them in the first place – but I've got no choice while they check the blood levels . . . Filled in that Beck depression inventory thing with a bit of imagination . . . God forgive me. – Six months? One year? . . . Two years? . . . Aaaargh! – I can feel myself getting knocked off by them already . . . Hmm . . . I'd rather be knocked off in a different way. – But I've lost the urge . . . And whatever the drug companies say, I'm putting on weight again and my head's fuzzy . . . This isn't me . . . Not me at all . . .

* * *

Wonder if I can get closer to Lucy again . . . But how? . . . Broke her trust. – Difficult to put it back together . . . Humpy Dumpty . . . God! – Stupid of me to shoot my mouth off like that – forgetting HALT after missing a few meetings and not working the Steps . . . Hmm . . . Too fragile – even now, after all this time . . . Carried away with reading about various therapies. Getting ahead of myself . . . Can't do without AA

... Should've known that .... So easy to forget. – Once an addict always an addict ...

* * *

'So how did this week's CBT session go?'

'Are you going to want a blow by blow account every week?'

'A blow job would be nice.'

'Roderick Finch, you're disgraceful!'

o O o

'Careful with the retractor when we get further in ... The carotid artery doesn't like to be tugged.'

'I s'pose not ... umm ... I imagine when things go wrong in this part of the body – surgically – it can be dramatic.'

'It's all a matter of practice ... Some teaching hospital consultants have so many commitments – research projects, committees, policy meetings, queries from the Department – they have real pressure on their clinical time ... Put your finger on that ... That's right ... with patients ... Maybe they wonder sometimes why they ever became doctors – particularly with some of the really dumb observations ... Cut – not too close to the knot – ... made by the Care Quality Commission people.'

'Such as?'

'Specialists at The Royal Marsden – the top cancer hospital ... Cut ... in the country – being told that their outcome figures were poor ... Cut ... That's it ... Getting the hang of it.'

'Cutting the suture's in the genes ... My mother's a gynaecologist.'

'That's good . . . Keep it in the family . . . We do that . . . Gujeratis.'

'Umm . . . Why would the outcome figures be poor at the Marsden?'

'Work it out for . . . Cut . . . yourself . . .. Where do they get their patients from? D'you think?'

'GPs.'

'Think again.'

'Oh . . . Other hospitals . . . The Marsden's a tertiary hospital, with patients coming from secondary care hospitals all over . . .'

'Cut.'

' . . . the country.'

'And therefore?'

'They've taken on extremely difficult patients. – The ones other consultant specialists couldn't manage.'

'That's right . . . Cut.'

* * *

'I see you've got an appointment with the consultant psychiatrist later this week . . . It's good to check in every so often . . . Good for me too – to have medical cover.'

'Yes.'

'How are things? . . . How are you in yourself?'

'Fine.'

'You don't sound it . . . And you know what "fine" stands for, don't you.'

'Yes . . . My son told me . . . He got it from the rehab he went to . . . "Effed up, insecure, neurotic and emotional.'

'Any of those apply to you?'

'All of them, probably.'

'Well on we go . . . How's the homework coming along?'

'I thought it was all my fault ... my reaction to the anaesthetic issue ... Bizarre. – How could it possibly be my fault?'

'Victims often blame themselves. That's the way it goes.'

'Well it's not going to go that way with me.'

'That's it! ... Got it! ... You really are doing very well ... talking back to your negative thoughts like that ... umm ... May I see your diary?   of the situations, thoughts, physical feelings, emotions and behaviour patterns you've experienced during this last week?'

'Here it is.'

'How did you find it? ... keeping a diary each day?'

'Strange at first – but then I got into it.'

'Interesting ... Not much about your children – nothing in fact – and yet you seem a very motherly person.'

'They're both busy at work.'

'Oh yes. So they are ... And how about your husband? ... How close are you to him?'

'Very. – He's a pillar of strength for me.'

'And you for him?'

'Y – yes.'

'You seem – to me – to be slightly hesitant.'

'We're fine ... I was just wondering where this is leading.'

'"Fine" again?'

'Not in that ... umm ... corrupt sense. – We're genuinely very happy ... personally ... with each other.'

'In what sense do you use the word "corrupt"?'

'Corrupted, distorted, peculiar.'

'Just asking. – You're really happy are you? ... despite all you've been through?'

'Yes.'

'Are you sure about that?'

'Yes.'

'You see . . . The approach we take – as CBT psycho-therapists – is to break down the larger problem into smaller components . . . Making problems more manageable helps to change negative thought patterns – and improve the way you feel . . . Then we try to identify particular problematic thoughts and behaviour . . . umm . . . As you have little personal contact – outside your work – other than with your husband, it's only reasonable to expect that tensions might arise . . . Don't you think?'

'Yes.'

'So there are tensions?'

'No more than in any other marriage – or any other long-term relationship.'

'I see . . . And has your behaviour towards each other been problematic . . . with all this dreadful pressure you've been under?'

'I don't think so . . . Nothing out of the ordinary – between us.'

'You might want to look at this . . . in the here and now . . . in your closest relationship.'

'Yes, if you say so.'

'Then – you and I together – might examine ways to intervene in the stresses you must be under . . . and explore the possibility of faulty reasoning underlying your personal belief system . . . and – inevitably – leading to your feelings becoming disturbed.'

'I follow.'

'Good . . . Good . . . Then we can establish new techniques – so it becomes less likely that you'll experience communication problems over this issue in future.'

'Yes . . . I see where you're going . . . now.'

'The starting position is for us to discuss the evidence . . .

for and against your negative beliefs . . . We can observe how they change – with the therapy – as time goes on.'

'Yes . . . That will certainly be interesting.'

'And – allied to your homework exercises – you'll be practising these incremental changes in your daily life.'

'I'm a very practical person. – That will suit me just f– . . . er . . . the ticket.'

'The eventual aim is to teach you how to apply the skills you've learned . . . so that you can manage your problems and stop them having a negative impact on your life – even after the course of therapy is finished.'

'Wonderful . . . I like the sense of time-limited therapy.'

'Yes indeed . . . In this respect CBT is as effective as medication . . . You can take it for as long as it's effective.'

'Indefinitely?'

'You'll have to ask your consultant psychiatrist about that.'

'And CBT?'

'As long as you like . . . When I've taught you how to administer it to yourself – along the same structured lines as the homework assignments – and possibly through inter-active software programmes.'

'That's encouraging . . . I always like to check things out on the web and see demonstrations on *YouTube*.'

'Yes . . . and your response is very encouraging. – Computerised CBT is very effective . . . Have a look at *Beating the Blues* – for mild to moderate depression like yours . . . It could be very effective – and it does away with the need for anything other than minimal contact with the therapist.'

'Independence at last!'

'Yes, that's right . . . That's the ultimate goal of all therapy . . . other than psychoanalysis maybe . . . Now then . . . This week's homework. – What would you suggest?'

'Well, now that you've got me thinking about it – in such a

constructive way – the relationship with my husband . . . and all the negative beliefs that may underlie it.'

'That's the way.'

* * *

Oh no, no, no . . . This really is too much . . . the indignity! . . . the pathetic dependency! – Huh! If the Garrick didn't have a special ramp, I'd top meself . . . if I thought I was always going to need a stick – like now – or eventually get stuck in a wheelchair for any length of time . . . or for the rest of me life . . . What's it all about? . . . It's the trials of Job – and Mrs Job if there was one . . . Don't remember . . . Lizzie would know . . .

* * *

'Even better this week . . . I've been on the web – *Positive Psychology* . . . Professor Martin Seligman . . . American. – University of Pensylvania.'

'Why all these Americans? – having all the bright ideas? . . . Haven't our people got any? . . . Anywhere?'

'Not nowadays . . . Seems to me . . . No originators.'

'Why not? . . . There are plenty of universities here. – And lots in Europe.'

'You'll have to ask them . . . Stuck in their own mind sets with psychoanalysis . . . And now CBT – since that took root.'

'But that's American. – Not European.'

'Yes. – Nothing this side of the pond in the last hundred years or more . . . since the days of Freud, Jung, Adler.'

'But why not?'

'Inertia . . . Just like there's been no real progress in healthcare and welfare ideas in the UK . . . since the NHS came in.'

'Can't we think for ourselves any more? . . . Anyway, what's this *Positive Psychology* stuff? What's it all about? . . . Isn't all psychology positive?'

'Should be . . . But it took a wrong turn with Freud – always looking at complete nutters and creating ids, egos, super-egos, complexes and God knows what else.'

'What was there before Freud? . . . and the others?'

'Doctors – and Freud himself was a doctor . . . a maverick in his day . . . They kept asking him to cut up a brain – from a dead patient – and show them the bit that had gone wrong.'

'And what did he say?'

'Dunno.'

'Come on, James . . . Where's your curiosity? – You'll be as fossilised as the rest of them.'

'Thanks for that.'

'Oh . . . Sorry. – My turn to apologise.'

'That's a relief . . . I thought I was the only one . . . making mistakes.'

'We all do . . . No harm – and a lot of good – in making mistakes.'

'Why "a lot of good"?'

'It shows we're still alive . . . mentally active . . . We can learn from mistakes. – Not the way politicians and inspectors are always going on about . . . but by keeping our minds open to where a new possibility might lead. – And the stimulus towards doing that might be a mistake.'

'Am I forgiven for mine?'

'Yes of course . . . Threw me for a bit . . . Not the James I thought I knew.'

'That's the real James, I'm afraid. – The one you know is artificial.'

'A fraud?'

'No . . . Hope not . . . One I . . . umm . . . try to superimpose on my basic addictive nature.'

'Sounds tricky.'

'Not really ... Just a daily reminder ... Like *Positive Psychology* really ... Looking at what people do successfully ... really well ... and copying that.'

'But that's obvious ... so simple.'

'I s'pose so ... But "simple" doesn't mean "easy" ... That's what I was taught in rehab...'

'That's remarkable. – Rehab teaching you all sorts of things that are way outside the standard loop in universities ... with their nit-picking "research" projects.'

Seems to me nowadays that "research" is just statistics, number crunching.'

'Yes ... I reckon it takes a Beck or a Glasser or a Seligman – three Americans – to observe and then have the courage to say that the emperor has no clothes.'

* * *

'Dear, dear Roddy ... It's such a bore for you – needing to use a stick – just for now, hopefully.'

'Fifty one shades of grey?'

'Roddy!'

'Hmm ... But I doubt it – over the stick being temporary ... I s'pose that's the way the cookie crumbles.'

'I haven't heard that expression for yonks.'

'And how long's a "yonk"?'

'As I've always said, a very long time – like the time I shall be having so-called "treatment" with CBT – when there was nothing wrong with me in the first place ... Unlike you, poor love ... umm ... Roddy?'

'Yes, me love?'

'I've got you on my conscience ... and my conscience is

already working overtime over the way I'm playing – almost toying – with the CBT lady.'

'I expect she asks for trouble.'

'Yes, she does . . . Asking me things like, "How are things?" and "How are you in yourself?" . . . It's exasperating, patronising.'

'Rather you than me . . . trying to stay cool under that onslaught . . . umm . . . Where do I come into this?'

'She was fishing around for something to get her teeth into . . . underlying problems. – She assumed there must be something between you and me and I was thinking . . .'

'There is.'

'Roddy! . . . Put that thing away – right now!'

* * *

'I'm glad to learn that you've started the CBT . . . Doing very well, I hear.'

'Thank you.'

'And the blood tests confirm that you're at the therapeutic level for the antidepressant . . . Can't be too careful . . . er . . . too precise in what we're trying to achieve for you.'

'Thank you . . . I'm most appreciative.'

'That's the way.'

'Umm . . . There is one thing that I'd like your reassurance about . . .'

'Yes?'

'The . . . er . . . suicide risk.'

'Vastly overblown . . . It's a self-selecting population. – If they hadn't been suicidal, they wouldn't have been given medication in the first place . . . As I said, can't be too careful, too precise.'

'And how long d'you think I'll be on these . . . er . . . pharmaceutical drugs?'

'As long as it takes, as long as a ball of string . . . Ha! –
Funny expression that. – Isn't it? – When did anyone last see
a ball of string?'

'Umm . . . For a few weeks – until the course of CBT is
complete? . . . for a few months? even longer?'

'Some people are on them for life . . . After all, if a treatment's going well, why change it?'

*   *   *

'What did you make of it?'

'After the first ten minutes I nearly walked out . . . In
general I don't like sex scenes that add nothing to the plot.'

'You clairvoyant, Phebe? . . . How would you know the plot
after only ten minutes?'

'I feared the worst . . . These Scandinavian films seem to
come in two categories – thrillers like *The Girl with the
Dragon Tattoo* and orgies . . . Fortunately there wasn't much
of an orgy in *Blind* . . . just a bit of statutory nudity – to
confirm their Scandinavian credentials.'

'It became relevant . . . when we got yet another insight
into what a blind person loses in life . . . It's far more than
sight.'

'You think blind people miss out on orgies?'

'Hey, Precious! You're simply being provocative . . .
possibly because you're a man.'

'What would a shy man like me do in an orgy. – I'd die of
embarrassment.'

'Then why did you ask that stupid question?'

'Dunno really . . . But I can't be on academic duty all the
time . . . Gotta be a flesh and blood human sometimes.'

'Yeah . . . Well we don't need to talk about that either. – I was thinking about disabilities generally, with both my parents in pretty poor shape one way or another at present.'

'Yes, that's one thing the film did for me – that I'd never thought about before. – Blind people forget what the world looks like . . . or even what they themselves look like . . . And the boundary between reality and imagination – fantasy – gets blurred.'

'Yes – and other people come to define them by their disabilities . . . Dad won't be a distinguished commercial barrister any more – although he still is . . . just . . . He'll be "That man who's got . . . umm . . . whatever it is he's got" . . . And mum will forever be "That lady who woke up under the anaesthetic – poor dear".'

'Do I detect a streak of bitterness?'

'Yes . . . er . . . Not really bitterness or resentment . . . kind of sadness and anger, fear and remorse all mixed in.'

'Why remorse?'

'Because I haven't made the best of my opportunities to be nice to them . . . Sometimes I've gone the other way . . . deliberately.'

'Yup . . . I'll buy that . . . I wasn't always sweetness and light to Mom – and she had lots of disabilities, God . . .'

' . . . rest her mortal soul.'

'Ha! – Yes.'

'Hmm . . . What it is to see ourselves as others see us! – That's the easy one. – The more difficult challenge, seems to me, is to see other people as they see themselves.'

o O o

'I'll come straight to the point, Mr Finch, so that we can have plenty of time for discussion.'

'That sounds like bad news.'

'All the evidence points to one of the motor neurone diseases . . . In technical terms you have signs of lesions – defects – in the upper motor neurones. These start in the brain and go to the spinal cord. They join up with the lower motor neurones. They start in the spinal cord and go to the muscles in the body – the voluntary muscles that you use to move around or breathe, not the automatic muscles like the heart or bowels and bladder . . . You also have the fasciculations – the flickerings we noted previously – but there are more of them now . . . I think ALS – Amyotrophic Lateral Sclerosis – is the most likely diagnosis.'

'Umm . . . Is that . . . er . . . – silly thing really – why I find it difficult . . . sometimes . . . to do up my shirt buttons?'

'Yes.'

'Hmm . . . What's the good news?'

'We can do whatever we can – with medicines and physiotherapy – to slow down the progression but the end result's going to be much the same.'

'Die, punk!'

'I beg your pardon?'

'Clint Eastwood . . . *Dirty Harry* . . . Something like that.'

'I think it was, "Make my day".'

'All much the same really . . . Don't remember the quote – or the scene – exactly . . . Still, the principle's much the same . . . er . . . fer me.'

'I wouldn't put it like that . . . But let's say we'll do whatever we can – do everything possible – to make you comfortable between now and then.'

'Umm . . . Thank you.'

'Now ask me all the questions you want and I'll do my best to answer them . . . My time's yours . . . And by the way, now that we know – as far as one ever can – the way the land lies, you really must make sure that your GP refers you to me on the Health.'

* * *

Stupid fucking idiot I was – losing it with Lucy like that . . . Wonder if she'll ever really be able to forget it . . . Ha! – "Fergedaboudit", as my room mate said in Hazelden . . . The point is . . . the important point is that *I* mustn't fergedaboudit . . . Yeah, I know what I'll do. – I'll snip the corner off the cover of my small copy of the *Big Book*. Ha! – the small *Big Book* . . . Never go anywhere without it – always in my left pocket – Won't forget that . . . and won't forget why I made that cut . . . Hmm . . . Should remind me of my priorities – sort myself out – if I ever want to make a difference . . .

* * *

'Hello Mum . . .'

'Just you hold it right there . . . Since telling you about Dad, I know perfectly well what you're planning to say and do now . . . and I won't hear of it . . . The answer's an absolute "no".'

'But Precious and I have talked it through.'

'Then bring him round, bring him here, and I'll tell him to his face.'

'Oh . . . but I . . .'

'No "if"s . . . No "but"s . . . Just "No" – Absolute "No".'

'Oh.'

'That's right . . . "Oh" says it all . . . We're very grateful for the offer . . . truly grateful – whatever it is – but we won't hear of it . . . We've got enough money in the bank – and sufficient savings and no mortgage – to be able to live in style for a few years until . . . until . . . Buggrit!'

'Mum!'

'Yes, well . . .'

'You don't have to explain yourself to me . . . I spent four months on the wards every day in "Care for the Elderly" . . . or whatever Dr Patel decides to call it now in order to make his personal mark – so that he stands a good chance of being appointed to the substantive post, rather than being a locum. – You don't have to avoid talking about death to me . . . or about what bereaved families go through.'

'Thanks . . . Thank you dear Phoebe, dear little one.'

* * *

'How did you get on with your homework this week?'

'Very well.'

'I recall you were going to monitor your relationship with your husband.'

'Yes.'

'What did you find? . . . Where were the negative thoughts? . . . or actions?'

'There were none . . . Only positive ones.'

'You may not have looked deeply enough into this.'

'I looked deeply into his eyes and found nothing but love.'

'Are you sure you've understood the nature of this exercise? – It's to look at what you really think and feel, rather than what you believe you should think and feel.'

'Yes, I understand . . . That really is what I think and feel . . . My husband says the same.'

'Extraordinary – under the circumstances – although there might be an element of denial in the reaction to trauma . . . For example, women would not go through a second childbirth if they remembered the full traumatic experience of the first . . . The body secretes its own natural opiates – to dull the pain and produce a sense of euphoria . . . That may have been an influence in your case.'

'I'm a gynaecologist but I'll have another look next week.'

'That's better. – A very good idea. – Now we're on the right lines.'

'That's very reassuring.'

'Good . . . It's so important to maintain your sense of comfort with the process of therapy . . . and your contact with reality.'

'Yes . . . I'll do that.'

'What we've been doing so far is to summarise the process of CBT . . . What we'll start doing next week – I'll help you with this and guide you carefully – is to start putting it all into practice.'

'I'll be glad to get involved . . . I want to show my husband that I can move on from this dreadful time.'

'He might also need to be involved in the assessment . . . with me guiding you both. The therapeutic alliance – between therapist and client and significant others – is at the core of all movement towards resolution.'

'I see . . . I'll have to take your word for it . . . Trust you.'

'That's it . . . Right. – Let's complete the familiarisation process this week . . . What we'll begin to do from next week on – in therapeutic practice – is to analyse your thoughts, feelings and behaviours in order to work out if they're unrealistic or unhelpful . . . Then we can determine the effects each of these components has on the others and also on you . . . From that we can ascertain how to change the unhelpful thoughts and behaviours.'

'That's all very logical.'

'Good . . . We're back on track now, aren't we?'

'Yes . . . We certainly are.'

'When you come to question your upsetting thoughts you gradually learn how to replace them with more helpful ones

. . . Then you practise these changes in your daily life. – And you'll come to recognise when you're about to do something that will make you feel worse rather than better . . . Then you do something more helpful. – D'you follow me?'

'Yes . . . All the way.'

'In your homework you will assess the effectiveness of your new thoughts and behaviours . . . D'you think you'll be able to do that?'

'I hope so.'

'Ah well . . . The process may need something more than hope.'

'Oh yes . . . Commitment . . . actually doing something – rather than saying, "I'll try.".'

'Very good . . . You've understood precisely what's needed . . . This will be important when we come to confront your fears . . . Anxieties, of one kind or another, at work or at home, can be very difficult . . . very disabling. But – be assured – you will not be asked to do things you don't want to do and we'll work at a comfortable pace – for you – within the time available . . . It's part of my responsibility to ensure that you are comfortable with the progress you make.'

'Thank you. That's very considerate of you.'

'Then – most importantly, when the formal therapeutic sessions are complete – you can continue to apply the principles of CBT in your daily life on your own – without me.'

'That's really important for me . . . for my long-term future.'

'It certainly is . . . But – in the here and now – I'll help you to break the negative thought cycles . . . There are helpful or unhelpful ways of reacting to any situation . . . And these reactions are often determined by what you think about the situation. – Change the thoughts and the reactions will change . . . Are you with me?'

'Yes . . . It all makes very good sense . . . Almost surgical in its precision.'

'Indeed . . . The negative thoughts may lead to you feeling lonely, hopeless, depressed and tired.'

'I've felt all of those things.'

'Yes – and you may isolate yourself . . . stop going out to meet people, stay stuck at home – on your own or with your husband.'

'Yes.'

'Then you feel bad about yourself and you remain trapped in a negative cycle of thoughts, physical sensations, feelings and actions . . . They come as a package.'

'They certainly do . . . and it's so difficult to unwrap it.'

'I'm here to help you with that . . . but later on you'll be able to achieve – and sustain – all these changes on your own.'

'And what do I . . . er . . . we . . . do to help me through the anaesthetic awareness after-shocks? . . . if they come again?'

'Hopefully they won't – if you've followed the structured process I've outlined to you.'

'Good.'

'But, if they do recur, we can involve you in some exposure therapy . . . As I said before, I believe, you will learn to face your fears in a methodical and structured way.'

'I remember.'

'Excellent . . . In the exposure therapy, we would start with issues and situations that cause tolerable anxiety. – Things that don't upset you too much. – We expose you to that for one or two hours or until you find that the length of time you feel any distress is reduced by half . . . Then we repeat this exposure three times a day – so that the sting is drawn very gradually . . . Then, when you're acclimatised to that level of challenging stimulus, we move to a more difficult situation . . . Altogether we may spend anything from six to fifteen hours together in these de-sensitising sessions.'

'Gosh! . . . That's an amazing commitment . . . from you.'

'Well – if I'm too busy with other clients – you can always do it yourself . . . using self-help books or computer programmes.'

'Oh . . . umm . . . Thank you.'

'There we are. – That's covered it. – Now then . . . Have another go at your homework exercise – seeing what's *really* there, underneath the surface, in your relationship with your husband – and we'll start the real work, putting all this into practice, next week.'

* * *

'She wouldn't hear of it? . . . Yeah, that fits.'

'Fits with what?'

'Fits with someone strong enough to be your mother.'

'Oh . . . I'm not that bad, am I?'

'Of course you are – and I love you for it . . . Your values, your principles, your courage . . . You and your mom are two peas in a pod . . . And your dad's right up there with you.'

'James is a bit of all right as well, turning himself round as he has done.'

'Sure thing . . . What did your mom actually say?'

'You've asked the wrong question . . . You should've asked what *I* said.'

'Okay . . . What did you say?'

'Nothing.'

'Nothing at all?'

'Nothing at all . . . She wouldn't let me get a word in edge-ways. – Stopped me before I'd even started.'

'I'll say this for you Finches . . . You got style.'

oOo

'So what d'you think is the most important thing we could ever tell our patients on this ward? . . . or any ward?'

'Give up smoking.'

'Yes . . . And will they do it? . . . as a result of us telling them that?'

'Probably not.'

'"Probably"?'

'Umm . . . I don't know.'

'We have government health warnings on every packet of cigarettes and now plans to introduce plain packs, posters in doctors' offices, rules against smoking indoors or in cars with children in them and a constant battering of eardrums and eyes – using every possible approach to persuade people to give up smoking . . . And still there's a hard core of inveterate smokers . . . And as they die off they're joined every year by new smokers . . . And women are catching up the men – in smoking habits and in death rates from cigarette smoking related illnesses . . . What d'you make of that?'

'It's grim.'

'Got any ideas?'

'It's something I want to tackle seriously when I'm a GP.'

'There already are GPs working very hard on this – just as you want to do . . . They have special sessions for people who want to quit . . . They dish out nicotine chewing gum and e-cigarettes . . . They do all sorts of things – but none of it works on the hard core or prevents youngsters from taking it up . . . especially young women who are frightened of putting on weight and young men who want to look cool.'

'My . . . er . . . man has some ideas on this.'

'Really? . . . I'd love to hear them . . . umm . . . If we could get people to give up smoking, we could empty half the wards

– not just the heart and lung wards but all over the hospital
. . . Cigarette smoking, obesity and heavy drinking are the
three big killers – in all the wards – and cigarette smoking's
the worst of all.'

'Yes . . . But he says nobody – certainly no politician –
would take up his idea.'

'Why not?'

'All right . . . I'll try it on you . . . er . . . He's a Libertarian
. . . umm . . . He says that he supports people's right to smoke
and he also supports their right to pay for the medical consequences of that choice.'

'Oh . . . umm . . . I see.'

*   *   *

'I thought I'd come to see you again . . . I've got some big decisions to make . . . I thought I'd run them past you'

'You know I don't give advice . . . I don't know enough
about you.'

'You know a darn sight more about me than the CBT
psychotherapist I've been seeing . . . She can talk for England
– but she's not hot on listening . . . By the way, what's the
difference between a counsellor, a therapist and a
psychotherapist?'

'Usually nothing other than the size of the fee.'

'But you call yourself a counsellor and you charge a
fortune.'

'Only in relative terms – relative to what other counsellors
charge.'

'Why?'

'Because of my experience.'

'How long d'you intend to go on for?'

'Until I drop off my perch . . . or get nailed to it.'

'Ha! – The "dead parrot" sketch.'

'Yup . . . Still as fresh today as it ever was in *Monty Python* . . . and I hope the same freshness – of mind – is true for me . . . and will be for years to come.'

'I hope not for the CBT lady – for the sake of her patients, clients, whatever . . . She spoke in formulae . . . reciting a script probably.'

'I don't know her so I won't judge . . . Wouldn't anyway . . . Now then . . . What did you want to run past me?'

'Whether I should continue working as a doctor.'

'I can't possibly answer that for you.'

'Guide me?'

'Nope.'

'What can you do?'

'Tell you my own experience.'

'Okay . . . Do that.'

'I didn't value being a doctor any more . . . I didn't want to be ruled and regulated by people who didn't have my experience or share my values. And I didn't want to prescribe . . . That's about it.'

'Don't you miss it?'

'I did at first but not now . . . I'm far too busy doing my counselling work – and loving every minute of it, just as I did when I worked as a doctor. I don't spend any time thinking about the past . . . It's over . . . I've moved on.'

'Could I move on?'

'It's up to you.'

'Aren't you going to look at the potential risks or benefits? . . . of my possible change of direction? . . . er . . . career?'

'No . . . You can do that for yourself – after talking with your husband . . . We're not free agents when we're married.'

'Ha! – It never occurred to me to ask the CBT lady if she's married.'

'You put yourself in her hands, asked for personal help, but didn't find out about her personal life?'

'No.'

'Why not?'

'Because I was the patient . . . umm . . . client . . . umm . . . professional etiquette.'

'Didn't it matter to you whether she had her own life in order – personally and professionally – before trusting her with yours?'

'No . . . Never occurred to me . . . It's not done.'

'Yeah, yeah . . . I know that. – But *who* is protected by that convention . . . the competent? . . . or the incompetent?'

'Oh.'

'Yes . . . "Oh".'

'But if you don't have conventions like that, isn't there a risk that you'd become over familiar and . . . umm . . .'

'Have sex with a patient?'

'I hadn't anticipated saying it quite so directly.'

'Why not? . . . People's behaviour directly corresponds with their values.'

'But how d'you assess that? . . . Surely you need ethical standards?'

'Yes, of course . . . But ethics are an inside job . . . You can't impose them from the outside . . . Look at the sheer number of doctors who finish up in front of the GMC professional conduct committee – or whatever it's called nowadays – despite all the GMC guidance booklets.'

'How about the Hippocratic oath?'

'Did you take it?'

'No. – Wasn't asked to.'

'Me neither . . . Wouldn't have signed it anyway.'

'Why not?'

'Try reading it for yourself . . . He was much more

interested in his own pension – and being revered and respected by his pupils – than anything much to do with patients . . . I make my own judgements and establish my own behaviour, based on my own values.'

'But how can anyone else assess them? . . . your values? You personally?'

'Not from a certificate on a wall. – That's for sure . . . I've already told you the answer – Observe my personal and professional behaviour.'

'But. That's expecting an awful lot . . . from the patients – making judgements like that.'

'Yes.'

'Oh.'

'"Oh" again.'

'Yes.'

'It's their lives . . . They're responsible for them . . . umm . . . Tell you what. – Let's look at this psychodramatically. – Your present predicament, not the ethical stuff we've been talking about.'

'Huh?'

'You'll get the hang of it as we go along . . . Here we go . . . I'll sit in this chair – and play the role of you . . . Anyone sitting in this chair is you . . . Got it?'

'Yes.'

'Now please place three or four chairs over there and imagine anyone sitting in any one of those chairs has a particular role.'

'Such as?'

'Your husband or another member of your family, the psychiatrist, the GMC, the CBT psychotherapist . . . You choose.'

'All of them – but just my husband from the family.'

'Okay . . . Who d'you want to start with?'

'My husband.'

'Okay . . . umm . . . Roddy – wasn't it?'

'Yes.'

'Okay, Roddy my love . . .'

'Ha!'

'Stay with it . . . Stay in role as Roddy – and I'm you . . . I'll start again . . . Okay Roddy my love, I've got some important decisions to make . . . and I'd like to go through them with you.'

'What decisions?'

'Umm . . . Change chairs with me now – I can't answer that question because I'm not really you . . . So now I move over there – as Roddy – and you sit here as yourself . . . umm . . . Ready?'

'Yes.'

'What decisions?'

'Huh?'

'I'm Roddy now . . . I'm replying to your previous state-ment about wanting to go through things with me . . .er . . . What decisions?'

'Got it . . . Umm . . . Whether I want to stay working as a doctor . . . Nothing's going right for either of us . . . I'm your wife . . . I have a duty to look after you . . . I want to look after you . . . Anyway there's too much grief from the shrink – God knows how long he'll keep me on the medicines . . . I'm caught in a double bind . . . He said he might keep me on them if I'm doing well . . . But if I come off them, my guess is that he'll get frightened of taking the rap if something goes wrong . . . What shall I do?'

'I can't answer that as Roddy. – I don't know him . . . You do . . . Change chairs again and reverse roles again . . . That's it . . . Now I'm you . . . and I'll put to you the statements I just heard – and the question you asked . . . Here we go . . . I don't know if I want to be a doctor any more . . . Nothing's going right for us . . . I'm your wife . . . I want to look after you . . . I'm getting grief from the shrink. – How long will he keep me on the medicines? . . . I'm caught in a double bind . . . If I'm doing well he'll keep me on them – but if I come off them – and something goes wrong – he'll take the rap . . . So what shall I do?'

'Oh . . . umm . . . Yes, I'm Roddy . . . umm . . . Well, me old fruit, it's up to you . . . Stuff the shrink . . . You're my wife, not his . . . We'll survive somehow . . . We've got each other. – That's what's important . . . We've got enough dosh to get by – at least until I pop me clogs . . . and there's more – to keep you secure afterwards . . . Do what you feel is best for you.'

'Reverse roles again.'

'I don't need to . . . I've got the answers I need . . . That was quite remarkable!'

'It's my work nowadays . . . psychodrama, EMDR and a bit of NLP – *Neuro Linguistic programming* . . . helping people to be aware of the words they use and what they signify and how to see things from a different perspective . . . and some guided imagery and hypnosis . . . That keeps me busy . . . I don't miss being a doctor at all . . . Maybe there's something out there – in the big wide world – that would be equally exciting for you . . . I don't know . . . It's your life – with your perspectives.'

'I'm certainly game to find out.'

'Good for you . . . And, while you're at it, you could continue these little psychodramas at home, with your husband playing the roles of the psychiatrist, the GMC and the CBT lady . . . You might have some fun – and learn something helpful.'

'That was great, really great.'

'You did the work . . . I sat in a chair and took my cues from you.'

'And you expect me to pay you for that?'

'You betcha!'

* * *

'Oh! . . . Hello James . . . Come in. – Everyone's out . . . Gives us a chance to get to know each other a bit better.'

'Thanks.'

'Umm . . . My sister tells me you're reading up on various psychotherapeutic models and techniques.'

'Yes . . . I've got to learn . . . I've got no clinical background . . . My mother and sister are both doctors but I'm a laundry-man and prescription fetcher.'

'Then you're the smart one in the family . . . Medicine's a political chess game nowadays. The high-ups in the Department of Health are the rooks. The bureaucrats – the administrators – are the bishops and knights, flying around all over the place, being self-important, getting in every-body's way . . . and escaping from tight corners. The doctors are the pawns.'

'Nice one . . . I like that a lot . . . Who are the king and queen?

'The king is the minister – the politician who has to be protected at all costs – and the queen, a right queen, is the Chief Medical Officer of Health – the head of the Department.'

'I'd be happy to be a pawn.'

'Interesting . . . Why?'

'Plenty of fun, building up a surprise attack when every-one takes me for granted.'

'That's wonderful.'

'You haven't heard the best bit.'

'What's that?'

'One day I might be a queen.'

338

'I'm one already.'

'Ha! – Yes . . . Lucy told me . . . I think that's great – finding your own place in the world . . . umm . . . I'm still looking for mine.'

'Sexually?'

'Professionally . . . I think my sexuality is well established – with a number of rather pathetic failed relationships under my belt – but as a care assistant . . . laundryman to be precise . . . I have ideas above my station.'

'Well good for you! . . . And which station are you aiming for.'

'I want to run a rehab.'

'Really? . . . It's a bed of nails s'far as I can see. – Never worked in one . . . Too much hassle . . . Patients nicking things and always pestering you for drugs.'

'I've done that . . . Well, pestered my parents for money and then bought the drugs.'

'Which ones?'

'Whatever was for sale, whatever I could afford.'

'And what scrip are you on now?'

'Nothing . . . Clean and serene since I went into the Mental Health Unit I was admitted to . . . Well – clean since then, with no drugs or alcohol . . . umm . . . Screne – feeling good about myself and about life – since going to a real rehab . . . Hazelden . . . in America.'

'Really?'

'Yeah . . . for real.'

'Remarkable . . . How did you do that? . . . How d'you stay clean? . . . and stay "serene".'

'It's just a saying for AA freaks like me.'

'I don't know anything about that stuff . . . Never taught about it . . . Never needed to find out . . . I tell the desperadoes to go to AA – What else could I do?'

'Go to a meeting – or to a rehab like the one Lucy and I work in . . . just to find out . . . umm . . . I had no choice. – Not really. – I had to stay in.'

'I couldn't go to a meeting . . . Patients might see me there.'

'So what? . . . They might work out you're a bit lezzie as well . . . D'you care about that?'

'Yes . . . I care a lot. – It's part of my identity . . . I'm content with it, proud of it.'

'Yeah, I feel the same – proud of being in recovery – along-side other addicts, not better than them or worse than them.

'Remarkable . . . Okay I'm up for that . . . Take me to a meeting.'

'Straight or gay and lesbian?'

'They have such things? . . . For people like me?'

'Why not? . . . Seen one drunk or druggie, you seen 'em all . . . All you need to know. Nobody gives a damn what else you might be – rich or poor, gay or straight, black or white or green.'

'Green?'

'In the autumn . . . On Halloween.'

* * *

'Joan . . . I've come to talk to you . . . You've been a good friend to me . . . over the years with all the anaesthetics you've given – safely – for my patients . . . and particularly recently – with this silly thing I've had.'

'We've had this conversation before – soon after it happened . . . when you became aware of what had happened to you. I told you then and I'll tell you now. It wasn't a "silly thing". It was a disaster – a crime really – although I shouldn't say that about a colleague.'

'Ha! – We never were politically correct, neither of us . . .

umm . . . I wanted to talk to you about whistleblowing.'
'Someone you're concerned about?'
'No . . . People being concerned about me.'
'Well I'm not . . . Can't wait to get you back into full harness.
– Ha! – Those were the days! . . . We did some good work
together. – A real team, not one of these fanciful get-togeth
ers to make everyone happy, make the books look good.'
'Which books? . . . You running a book on when I'll be
back up to speed?'
'Nah . . . Wouldn't do that . . . You're a mate, a mucker.'
'Well someone's got it in for me . . . I think someone blew
the whistle on me when I tried it out . . . thought I might be
able to start again. But I took one look at you and your
machine – and I couldn't get anywhere near the patient.'
'I remember . . . I thought I was going to have to resuscitate you.'
'That would have been sweet of you – but thank God I
didn't need it . . . But someone in this close group may not
want me to . . . er . . .'
'Yes . . . That's the way it is with medical politics. – Care for
the patients – maybe – but fight to the death with each other.'
'The thing is . . . I'm completely over the anaesthetic awareness . . . I was lucky. – Had some EMDR . . . strange business,
getting the thinking brain to reassure the feeling brain . . . I
sorted it completely . . . But I made one tiny slip . . . trying to
get better my own way . . . and there's someone – right here
– gunning for me . . . One more slip and I'm up in front of the
GMC quick as a knife – and I'm outa here.'
'Horrid . . . umm . . . I can't think of anyone . . . Haven't
heard anything . . . But you just can't tell.'
'Hmm . . . 'fraid that's what you would say . . . umm . . .
What was the book you were referring to earlier? . . . "making
the books look good".'

'Oh that . . . umm . . . being diverse – ticking all the right boxes for minority groups . . . Diversity . . . Doesn't apply to you and me . . . Does it? . . . Yet?'

*   *   *

'I'm concerned about your father . . . And therefore for your mother – and you.'

'Thanks.'

'What's going to become of him? . . . D'you reckon? . . . Hmm . . .Strange that I refer to ALS in one of my lectures.'

'Yes.'

'It's so long since I did any clinical work, I'm out of the loop . . . Wouldn't know nowadays what's likely to happen.'

'He'll die.'

'When?'

'Sometime . . . We all do.'

'But he's going to die nearer to now than we are – hopefully.'

'Yes.'

'You upset with me?'

'No.'

'Who then? . . . Something or somebody's bugging you.'

'It's just that life's so unfair . . . Dad's a good man . . . Mum's a good woman . . . and all this happens.'

*   *   *

'I met your sister. – I came round, hoping to see you. But you were out somewhere – and she'd come round to talk to your mother about something . . . don't know what . . . but she was out so we chatted together.'

'She told me . . . and you invited her to an AA meeting . . .

She told me.'

'Yes . . . She seemed quite keen. – Surprised me.'

'Surprised me too . . . You telling her everything . . . Doesn't your anonymity mean anything to you?'

'Not really . . . If I'm going to run a rehab . . . one day . . . I need to nail my flag to the mast. Show which side I'm on.'

'Yes . . . I s'pose so – but that takes me down with you.'

'But there's no "up" or "down" . . . Is there?'

'A bit.'

'Which bit?'

'The part of me that likes a bit of privacy.'

'Oh.'

'Didn't think of that . . . Did you?'

'No . . . Sorry.'

'And – to cap it all – you invited her to a meeting . . . You've never invited me to one . . . Doesn't my opinion – and sharing experiences with me – matter to you? . . . You're so wrapped up in yourself. . . Is that what these "Anonymous Fellowships" – what a bizarre phrase! – do to you?'

'Sorry.'

'Again.'

* * *

'I'm worried, Roddy.'

'What about?'

'"Abstain from doing harm." – That's the one part of the Hippocratic Oath that matters to me.'

'You weren't thinking of harming anyone? . . . Were you?'

'No . . . But someone at work may be out to harm me.'

'Surely not . . . in the state you're in already?'

'I still occupy a consultant post . . . They're highly sought after . . . Worth a lot of money.'

'That's very cloak and dagger . . . Have a look in the library . . . for a body . . . Maybe the butler done it.'

'Don't joke about it, love . . . You know – from those little psychodramas we did together the other night – I've got a lot on my mind.'

'You certainly have . . . and I'm no help.'

'You were a lot of help . . . in those psychodramas . . . umm . . . role reversals.'

'Thank you . . . Glad to help . . . I found it fascinating . . . Certainly seems a lot more constructive than the CBT you had.'

'That may simply be the particular practitioner . . . There are some major players in the psychology world – I gather – who swear by CBT . . . But anyone who uses words or phrases like "element of denial", "ascertain", "therapeutic alliance" may know her stuff – but she's robotic . . . not human at all . . . She makes assumptions – "must have been". – She talked about "empathy" but with no sign of knowing what it is . . . No wonder she thinks computerised CBT is sufficient . . . which it damn well would be in her case.'

'I can imagine.'

'Ha! – When you use that phrase it sounds genuine. But when she uses it she sounds – to me – as if she's following a formula . . . not being real . . . Yes – and another thing – she referred to President Obama as "Obama". I find that both arrogant and familiar . . . I don't warm to her at all.'

'That's tiresome – and not at all helpful in her profession.'

'And she wouldn't let go of the idea that there's something wrong in our marital relationship . . . Ha! – You're the love of my life – and always will be . . . whatever state we're in.'

'That's very unfortunate – her attitude – to say the least.'

'The whole performance is unfortunate . . . The anaesthetic awareness itself, the lack of knowledge of EMDR in the NHS, the self-serving attitudes of the psychiatrist and the GMC . . . There's the humiliation of supervision and I'm losing my familiarity with surgical techniques . . . Then there's the prospect of being on antidepressants for God knows how long . . . My head's fuzzy, I'm putting on weight and losing my whoomph. – And I'm going to have to let Alice go . . . I've got no patients – My referral sources have moved on . . . And now – on top of all that – there's the possibility of a whistleblower stalking me.'

'But why?'

'Have a talk with your friends in The Garrick . . . applicable to the criminal bar . . . Ha! – Don't tell me I know their maxim better than you do.'

'There are lots . . . which one did you have in mind?'

'Follow the money.'

'Oh . . . Yes . . . Oh Gawd! . . . You poor love.'

'I've come to my conclusion, Roddy . . .'

'Yes?'

'I want to be with you. – You're my husband and I love you . . . I just don't want to be a doctor any more . . . I've had enough . . . There's a better life for me than this one.'

'Not in the next world just yet, I hope.'

'Certainly not . . . In this one.'

'Doing what?'

'I don't know . . . But what I do know is this . . . If I go on hankering over re-creating the past, I'm done for . . . I've got to jump first – so that I can look at all the possibilities.'

'Hmm . . . That sounds like another maxim applicable to the criminal bar – from the old days . . . Dr Johnson.'

'Which one?'

'"When a man knows he is to be hanged in a fortnight, it concentrates his mind wonderfully.".'

o O o

www.ingramcontent.com/pod-product-compliance
Lightning Source LLC
Chambersburg PA
CBHW061321170626
46817CB00001B/261

*9 7 8 1 8 7 1 0 1 3 9 2 4 *